ORPHAN AND THE FIVE BEASTS™

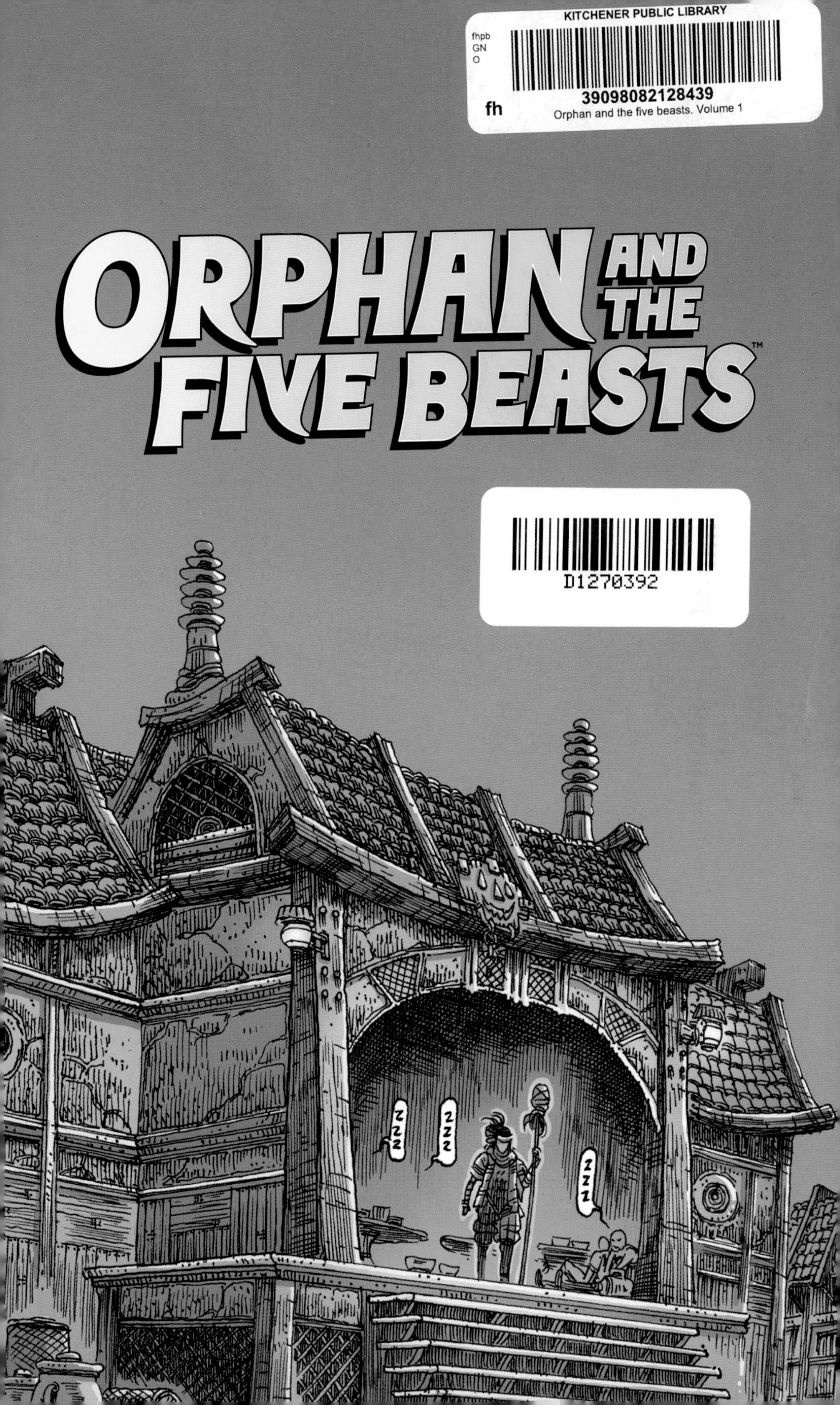
ZZZ
ZZZ
ZZZ

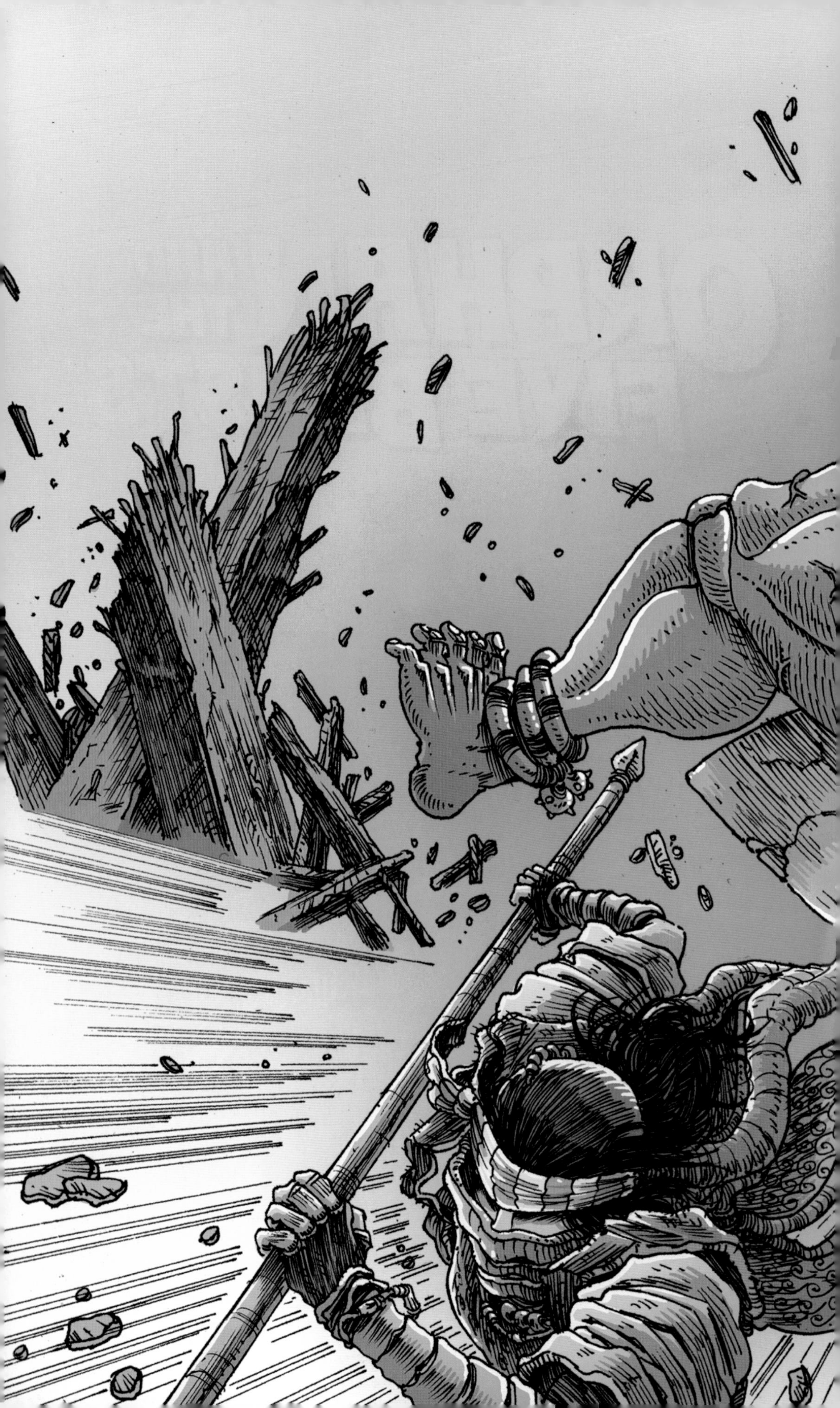

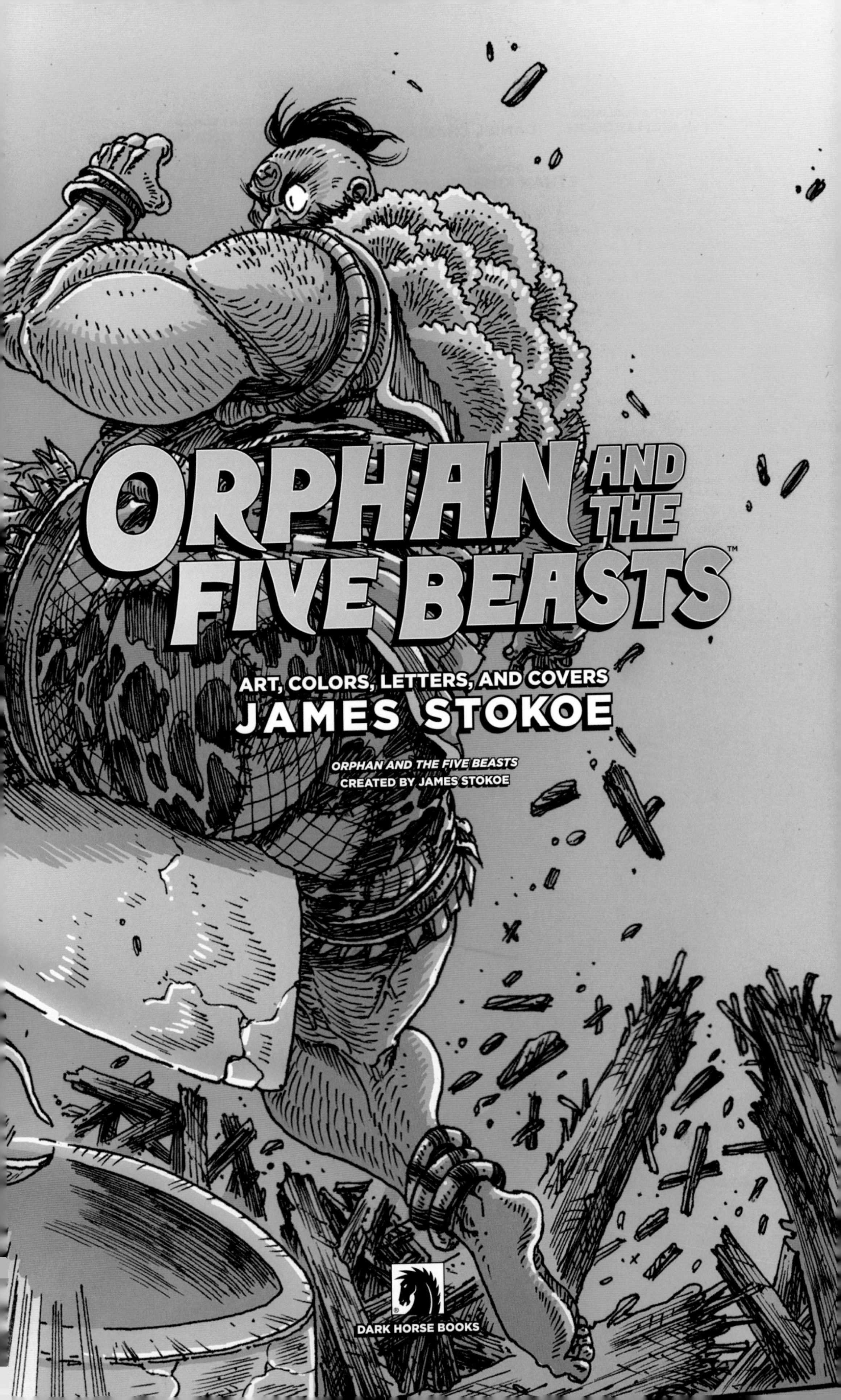

ORPHAN AND THE FIVE BEASTS™

ART, COLORS, LETTERS, AND COVERS

JAMES STOKOE

ORPHAN AND THE FIVE BEASTS

CREATED BY JAMES STOKOE

DARK HORSE BOOKS

PRESIDENT & PUBLISHER
MIKE RICHARDSON

EDITOR
DANIEL CHABON

ASSISTANT EDITORS
CHUCK HOWITT AND MISHA GEHR

DESIGNER
ETHAN KIMBERLING

DIGITAL ART TECHNICIAN
ADAM PRUETT

Orphan and the Five Beasts Volume One

Neil Hankerson, *Executive Vice President* Tom Weddle, *Chief Financial Officer* • Dale LaFountain, *Chief Information Officer* • Tim Wiesch, *Vice President of Licensing* • Matt Parkinson, *Vice President of Marketing* Vanessa Todd-Holmes, *Vice President of Production and Scheduling* • Mark Bernardi, *Vice President of Book Trade and Digital Sales* • Randy Lahrman, *Vice President of Product Development* • Ken Lizzi, *General Counsel* • Dave Marshall, *Editor in Chief* • Davey Estrada, *Editorial Director* • Chris Warner, *Senior Books Editor* • Cary Grazzini, *Director of Specialty Projects* • Lia Ribacchi, *Art Director* • Matt Dryer, *Director of Digital Art and Prepress* Michael Gombos, *Senior Director of Licensed Publications* • Kari Yadro, *Director of Custom Programs* • Kari Torson, *Director of International Licensing*

Library of Congress Cataloging-in-Publication Data

Names: Stokoe, James, author, artist.
Title: Orphan and the five beasts / art, colors, letters, and covers, James Stokoe.
Description: First edition. | Milwaukie, OR : Dark Horse Books, 2021. | "Orphan and the Five Beasts created by James Stakoe" | Summary: "Spurred on by her master's dying words, the adopted warrior "Orphan Mo" seeks to find and kill five former disciples who now threaten the land with corruption from their demonic powers"-- Provided by publisher.
Identifiers: LCCN 2021022068 (print) | LCCN 2021022069 (ebook) | ISBN 9781506715179 (trade paperback) | ISBN 9781506715148 (ebook)
Subjects: LCSH: Comic books, strips, etc. | LCGFT: Comics (Graphic works)
Classification: LCC PN6728.O766 S86 2021 (print) | LCC PN6728.O766 (ebook) | DDC 741.5/973--dc23
LC record available at https://lccn.loc.gov/2021022068
LC ebook record available at https://lccn.loc.gov/2021022069

Collects Orphan and the Five Beasts #1–#4.

Published by
Dark Horse Books
A division of Dark Horse Comics LLC
10956 SE Main Street
Milwaukie, OR 97222

DarkHorse.com

To find a comics shop in your area, visit comicshoplocator.com

First edition: July 2022
Ebook ISBN 978-1-50671-514-8
Trade paperback ISBN 978-1-50671-517-9

MIX
Paper from
responsible sources
FSC® C169962
FSC
www.fsc.org

1 3 5 7 9 10 8 6 4 2
Printed in China

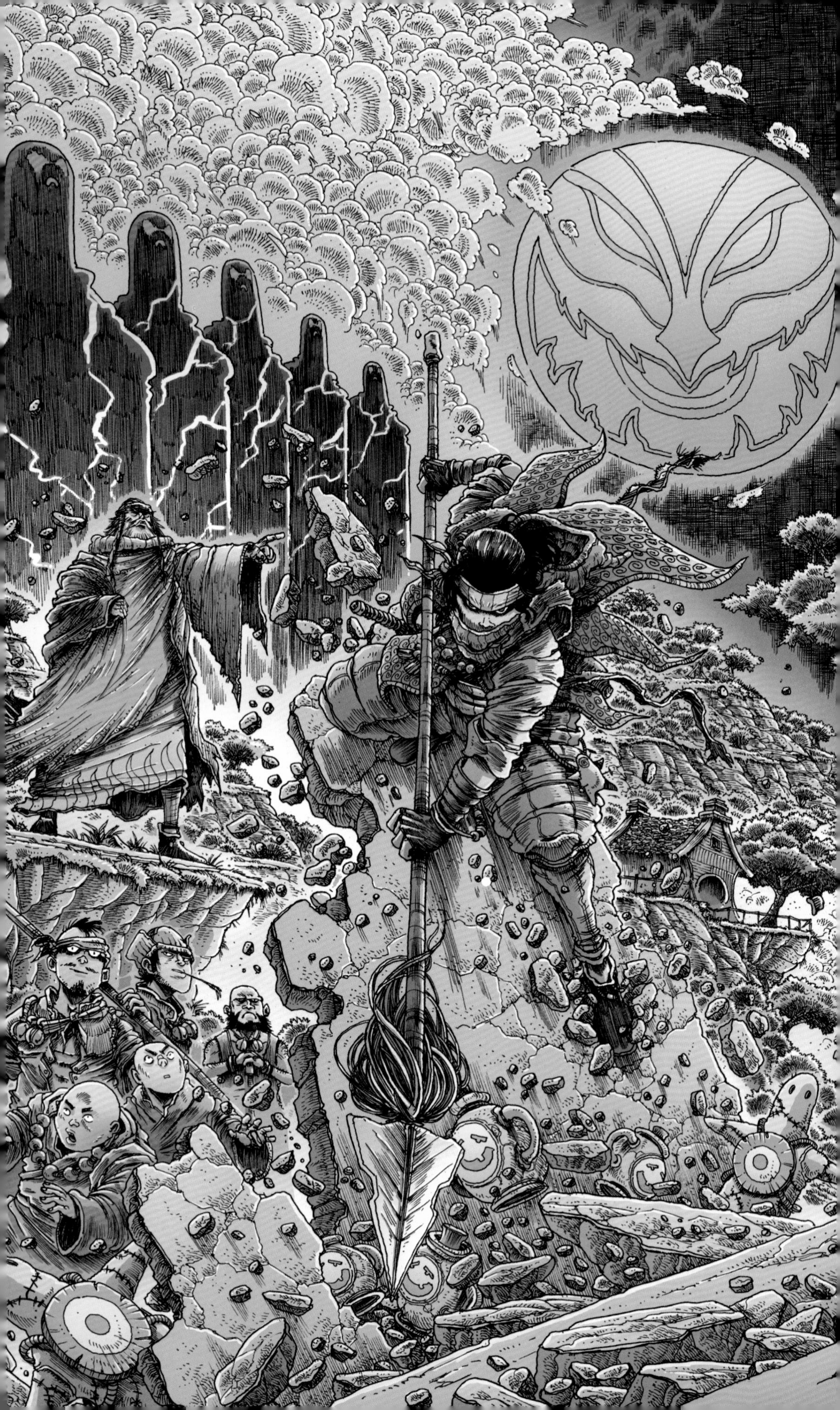

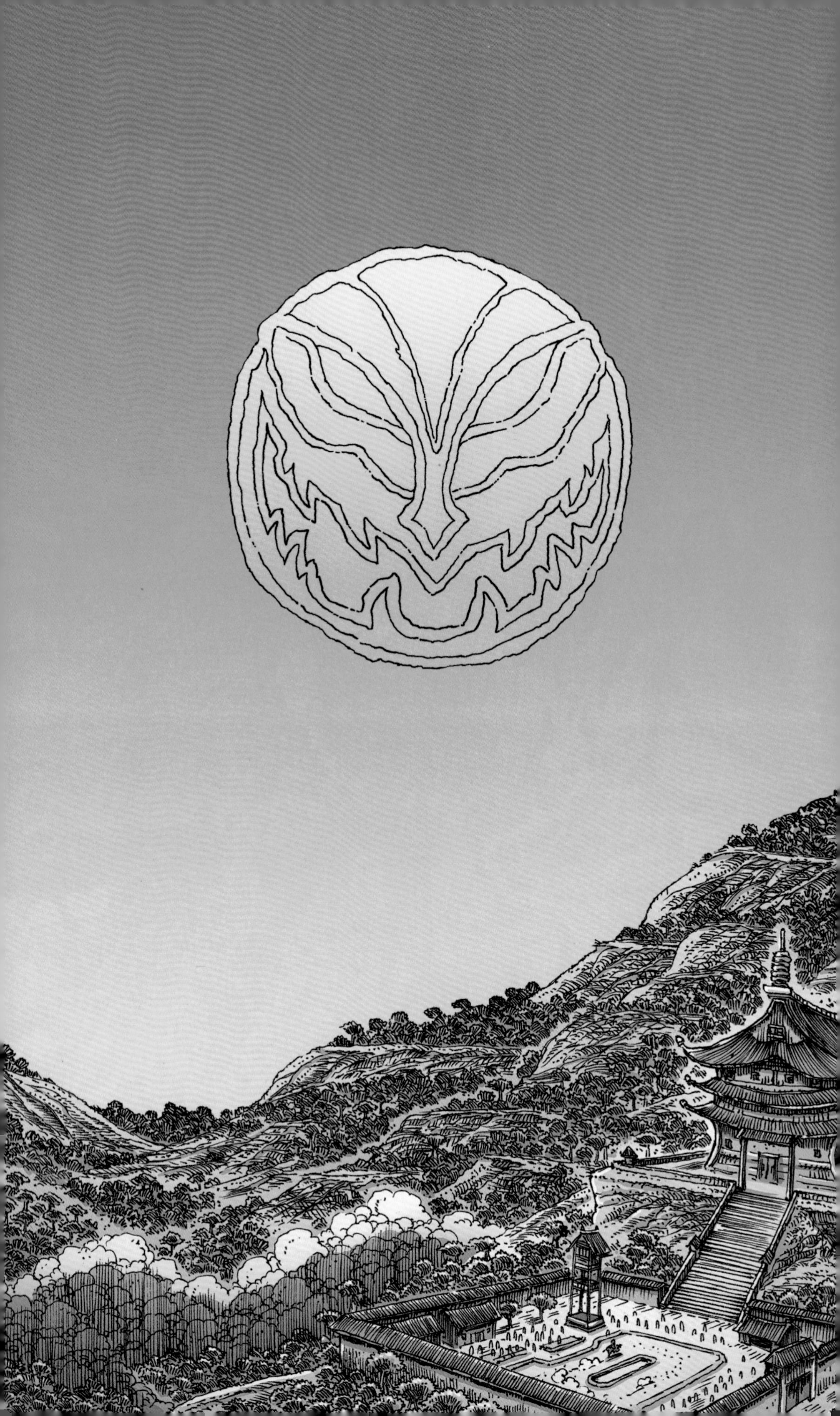

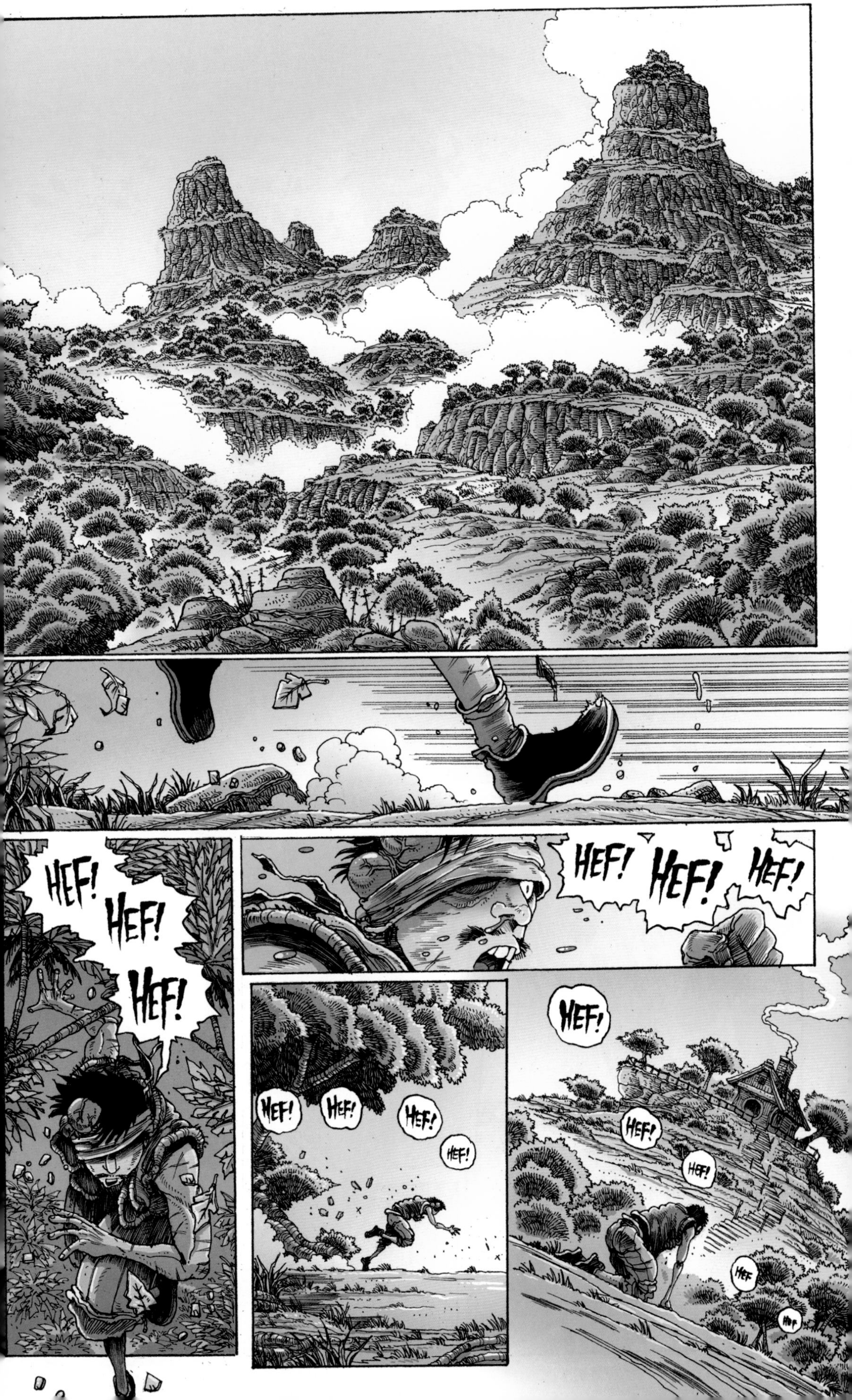
HEF!
HEF!
HEF!
HEF!
HEF!
HEF!
HEF!
HEF!
HEF!
HEF!
HEF!
HEF!
HEF!
HEF!
HEF

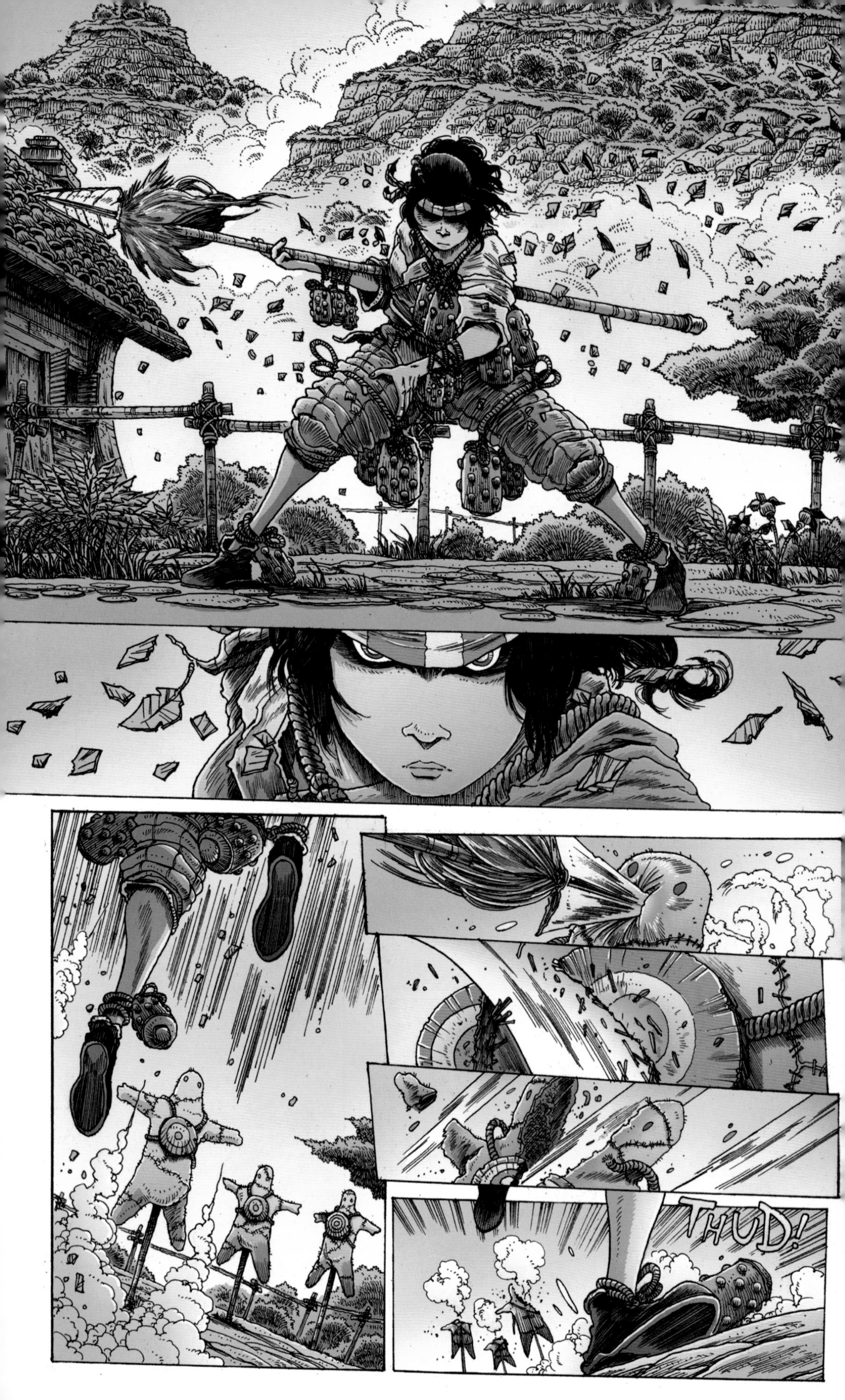
THUD!

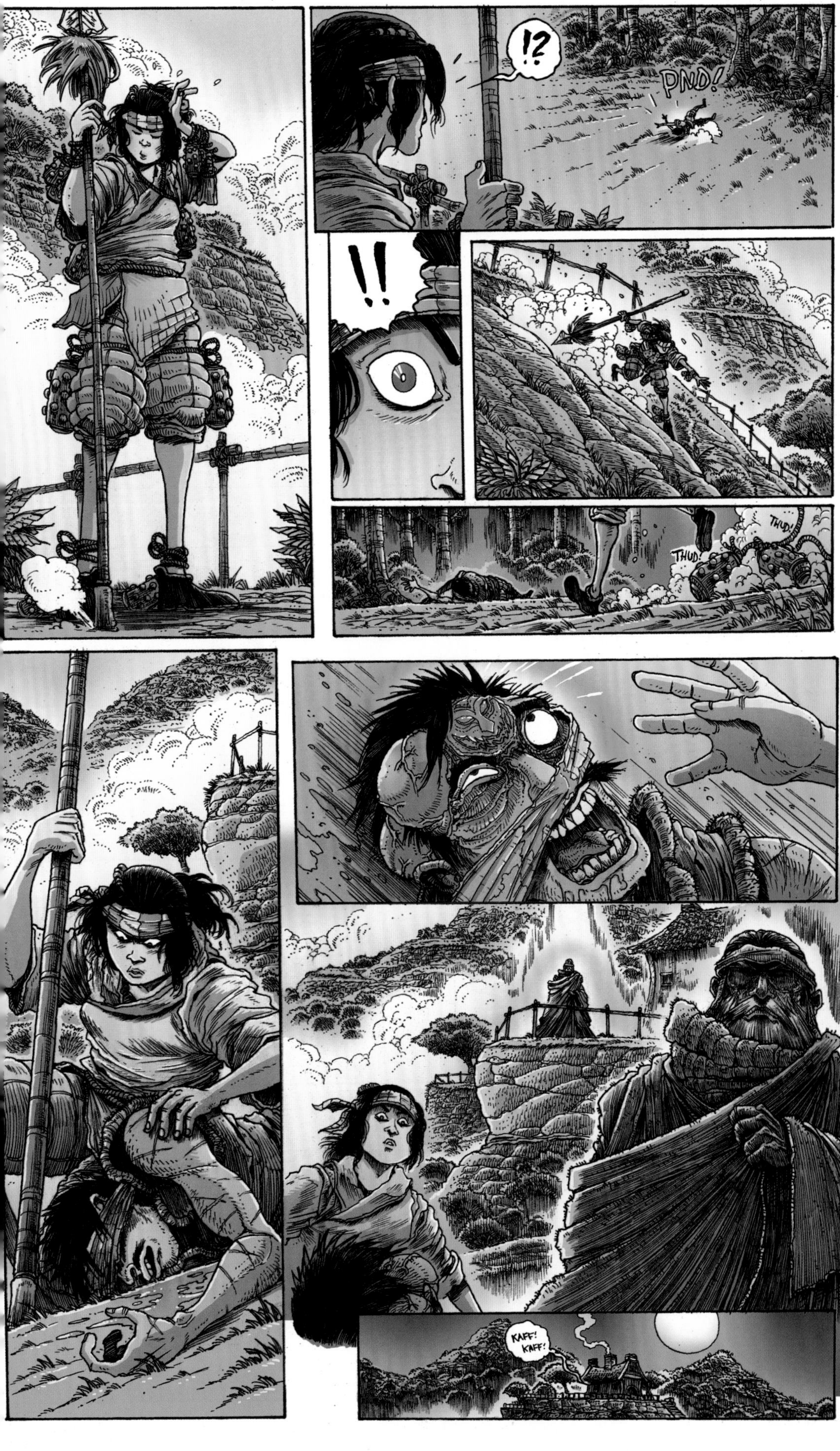
!?
PND!
!!
THUD!
THUD!
KAFF!
KAFF!

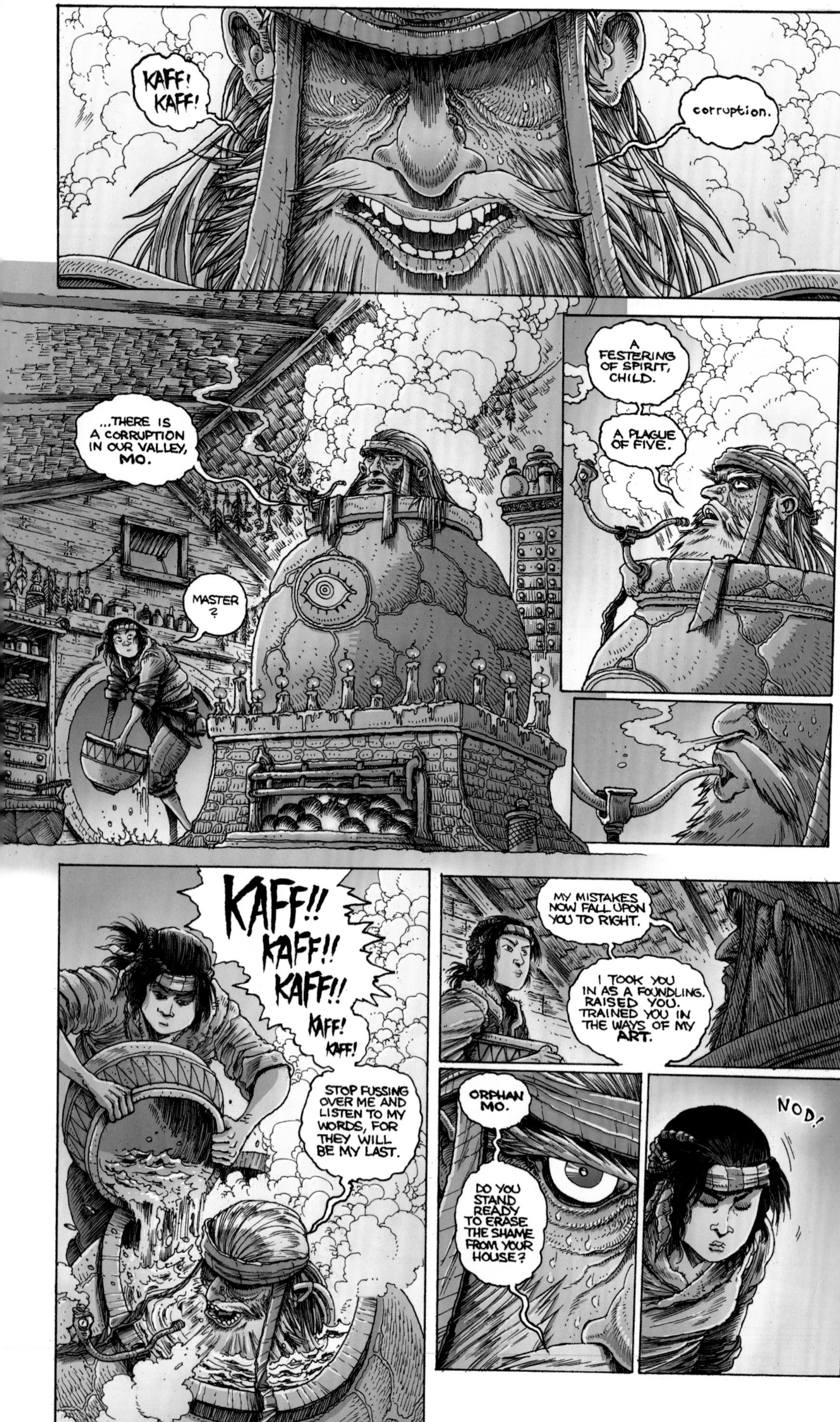
KAFF! KAFF!
corruption.
...THERE IS A CORRUPTION IN OUR VALLEY, MO.
MASTER?
A FESTERING OF SPIRIT, CHILD.
A PLAGUE OF FIVE.
KAFF!! KAFF!! KAFF!! KAFF! KAFF!
STOP FUSSING OVER ME AND LISTEN TO MY WORDS, FOR THEY WILL BE MY LAST.
MY MISTAKES NOW FALL UPON YOU TO RIGHT.
I TOOK YOU IN AS A FOUNDLING. RAISED YOU. TRAINED YOU IN THE WAYS OF MY ART.
ORPHAN MO.
DO YOU STAND READY TO ERASE THE SHAME FROM YOUR HOUSE?
NOD!

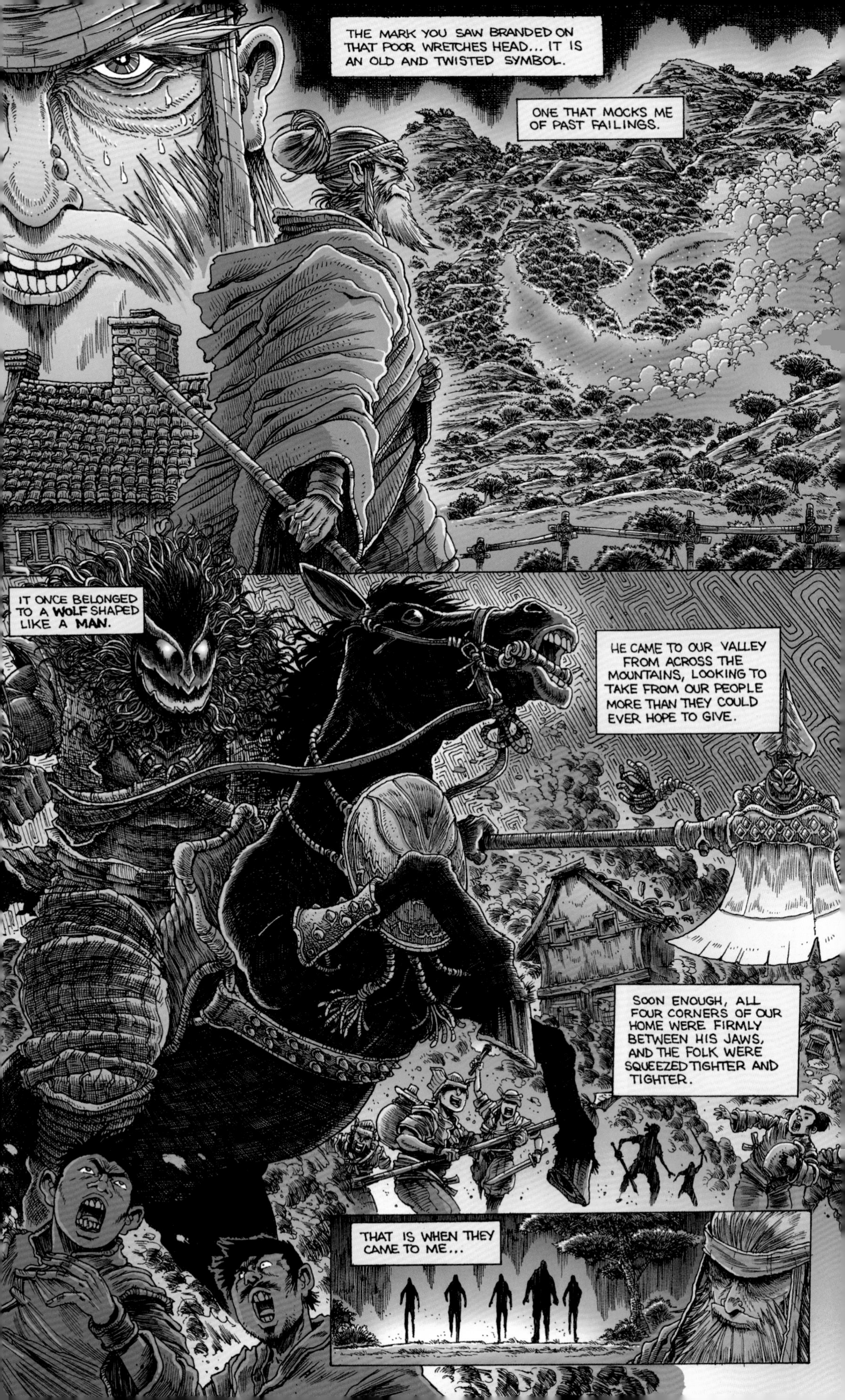
THE MARK YOU SAW BRANDED ON THAT POOR WRETCHES HEAD... IT IS AN OLD AND TWISTED SYMBOL.
ONE THAT MOCKS ME OF PAST FAILINGS.
IT ONCE BELONGED TO A **WOLF** SHAPED LIKE A **MAN**.
HE CAME TO OUR VALLEY FROM ACROSS THE MOUNTAINS, LOOKING TO TAKE FROM OUR PEOPLE MORE THAN THEY COULD EVER HOPE TO GIVE.
SOON ENOUGH, ALL FOUR CORNERS OF OUR HOME WERE FIRMLY BETWEEN HIS JAWS, AND THE FOLK WERE SQUEEZED TIGHTER AND TIGHTER.
THAT IS WHEN THEY CAME TO ME...

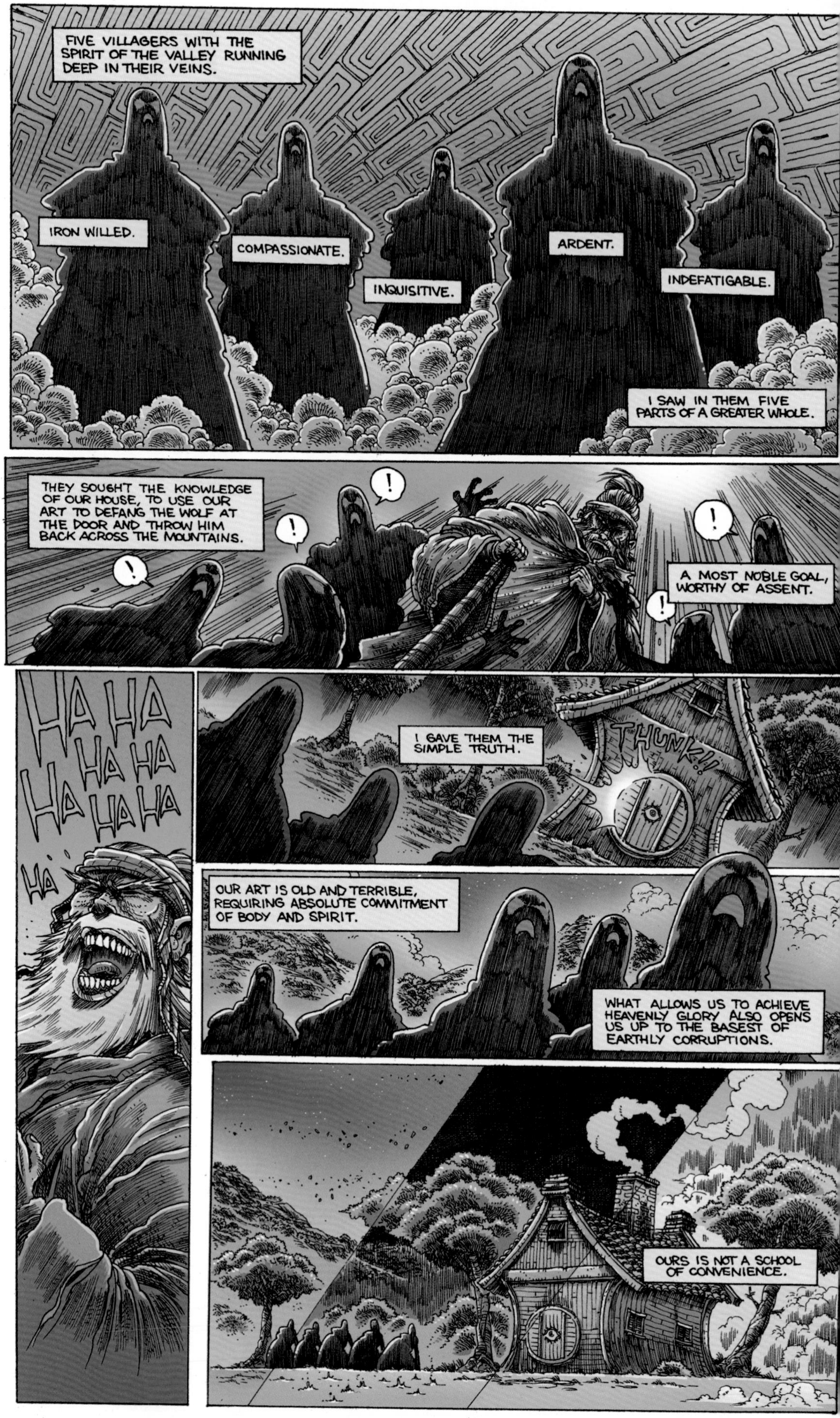

FIVE VILLAGERS WITH THE SPIRIT OF THE VALLEY RUNNING DEEP IN THEIR VEINS.
IRON WILLED.
COMPASSIONATE.
INQUISITIVE.
ARDENT.
INDEFATIGABLE.
I SAW IN THEM FIVE PARTS OF A GREATER WHOLE.
THEY SOUGHT THE KNOWLEDGE OF OUR HOUSE, TO USE OUR ART TO DEFANG THE WOLF AT THE DOOR AND THROW HIM BACK ACROSS THE MOUNTAINS.
!
!
!
!
!
A MOST NOBLE GOAL, WORTHY OF ASSENT.
HA HA HA HA HA HA HA HA
HA
I GAVE THEM THE SIMPLE TRUTH.
THUNK!!
OUR ART IS OLD AND TERRIBLE, REQUIRING ABSOLUTE COMMITMENT OF BODY AND SPIRIT.
WHAT ALLOWS US TO ACHIEVE HEAVENLY GLORY ALSO OPENS US UP TO THE BASEST OF EARTHLY CORRUPTIONS.
OURS IS NOT A SCHOOL OF CONVENIENCE.

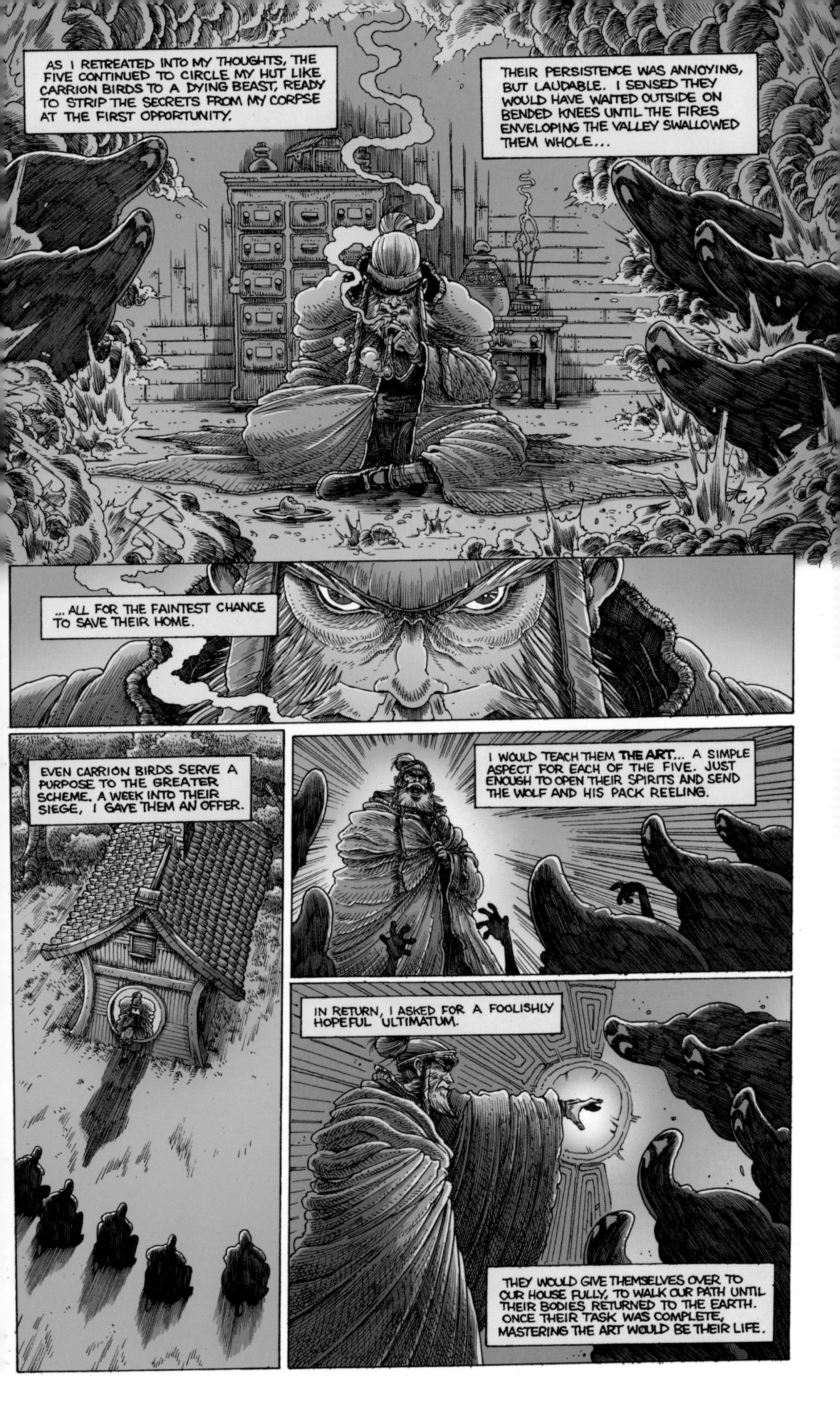
AS I RETREATED INTO MY THOUGHTS, THE FIVE CONTINUED TO CIRCLE MY HUT LIKE CARRION BIRDS TO A DYING BEAST, READY TO STRIP THE SECRETS FROM MY CORPSE AT THE FIRST OPPORTUNITY.
THEIR PERSISTENCE WAS ANNOYING, BUT LAUDABLE. I SENSED THEY WOULD HAVE WAITED OUTSIDE ON BENDED KNEES UNTIL THE FIRES ENVELOPING THE VALLEY SWALLOWED THEM WHOLE...
...ALL FOR THE FAINTEST CHANCE TO SAVE THEIR HOME.
EVEN CARRION BIRDS SERVE A PURPOSE TO THE GREATER SCHEME. A WEEK INTO THEIR SIEGE, I GAVE THEM AN OFFER.
I WOULD TEACH THEM **THE ART**... A SIMPLE ASPECT FOR EACH OF THE FIVE. JUST ENOUGH TO OPEN THEIR SPIRITS AND SEND THE WOLF AND HIS PACK REELING.
IN RETURN, I ASKED FOR A FOOLISHLY HOPEFUL ULTIMATUM.
THEY WOULD GIVE THEMSELVES OVER TO OUR HOUSE FULLY, TO WALK OUR PATH UNTIL THEIR BODIES RETURNED TO THE EARTH. ONCE THEIR TASK WAS COMPLETE, MASTERING THE ART WOULD BE THEIR LIFE.

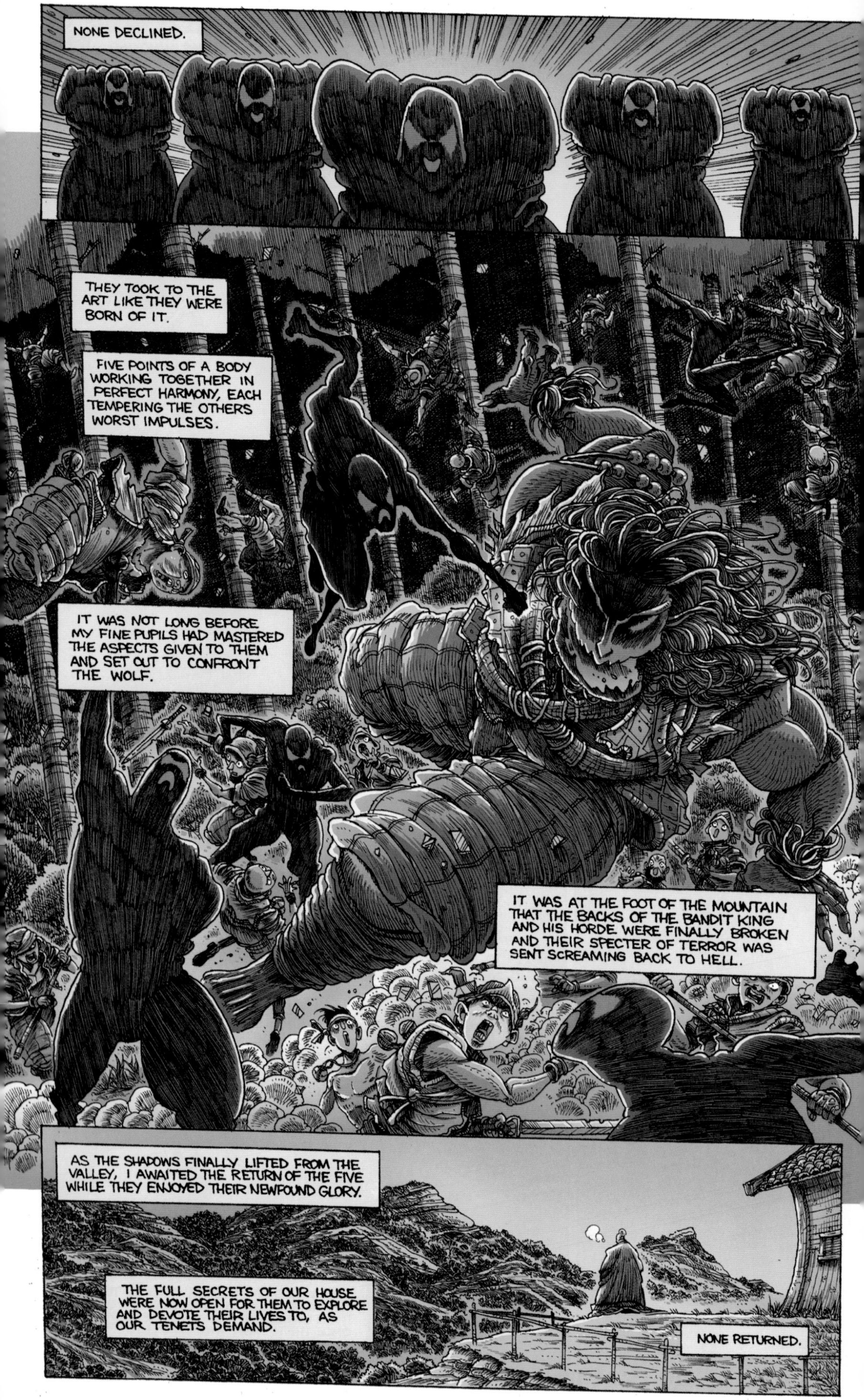
NONE DECLINED.
THEY TOOK TO THE ART LIKE THEY WERE BORN OF IT.
FIVE POINTS OF A BODY WORKING TOGETHER IN PERFECT HARMONY, EACH TEMPERING THE OTHERS WORST IMPULSES.
IT WAS NOT LONG BEFORE MY FINE PUPILS HAD MASTERED THE ASPECTS GIVEN TO THEM AND SET OUT TO CONFRONT THE WOLF.
IT WAS AT THE FOOT OF THE MOUNTAIN THAT THE BACKS OF THE BANDIT KING AND HIS HORDE WERE FINALLY BROKEN AND THEIR SPECTER OF TERROR WAS SENT SCREAMING BACK TO HELL.
AS THE SHADOWS FINALLY LIFTED FROM THE VALLEY, I AWAITED THE RETURN OF THE FIVE WHILE THEY ENJOYED THEIR NEWFOUND GLORY.
THE FULL SECRETS OF OUR HOUSE WERE NOW OPEN FOR THEM TO EXPLORE AND DEVOTE THEIR LIVES TO, AS OUR TENETS DEMAND.
NONE RETURNED.

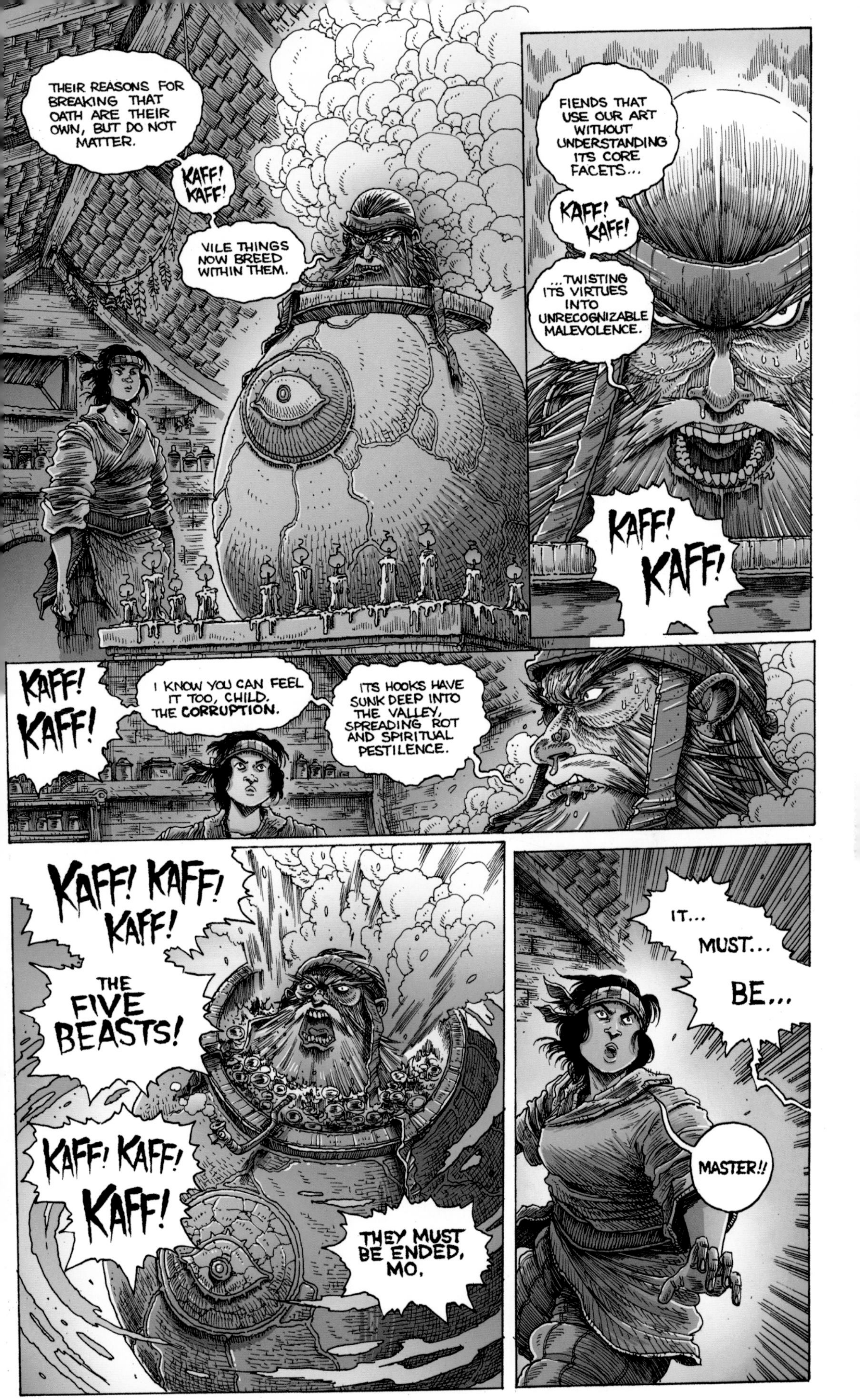
THEIR REASONS FOR BREAKING THAT OATH ARE THEIR OWN, BUT DO NOT MATTER.
KAFF! KAFF!
VILE THINGS NOW BREED WITHIN THEM.
FIENDS THAT USE OUR ART WITHOUT UNDERSTANDING ITS CORE FACETS...
KAFF! KAFF!
...TWISTING ITS VIRTUES INTO UNRECOGNIZABLE MALEVOLENCE.
KAFF! KAFF!
KAFF! KAFF!
I KNOW YOU CAN FEEL IT TOO, CHILD. THE CORRUPTION.
ITS HOOKS HAVE SUNK DEEP INTO THE VALLEY, SPREADING ROT AND SPIRITUAL PESTILENCE.
KAFF! KAFF! KAFF!
THE FIVE BEASTS!
KAFF! KAFF! KAFF!
THEY MUST BE ENDED, MO.
IT...
MUST...
BE...
MASTER!!

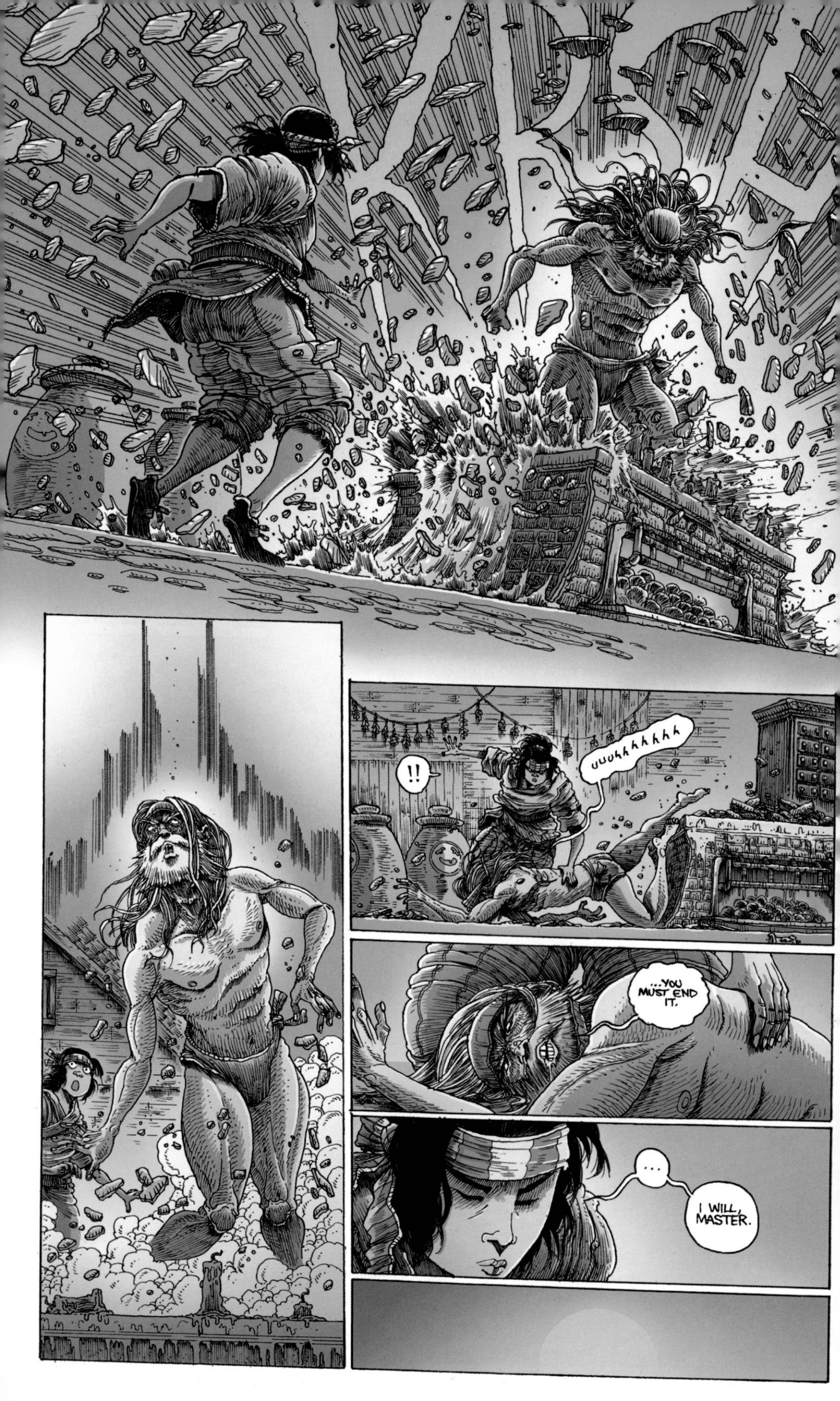

!!
uuuhhhhhh
...YOU MUST END IT.
...
I WILL, MASTER.

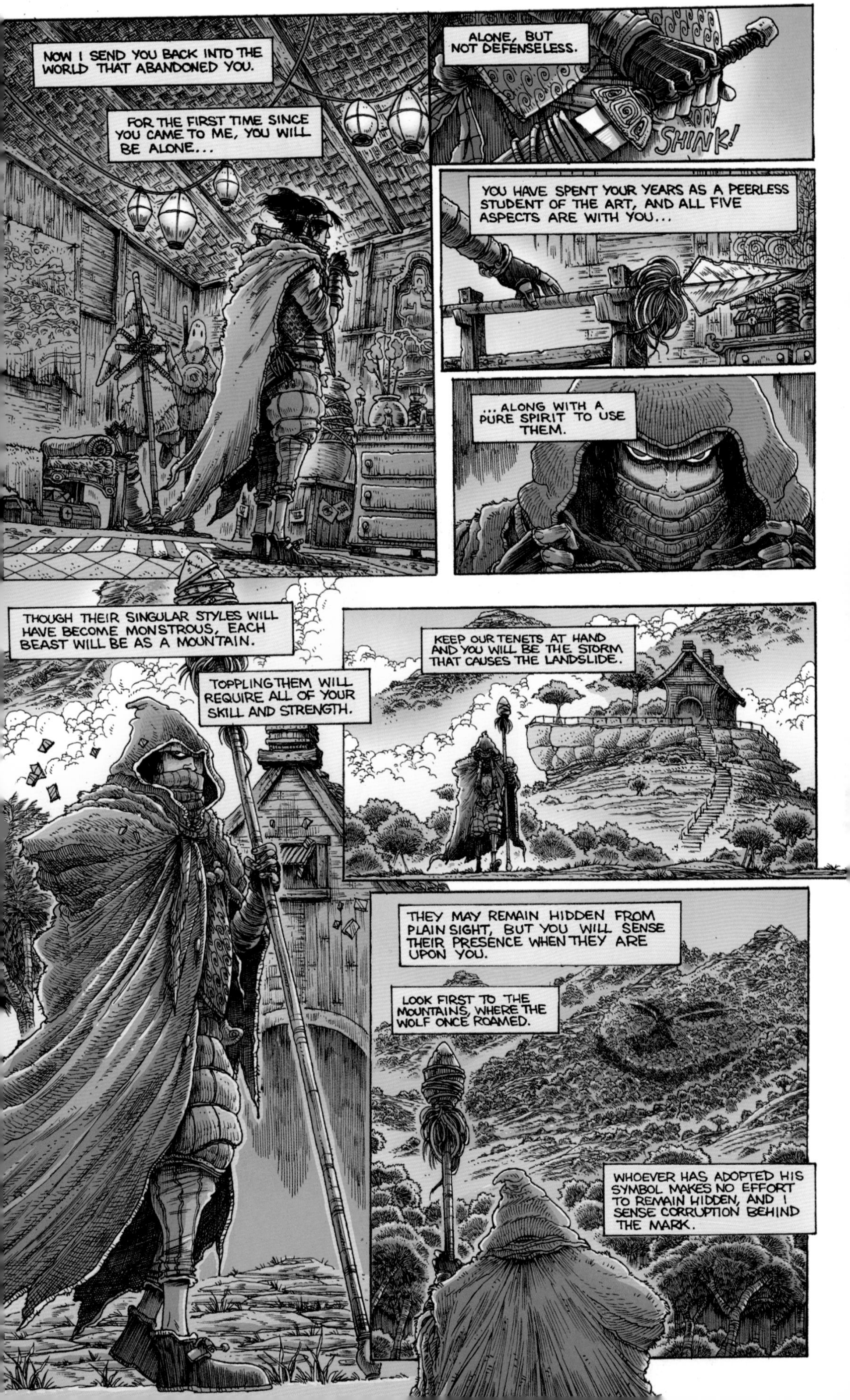
NOW I SEND YOU BACK INTO THE WORLD THAT ABANDONED YOU.
FOR THE FIRST TIME SINCE YOU CAME TO ME, YOU WILL BE ALONE...
ALONE, BUT NOT DEFENSELESS.
SHINK!
YOU HAVE SPENT YOUR YEARS AS A PEERLESS STUDENT OF THE ART, AND ALL FIVE ASPECTS ARE WITH YOU...
...ALONG WITH A PURE SPIRIT TO USE THEM.
THOUGH THEIR SINGULAR STYLES WILL HAVE BECOME MONSTROUS, EACH BEAST WILL BE AS A MOUNTAIN.
TOPPLING THEM WILL REQUIRE ALL OF YOUR SKILL AND STRENGTH.
KEEP OUR TENETS AT HAND AND YOU WILL BE THE STORM THAT CAUSES THE LANDSLIDE.
THEY MAY REMAIN HIDDEN FROM PLAIN SIGHT, BUT YOU WILL SENSE THEIR PRESENCE WHEN THEY ARE UPON YOU.
LOOK FIRST TO THE MOUNTAINS, WHERE THE WOLF ONCE ROAMED.
WHOEVER HAS ADOPTED HIS SYMBOL MAKES NO EFFORT TO REMAIN HIDDEN, AND I SENSE CORRUPTION BEHIND THE MARK.

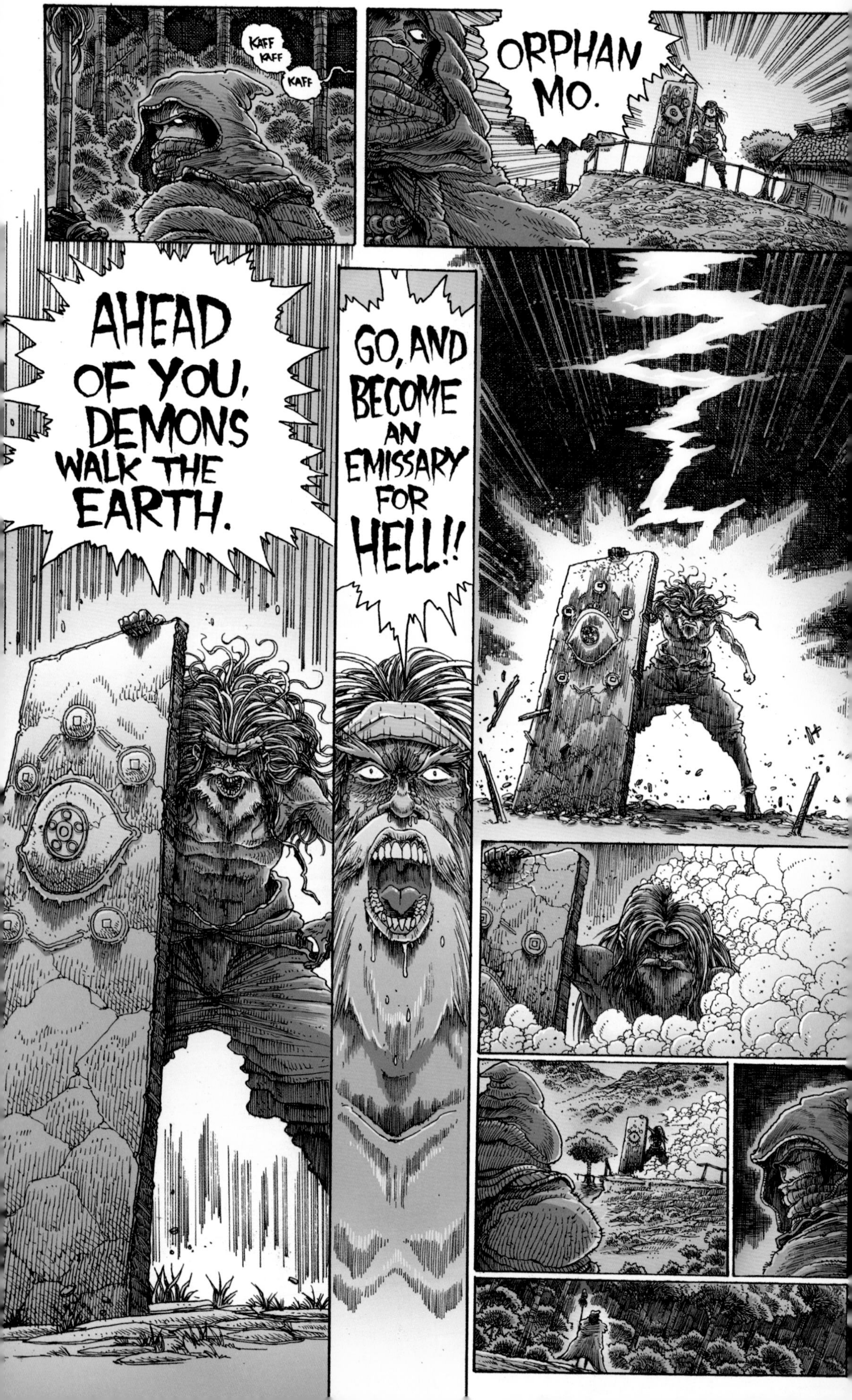
KAFF KAFF
KAFF
ORPHAN MO.
AHEAD OF YOU, DEMONS WALK THE EARTH.
GO, AND BECOME AN EMISSARY FOR HELL!!

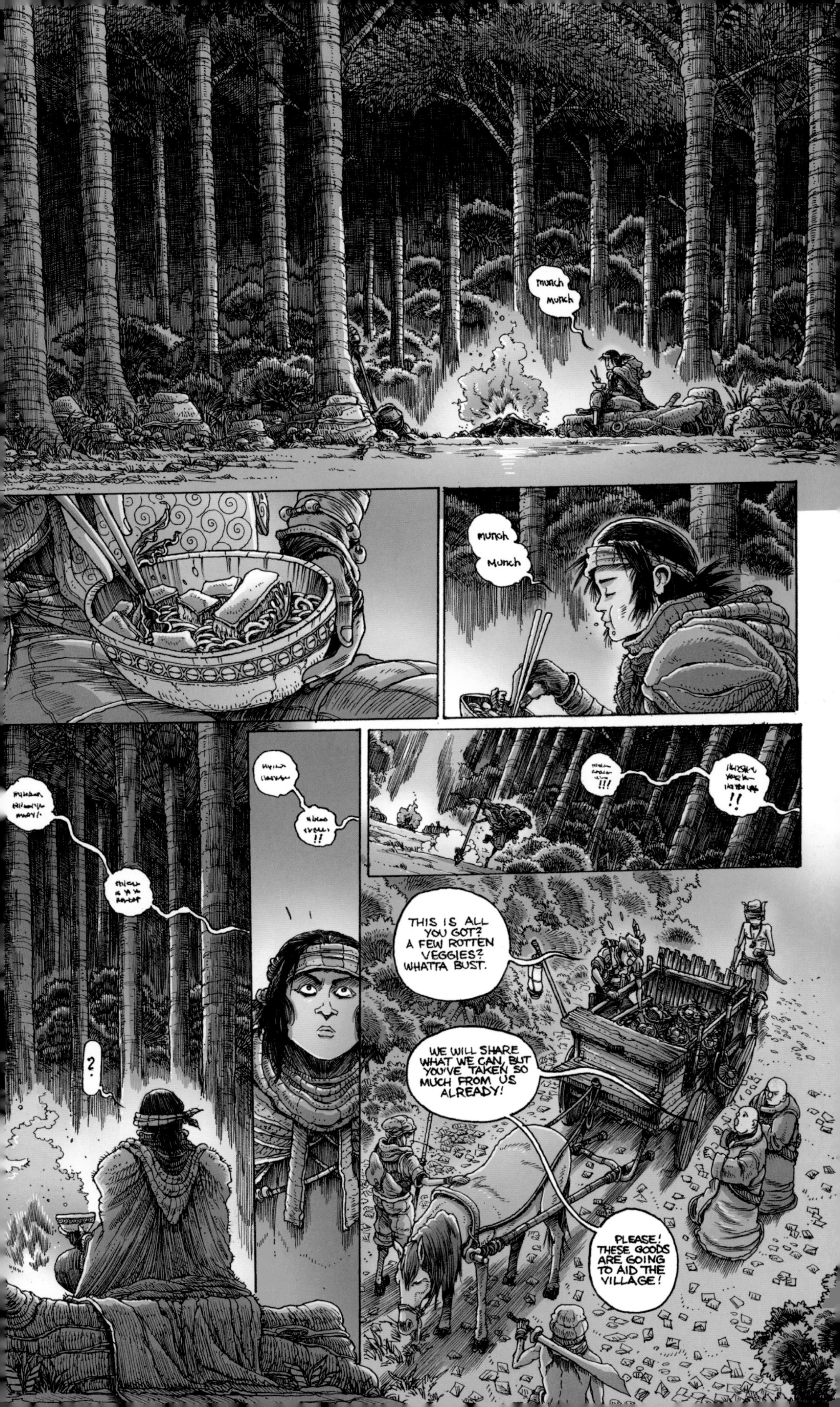
munch
munch
munch
munch
?
THIS IS ALL YOU GOT? A FEW ROTTEN VEGGIES? WHATTA BUST.
WE WILL SHARE WHAT WE CAN, BUT YOU'VE TAKEN SO MUCH FROM US ALREADY!
PLEASE! THESE GOODS ARE GOING TO AID THE VILLAGE!

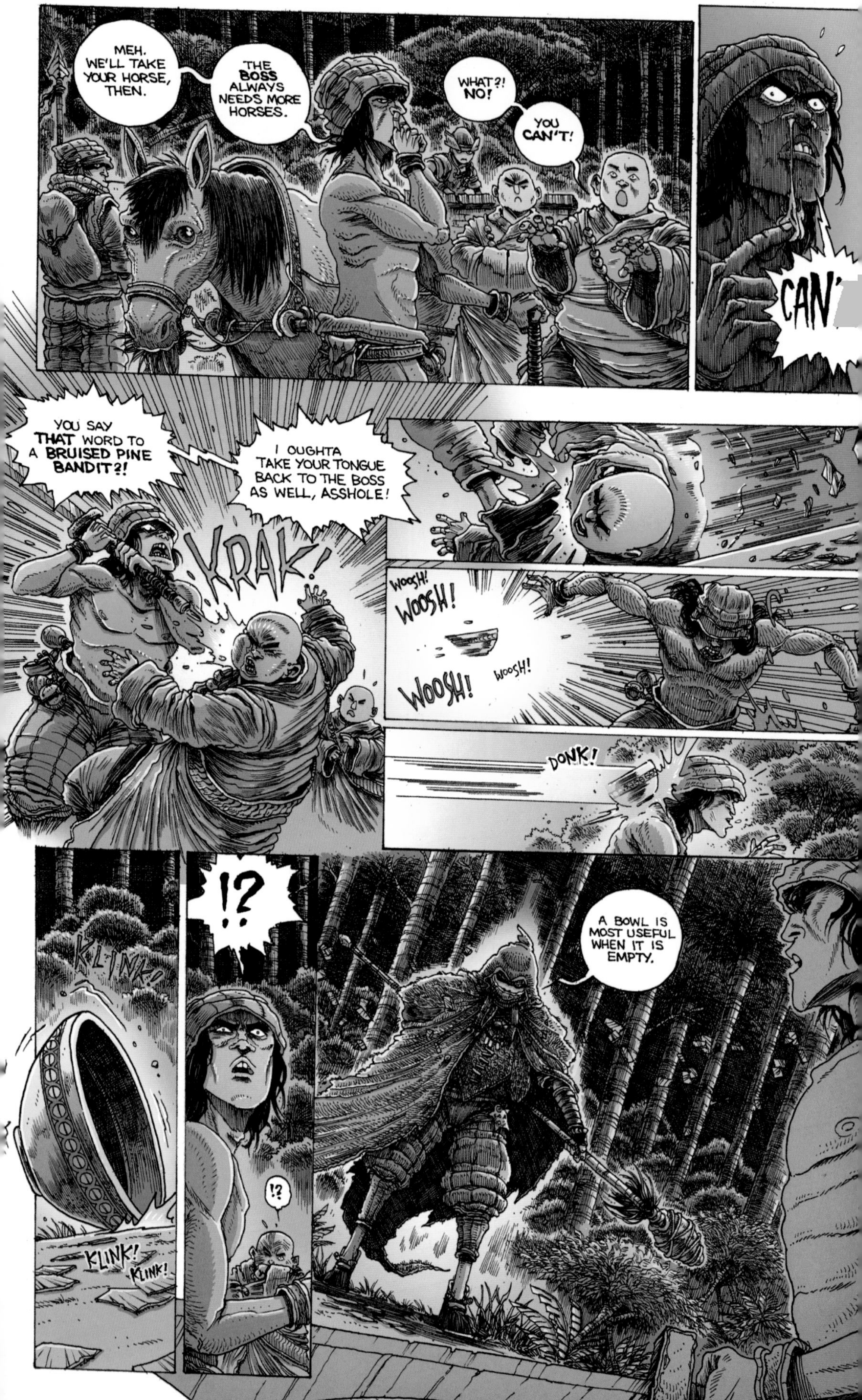
MEH. WE'LL TAKE YOUR HORSE, THEN.
THE BOSS ALWAYS NEEDS MORE HORSES.
WHAT?! NO!
YOU CAN'T!
CAN'
YOU SAY THAT WORD TO A BRUISED PINE BANDIT?!
I OUGHTA TAKE YOUR TONGUE BACK TO THE BOSS AS WELL, ASSHOLE!
KRAK!
WOOSH!
WOOSH!
WOOSH!
WOOSH!
DONK!
KLINK!
KLINK!
KLINK!
!?
!?
A BOWL IS MOST USEFUL WHEN IT IS EMPTY.

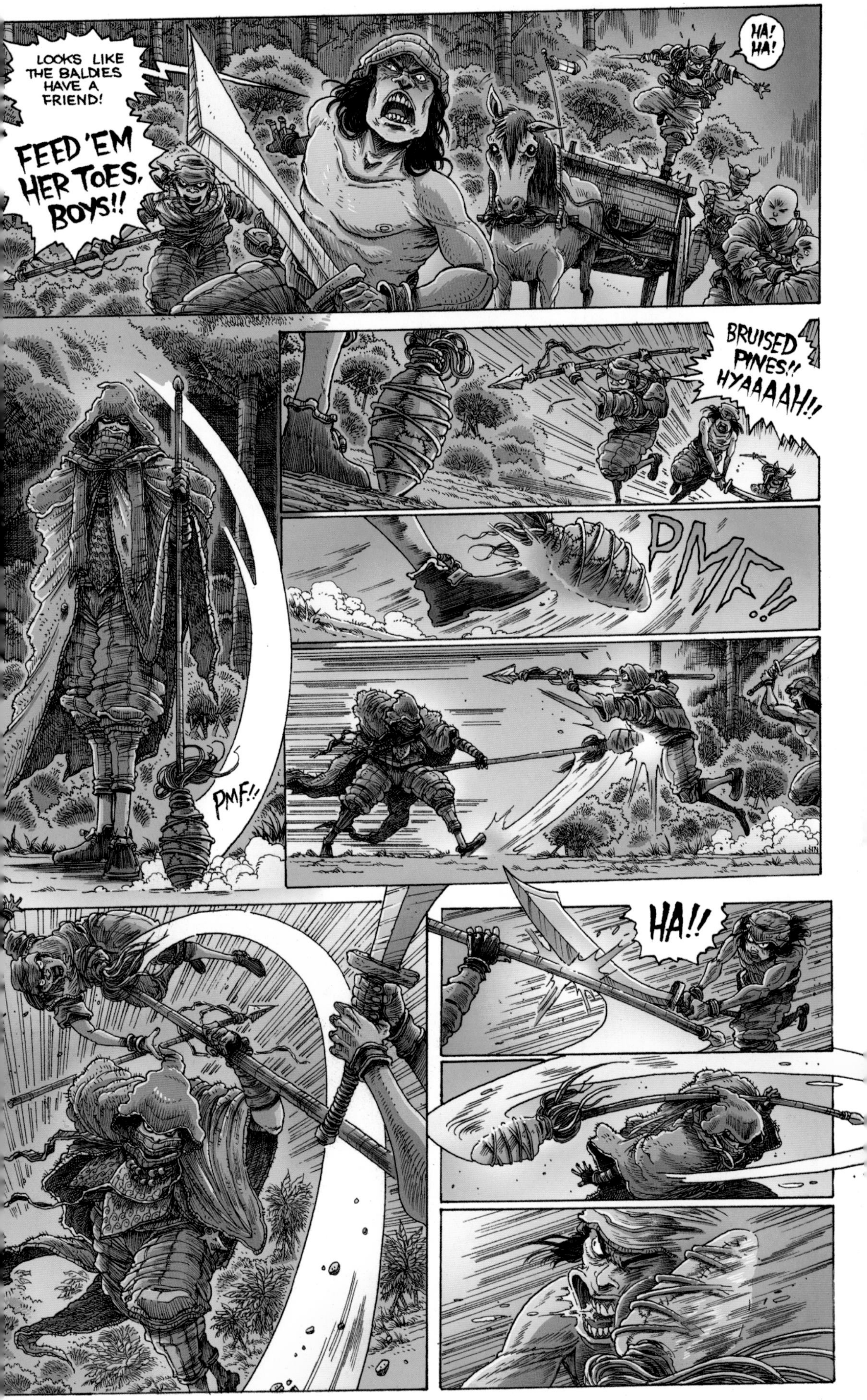
LOOKS LIKE THE BALDIES HAVE A FRIEND!
FEED 'EM HER TOES, BOYS!!
HA! HA!
BRUISED PINES!! HYAAAAH!!
PMF!!
PMF!!
HA!!

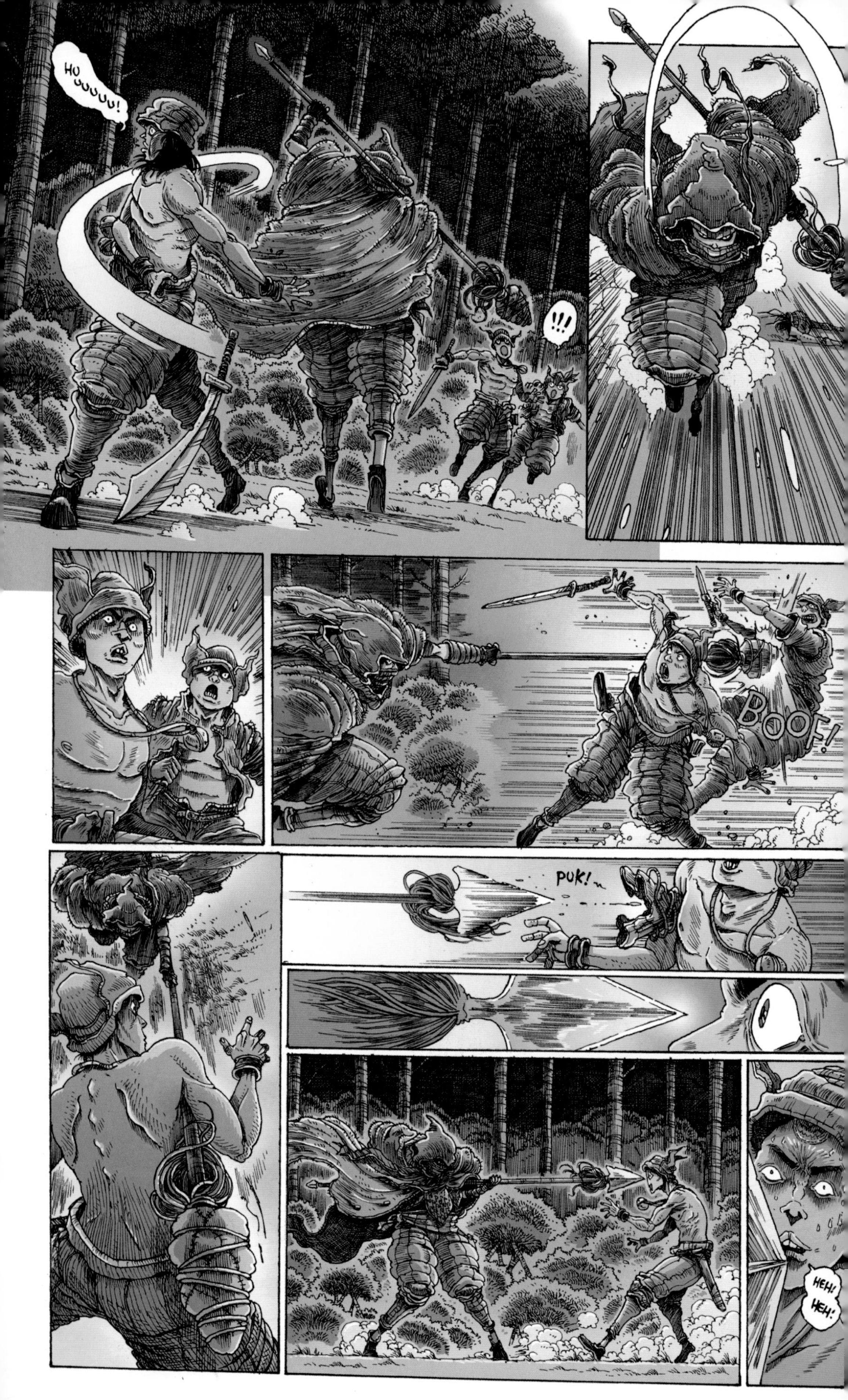
HUUUUUU!
!!!
BOOF!
PUK!
HEH! HEH!

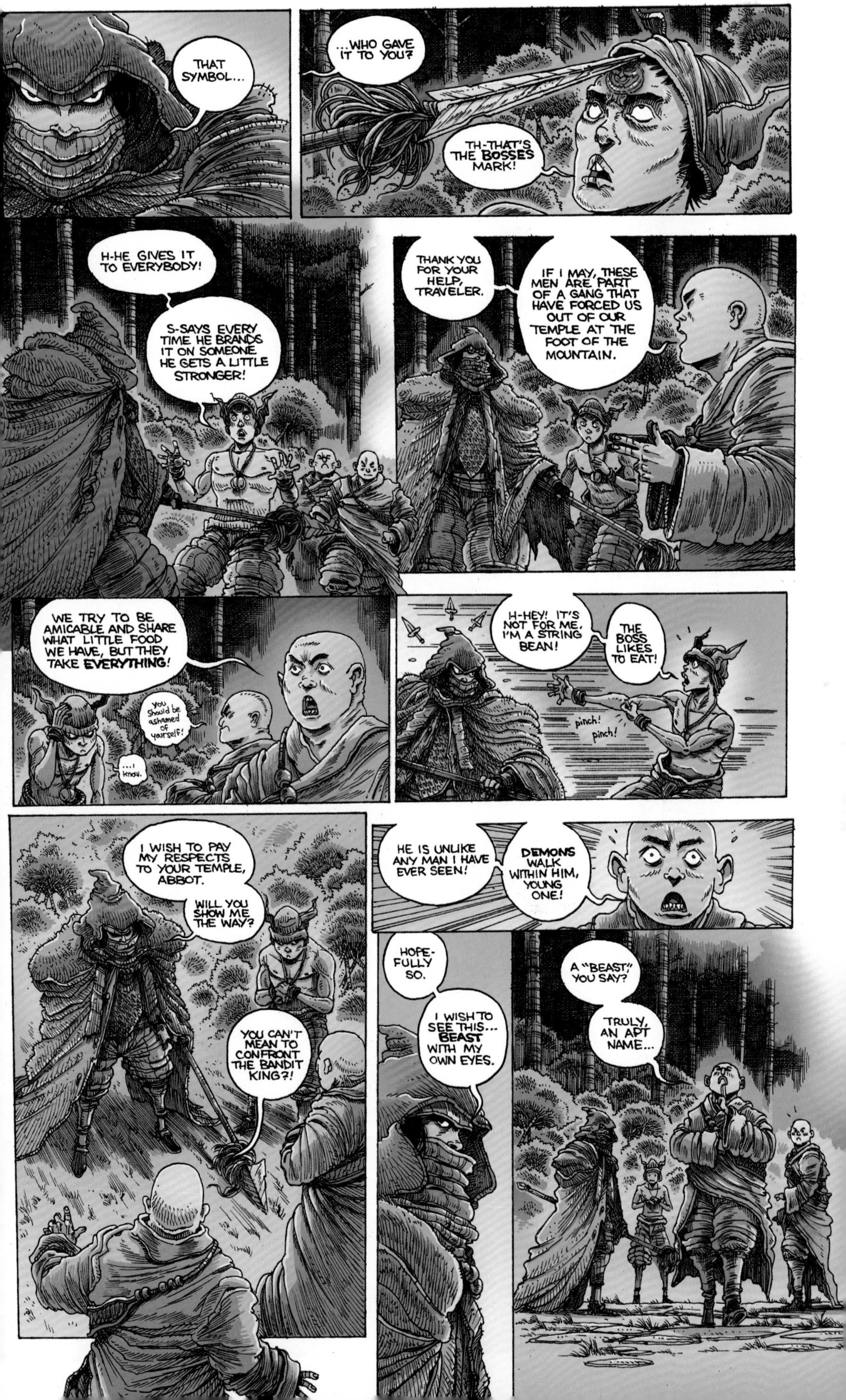
THAT SYMBOL...
...WHO GAVE IT TO YOU?
TH-THAT'S THE **BOSSES** MARK!
H-HE GIVES IT TO EVERYBODY!
S-SAYS EVERY TIME HE BRANDS IT ON SOMEONE HE GETS A LITTLE STRONGER!
THANK YOU FOR YOUR HELP, TRAVELER.
IF I MAY, THESE MEN ARE PART OF A GANG THAT HAVE FORCED US OUT OF OUR TEMPLE AT THE FOOT OF THE MOUNTAIN.
WE TRY TO BE AMICABLE AND SHARE WHAT LITTLE FOOD WE HAVE, BUT THEY TAKE **EVERYTHING**!
You should be ashamed of yourself!
...I know.
H-HEY! IT'S NOT FOR ME, I'M A STRING BEAN!
THE BOSS LIKES TO EAT!
pinch! pinch!
I WISH TO PAY MY RESPECTS TO YOUR TEMPLE, ABBOT.
WILL YOU SHOW ME THE WAY?
YOU CAN'T MEAN TO CONFRONT THE BANDIT KING?!
HE IS UNLIKE ANY MAN I HAVE EVER SEEN!
DEMONS WALK WITHIN HIM, YOUNG ONE!
HOPE-FULLY SO.
I WISH TO SEE THIS... **BEAST** WITH MY OWN EYES.
A "BEAST," YOU SAY?
TRULY, AN APT NAME...

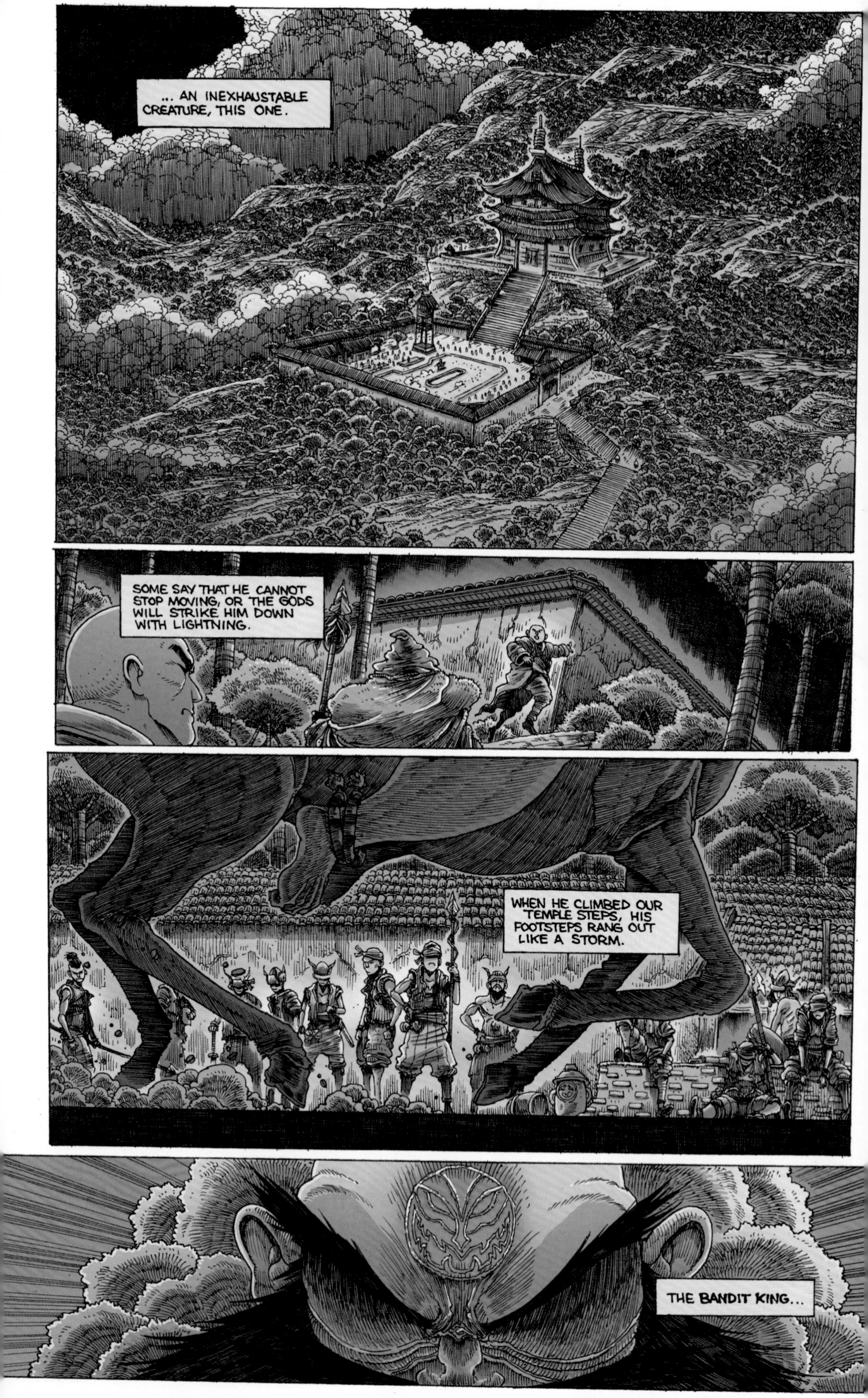
... AN INEXHAUSTABLE CREATURE, THIS ONE.
SOME SAY THAT HE CANNOT STOP MOVING, OR THE GODS WILL STRIKE HIM DOWN WITH LIGHTNING.
WHEN HE CLIMBED OUR TEMPLE STEPS, HIS FOOTSTEPS RANG OUT LIKE A STORM.
THE BANDIT KING...

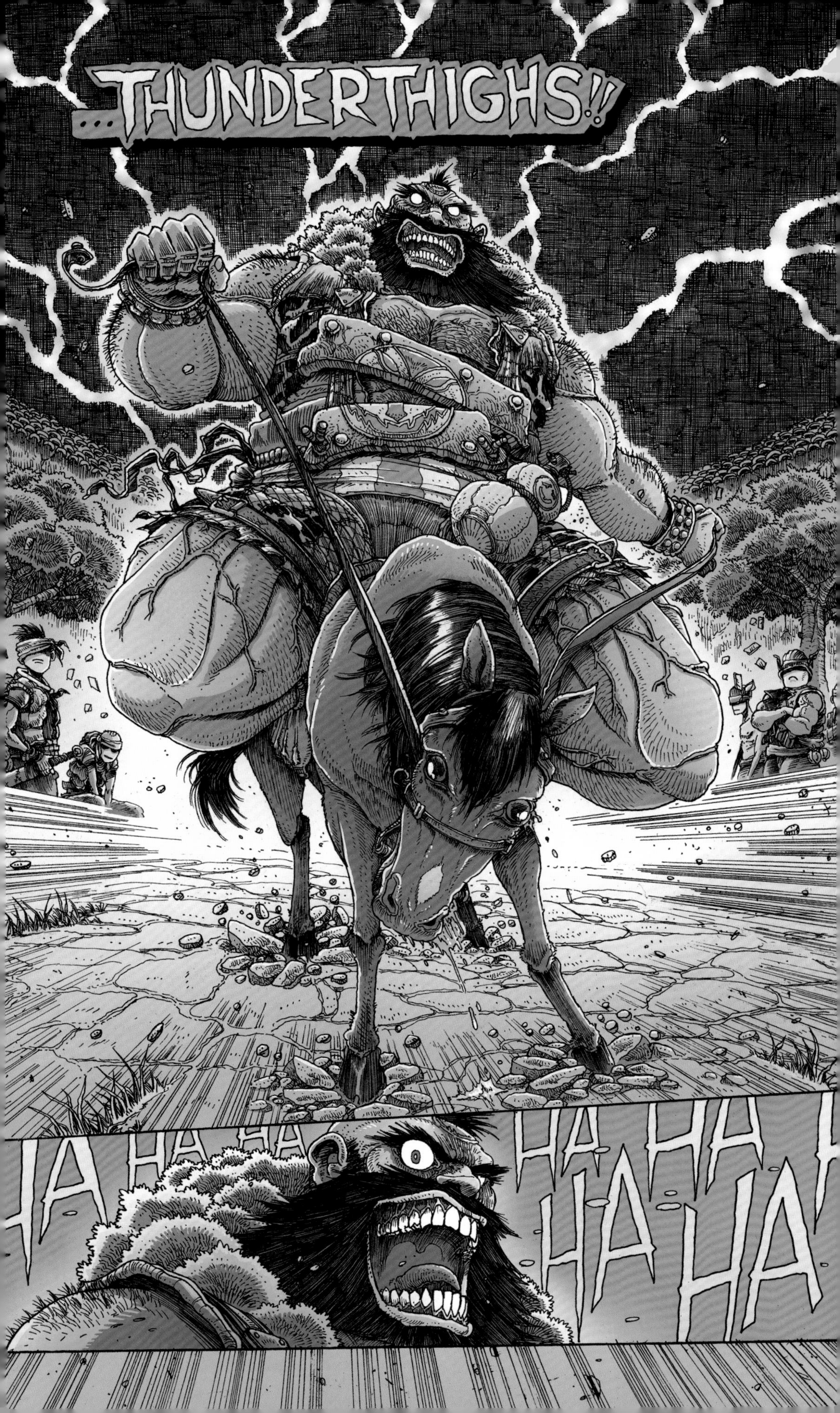
...THUNDERTHIGHS!!
HA HA HA HA HA HA HA HA HA

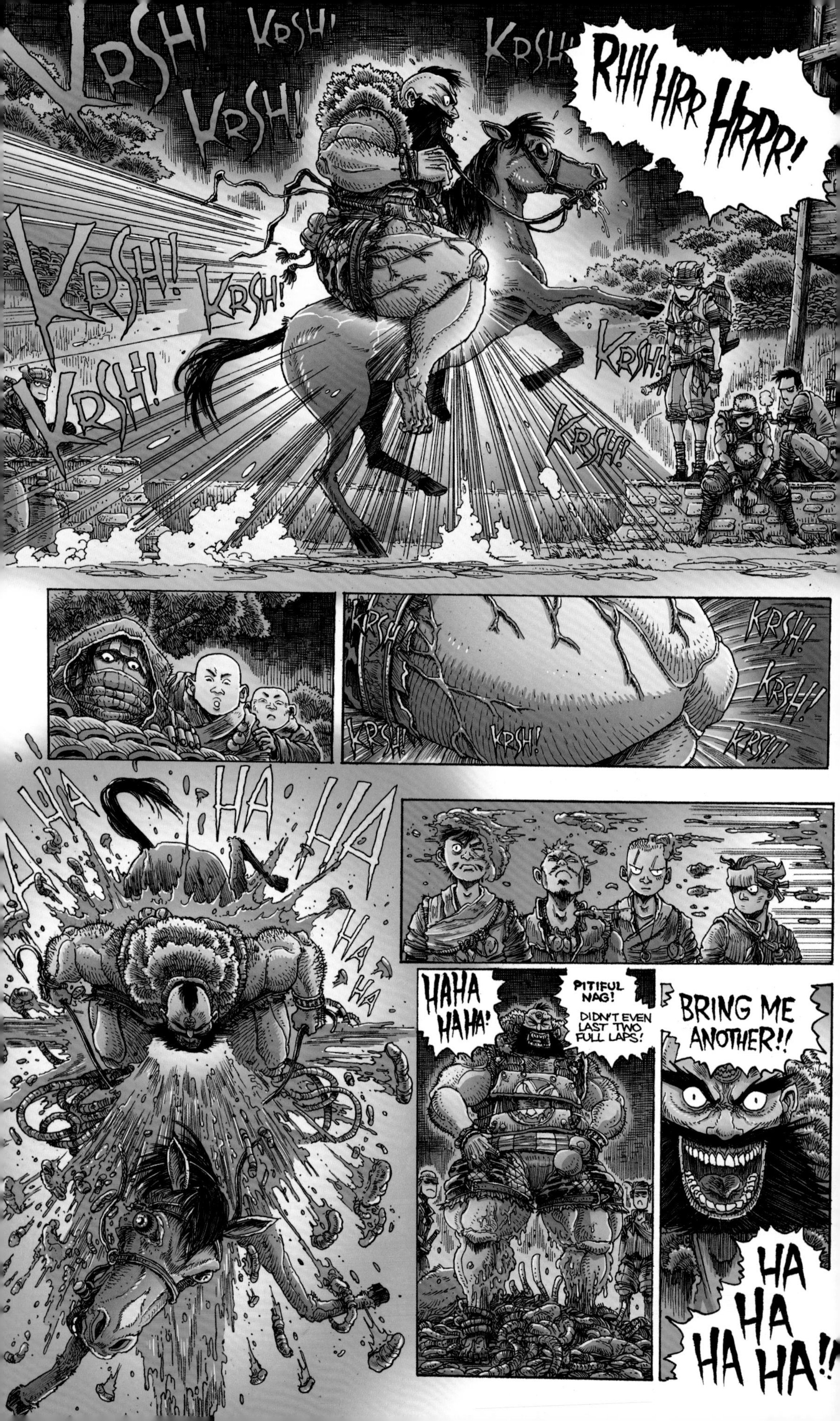
KRSH! KRSH! KRSH!
KRSH!
RHH HRR HRRR!
KRSH! KRSH!
KRSH!
KRSH!
KRSH!
KRSH! KRSH! KRSH! KRSH! KRSH! KRSH!
HA HA HA HA HA
HA HA
HAHA HAHA!
PITIFUL NAG!
DIDN'T EVEN LAST TWO FULL LAPS!
BRING ME ANOTHER!!
HA HA HA HA HA!!

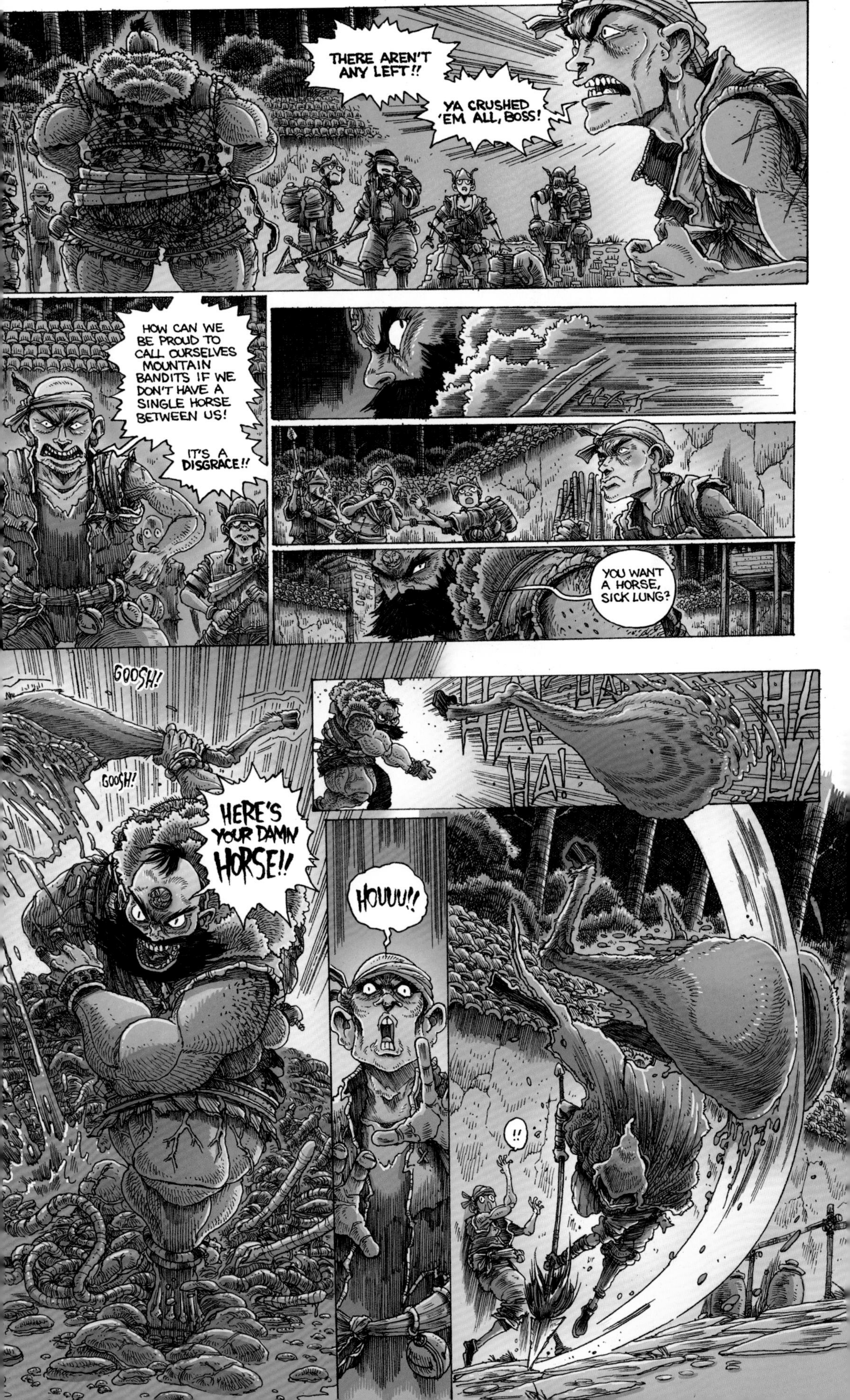
THERE AREN'T ANY LEFT!!
YA CRUSHED 'EM ALL, BOSS!
HOW CAN WE BE PROUD TO CALL OURSELVES MOUNTAIN BANDITS IF WE DON'T HAVE A SINGLE HORSE BETWEEN US!
IT'S A DISGRACE!!
YOU WANT A HORSE, SICK LUNG?
GOOSH!
GOOSH!
HERE'S YOUR DAMN HORSE!!
HA! HA! HA!
HOUUU!!
!!

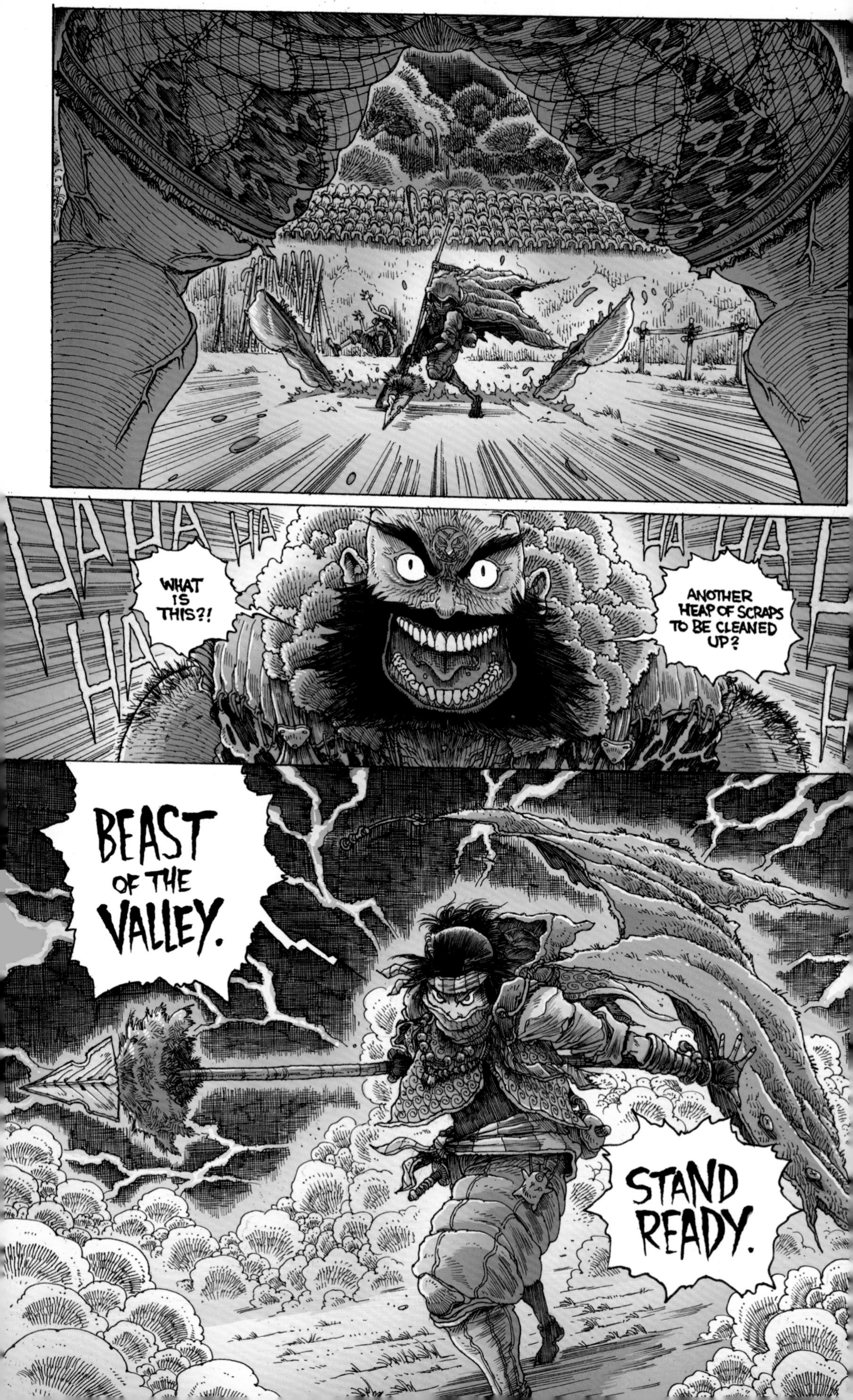
HA HA HA HA
HA HA
WHAT IS THIS?!
ANOTHER HEAP OF SCRAPS TO BE CLEANED UP?
HA HA!
HA
BEAST OF THE VALLEY.
STAND READY.

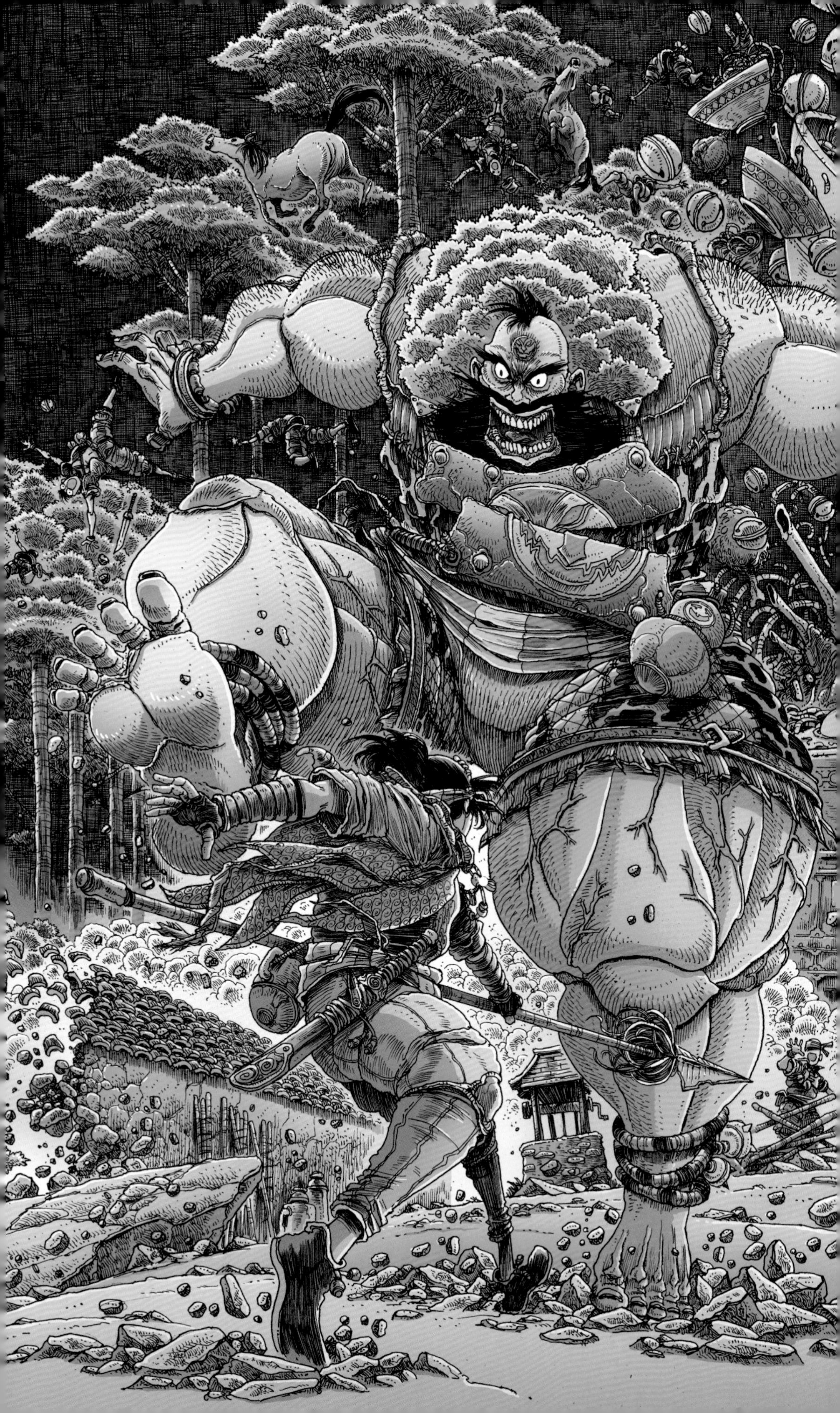

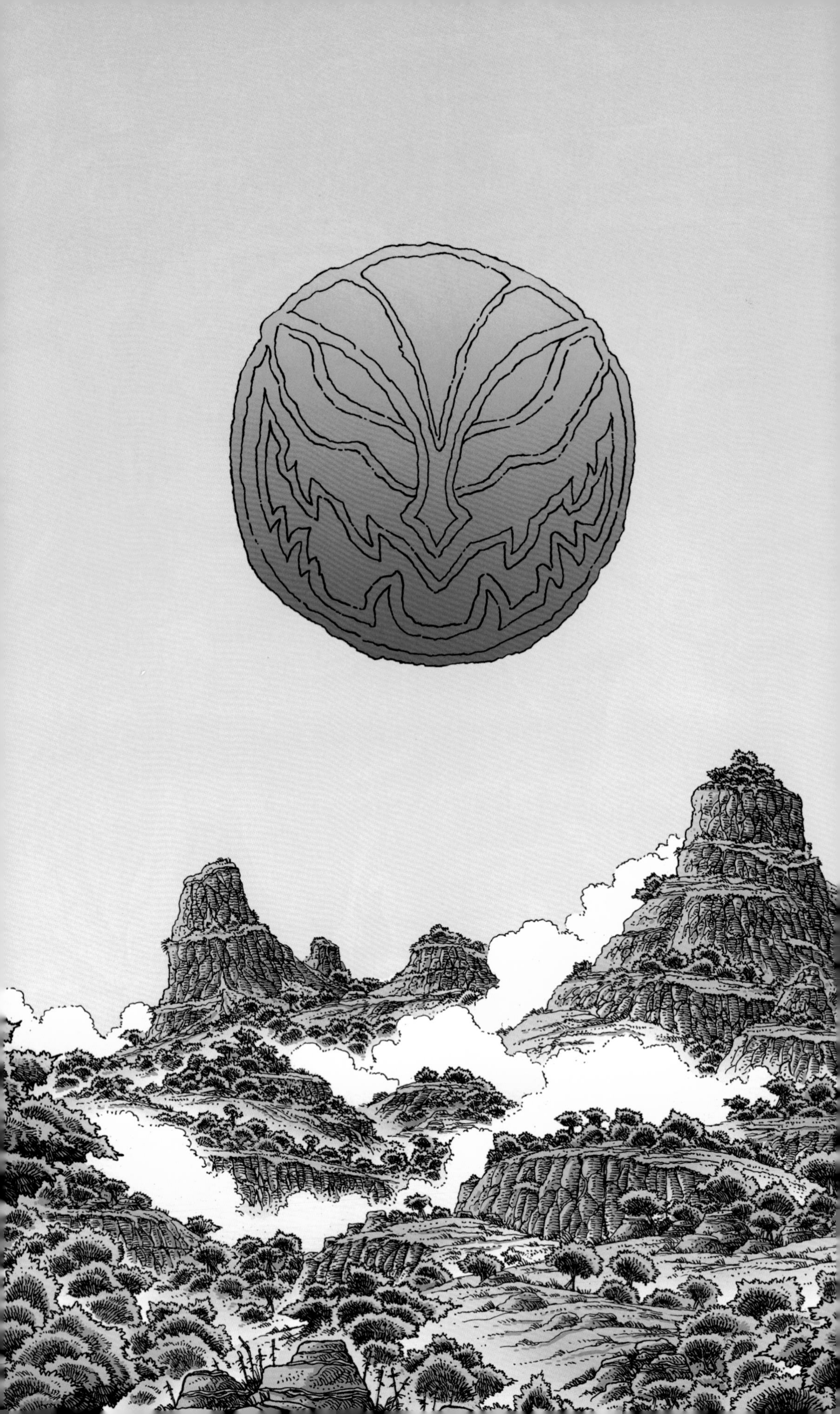

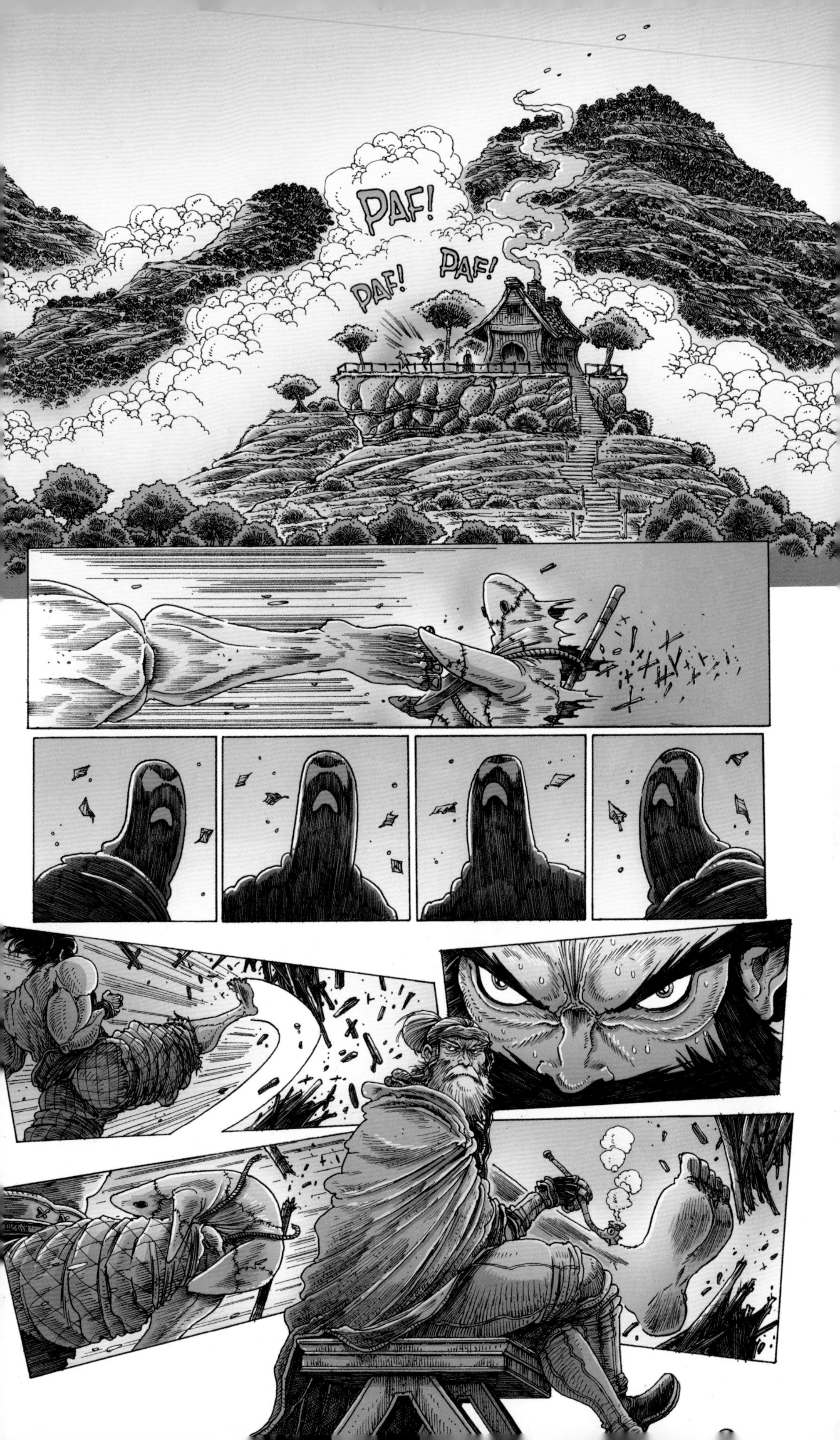
PAF!
PAF!
PAF!

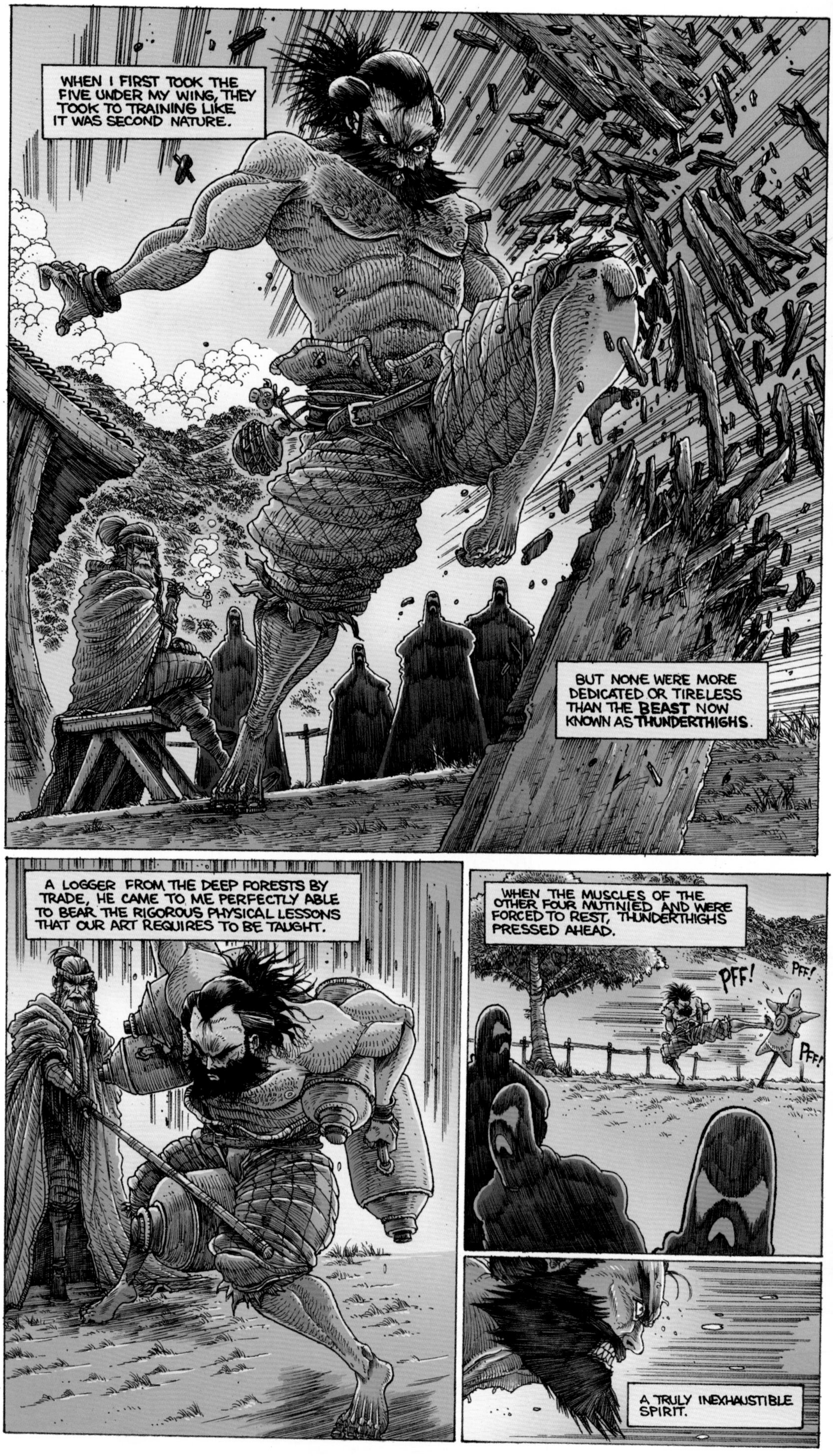
WHEN I FIRST TOOK THE FIVE UNDER MY WING, THEY TOOK TO TRAINING LIKE IT WAS SECOND NATURE.
BUT NONE WERE MORE DEDICATED OR TIRELESS THAN THE BEAST NOW KNOWN AS THUNDERTHIGHS.
A LOGGER FROM THE DEEP FORESTS BY TRADE, HE CAME TO ME PERFECTLY ABLE TO BEAR THE RIGOROUS PHYSICAL LESSONS THAT OUR ART REQUIRES TO BE TAUGHT.
WHEN THE MUSCLES OF THE OTHER FOUR MUTINIED AND WERE FORCED TO REST, THUNDERTHIGHS PRESSED AHEAD.
PFF!
PFF!
PFF!
A TRULY INEXHAUSTIBLE SPIRIT.

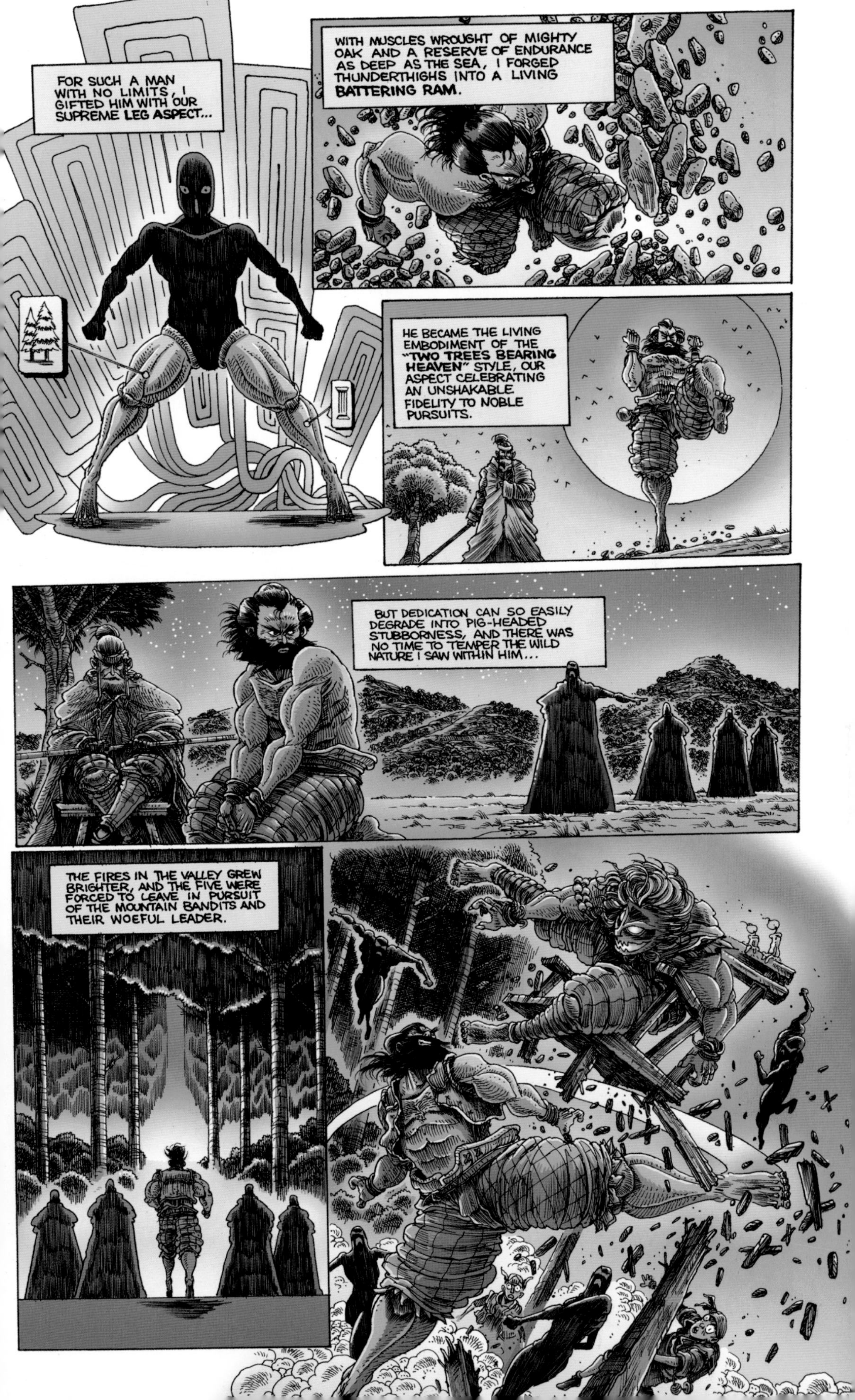
FOR SUCH A MAN WITH NO LIMITS, I GIFTED HIM WITH OUR SUPREME LEG ASPECT...
WITH MUSCLES WROUGHT OF MIGHTY OAK AND A RESERVE OF ENDURANCE AS DEEP AS THE SEA, I FORGED THUNDERTHIGHS INTO A LIVING BATTERING RAM.
HE BECAME THE LIVING EMBODIMENT OF THE "TWO TREES BEARING HEAVEN" STYLE, OUR ASPECT CELEBRATING AN UNSHAKABLE FIDELITY TO NOBLE PURSUITS.
BUT DEDICATION CAN SO EASILY DEGRADE INTO PIG-HEADED STUBBORNESS, AND THERE WAS NO TIME TO TEMPER THE WILD NATURE I SAW WITHIN HIM...
THE FIRES IN THE VALLEY GREW BRIGHTER, AND THE FIVE WERE FORCED TO LEAVE IN PURSUIT OF THE MOUNTAIN BANDITS AND THEIR WOEFUL LEADER.

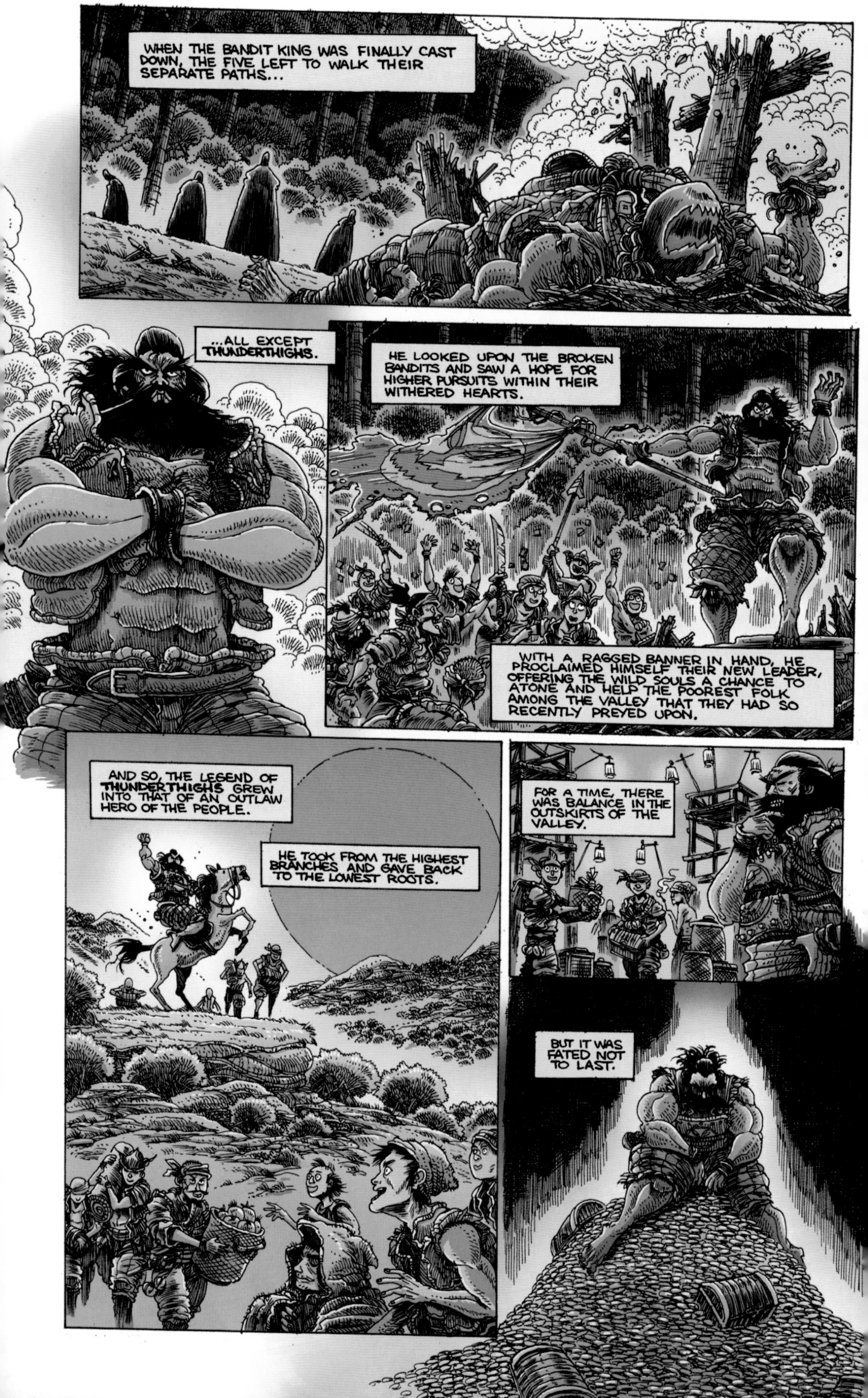

WHEN THE BANDIT KING WAS FINALLY CAST DOWN, THE FIVE LEFT TO WALK THEIR SEPARATE PATHS...
...ALL EXCEPT THUNDERTHIGHS.
HE LOOKED UPON THE BROKEN BANDITS AND SAW A HOPE FOR HIGHER PURSUITS WITHIN THEIR WITHERED HEARTS.
WITH A RAGGED BANNER IN HAND, HE PROCLAIMED HIMSELF THEIR NEW LEADER, OFFERING THE WILD SOULS A CHANCE TO ATONE AND HELP THE POOREST FOLK AMONG THE VALLEY THAT THEY HAD SO RECENTLY PREYED UPON.
AND SO, THE LEGEND OF THUNDERTHIGHS GREW INTO THAT OF AN OUTLAW HERO OF THE PEOPLE.
HE TOOK FROM THE HIGHEST BRANCHES AND GAVE BACK TO THE LOWEST ROOTS.
FOR A TIME, THERE WAS BALANCE IN THE OUTSKIRTS OF THE VALLEY.
BUT IT WAS FATED NOT TO LAST.

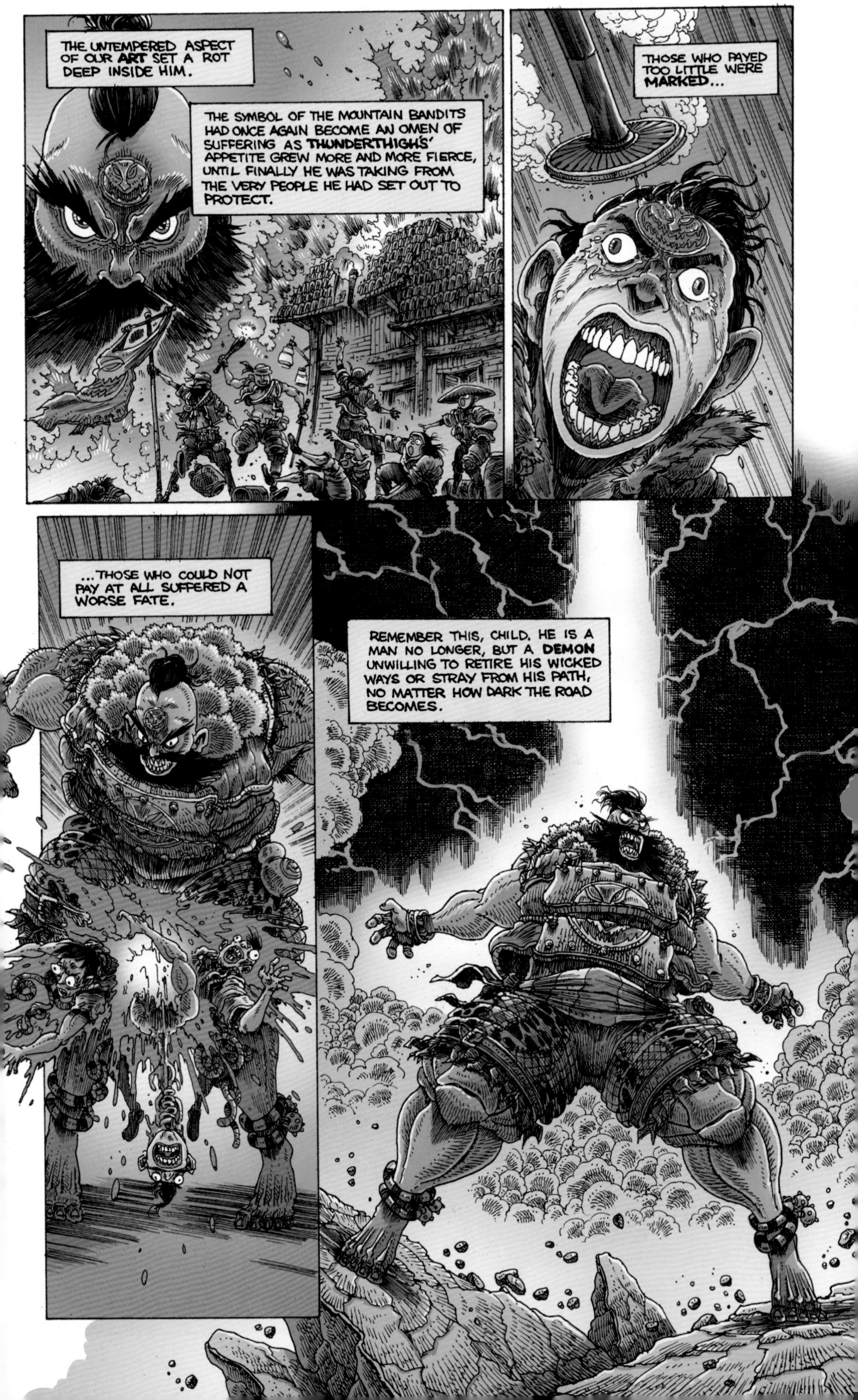
THE UNTEMPERED ASPECT OF OUR **ART** SET A ROT DEEP INSIDE HIM.
THE SYMBOL OF THE MOUNTAIN BANDITS HAD ONCE AGAIN BECOME AN OMEN OF SUFFERING AS **THUNDERTHIGHS'** APPETITE GREW MORE AND MORE FIERCE, UNTIL FINALLY HE WAS TAKING FROM THE VERY PEOPLE HE HAD SET OUT TO PROTECT.
THOSE WHO PAYED TOO LITTLE WERE **MARKED**...
...THOSE WHO COULD NOT PAY AT ALL SUFFERED A WORSE FATE.
REMEMBER THIS, CHILD. HE IS A MAN NO LONGER, BUT A **DEMON** UNWILLING TO RETIRE HIS WICKED WAYS OR STRAY FROM HIS PATH, NO MATTER HOW DARK THE ROAD BECOMES.

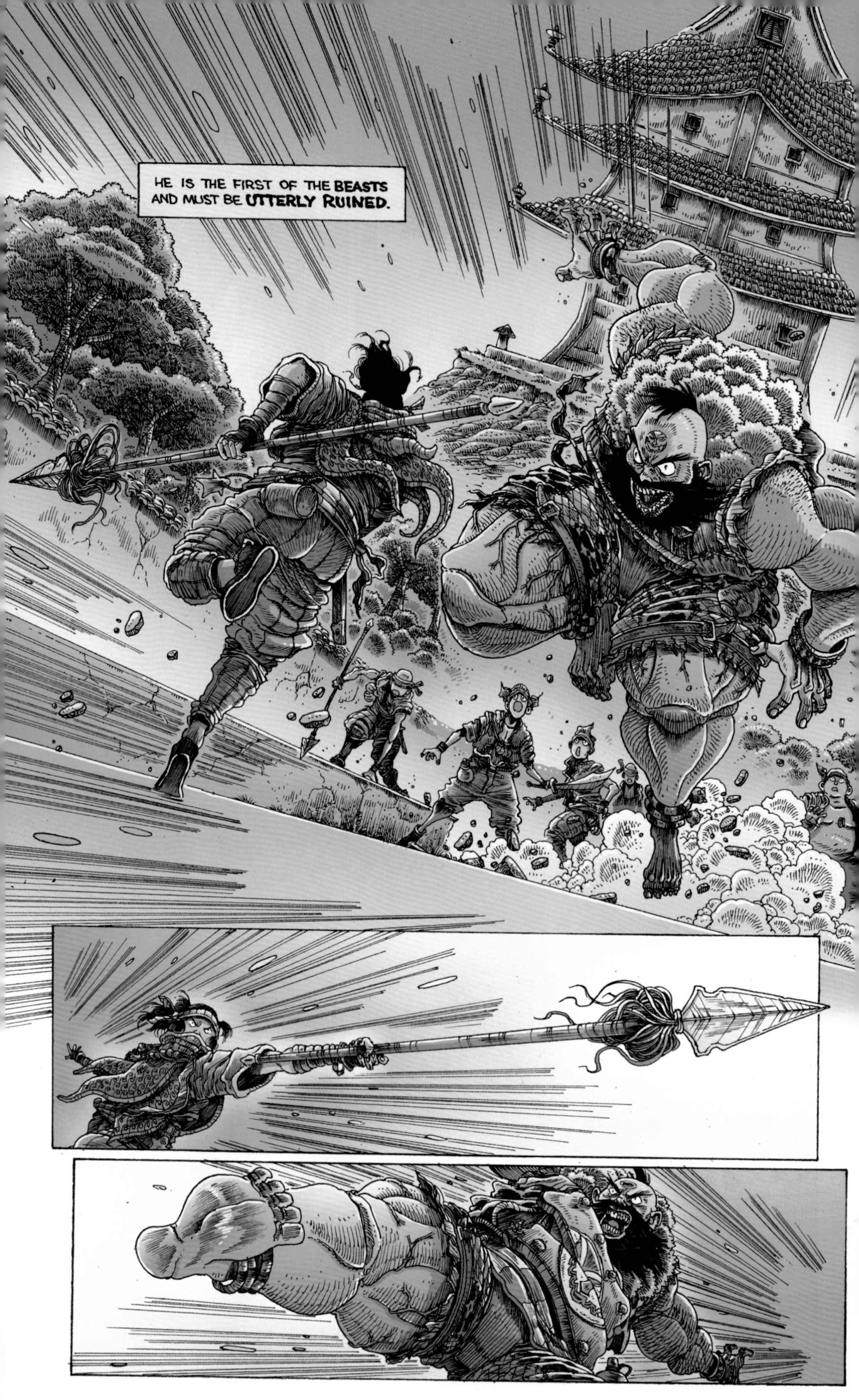
HE IS THE FIRST OF THE BEASTS AND MUST BE UTTERLY RUINED.

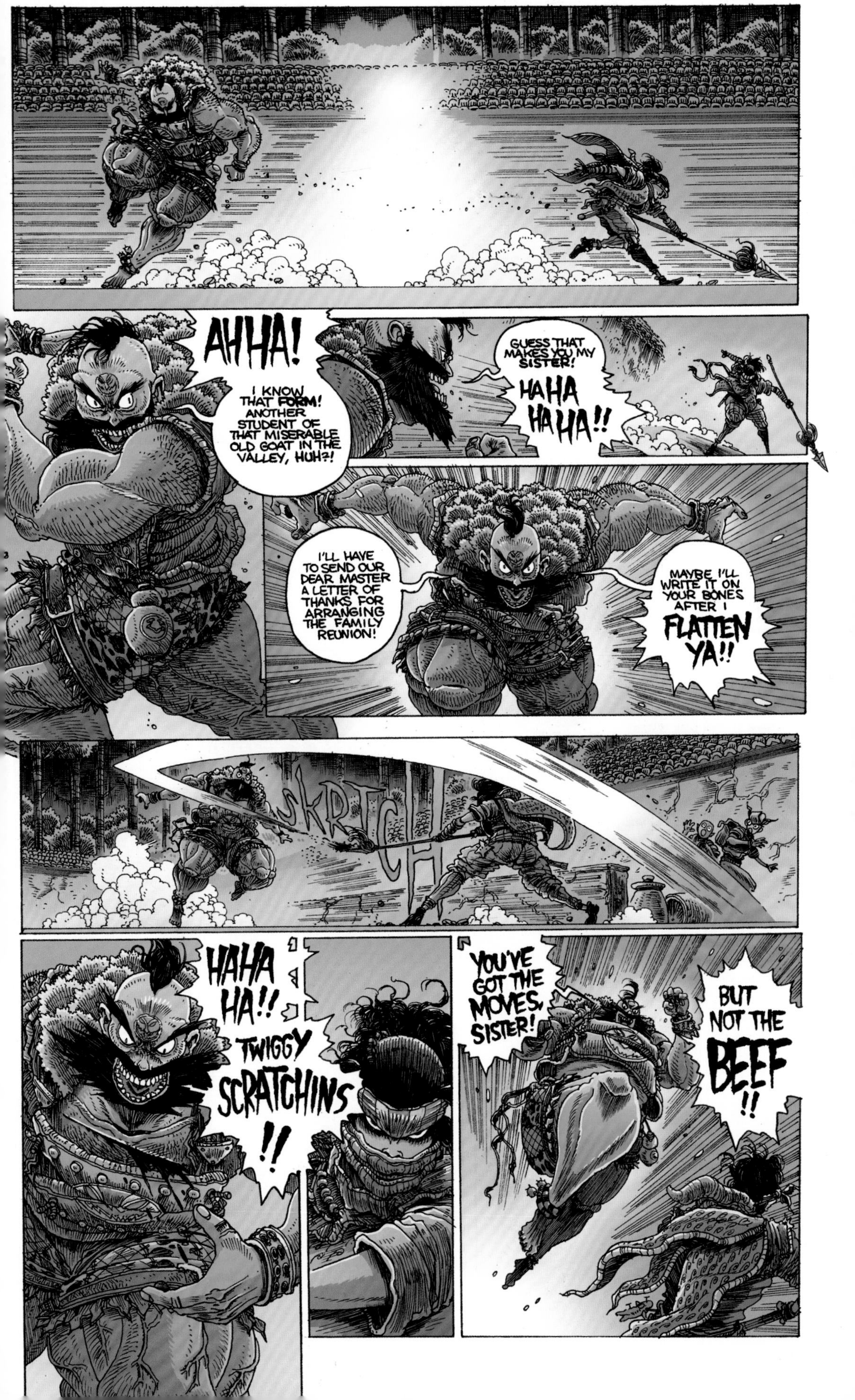
AHHA!
I KNOW THAT FORM! ANOTHER STUDENT OF THAT MISERABLE OLD GOAT IN THE VALLEY, HUH?!
GUESS THAT MAKES YOU MY SISTER!
HAHA HAHA!!
I'LL HAVE TO SEND OUR DEAR MASTER A LETTER OF THANKS FOR ARRANGING THE FAMILY REUNION!
MAYBE I'LL WRITE IT ON YOUR BONES AFTER I FLATTEN YA!!
SKRTCH
HAHA HA!! TWIGGY SCRATCHINS !!
YOU'VE GOT THE MOVES, SISTER!
BUT NOT THE BEEF !!

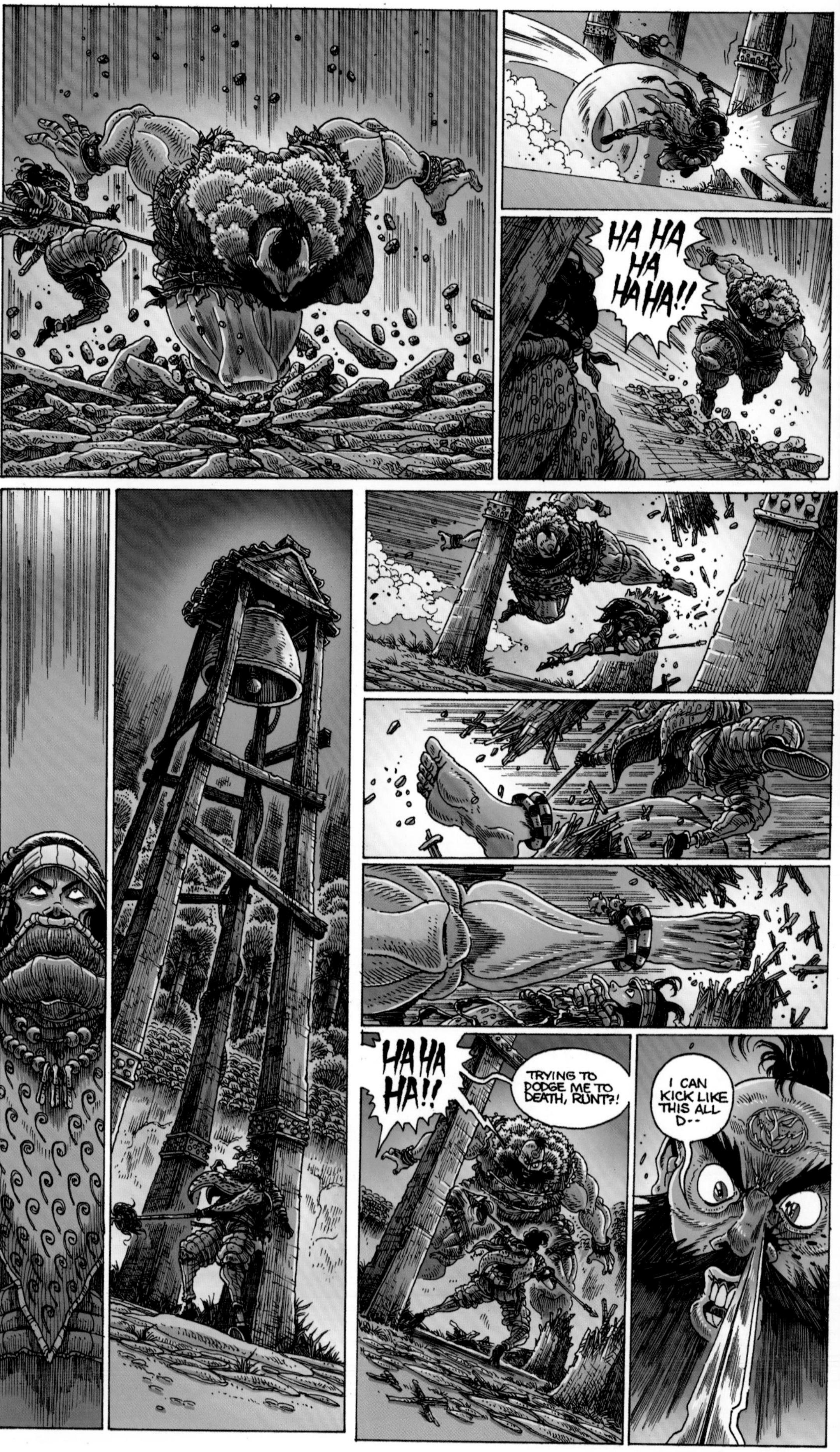
HA HA
HA
HA HA!!
HA HA
HA!!
TRYING TO DODGE ME TO DEATH, RUNT?!
I CAN KICK LIKE THIS ALL D--

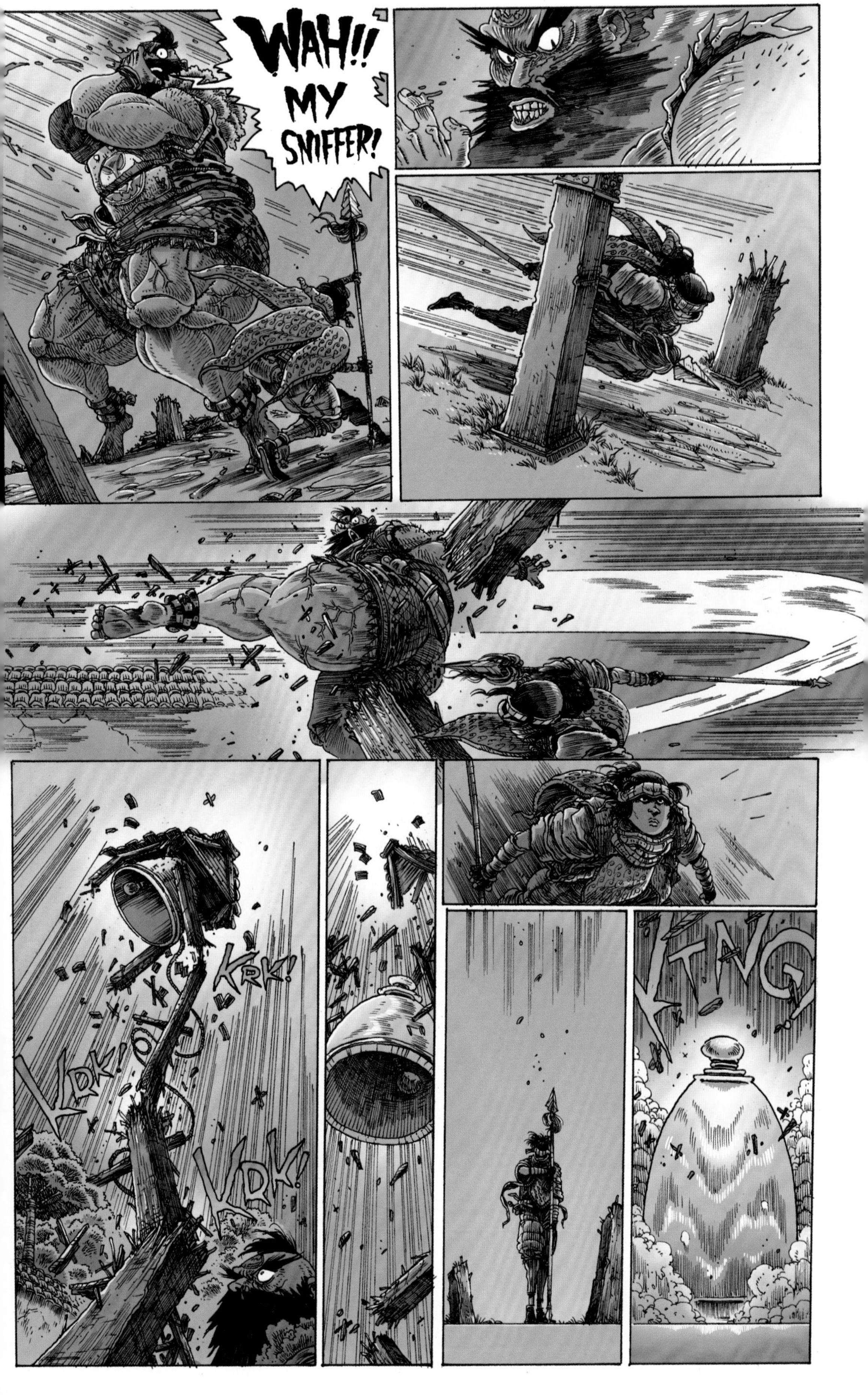
WAH!! MY SNIFFER!
KRK!
KRK!
KRK!
KTNG!

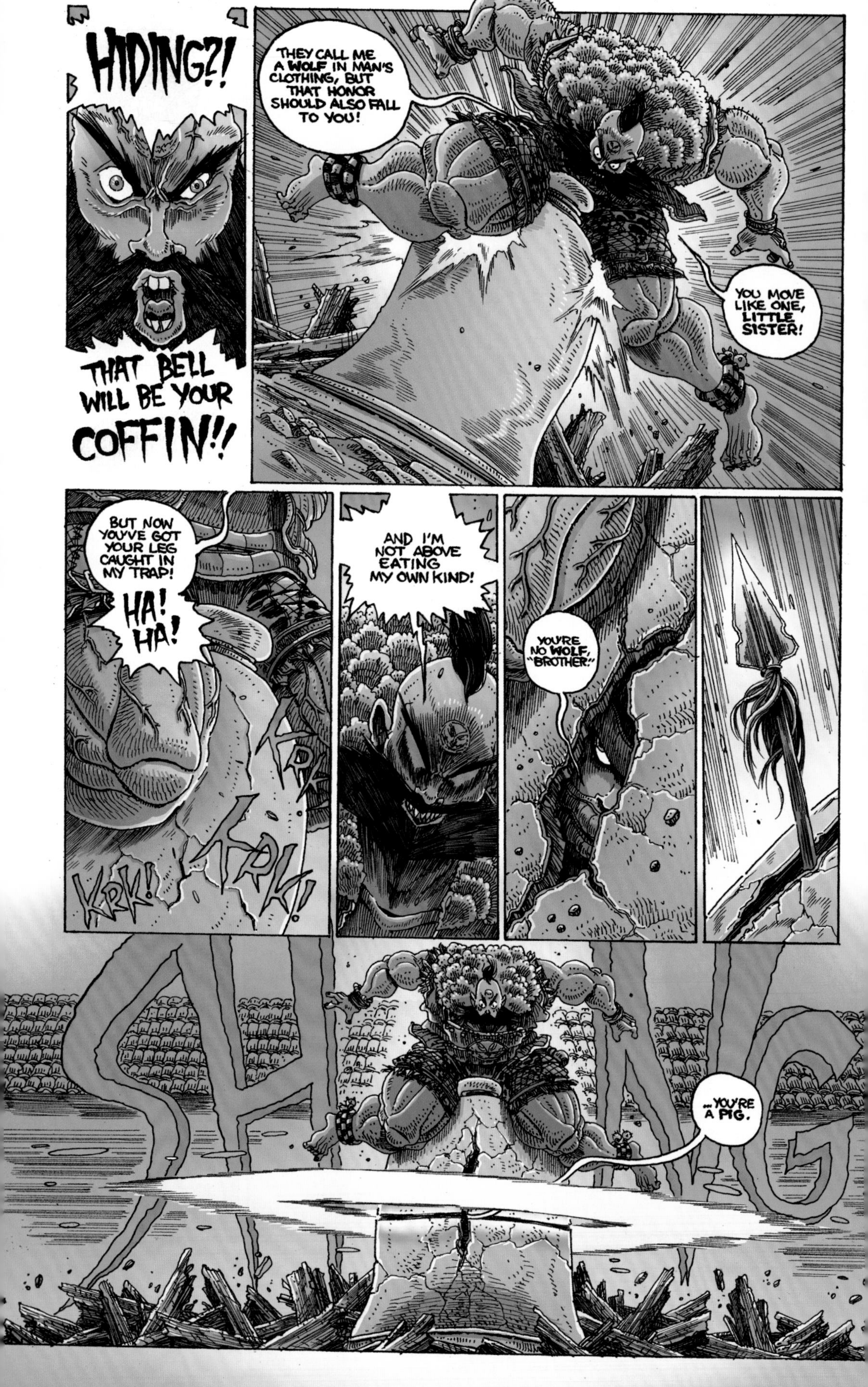
HIDING?!
THAT BELL WILL BE YOUR COFFIN!!
THEY CALL ME A WOLF IN MAN'S CLOTHING, BUT THAT HONOR SHOULD ALSO FALL TO YOU!
YOU MOVE LIKE ONE, LITTLE SISTER!
BUT NOW YOU'VE GOT YOUR LEG CAUGHT IN MY TRAP!
HA! HA!
KRK!
KRK!
KRK!
AND I'M NOT ABOVE EATING MY OWN KIND!
YOU'RE NO WOLF, "BROTHER."
...YOU'RE A PIG.

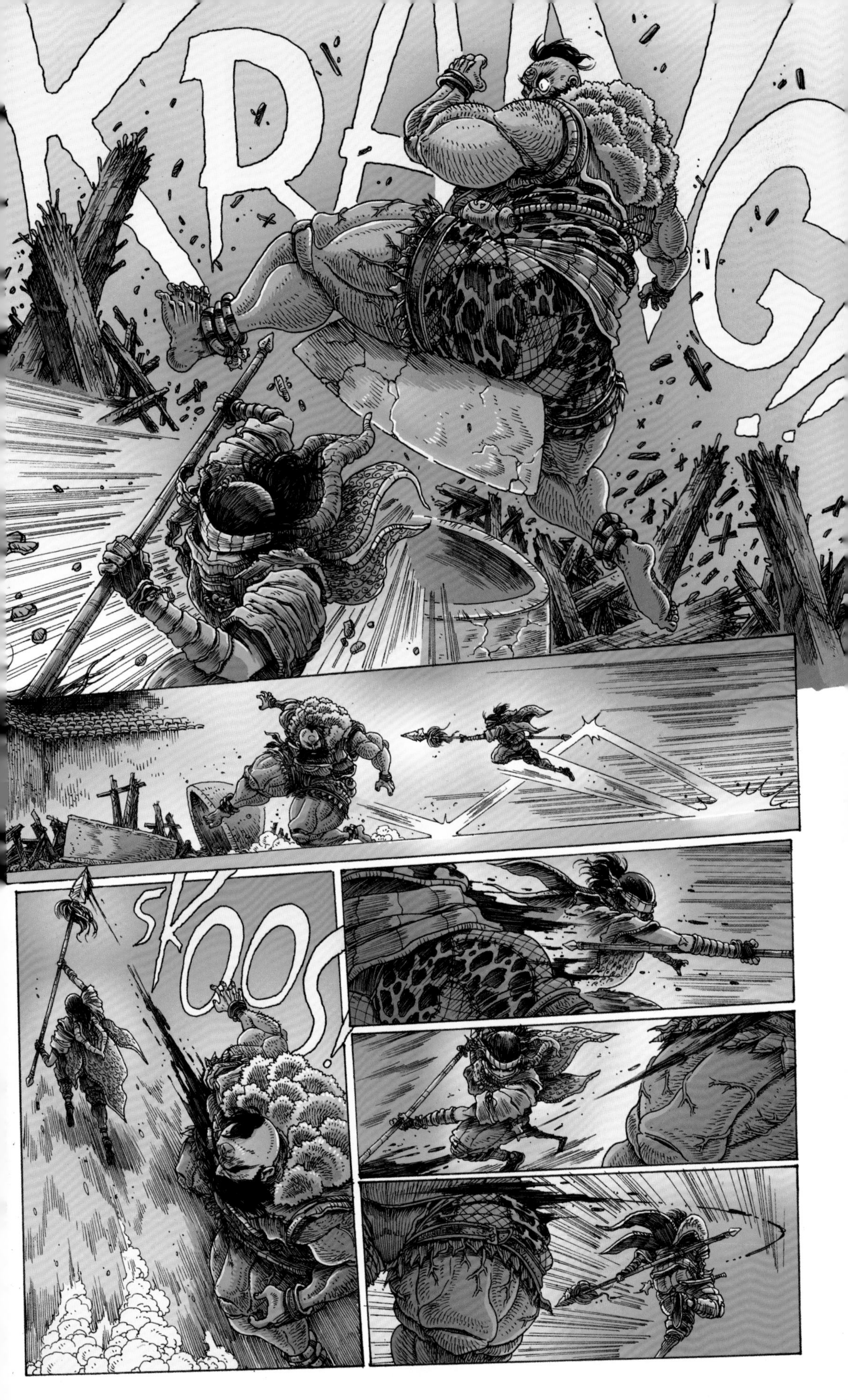
KRANG!
SKOOS

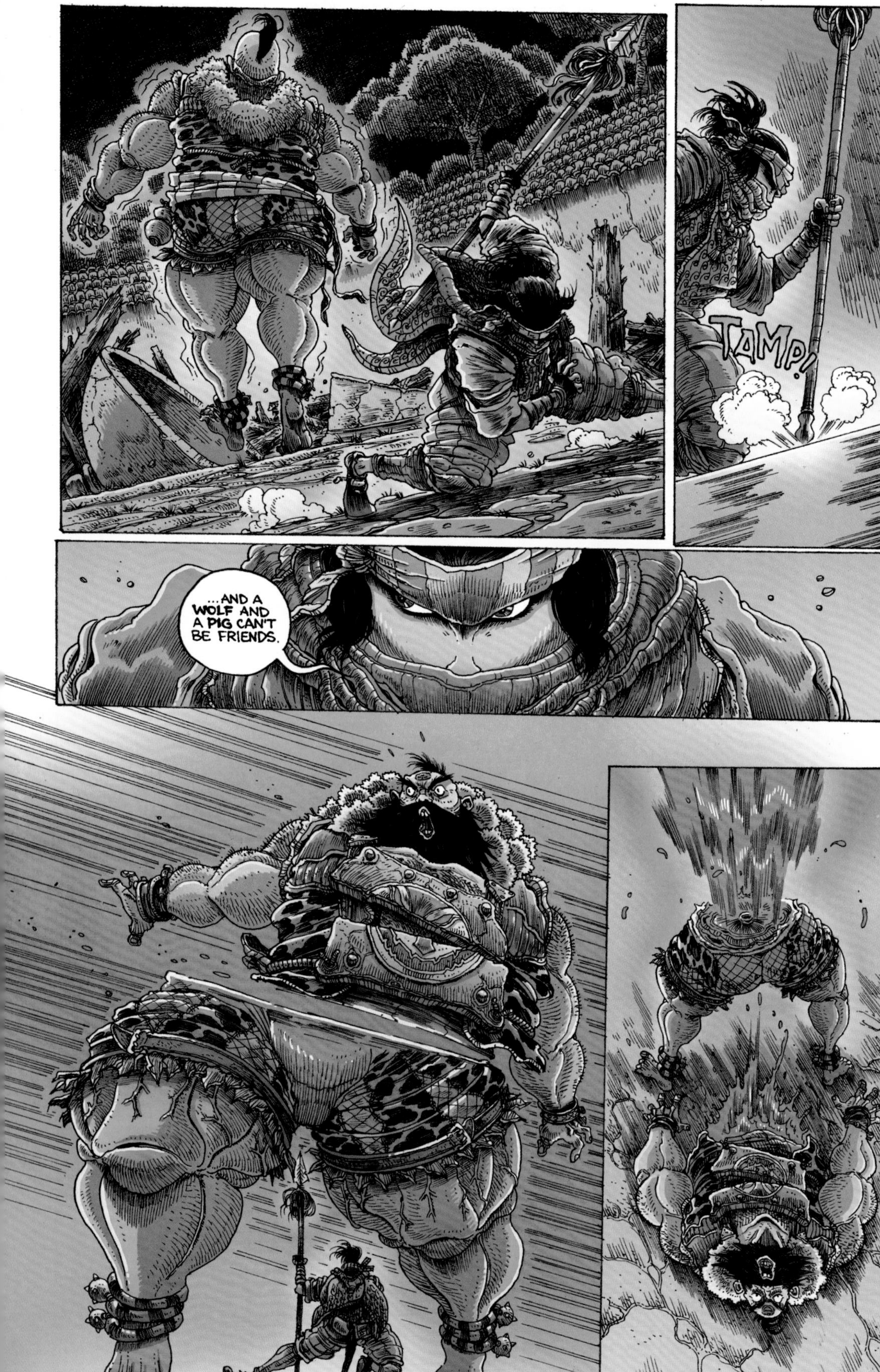

TAMP!
...AND A WOLF AND A PIG CAN'T BE FRIENDS.

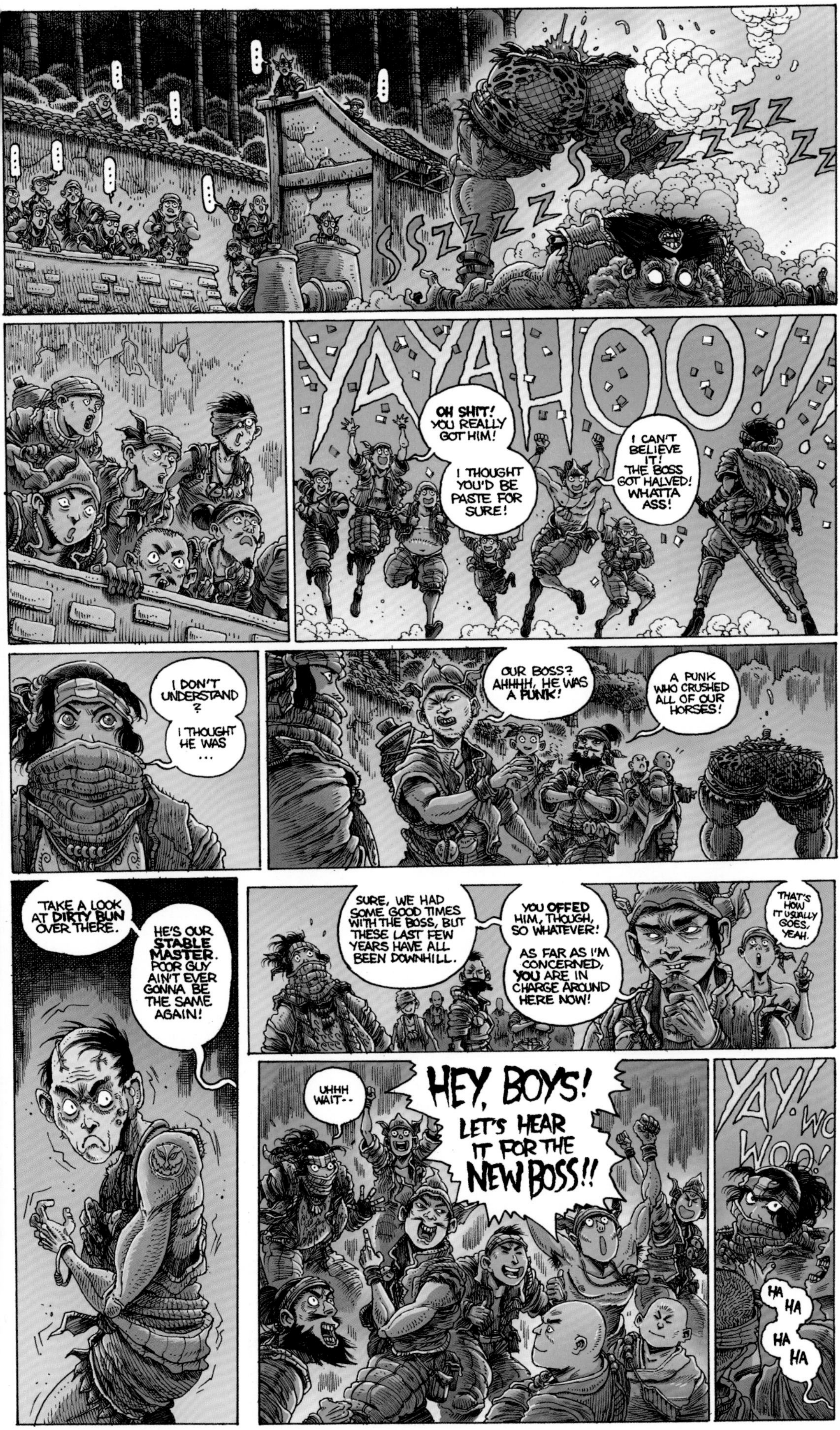
...
...
...
...
...
...
...
...
SSZZZZZ
ZZZZZZZ
YAYAHOO!!
OH SHIT! YOU REALLY GOT HIM!
I THOUGHT YOU'D BE PASTE FOR SURE!
I CAN'T BELIEVE IT! THE BOSS GOT HALVED! WHATTA ASS!
I DON'T UNDERSTAND?
I THOUGHT HE WAS ...
OUR BOSS? AHHHHH, HE WAS A PUNK!
A PUNK WHO CRUSHED ALL OF OUR HORSES!
TAKE A LOOK AT DIRTY BUN OVER THERE.
HE'S OUR STABLE MASTER. POOR GUY AIN'T EVER GONNA BE THE SAME AGAIN!
SURE, WE HAD SOME GOOD TIMES WITH THE BOSS, BUT THESE LAST FEW YEARS HAVE ALL BEEN DOWNHILL.
YOU OFFED HIM, THOUGH, SO WHATEVER!
AS FAR AS I'M CONCERNED, YOU ARE IN CHARGE AROUND HERE NOW!
THAT'S HOW IT USUALLY GOES, YEAH.
UHHH WAIT--
HEY, BOYS! LET'S HEAR IT FOR THE NEW BOSS!!
YAY! WOO!
HA HA HA HA

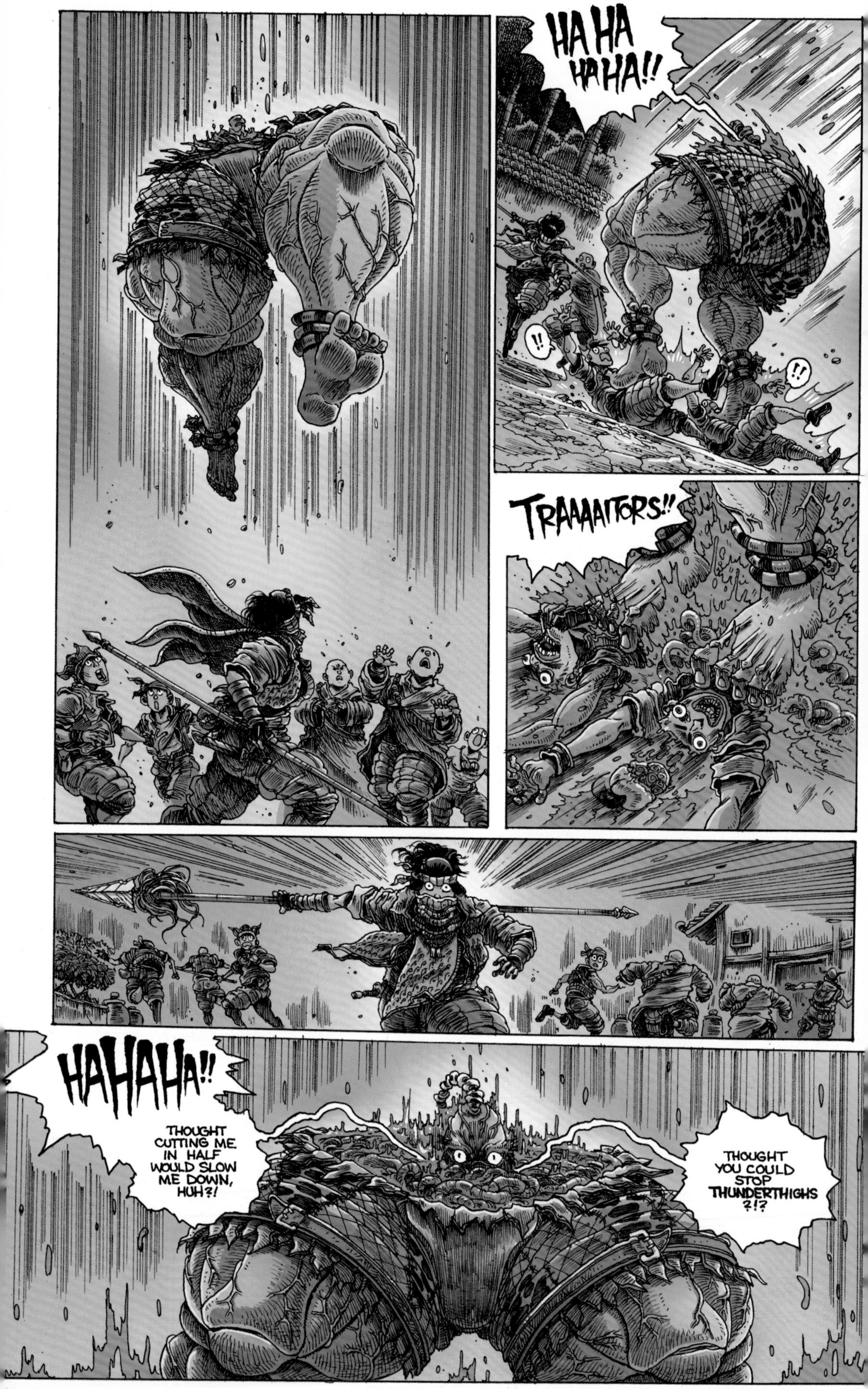
HA HA
HA HA!!
!!
!!
TRAAAAITORS!!
HAHAHA!!
THOUGHT CUTTING ME IN HALF WOULD SLOW ME DOWN, HUH?!
THOUGHT YOU COULD STOP THUNDERTHIGHS ?!?

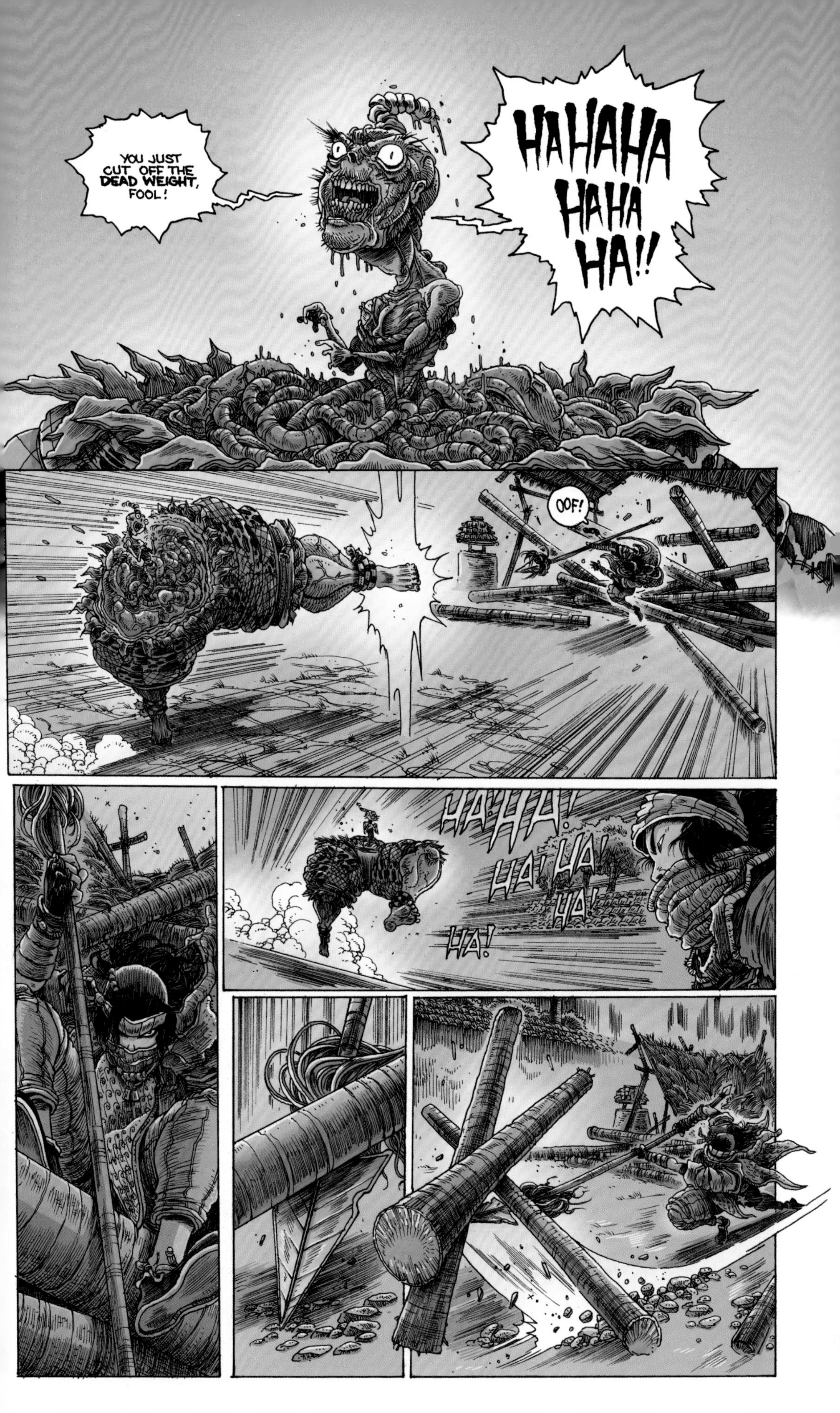
YOU JUST CUT OFF THE DEAD WEIGHT, FOOL!
HAHAHA HAHA HA!!
OOF!
HA! HA! HA! HA! HA! HA!

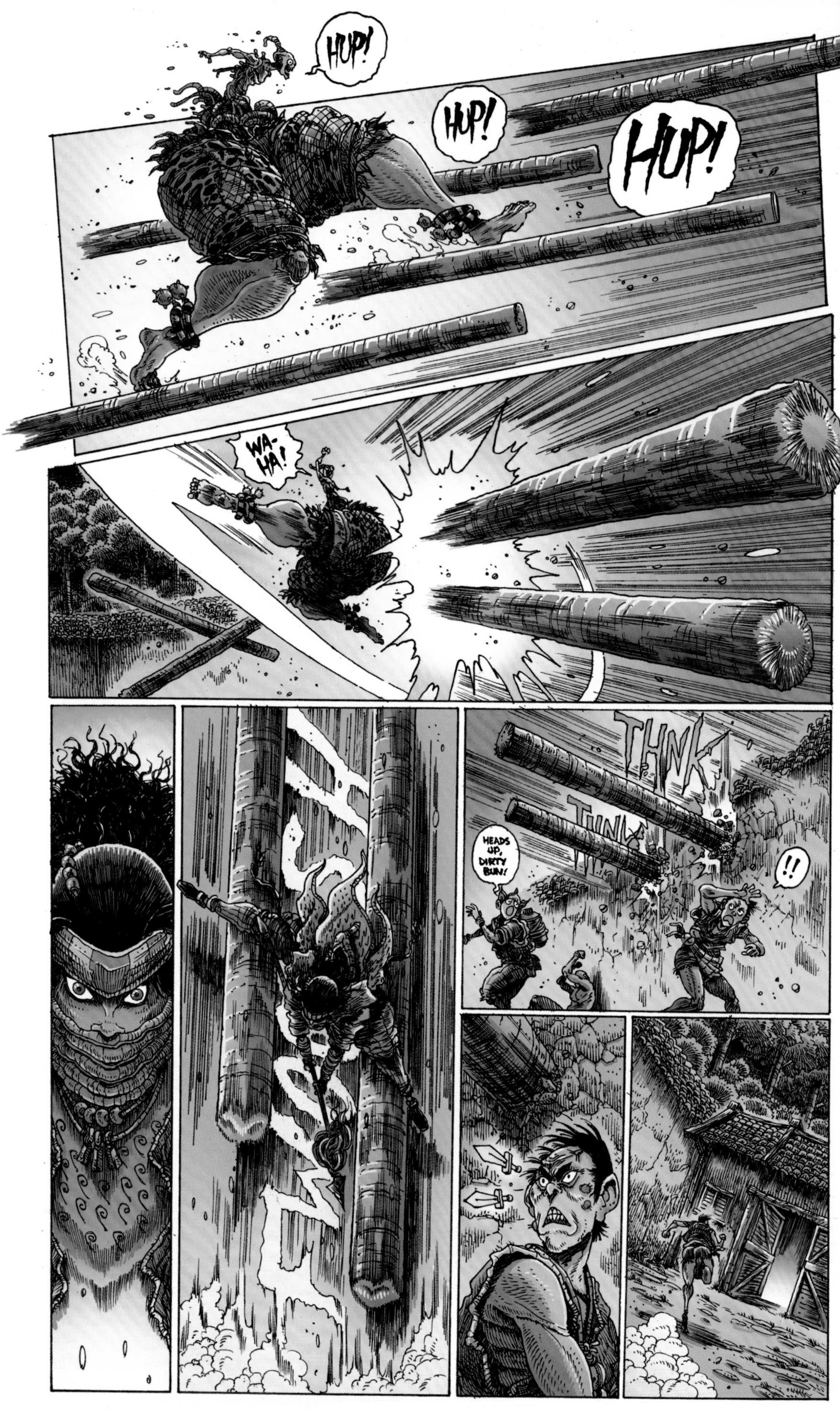
HUP!
HUP!
HUP!
WA-HA!
THNK
THNK
HEADS UP, DIRTY BUN!
!!

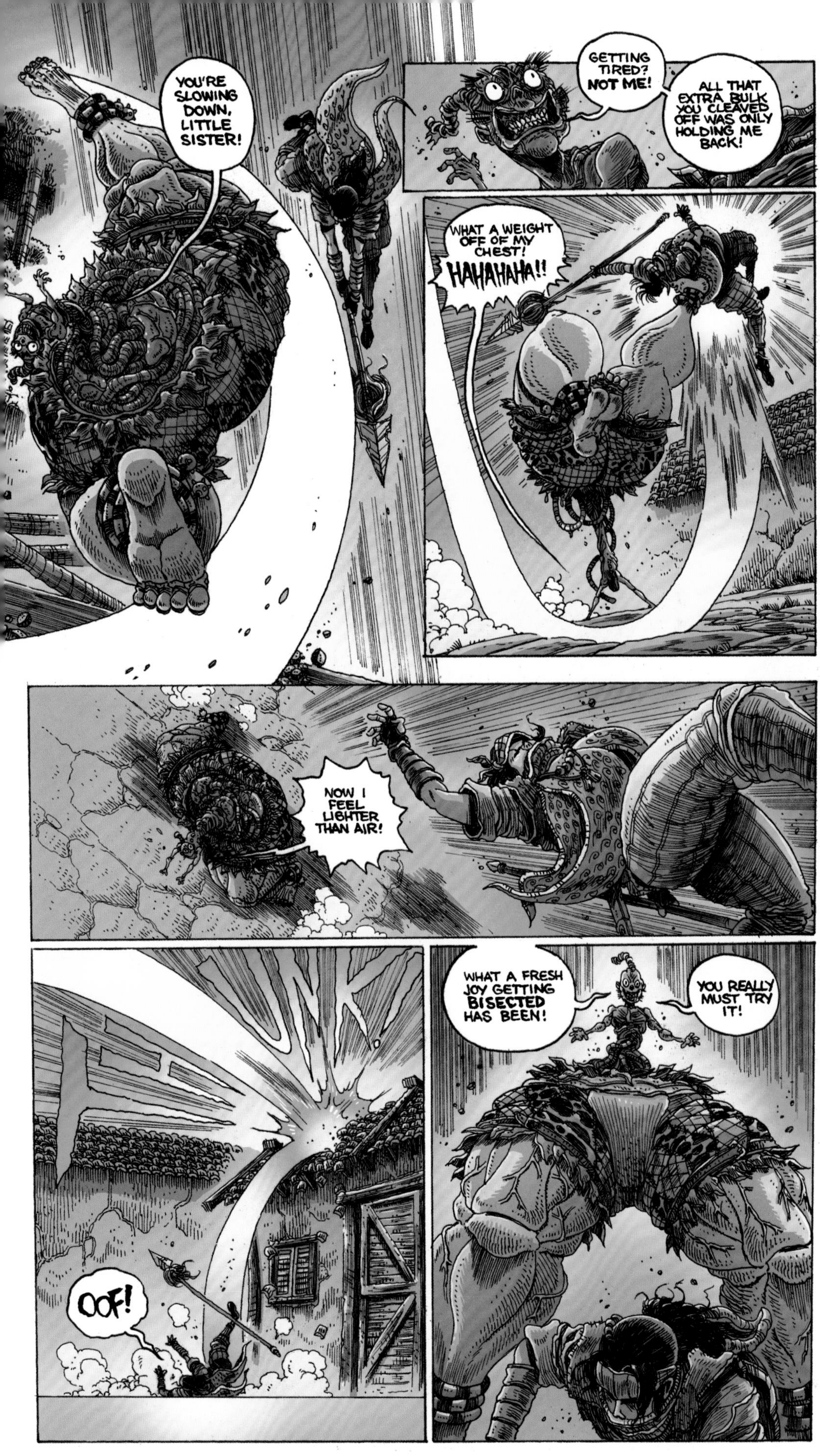

YOU'RE SLOWING DOWN, LITTLE SISTER!
GETTING TIRED? NOT ME!
ALL THAT EXTRA BULK YOU CLEAVED OFF WAS ONLY HOLDING ME BACK!
WHAT A WEIGHT OFF OF MY CHEST!
HAHAHAHA!!
NOW I FEEL LIGHTER THAN AIR!
OOF!
WHAT A FRESH JOY GETTING BISECTED HAS BEEN!
YOU REALLY MUST TRY IT!

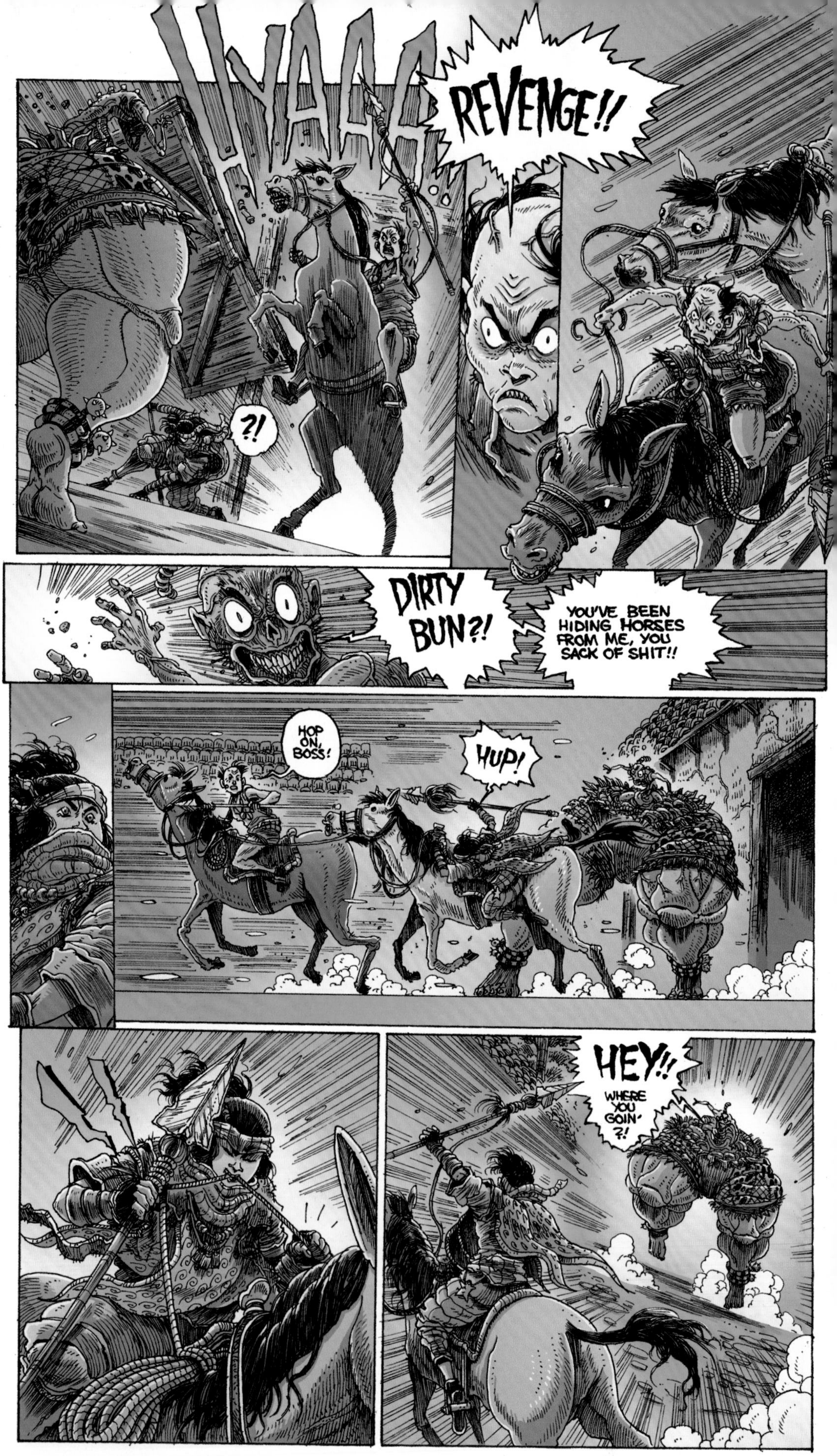
HYAAA
REVENGE!!
?!
DIRTY BUN?!
YOU'VE BEEN HIDING HORSES FROM ME, YOU SACK OF SHIT!!
HOP ON, BOSS!
HUP!
HEY!!
WHERE YOU GOIN'?!

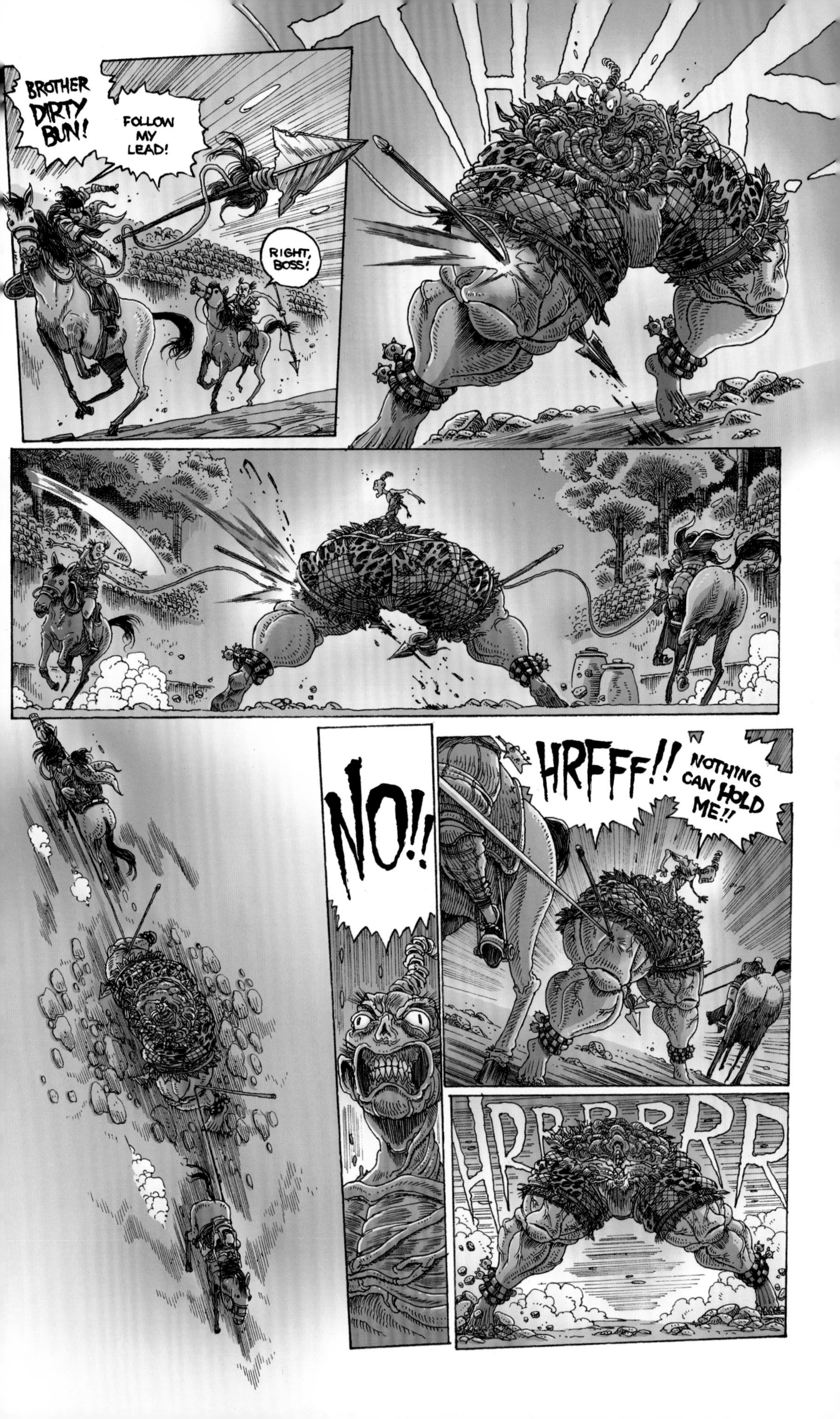
BROTHER DIRTY BUN!
FOLLOW MY LEAD!
RIGHT, BOSS!
NO!!
HRFFF!!
NOTHING CAN HOLD ME!!
HRRRRRR

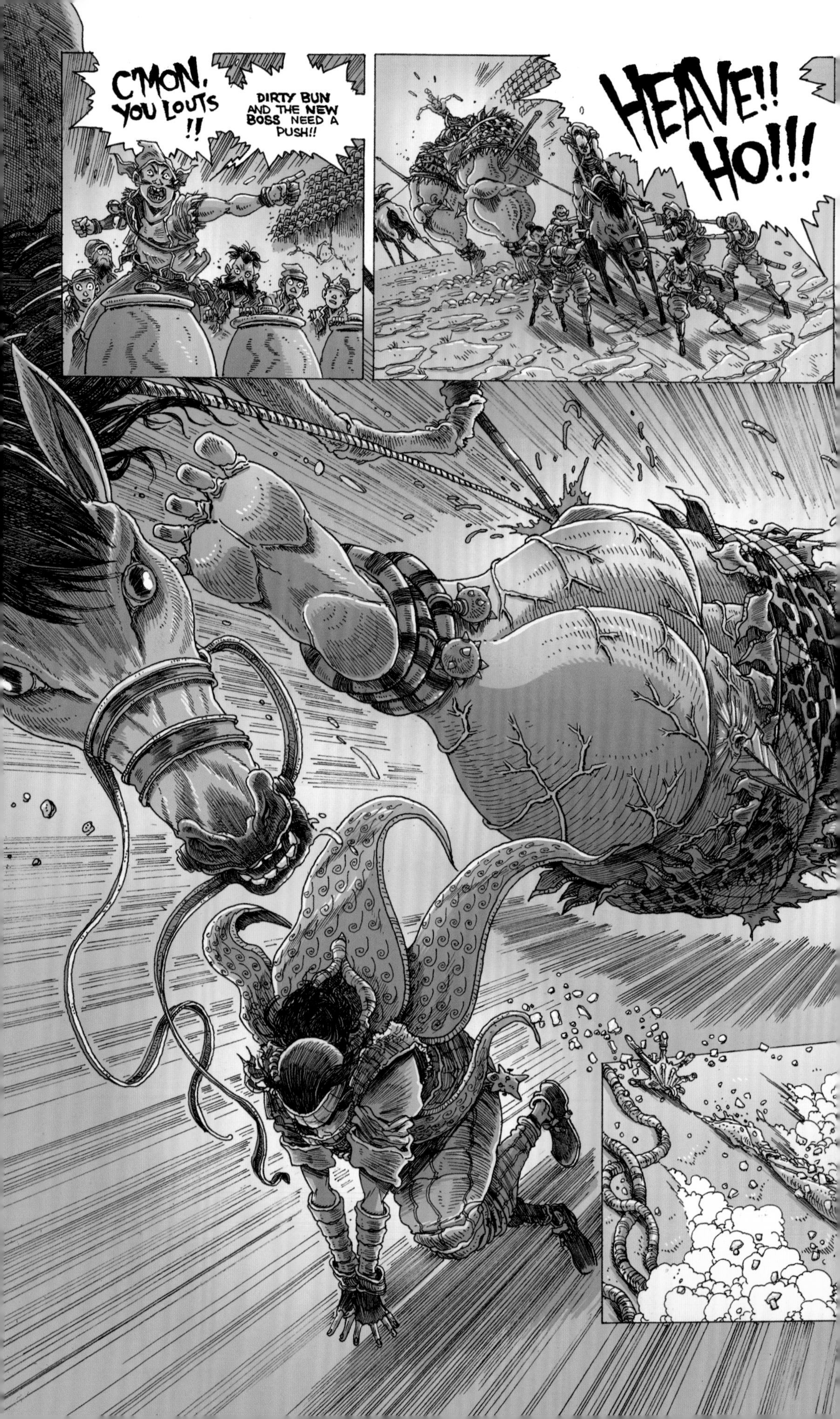
C'MON, YOU LOUTS !!
DIRTY BUN AND THE NEW BOSS NEED A PUSH!!
HEAVE!! HO!!!

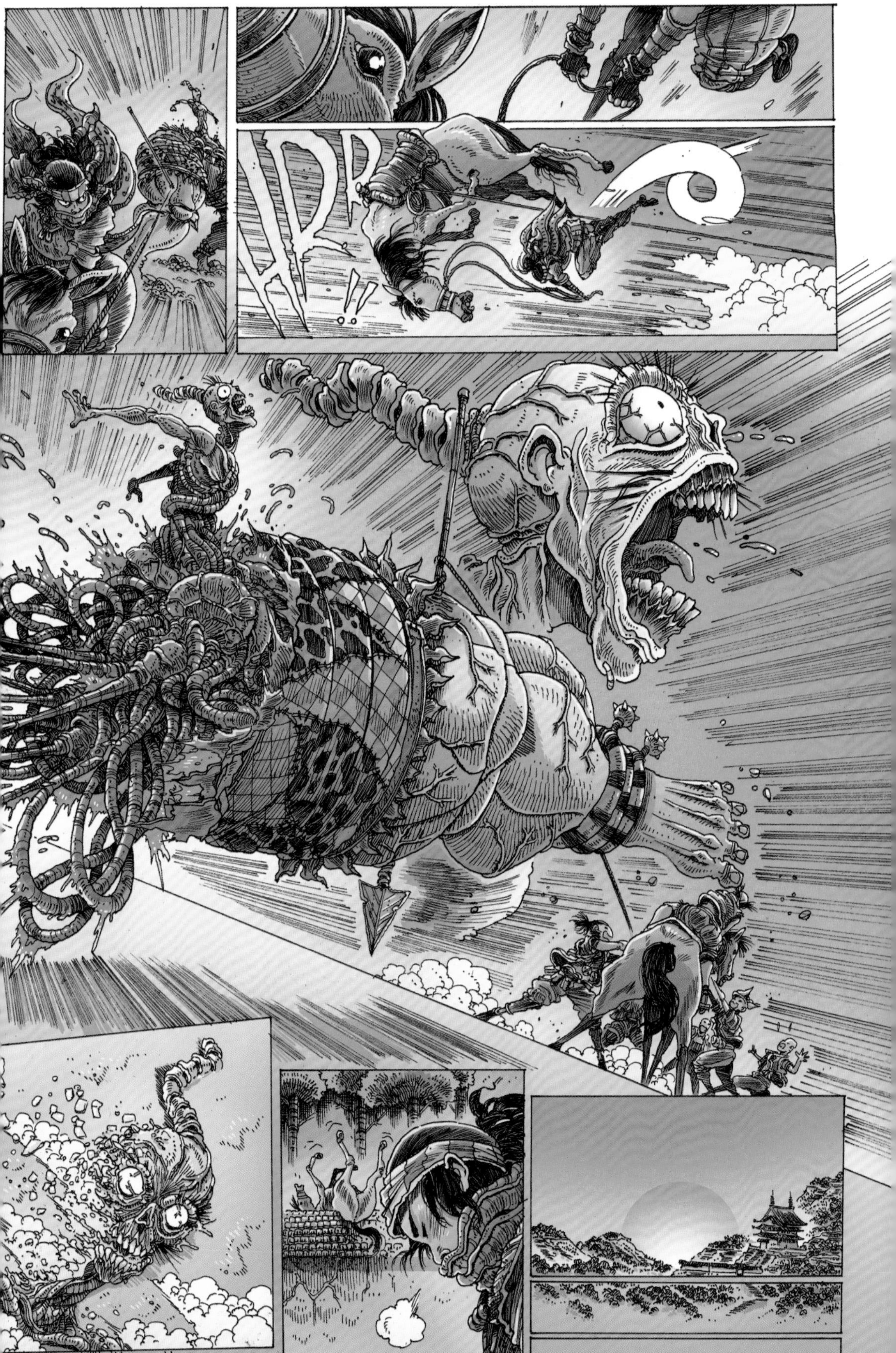

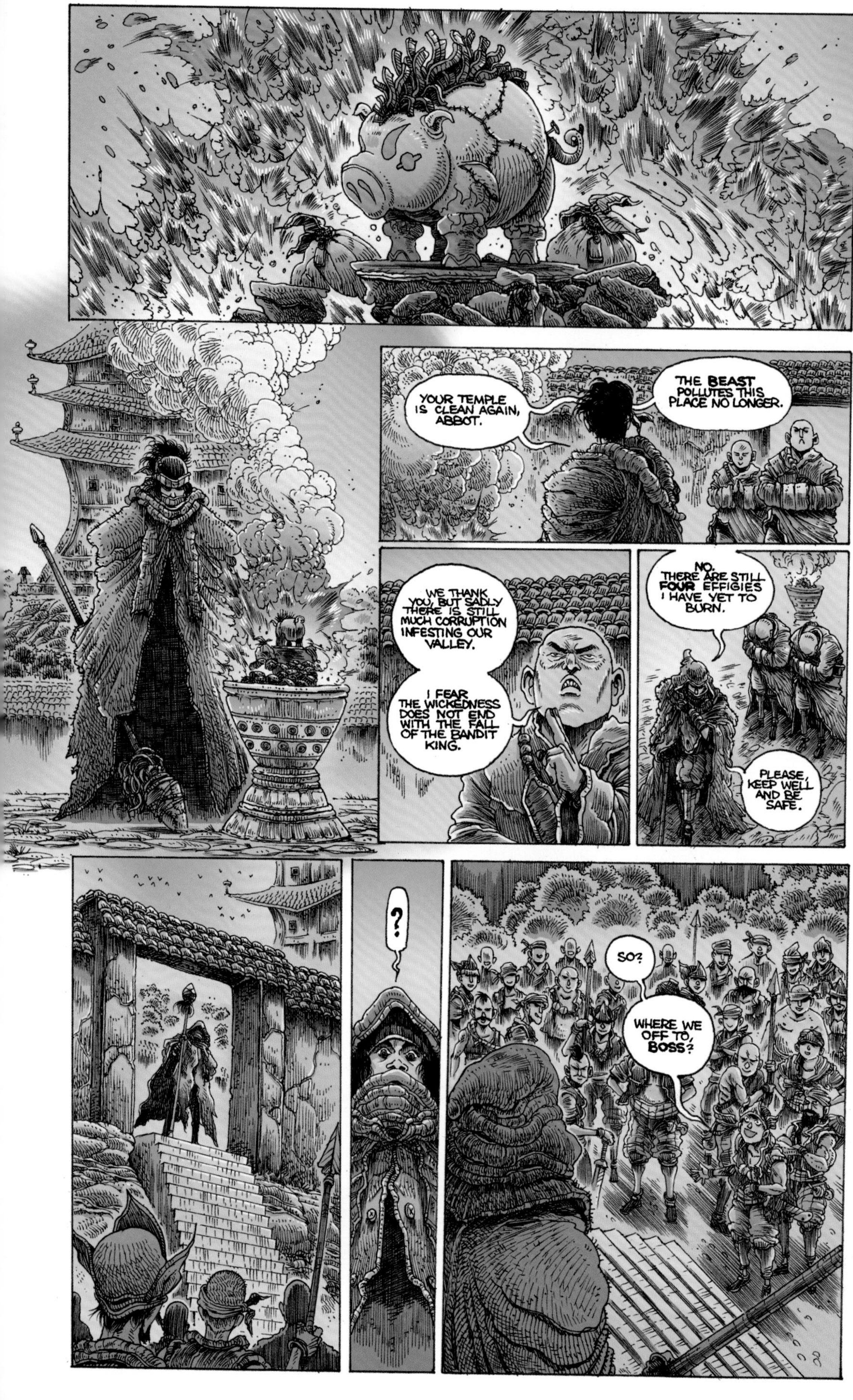
YOUR TEMPLE IS CLEAN AGAIN, ABBOT.
THE **BEAST** POLLUTES THIS PLACE NO LONGER.
WE THANK YOU, BUT SADLY THERE IS STILL MUCH CORRUPTION INFESTING OUR VALLEY.
I FEAR THE WICKEDNESS DOES NOT END WITH THE FALL OF THE BANDIT KING.
NO. THERE ARE STILL **FOUR** EFFIGIES I HAVE YET TO BURN.
PLEASE, KEEP WELL AND BE SAFE.
?
SO?
WHERE WE OFF TO, **BOSS**?

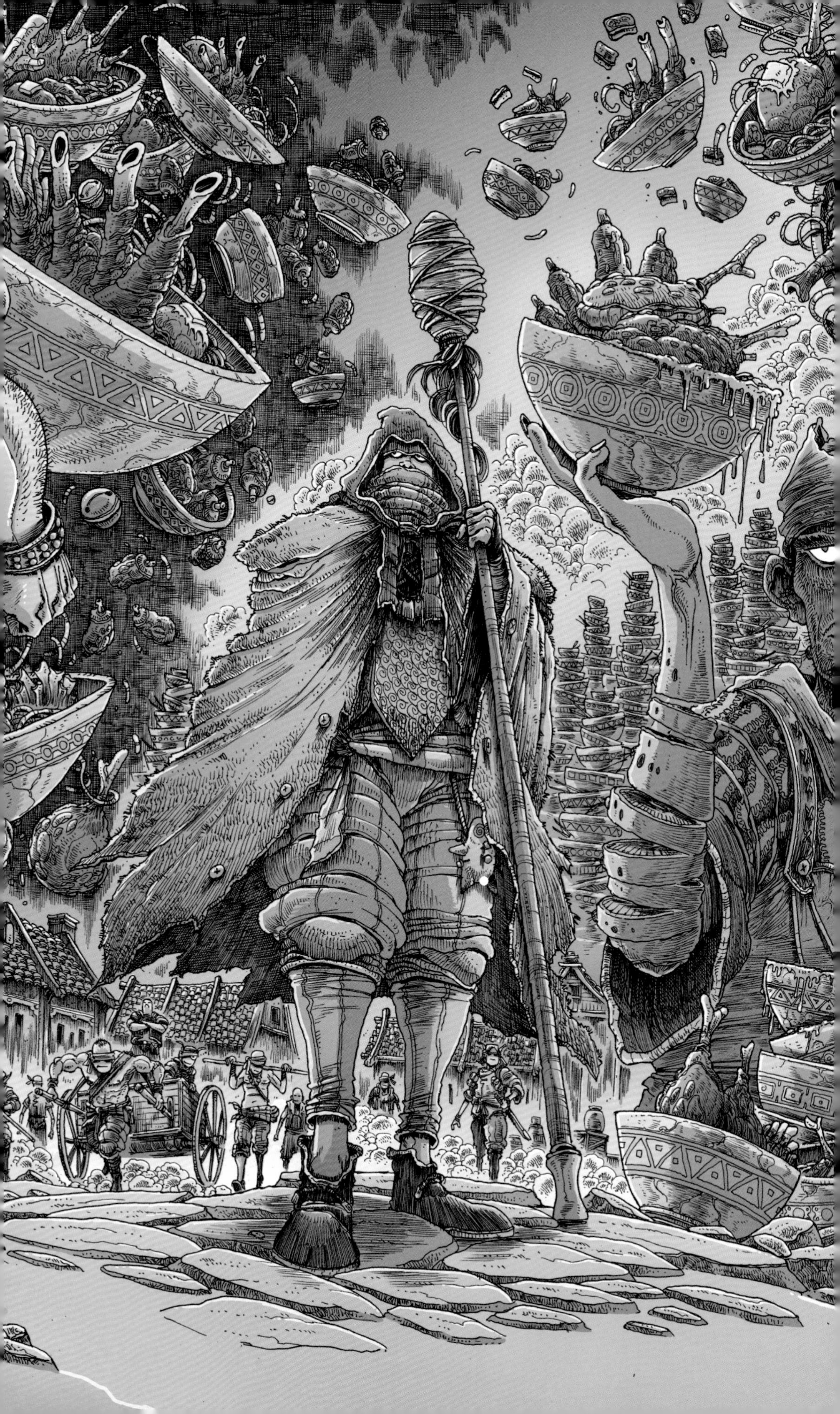

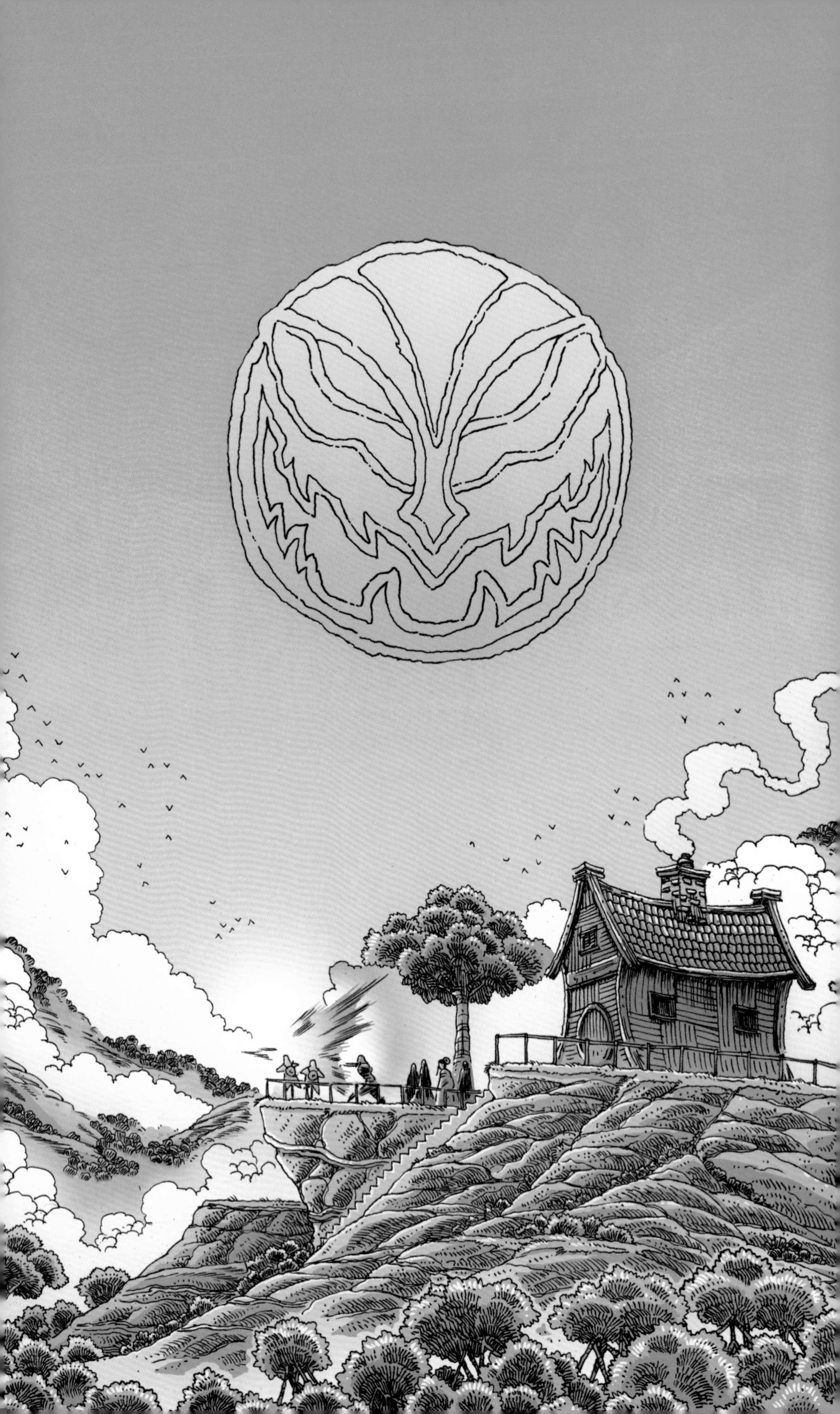

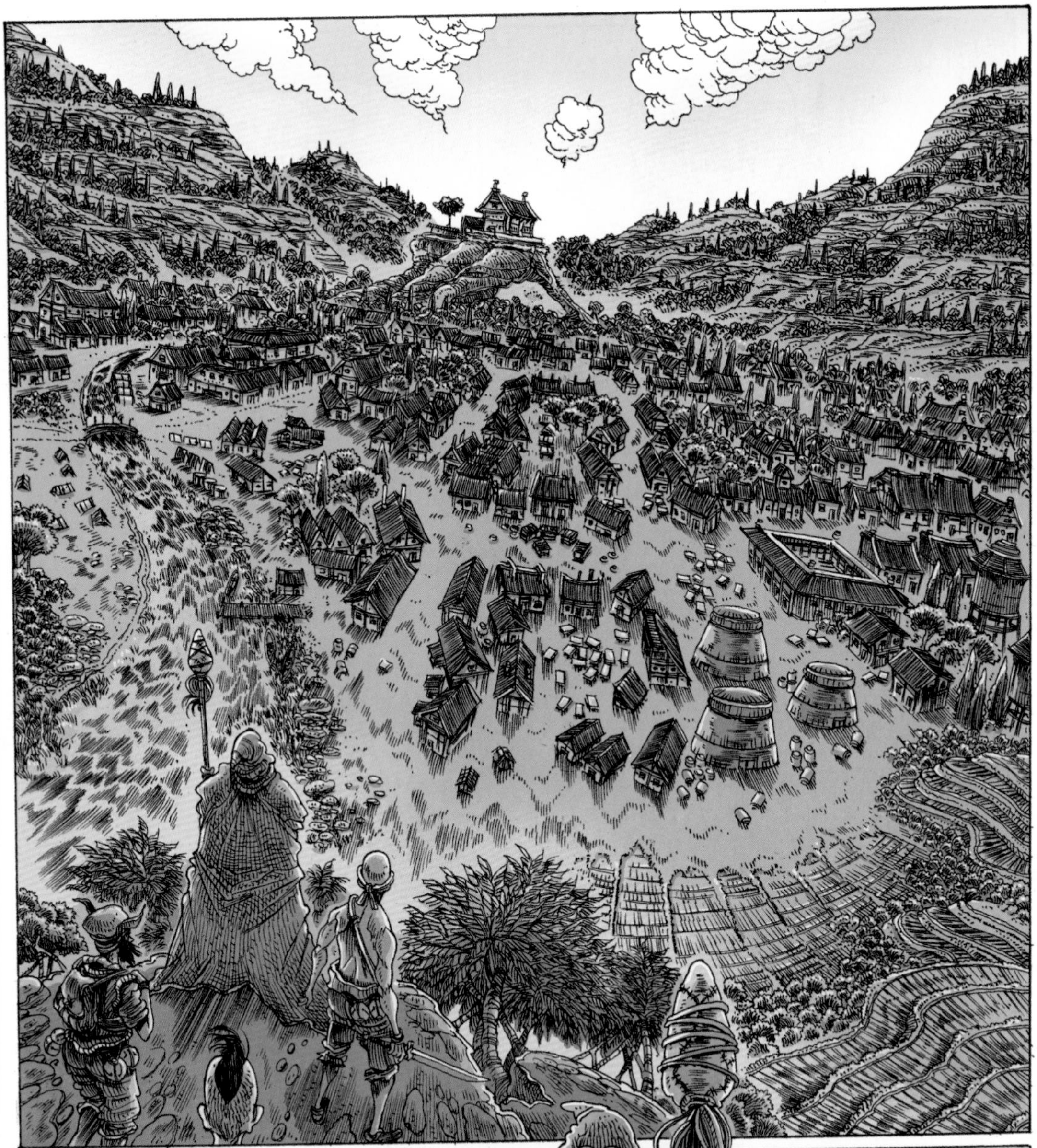

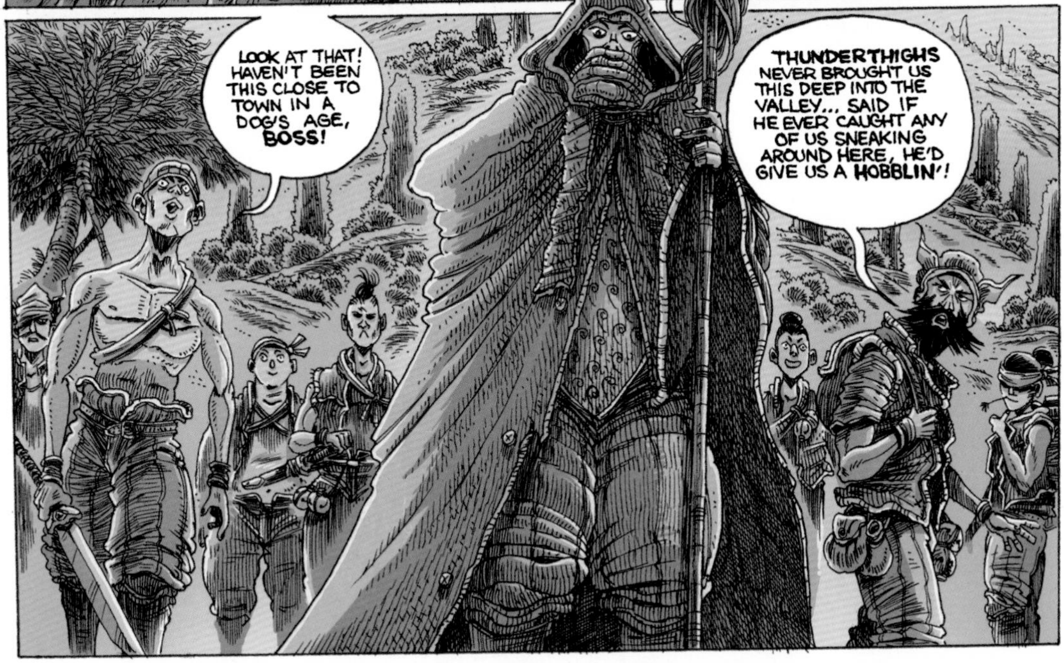

LOOK AT THAT! HAVEN'T BEEN THIS CLOSE TO TOWN IN A DOG'S AGE, BOSS!
THUNDERTHIGHS NEVER BROUGHT US THIS DEEP INTO THE VALLEY... SAID IF HE EVER CAUGHT ANY OF US SNEAKING AROUND HERE, HE'D GIVE US A HOBBLIN'!

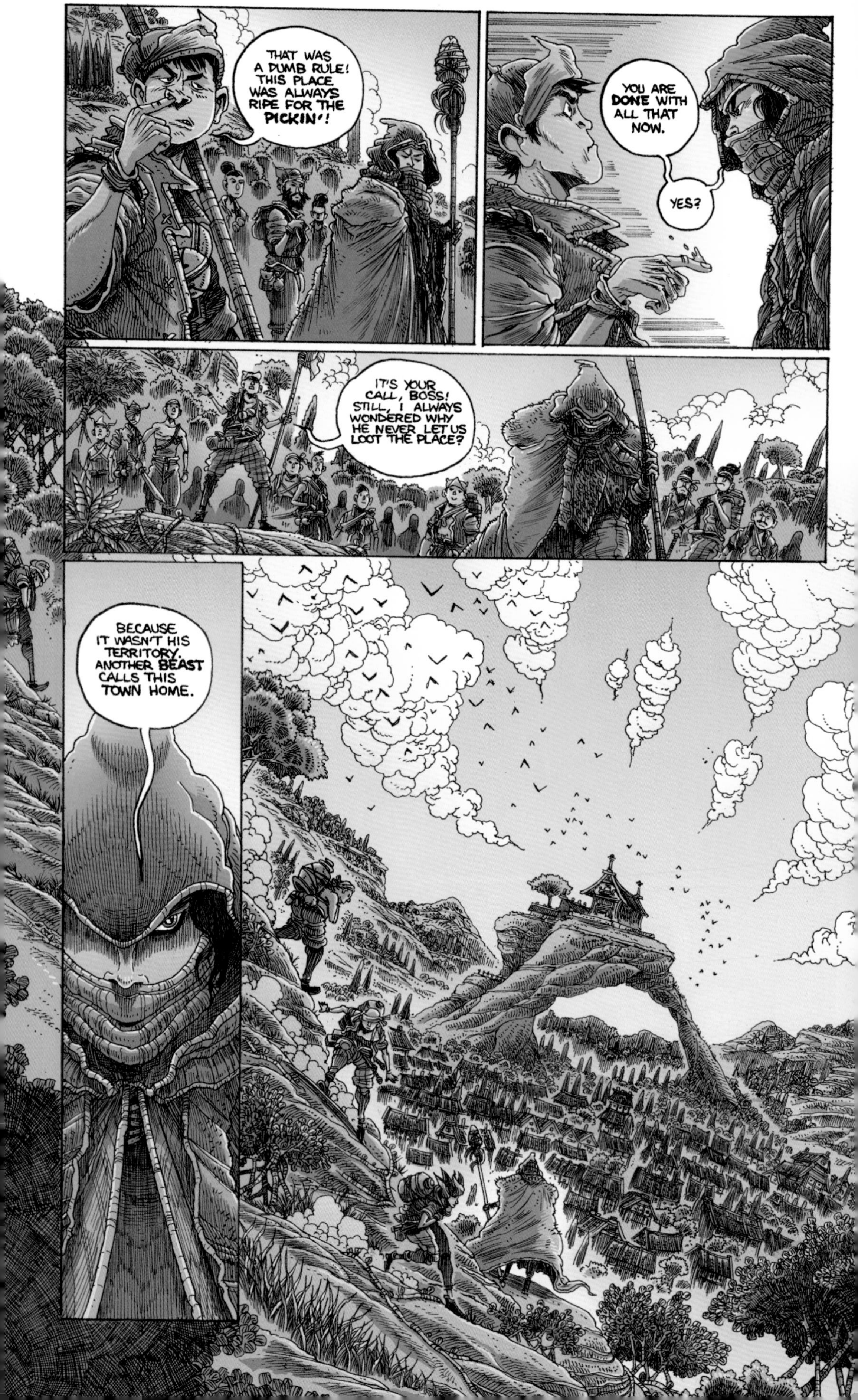
THAT WAS A DUMB RULE! THIS PLACE WAS ALWAYS RIPE FOR THE PICKIN'!
YOU ARE DONE WITH ALL THAT NOW.
YES?
IT'S YOUR CALL, BOSS! STILL, I ALWAYS WONDERED WHY HE NEVER LET US LOOT THE PLACE?
BECAUSE IT WASN'T HIS TERRITORY. ANOTHER BEAST CALLS THIS TOWN HOME.

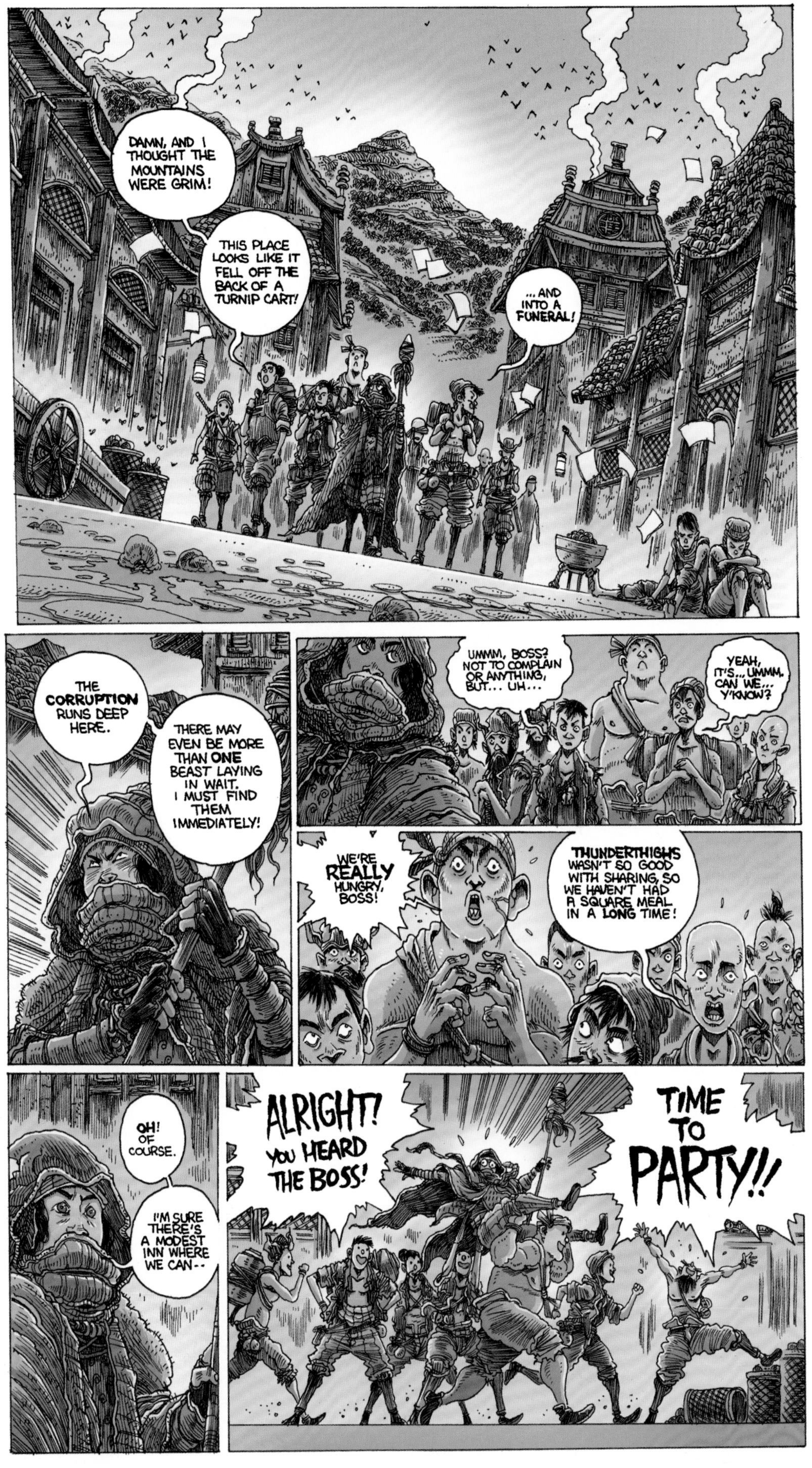
DAMN, AND I THOUGHT THE MOUNTAINS WERE GRIM!
THIS PLACE LOOKS LIKE IT FELL OFF THE BACK OF A TURNIP CART!
...AND INTO A FUNERAL!
THE CORRUPTION RUNS DEEP HERE.
THERE MAY EVEN BE MORE THAN ONE BEAST LAYING IN WAIT. I MUST FIND THEM IMMEDIATELY!
UMMM, BOSS? NOT TO COMPLAIN OR ANYTHING, BUT... UH...
YEAH, IT'S... UMMM. CAN WE... Y'KNOW?
WE'RE REALLY HUNGRY, BOSS!
THUNDERTHIGHS WASN'T SO GOOD WITH SHARING, SO WE HAVEN'T HAD A SQUARE MEAL IN A LONG TIME!
OH! OF COURSE.
I'M SURE THERE'S A MODEST INN WHERE WE CAN--
ALRIGHT! YOU HEARD THE BOSS!
TIME TO PARTY!!

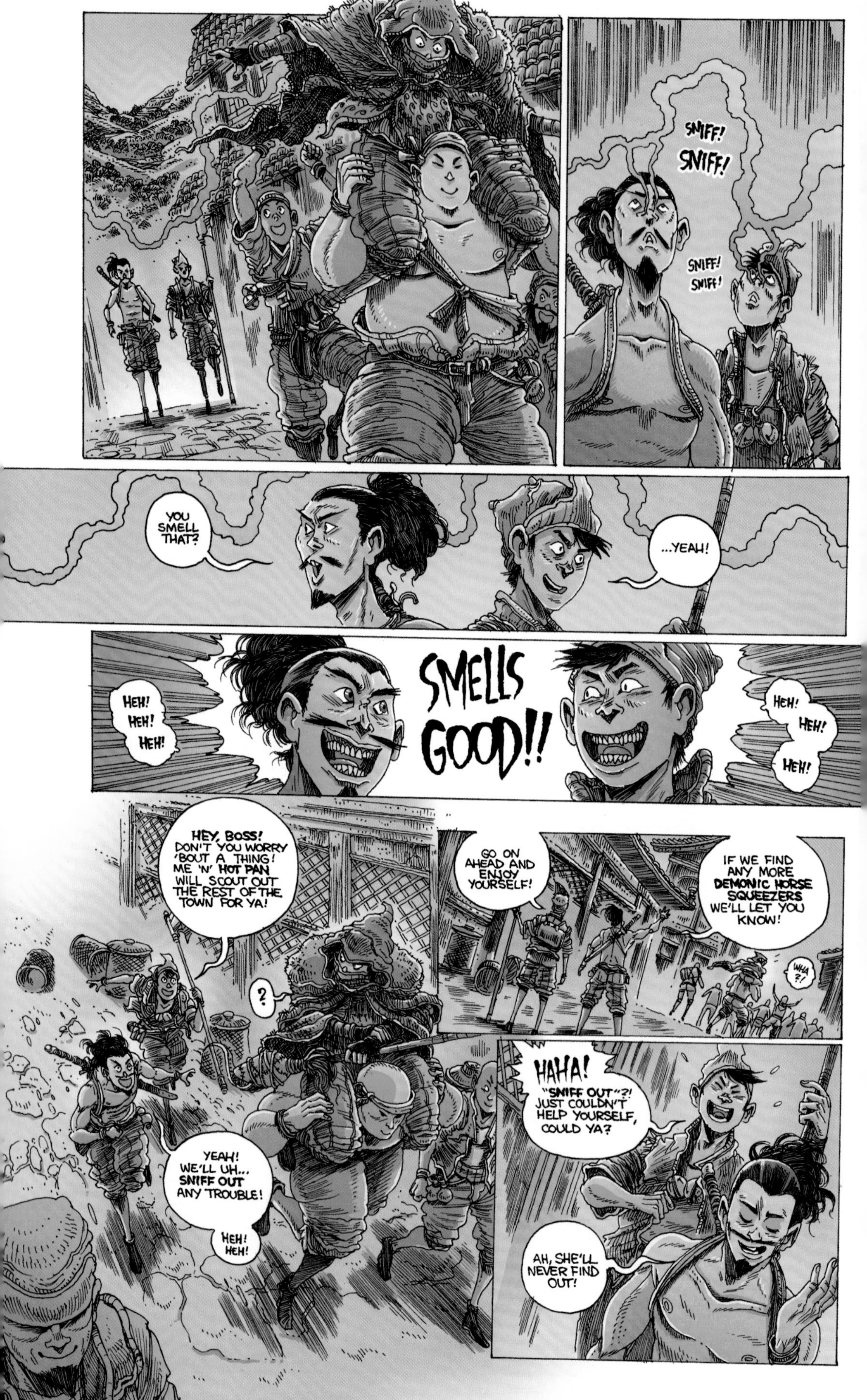
SNIFF!
SNIFF!
SNIFF!
SNIFF!
YOU SMELL THAT?
...YEAH!
SMELLS GOOD!!
HEH! HEH! HEH!
HEH! HEH! HEH!
HEY, BOSS! DON'T YOU WORRY 'BOUT A THING! ME 'N' HOT PAN WILL SCOUT OUT THE REST OF THE TOWN FOR YA!
?
GO ON AHEAD AND ENJOY YOURSELF!
IF WE FIND ANY MORE DEMONIC HORSE SQUEEZERS WE'LL LET YOU KNOW!
WHA?!
YEAH! WE'LL UH... SNIFF OUT ANY TROUBLE!
HEH! HEH!
HAHA! "SNIFF OUT"?! JUST COULDN'T HELP YOURSELF, COULD YA?
AH, SHE'LL NEVER FIND OUT!

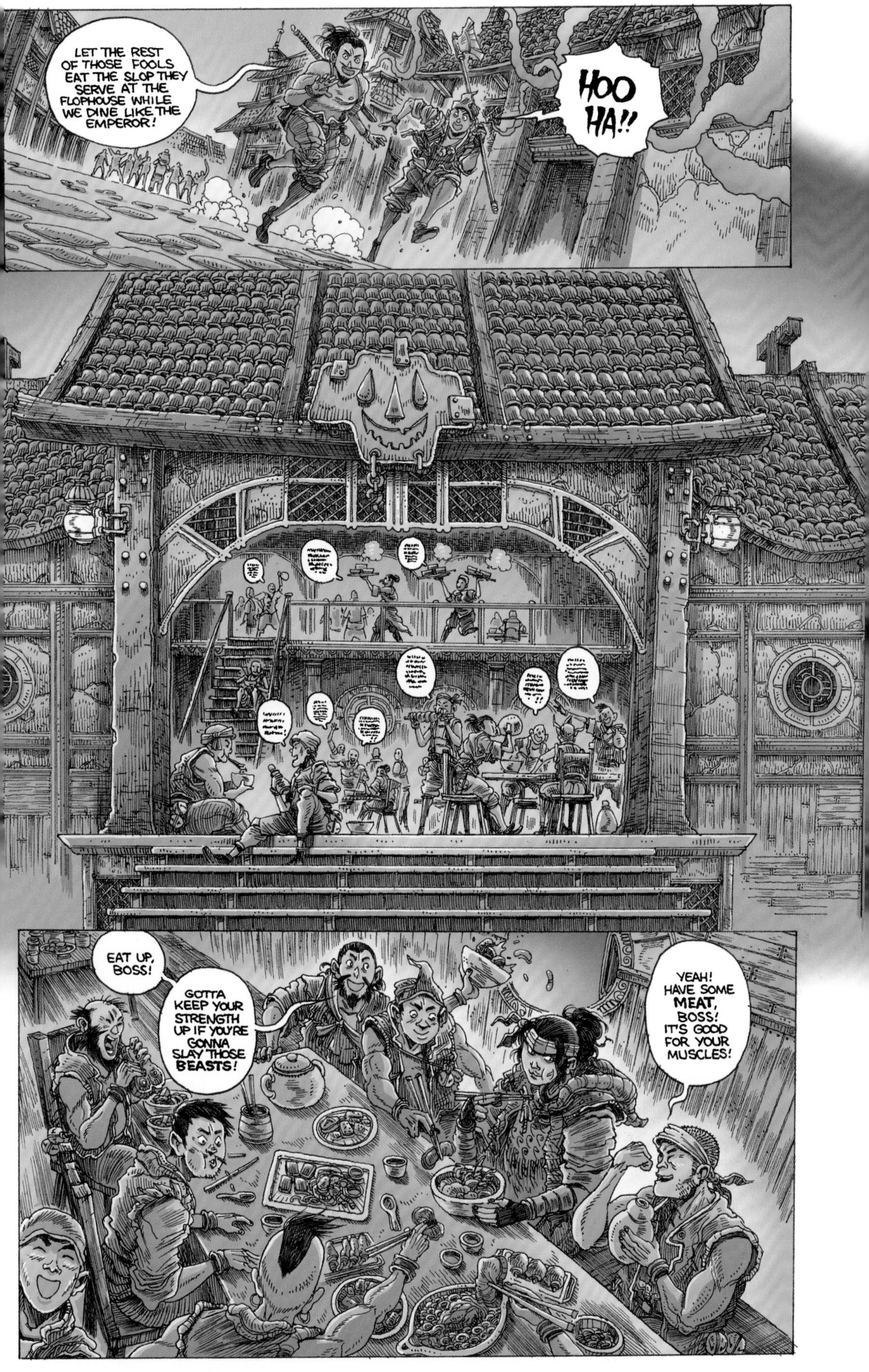
LET THE REST OF THOSE FOOLS EAT THE SLOP THEY SERVE AT THE FLOPHOUSE WHILE WE DINE LIKE THE EMPEROR!
HOO HA!!
EAT UP, BOSS!
GOTTA KEEP YOUR STRENGTH UP IF YOU'RE GONNA SLAY THOSE BEASTS!
YEAH! HAVE SOME MEAT, BOSS! IT'S GOOD FOR YOUR MUSCLES!

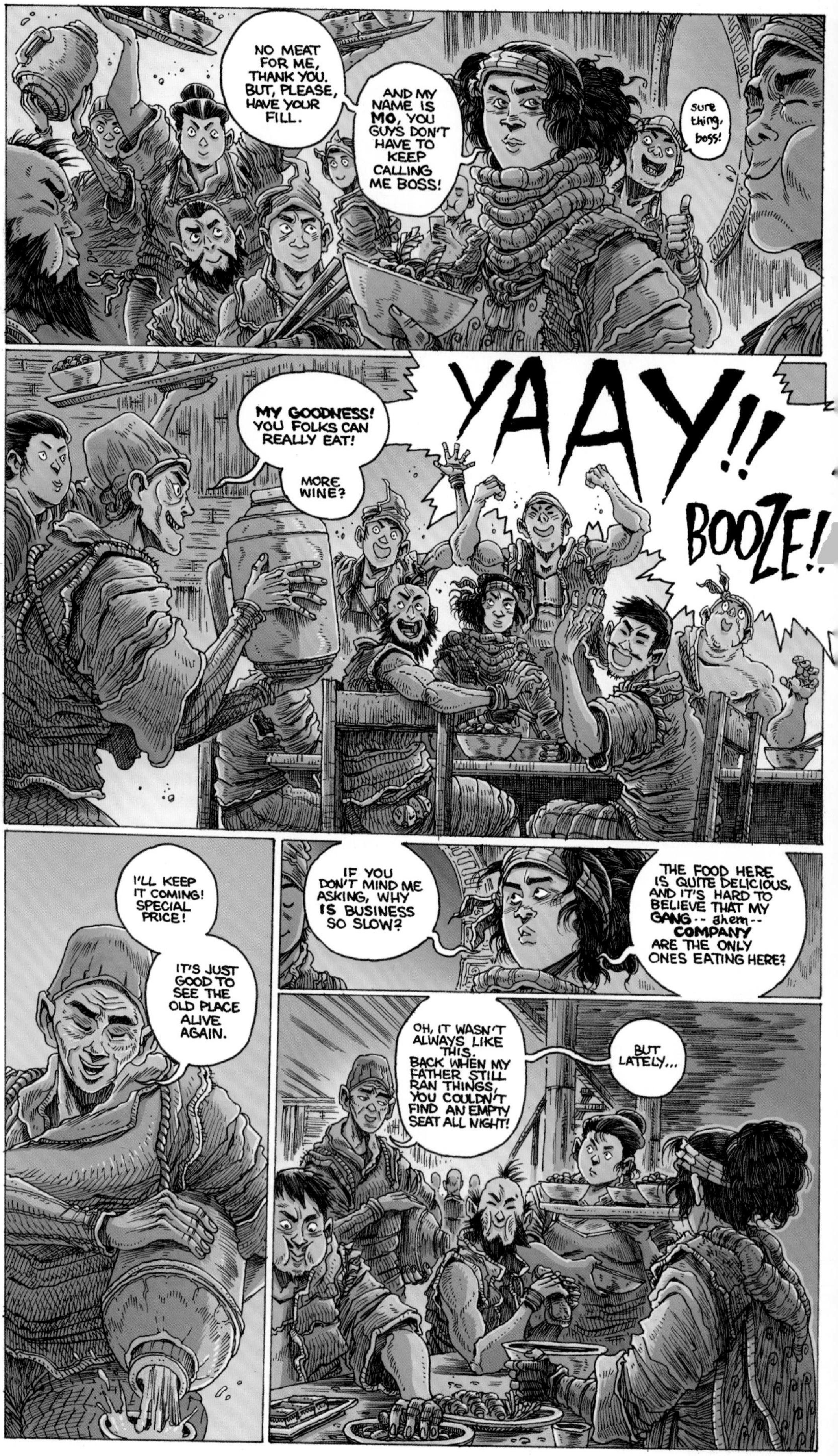
NO MEAT FOR ME, THANK YOU. BUT, PLEASE, HAVE YOUR FILL.
AND MY NAME IS MO, YOU GUYS DON'T HAVE TO KEEP CALLING ME BOSS!
sure thing, boss!
YAAY!!
BOOZE!!
MY GOODNESS! YOU FOLKS CAN REALLY EAT!
MORE WINE?
I'LL KEEP IT COMING! SPECIAL PRICE!
IT'S JUST GOOD TO SEE THE OLD PLACE ALIVE AGAIN.
IF YOU DON'T MIND ME ASKING, WHY IS BUSINESS SO SLOW?
THE FOOD HERE IS QUITE DELICIOUS, AND IT'S HARD TO BELIEVE THAT MY GANG-- ahem-- COMPANY ARE THE ONLY ONES EATING HERE?
OH, IT WASN'T ALWAYS LIKE THIS. BACK WHEN MY FATHER STILL RAN THINGS, YOU COULDN'T FIND AN EMPTY SEAT ALL NIGHT!
BUT LATELY...

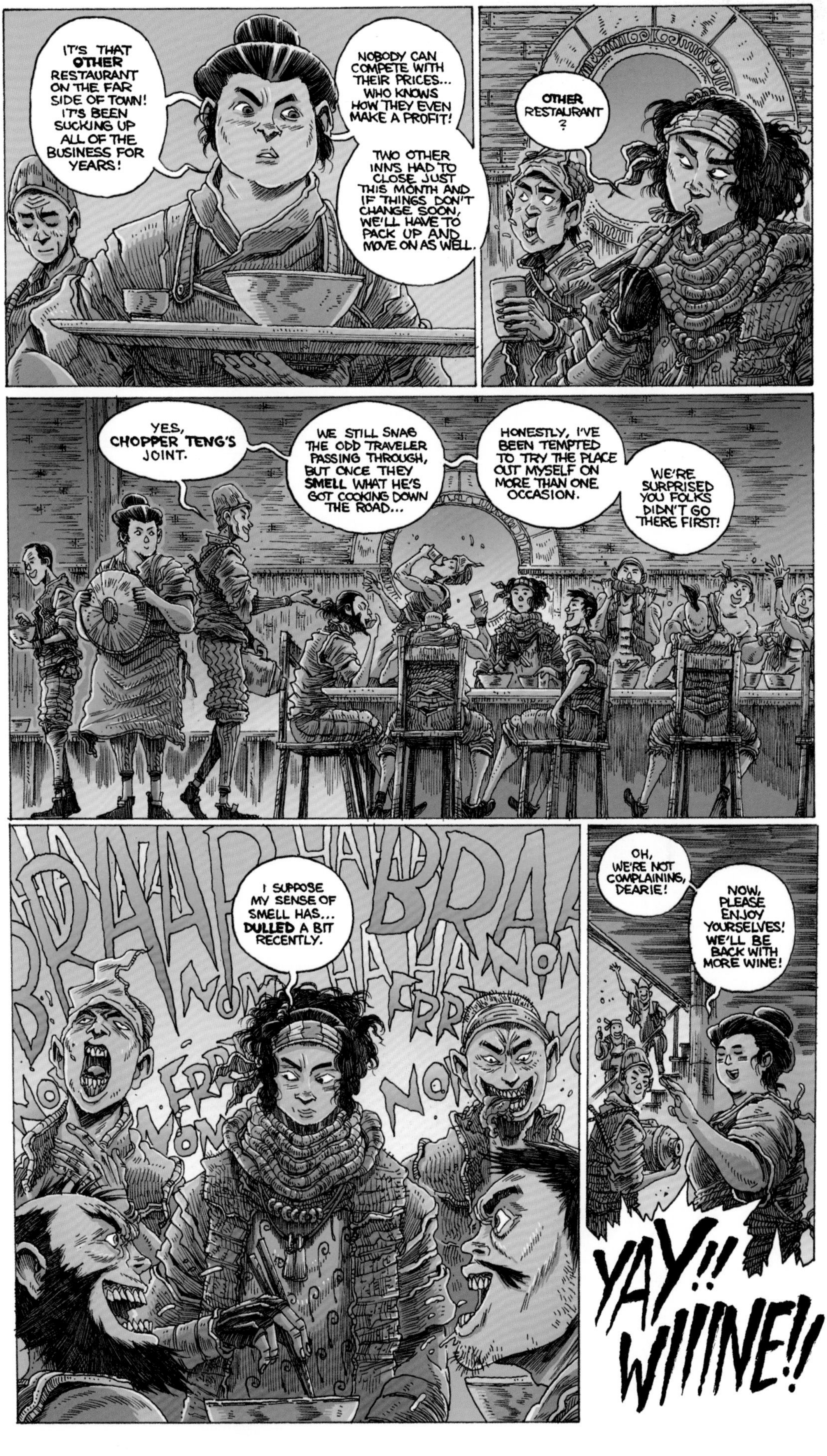
IT'S THAT **OTHER** RESTAURANT ON THE FAR SIDE OF TOWN! IT'S BEEN SUCKING UP ALL OF THE BUSINESS FOR YEARS!
NOBODY CAN COMPETE WITH THEIR PRICES... WHO KNOWS HOW THEY EVEN MAKE A PROFIT!
TWO OTHER INNS HAD TO CLOSE JUST THIS MONTH AND IF THINGS DON'T CHANGE SOON, WE'LL HAVE TO PACK UP AND MOVE ON AS WELL.
OTHER RESTAURANT?
YES, **CHOPPER TENG'S** JOINT.
WE STILL SNAG THE ODD TRAVELER PASSING THROUGH, BUT ONCE THEY **SMELL** WHAT HE'S GOT COOKING DOWN THE ROAD...
HONESTLY, I'VE BEEN TEMPTED TO TRY THE PLACE OUT MYSELF ON MORE THAN ONE OCCASION.
WE'RE SURPRISED YOU FOLKS DIDN'T GO THERE FIRST!
I SUPPOSE MY SENSE OF SMELL HAS... **DULLED** A BIT RECENTLY.
OH, WE'RE NOT COMPLAINING, DEARIE!
NOW, PLEASE ENJOY YOURSELVES! WE'LL BE BACK WITH MORE WINE!
YAY!! WIIINE!!

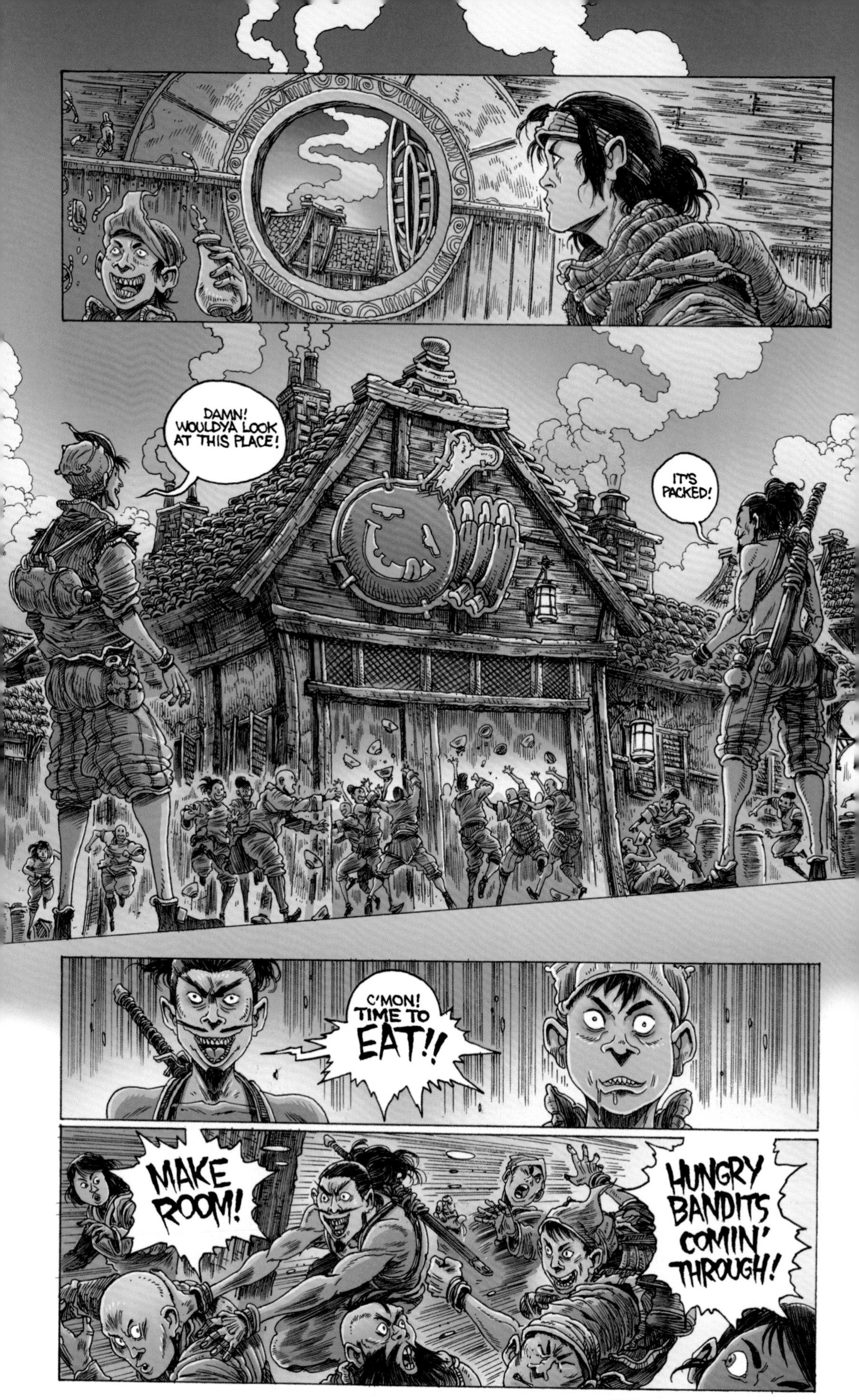
DAMN! WOULDYA LOOK AT THIS PLACE!
IT'S PACKED!
C'MON! TIME TO EAT!!
MAKE ROOM!
HUNGRY BANDITS COMIN' THROUGH!

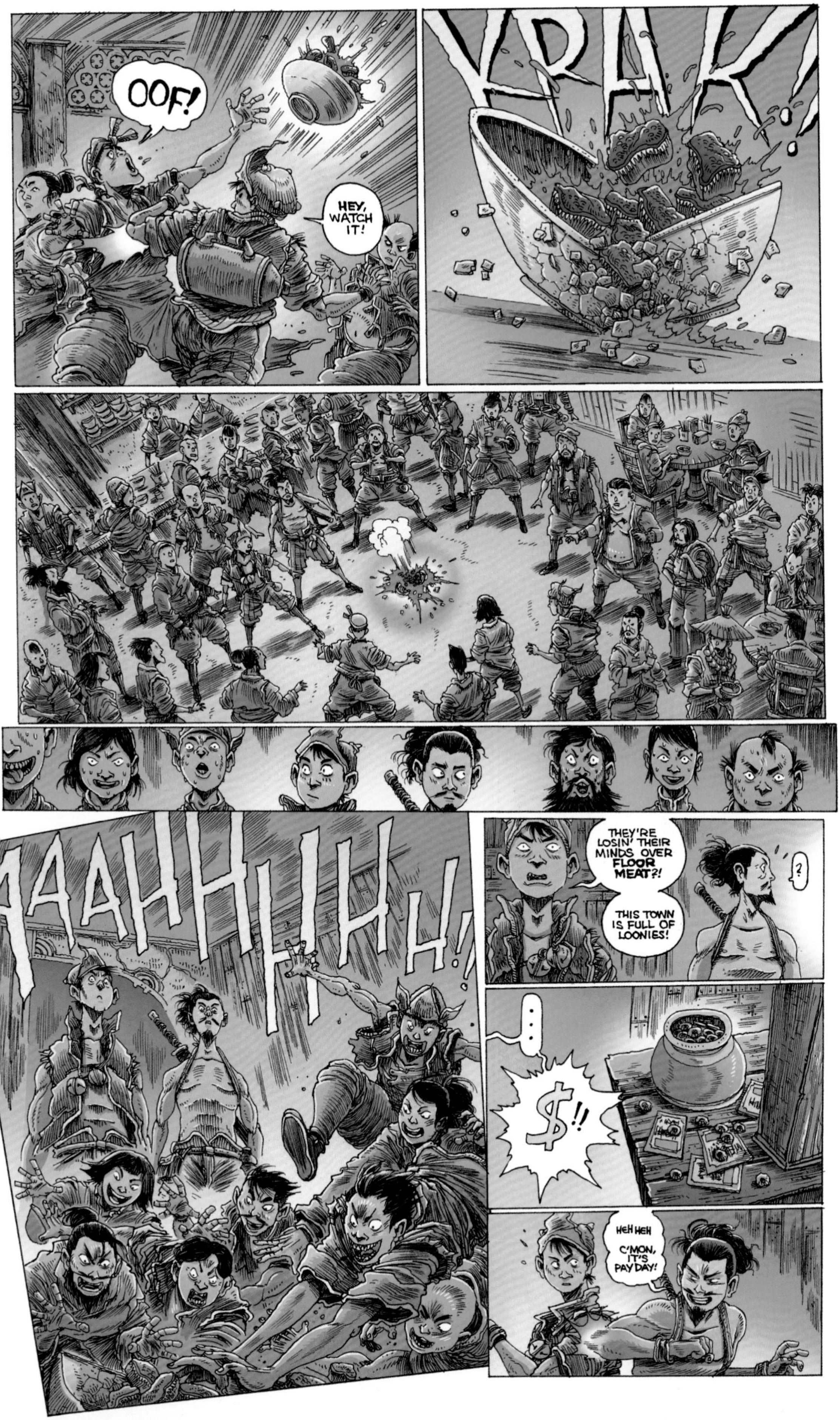
OOF!
HEY, WATCH IT!
KRAK!
AAHHHHH!
THEY'RE LOSIN' THEIR MINDS OVER **FLOOR MEAT**?!
THIS TOWN IS FULL OF LOONIES!
?
...
$!!
HEH HEH
C'MON, IT'S PAYDAY!

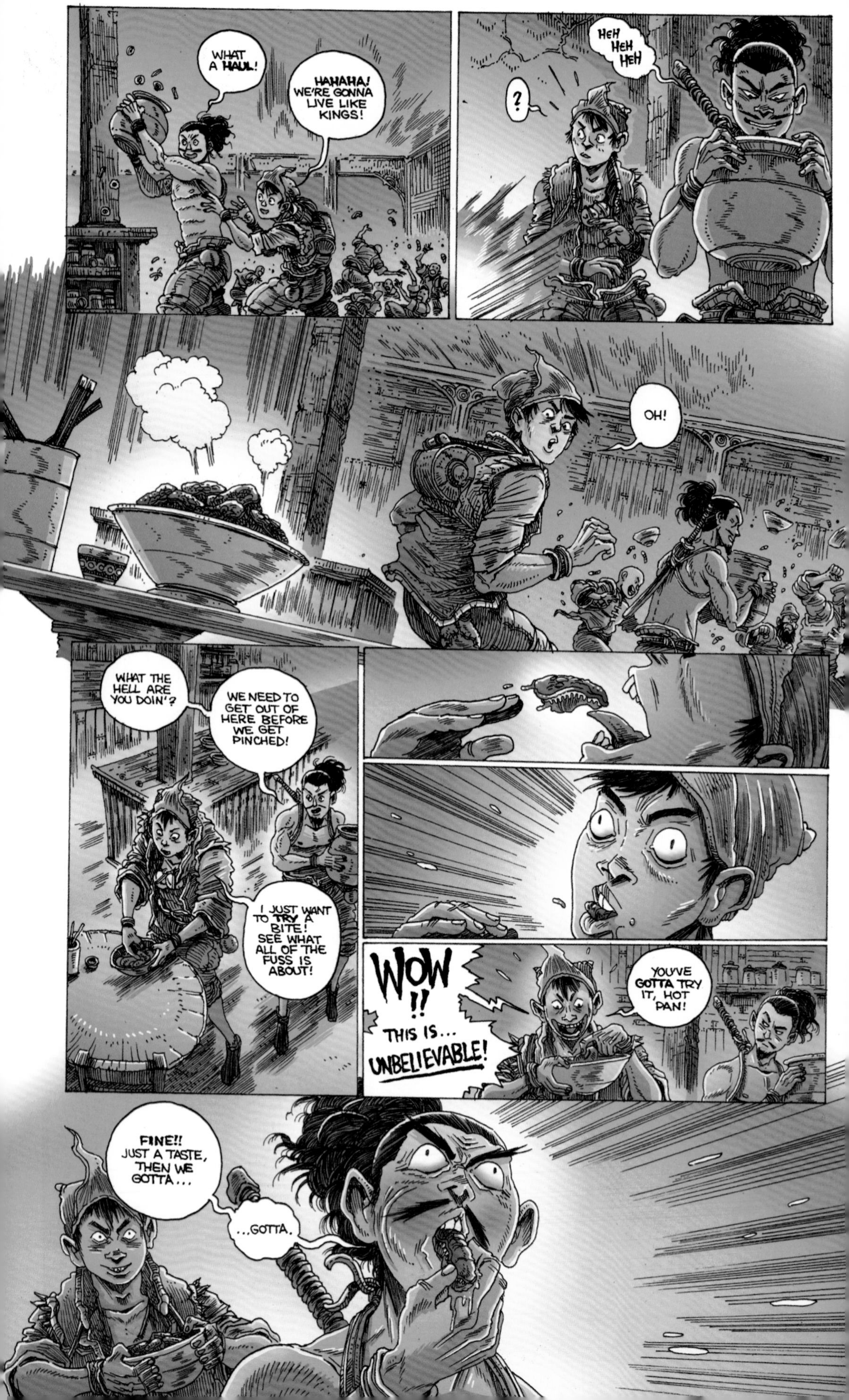
WHAT A HAUL!
HAHAHA! WE'RE GONNA LIVE LIKE KINGS!
HEH HEH HEH
?
OH!
WHAT THE HELL ARE YOU DOIN'?
WE NEED TO GET OUT OF HERE BEFORE WE GET PINCHED!
I JUST WANT TO TRY A BITE! SEE WHAT ALL OF THE FUSS IS ABOUT!
WOW !! THIS IS... UNBELIEVABLE!
YOU'VE GOTTA TRY IT, HOT PAN!
FINE!! JUST A TASTE, THEN WE GOTTA...
...GOTTA.

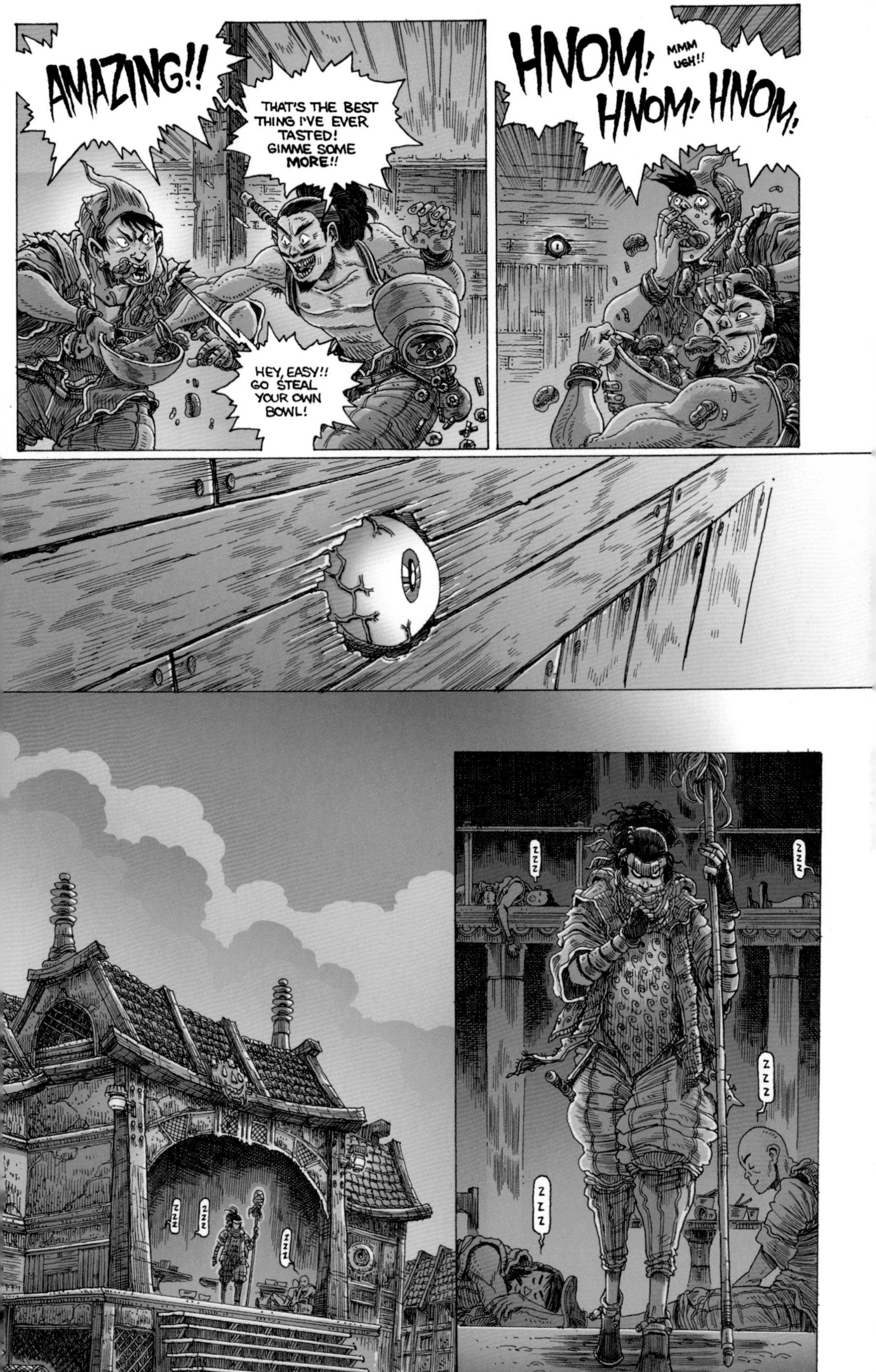
AMAZING!!
THAT'S THE BEST THING I'VE EVER TASTED! GIMME SOME MORE!!
HEY, EASY!! GO STEAL YOUR OWN BOWL!
HNOM! HNOM! HNOM!
MMM UGH!!
ZZZ
ZZZ
ZZZ
ZZZ
ZZZ
ZZZ
ZZZ

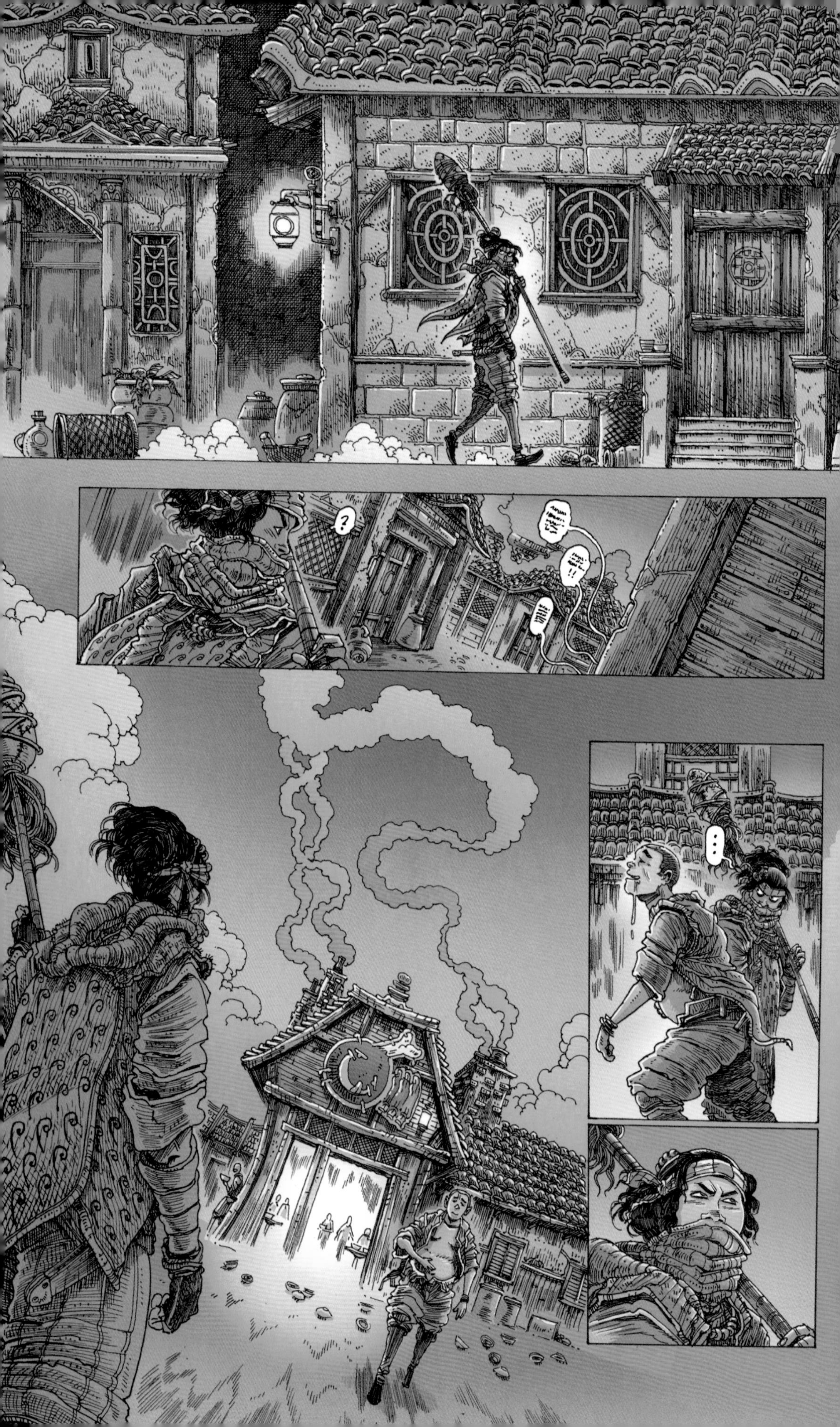
?
...

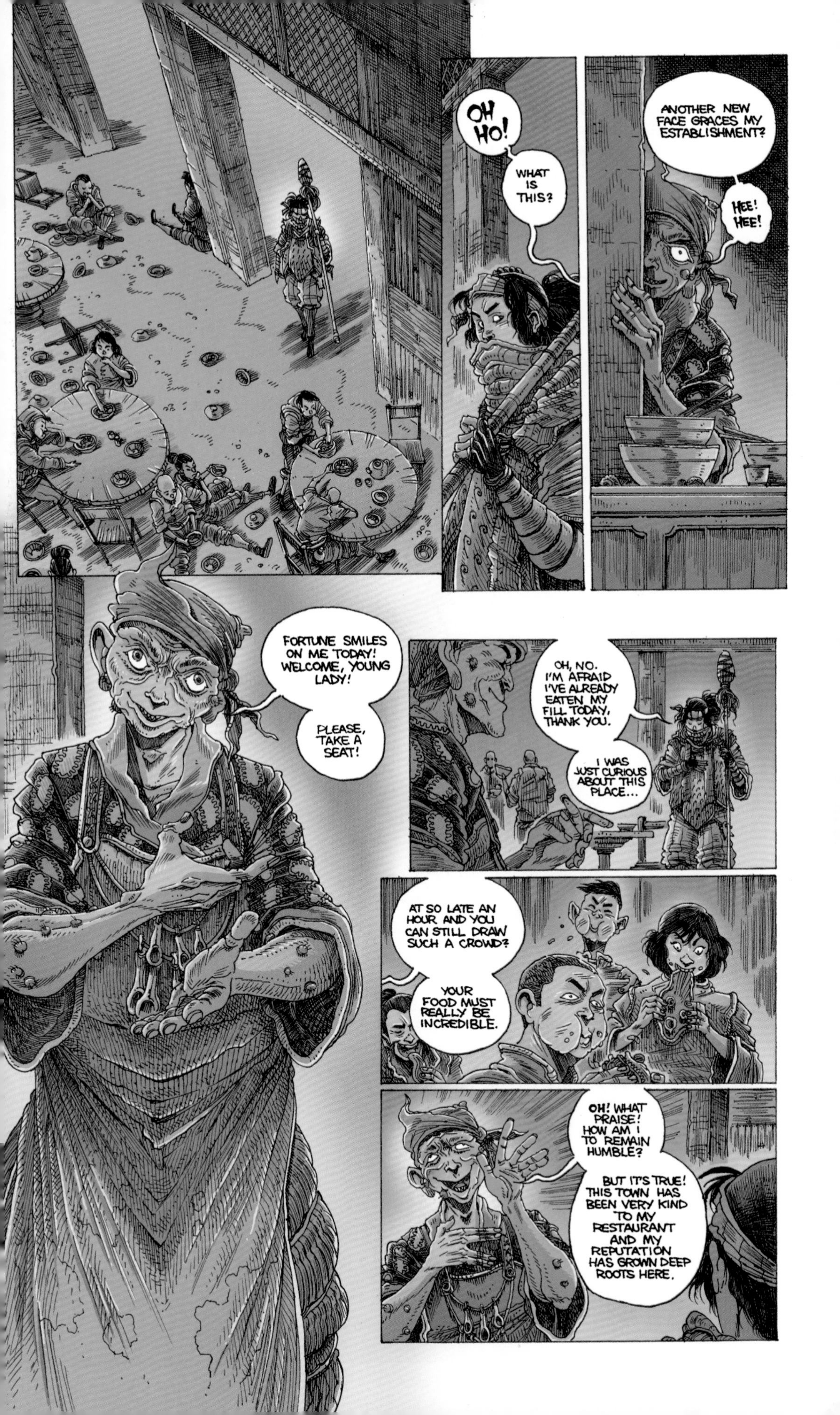
OH HO!
WHAT IS THIS?
ANOTHER NEW FACE GRACES MY ESTABLISHMENT?
HEE! HEE!
FORTUNE SMILES ON ME TODAY! WELCOME, YOUNG LADY!
PLEASE, TAKE A SEAT!
OH, NO. I'M AFRAID I'VE ALREADY EATEN MY FILL TODAY, THANK YOU.
I WAS JUST CURIOUS ABOUT THIS PLACE...
AT SO LATE AN HOUR AND YOU CAN STILL DRAW SUCH A CROWD?
YOUR FOOD MUST REALLY BE INCREDIBLE.
OH! WHAT PRAISE! HOW AM I TO REMAIN HUMBLE?
BUT IT'S TRUE! THIS TOWN HAS BEEN VERY KIND TO MY RESTAURANT AND MY REPUTATION HAS GROWN DEEP ROOTS HERE.

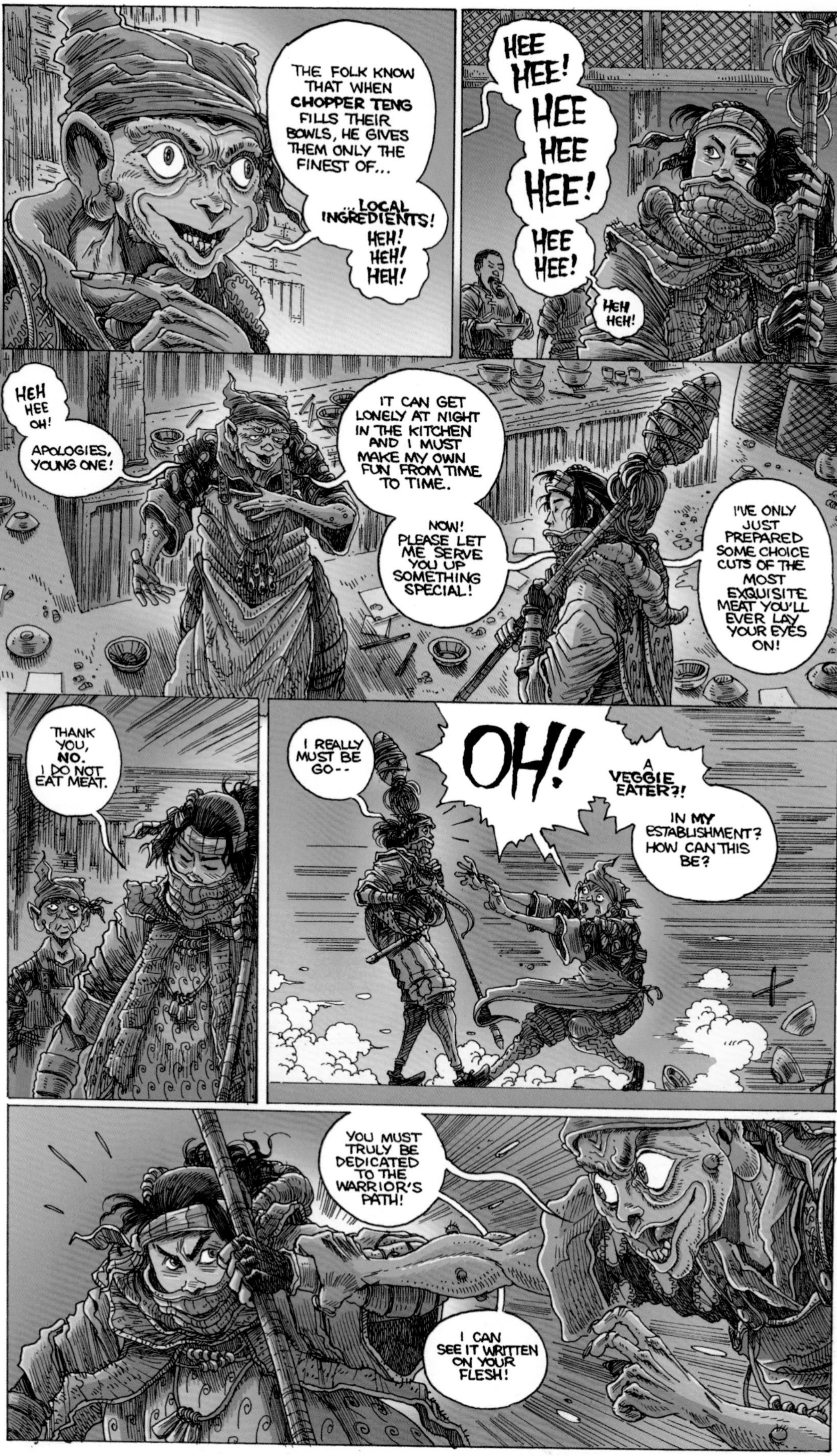
THE FOLK KNOW THAT WHEN **CHOPPER TENG** FILLS THEIR BOWLS, HE GIVES THEM ONLY THE FINEST OF...
...LOCAL INGREDIENTS! HEH! HEH! HEH!
HEE HEE! HEE HEE HEE! HEE HEE!
HEH HEH!
HEH HEE OH!
APOLOGIES, YOUNG ONE!
IT CAN GET LONELY AT NIGHT IN THE KITCHEN AND I MUST MAKE MY OWN FUN FROM TIME TO TIME.
NOW! PLEASE LET ME SERVE YOU UP SOMETHING SPECIAL!
I'VE ONLY JUST PREPARED SOME CHOICE CUTS OF THE MOST EXQUISITE MEAT YOU'LL EVER LAY YOUR EYES ON!
THANK YOU, **NO.** I DO NOT EAT MEAT.
I REALLY MUST BE GO--
OH!
A **VEGGIE EATER?!**
IN **MY** ESTABLISHMENT? HOW CAN THIS BE?
YOU MUST TRULY BE DEDICATED TO THE WARRIOR'S PATH!
I CAN SEE IT WRITTEN ON YOUR FLESH!

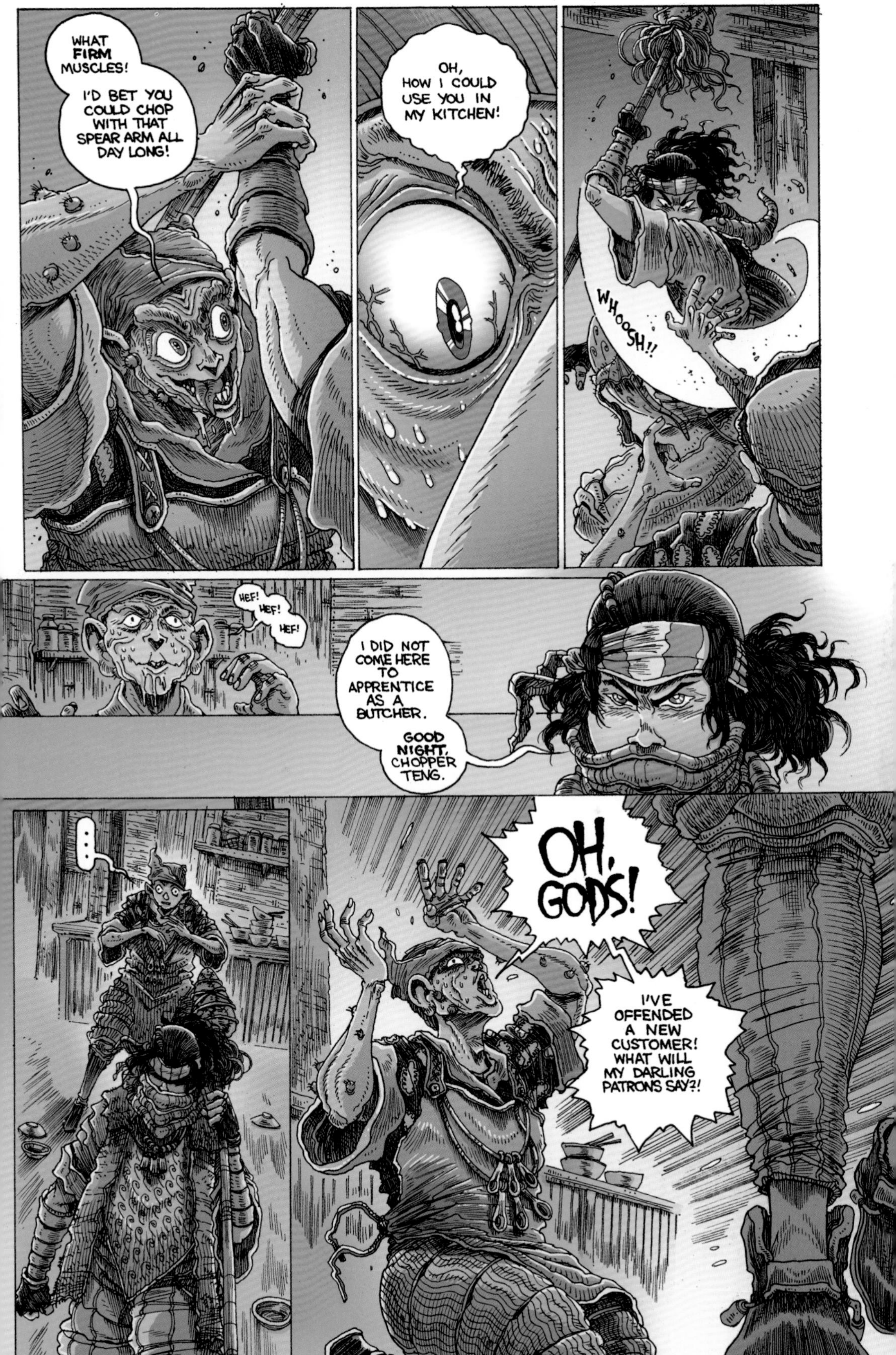
WHAT FIRM MUSCLES!
I'D BET YOU COULD CHOP WITH THAT SPEAR ARM ALL DAY LONG!
OH, HOW I COULD USE YOU IN MY KITCHEN!
WHOOSH!!
HEF! HEF! HEF!
I DID NOT COME HERE TO APPRENTICE AS A BUTCHER.
GOOD NIGHT, CHOPPER TENG.
...
OH, GODS!
I'VE OFFENDED A NEW CUSTOMER! WHAT WILL MY DARLING PATRONS SAY?!

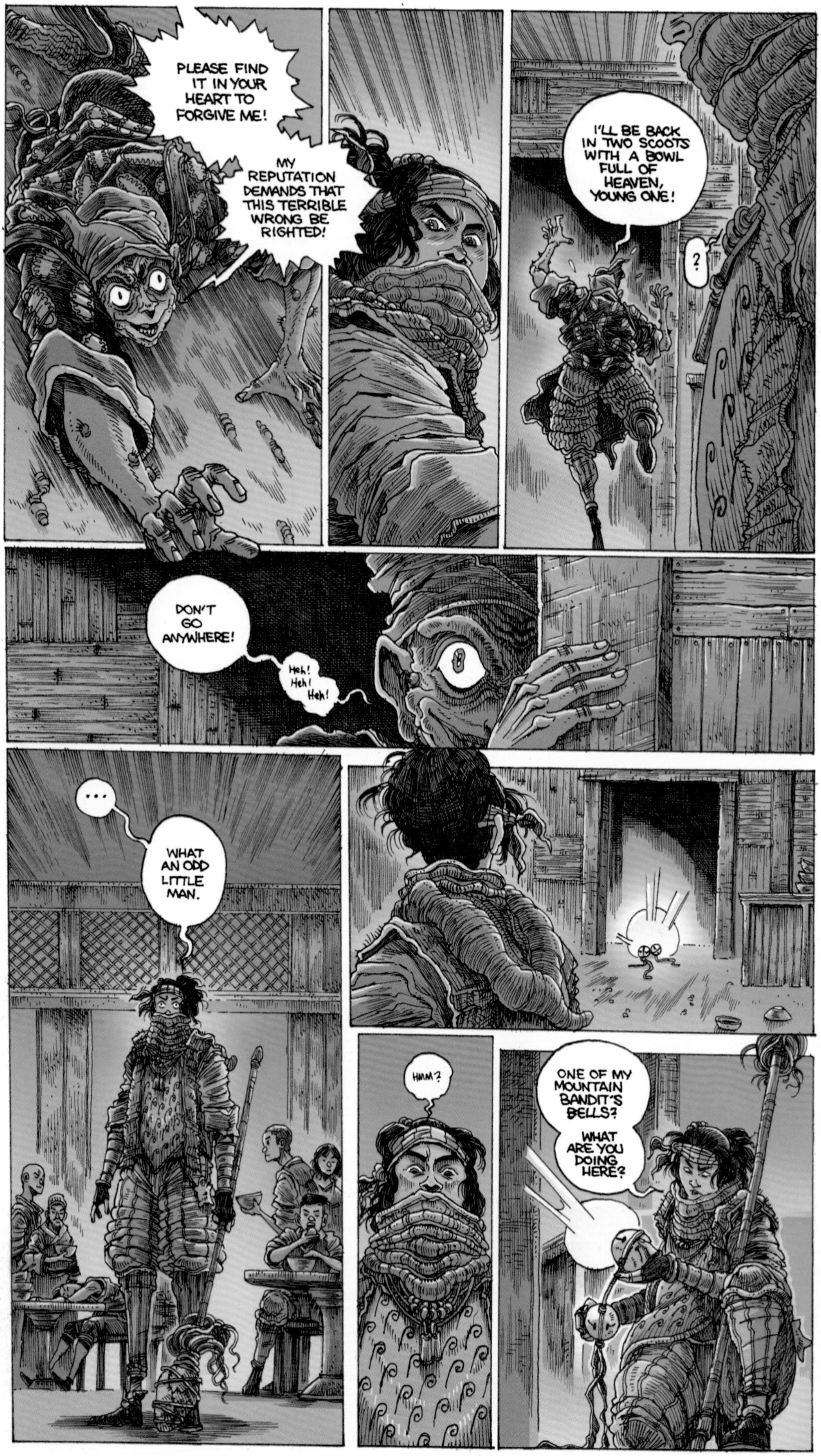
PLEASE FIND IT IN YOUR HEART TO FORGIVE ME!
MY REPUTATION DEMANDS THAT THIS TERRIBLE WRONG BE RIGHTED!
I'LL BE BACK IN TWO SCOOTS WITH A BOWL FULL OF HEAVEN, YOUNG ONE!
?
DON'T GO ANYWHERE!
Heh! Heh! Heh!
...
WHAT AN ODD LITTLE MAN.
HMM?
ONE OF MY MOUNTAIN BANDIT'S BELLS?
WHAT ARE YOU DOING HERE?

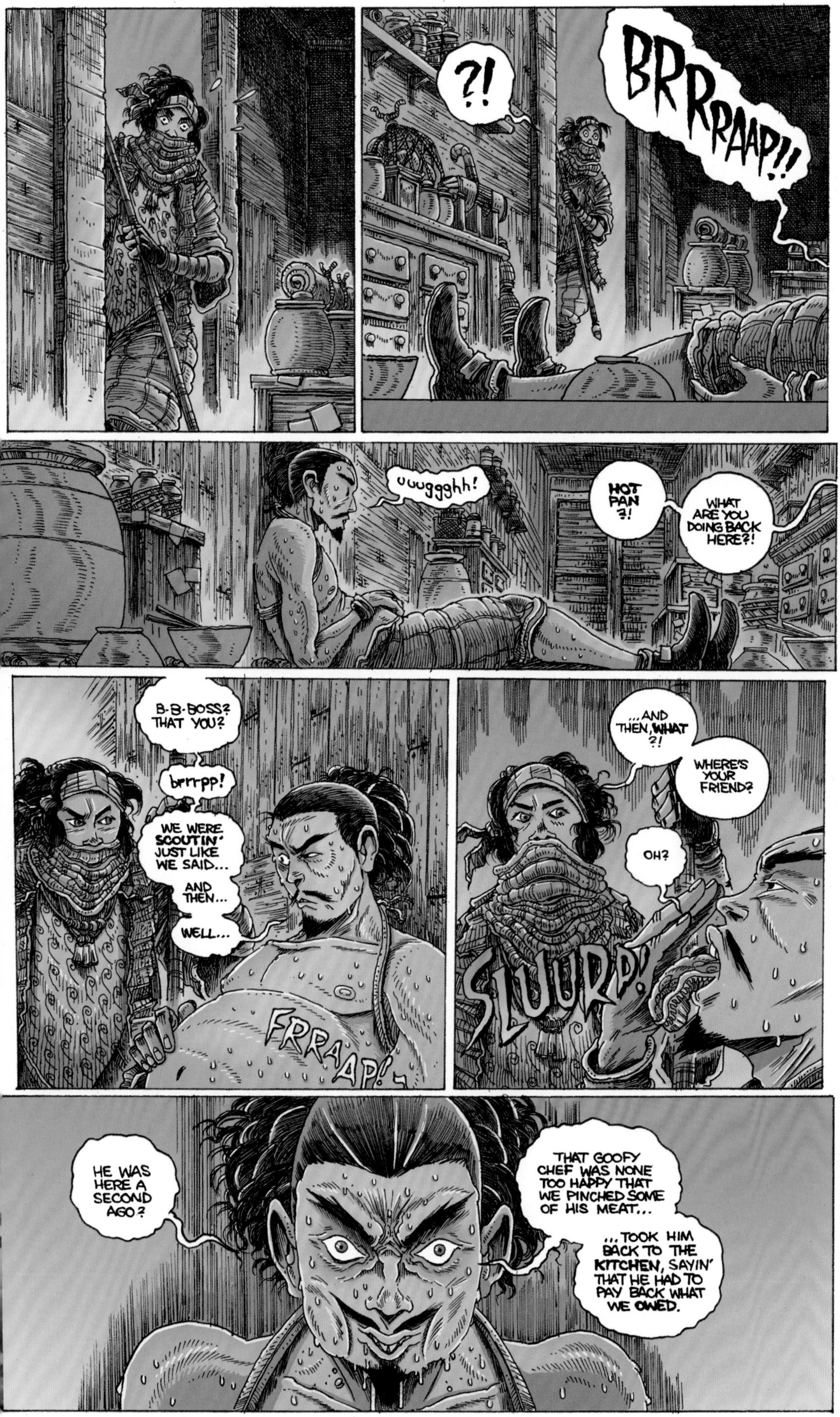
?!
BRRRAAP!!
uuuggghh!
HOT PAN ?!
WHAT ARE YOU DOING BACK HERE?!
B-B-BOSS? THAT YOU?
brrrpp!
WE WERE SCOUTIN' JUST LIKE WE SAID...
AND THEN...
WELL...
FRRAAP!
...AND THEN, WHAT ?!
WHERE'S YOUR FRIEND?
OH?
SLUURP!
HE WAS HERE A SECOND AGO?
THAT GOOFY CHEF WAS NONE TOO HAPPY THAT WE PINCHED SOME OF HIS MEAT...
...TOOK HIM BACK TO THE KITCHEN, SAYIN' THAT HE HAD TO PAY BACK WHAT WE OWED.

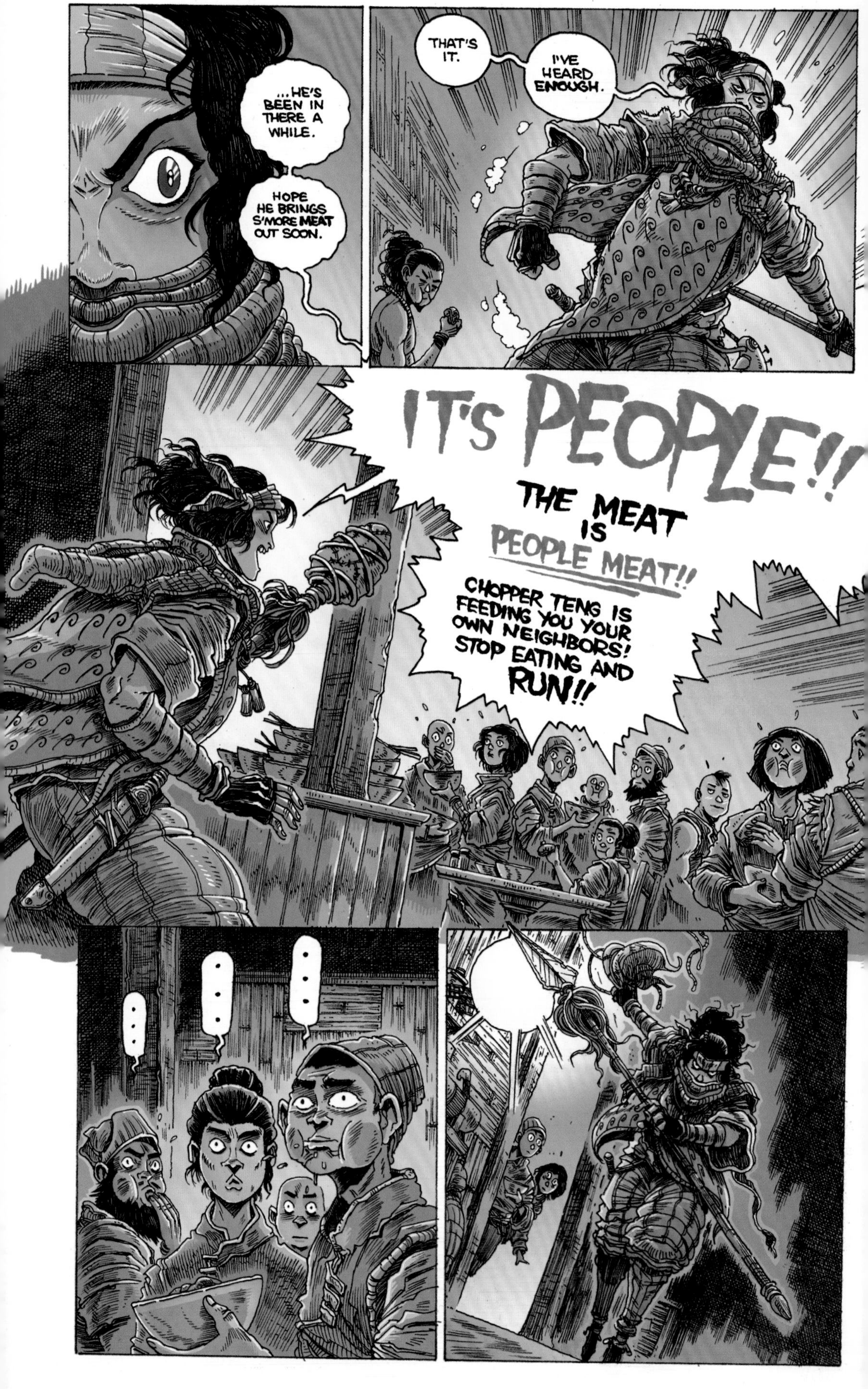
...HE'S BEEN IN THERE A WHILE.
HOPE HE BRINGS S'MORE MEAT OUT SOON.
THAT'S IT.
I'VE HEARD ENOUGH.
IT'S PEOPLE!!
THE MEAT IS PEOPLE MEAT!!
CHOPPER TENG IS FEEDING YOU YOUR OWN NEIGHBORS! STOP EATING AND RUN!!
...
...
...
...

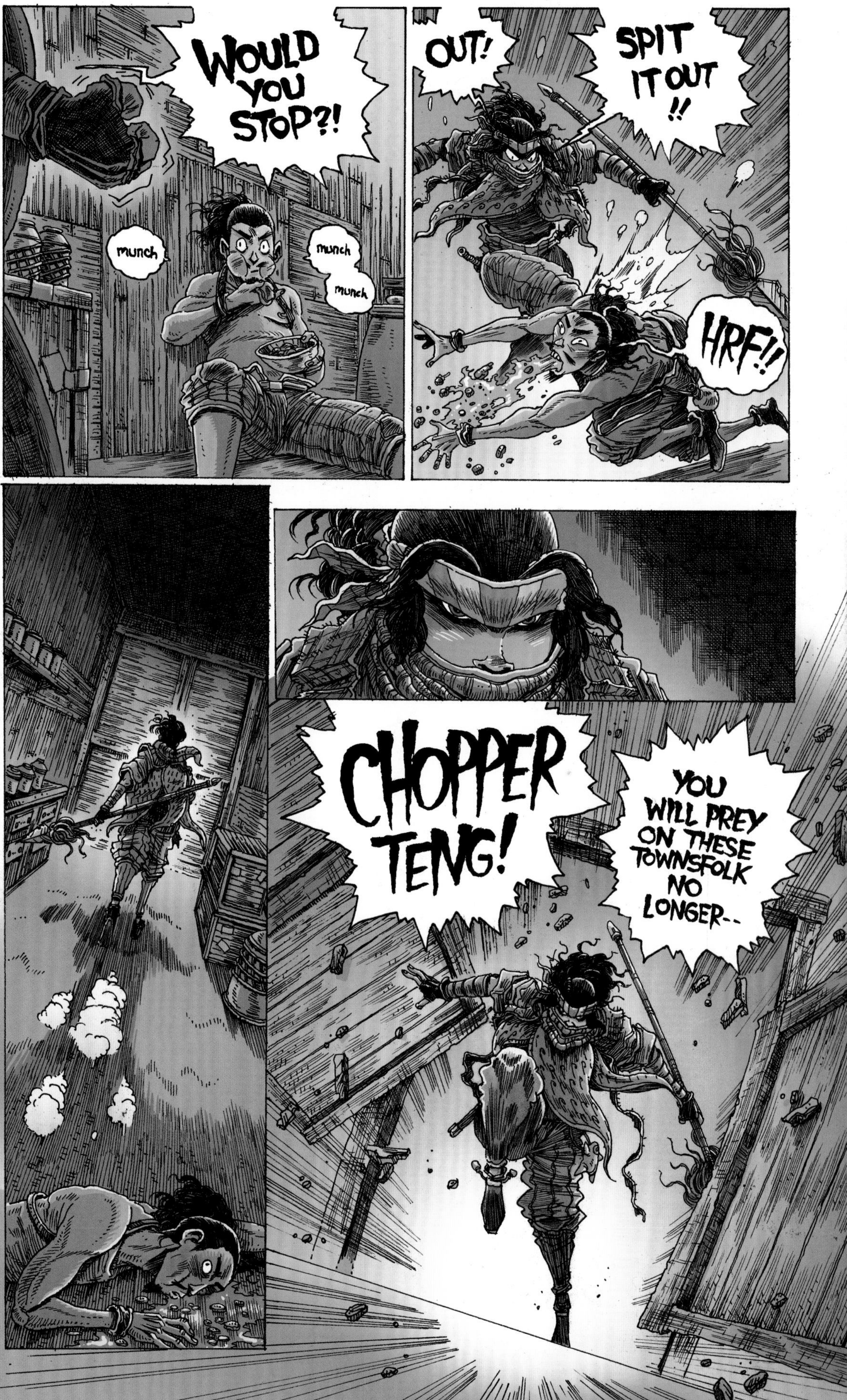
WOULD YOU STOP?!
munch
munch
munch
OUT!
SPIT IT OUT !!
HRF!!
CHOPPER TENG!
YOU WILL PREY ON THESE TOWNSFOLK NO LONGER--

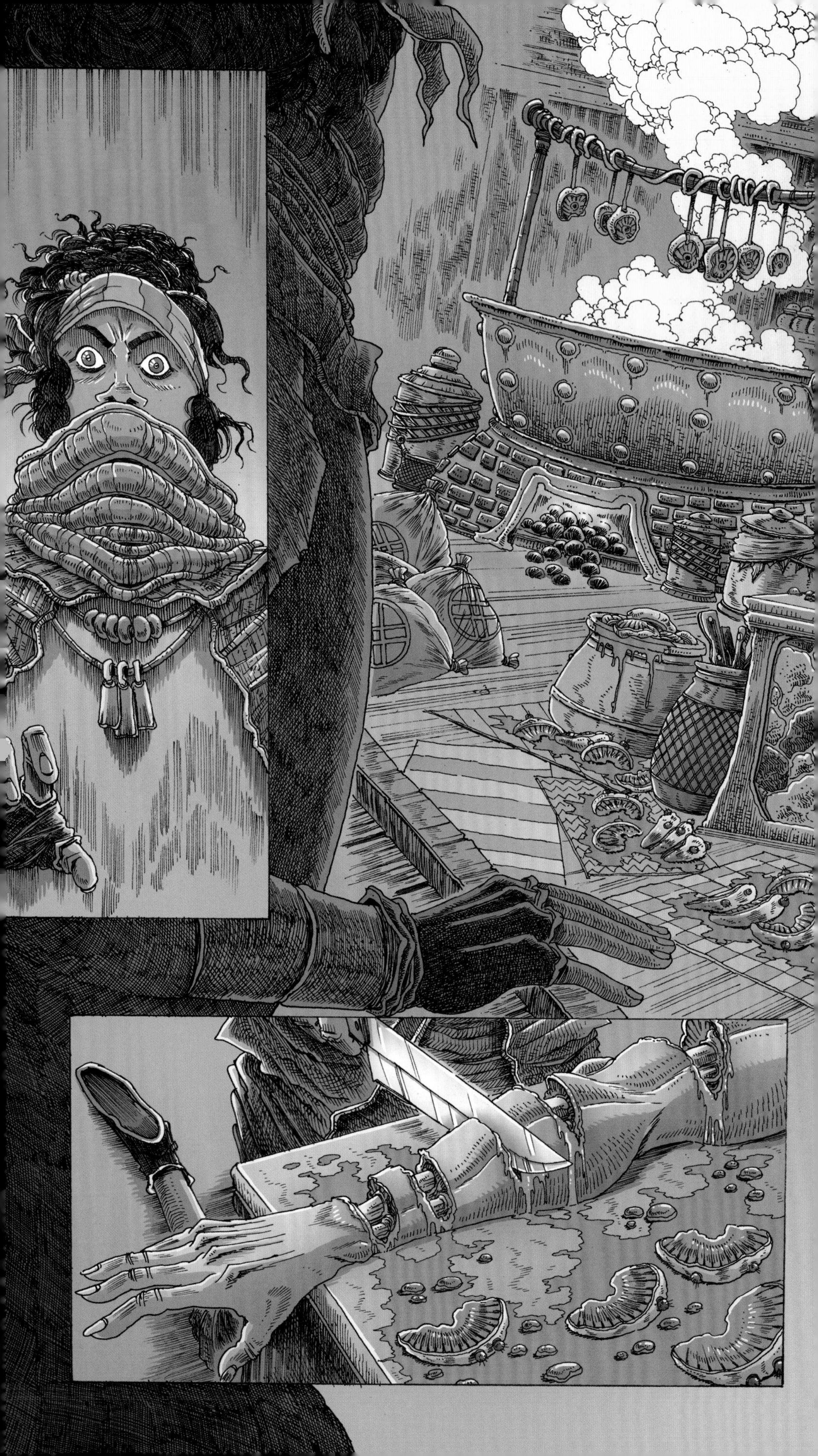

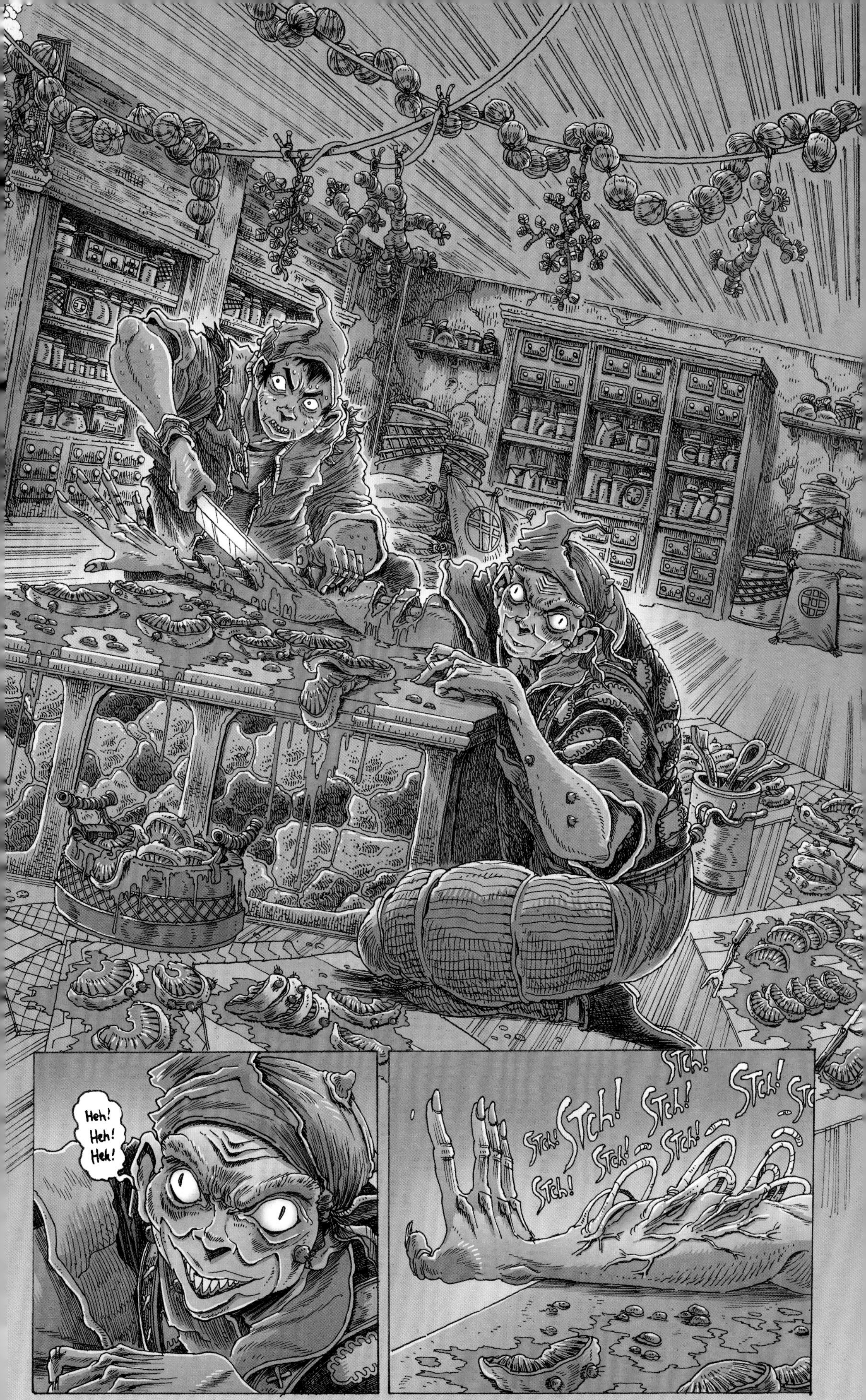
Heh!
Heh!
Heh!
STCH!

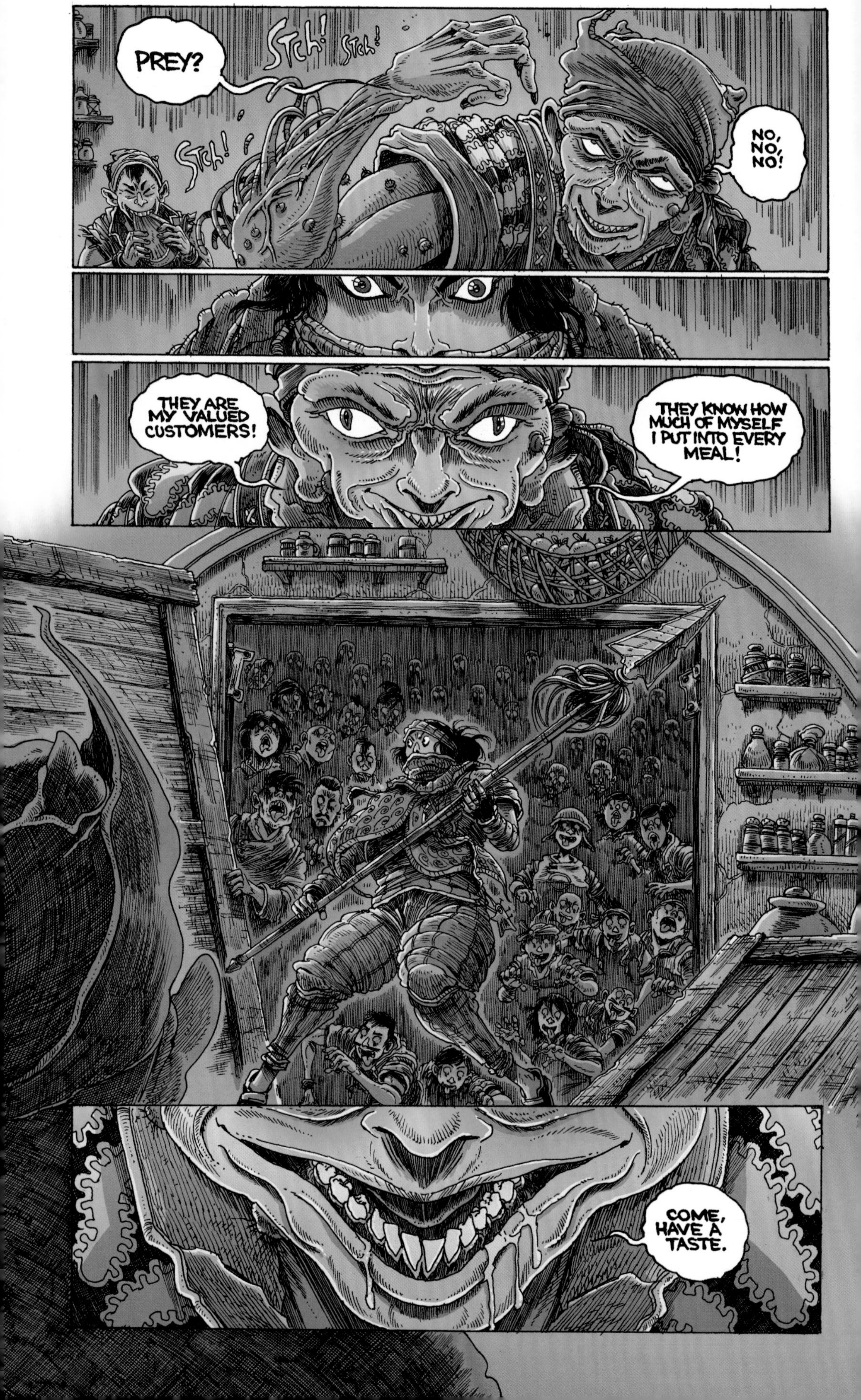
PREY?
Stch! Stch!
Stch!
NO, NO, NO!
THEY ARE MY VALUED CUSTOMERS!
THEY KNOW HOW MUCH OF MYSELF I PUT INTO EVERY MEAL!
COME, HAVE A TASTE.

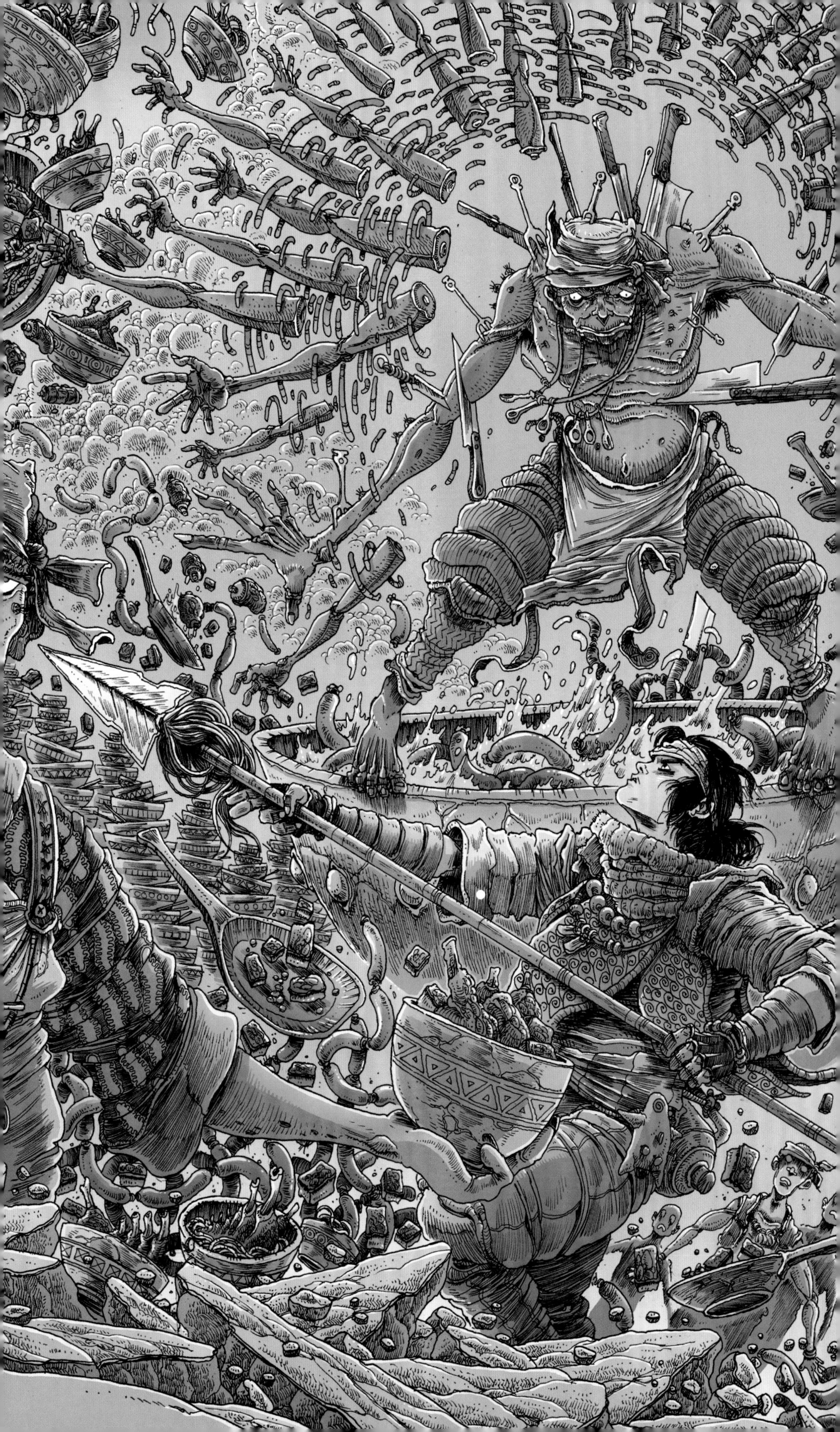

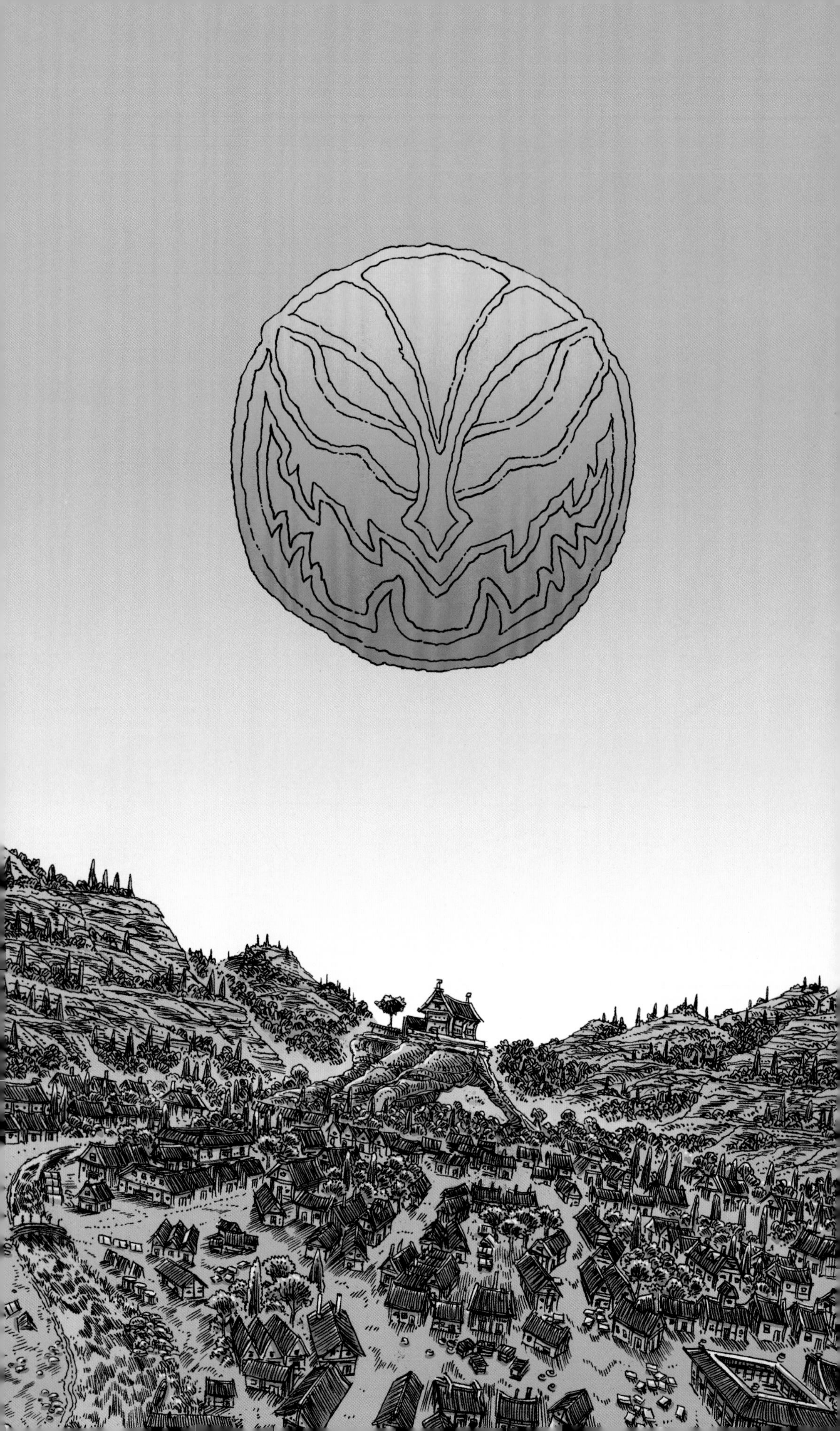

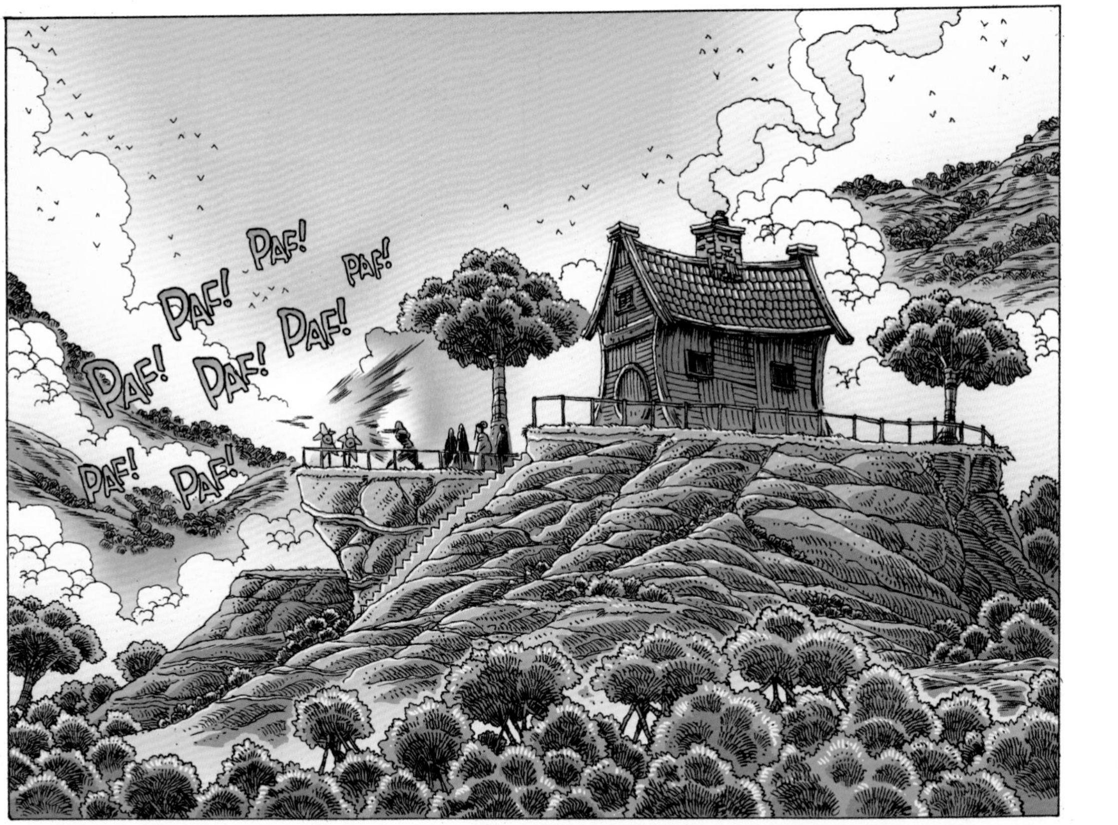
PAF!
PAF!
PAF!
PAF!
PAF!
PAF!
PAF!
PAF!

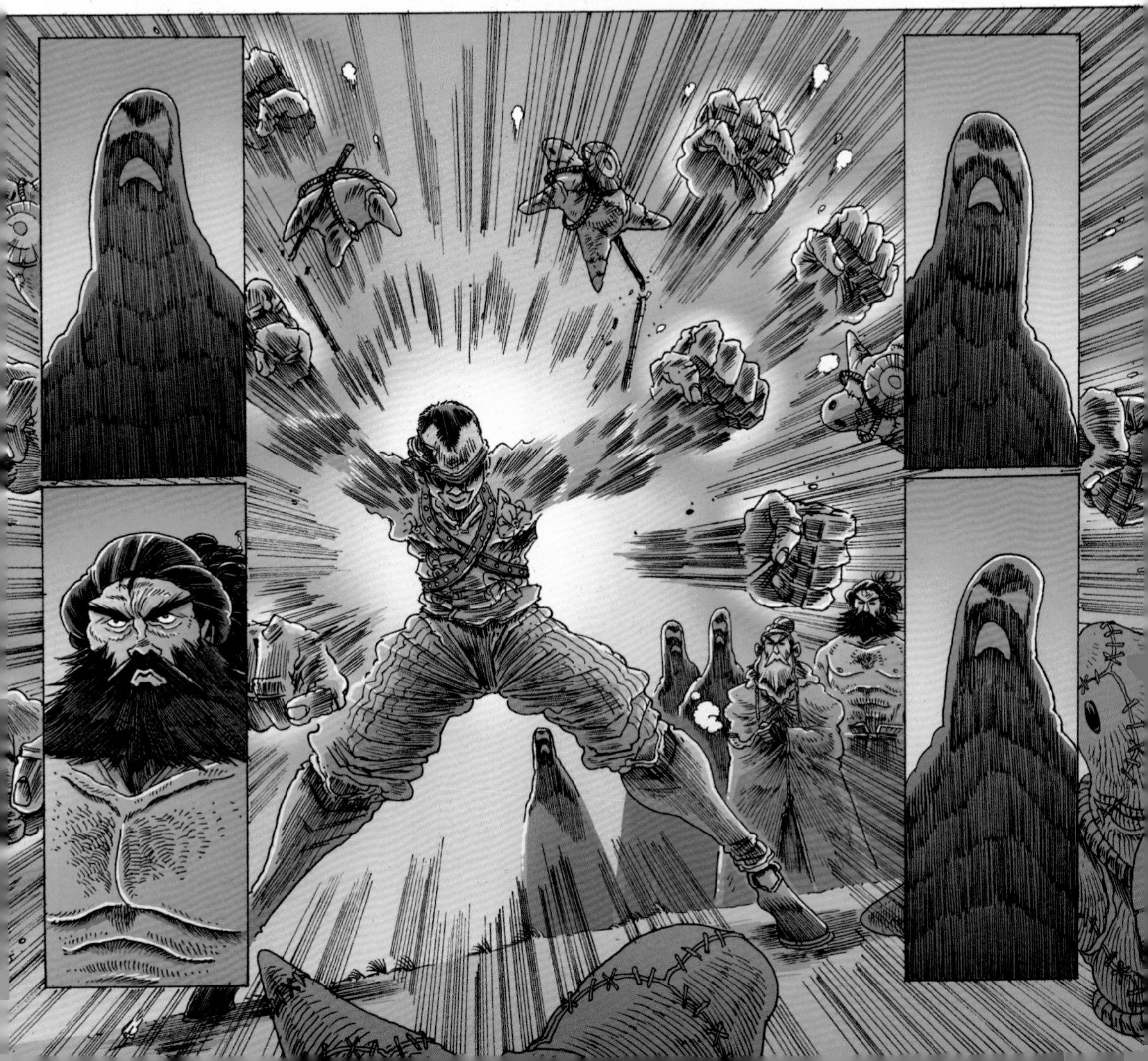

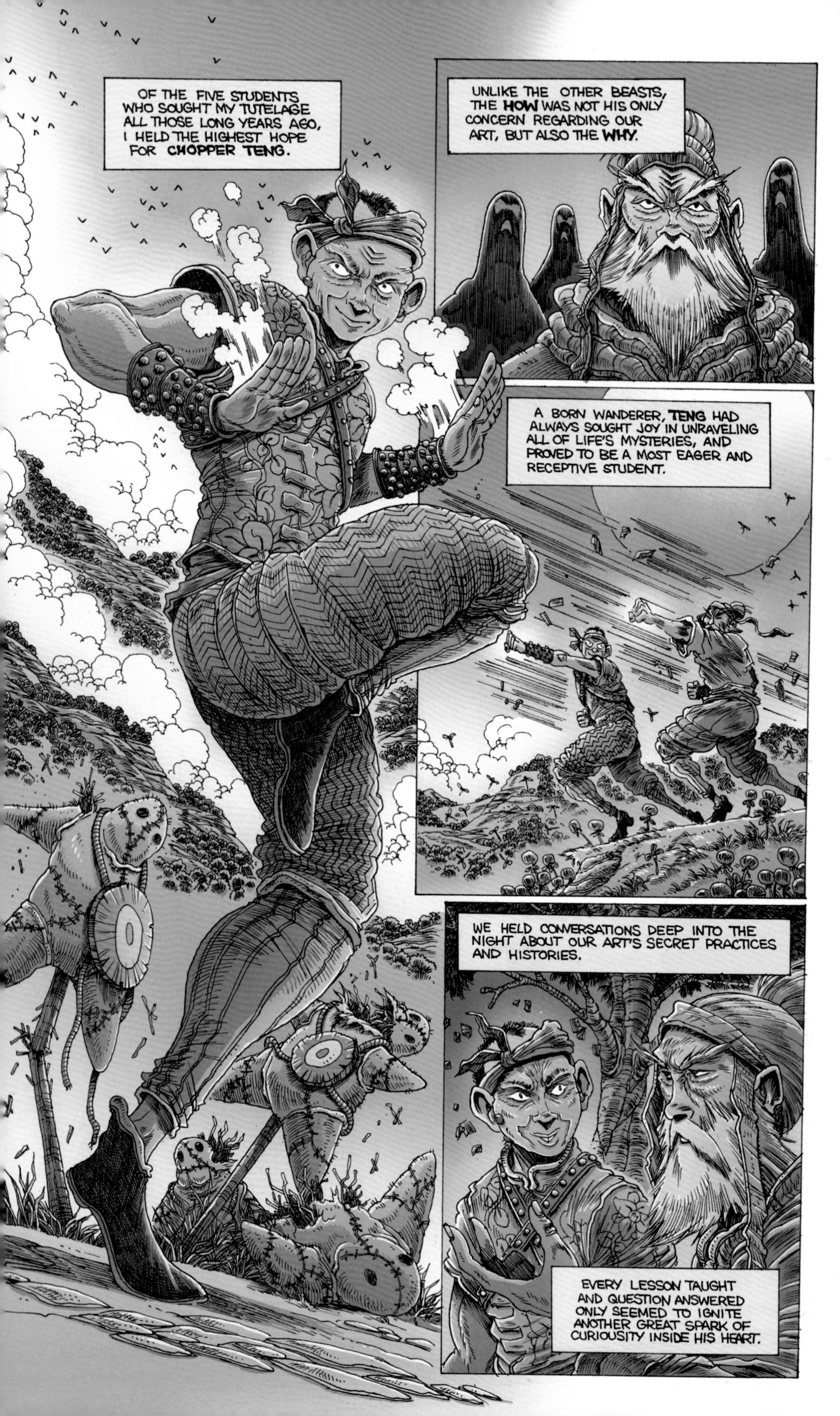

OF THE FIVE STUDENTS WHO SOUGHT MY TUTELAGE ALL THOSE LONG YEARS AGO, I HELD THE HIGHEST HOPE FOR CHOPPER TENG.
UNLIKE THE OTHER BEASTS, THE HOW WAS NOT HIS ONLY CONCERN REGARDING OUR ART, BUT ALSO THE WHY.
A BORN WANDERER, TENG HAD ALWAYS SOUGHT JOY IN UNRAVELING ALL OF LIFE'S MYSTERIES, AND PROVED TO BE A MOST EAGER AND RECEPTIVE STUDENT.
WE HELD CONVERSATIONS DEEP INTO THE NIGHT ABOUT OUR ART'S SECRET PRACTICES AND HISTORIES.
EVERY LESSON TAUGHT AND QUESTION ANSWERED ONLY SEEMED TO IGNITE ANOTHER GREAT SPARK OF CURIOUSITY INSIDE HIS HEART.

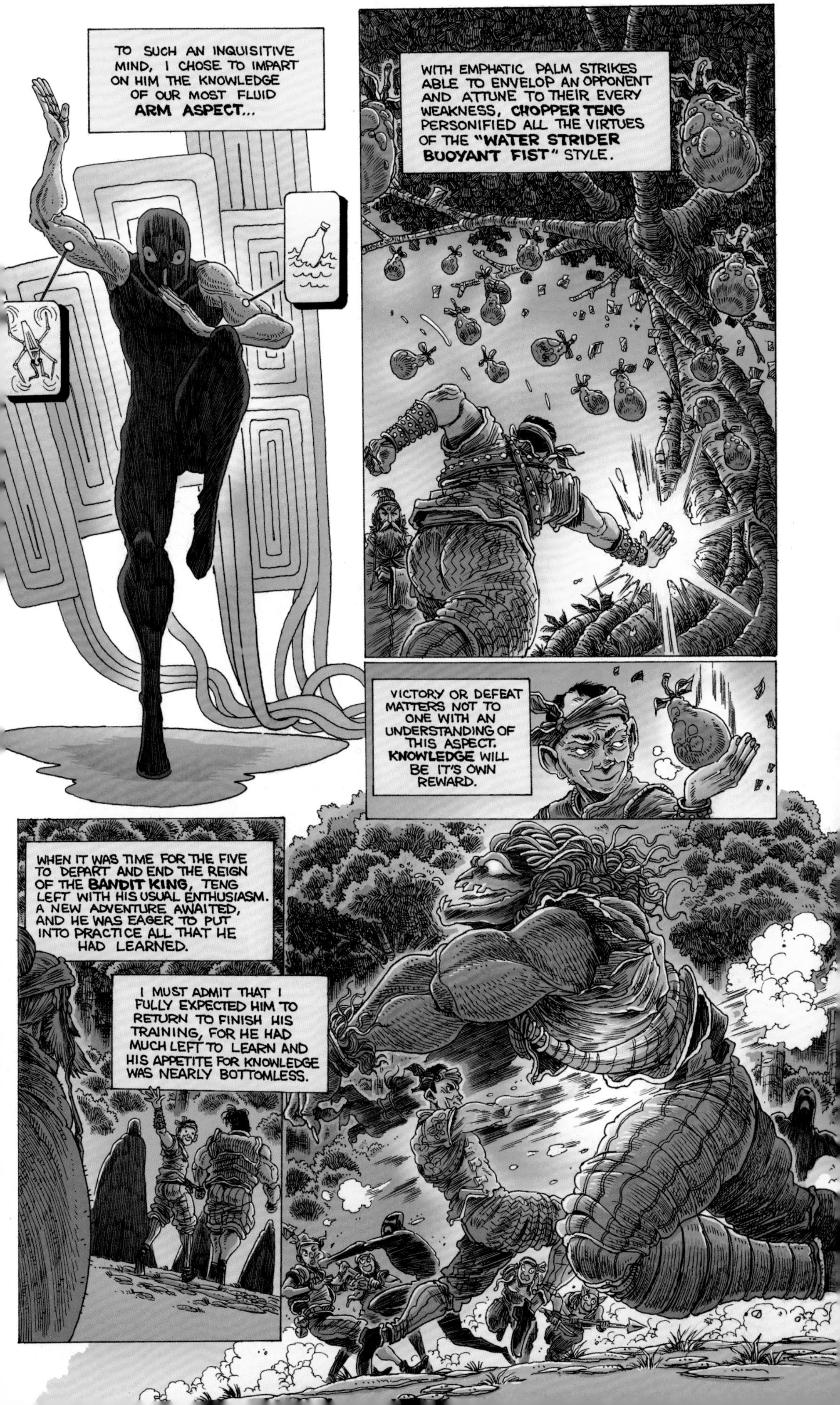

TO SUCH AN INQUISITIVE MIND, I CHOSE TO IMPART ON HIM THE KNOWLEDGE OF OUR MOST FLUID **ARM ASPECT**...
WITH EMPHATIC PALM STRIKES ABLE TO ENVELOP AN OPPONENT AND ATTUNE TO THEIR EVERY WEAKNESS, **CHOPPER TENG** PERSONIFIED ALL THE VIRTUES OF THE **"WATER STRIDER BUOYANT FIST"** STYLE.
VICTORY OR DEFEAT MATTERS NOT TO ONE WITH AN UNDERSTANDING OF THIS ASPECT. **KNOWLEDGE** WILL BE IT'S OWN REWARD.
WHEN IT WAS TIME FOR THE FIVE TO DEPART AND END THE REIGN OF THE **BANDIT KING**, TENG LEFT WITH HIS USUAL ENTHUSIASM. A NEW ADVENTURE AWAITED, AND HE WAS EAGER TO PUT INTO PRACTICE ALL THAT HE HAD LEARNED.
I MUST ADMIT THAT I FULLY EXPECTED HIM TO RETURN TO FINISH HIS TRAINING, FOR HE HAD MUCH LEFT TO LEARN AND HIS APPETITE FOR KNOWLEDGE WAS NEARLY BOTTOMLESS.

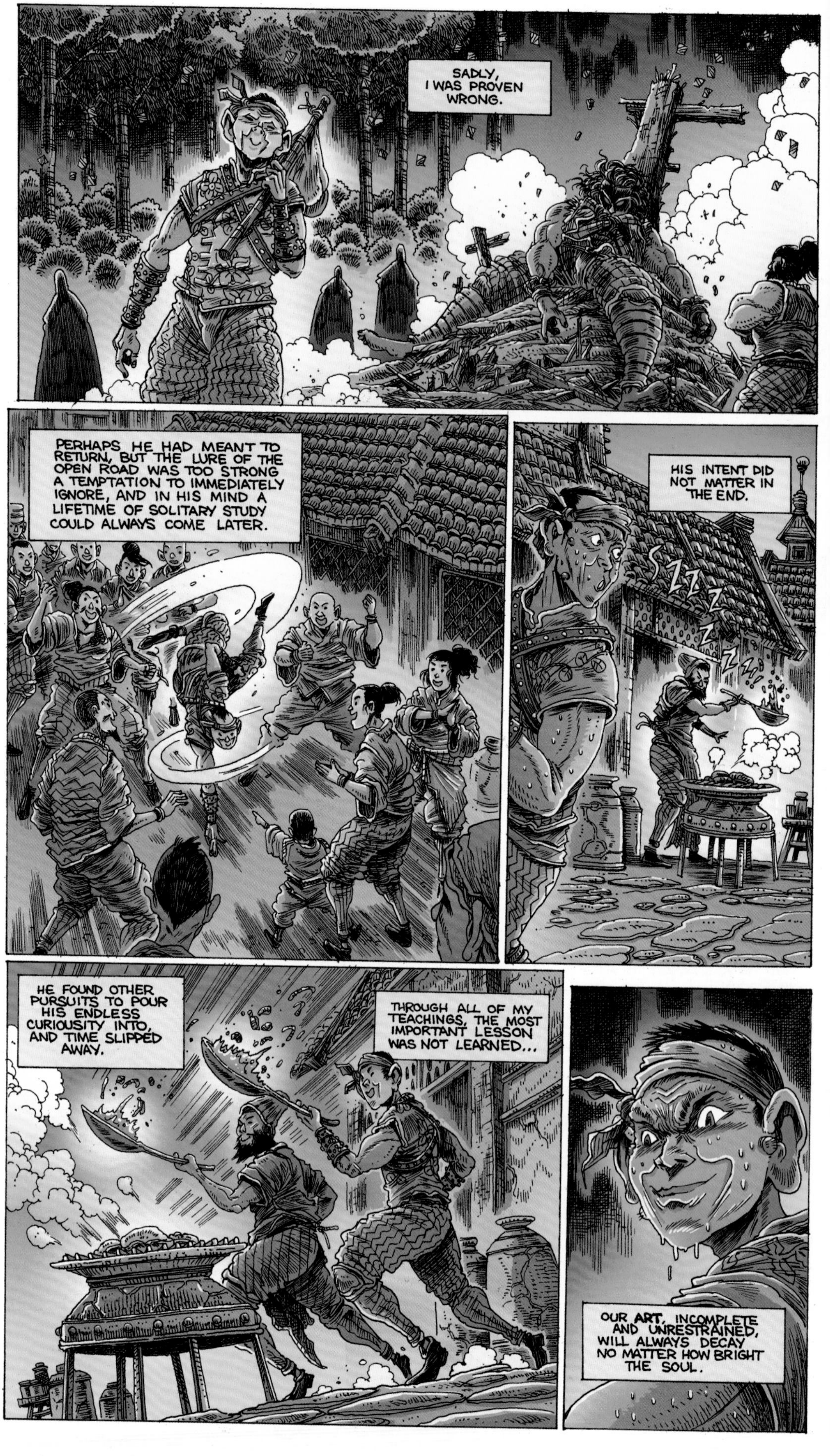
SADLY, I WAS PROVEN WRONG.
PERHAPS HE HAD MEANT TO RETURN, BUT THE LURE OF THE OPEN ROAD WAS TOO STRONG A TEMPTATION TO IMMEDIATELY IGNORE, AND IN HIS MIND A LIFETIME OF SOLITARY STUDY COULD ALWAYS COME LATER.
HIS INTENT DID NOT MATTER IN THE END.
HE FOUND OTHER PURSUITS TO POUR HIS ENDLESS CURIOUSITY INTO, AND TIME SLIPPED AWAY.
THROUGH ALL OF MY TEACHINGS, THE MOST IMPORTANT LESSON WAS NOT LEARNED...
OUR ART, INCOMPLETE AND UNRESTRAINED, WILL ALWAYS DECAY NO MATTER HOW BRIGHT THE SOUL.

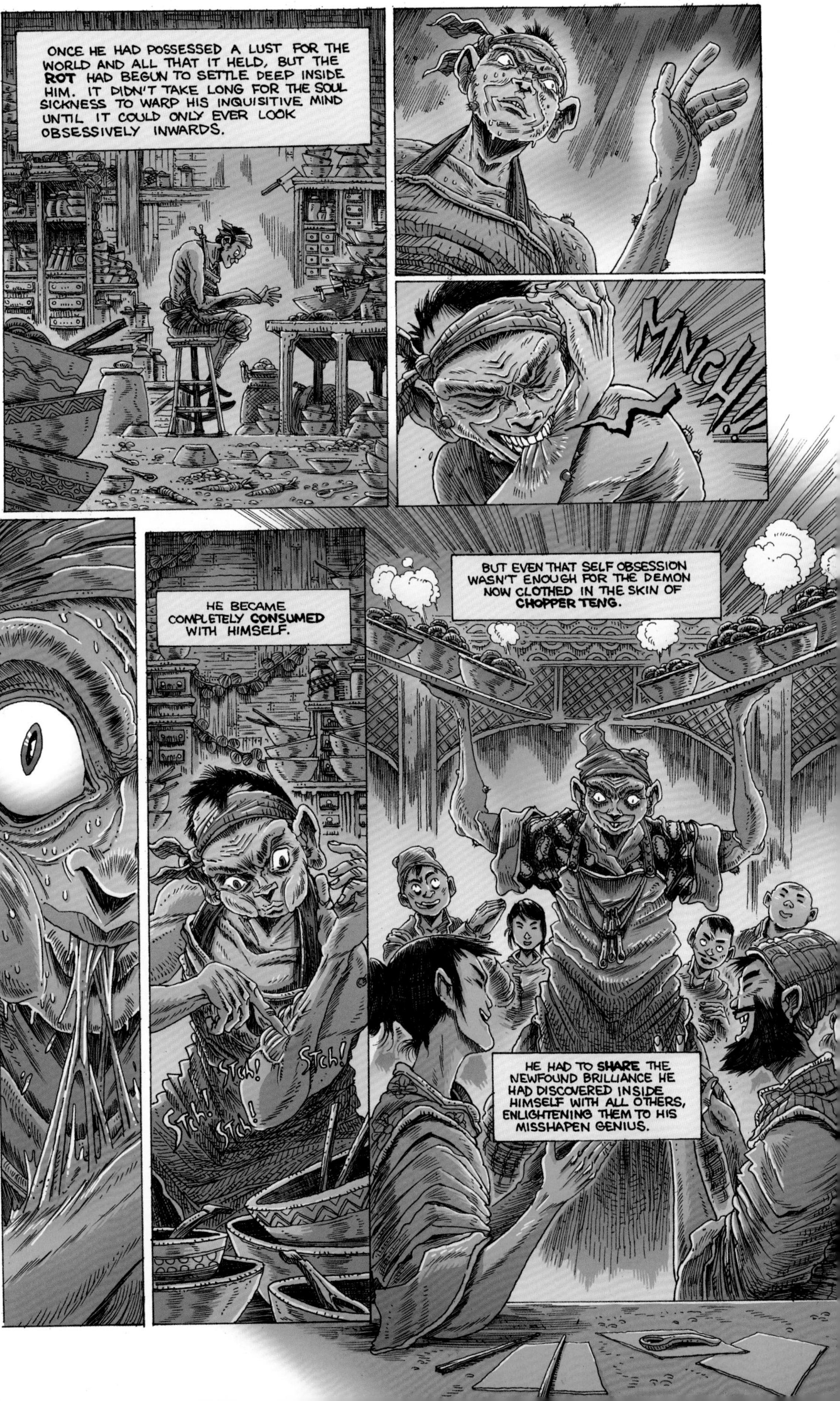
ONCE HE HAD POSSESSED A LUST FOR THE WORLD AND ALL THAT IT HELD, BUT THE ROT HAD BEGUN TO SETTLE DEEP INSIDE HIM. IT DIDN'T TAKE LONG FOR THE SOUL SICKNESS TO WARP HIS INQUISITIVE MIND UNTIL IT COULD ONLY EVER LOOK OBSESSIVELY INWARDS.
MNCH!!
HE BECAME COMPLETELY CONSUMED WITH HIMSELF.
STCH! STCH! STCH! STCH!
BUT EVEN THAT SELF OBSESSION WASN'T ENOUGH FOR THE DEMON NOW CLOTHED IN THE SKIN OF CHOPPER TENG.
HE HAD TO SHARE THE NEWFOUND BRILLIANCE HE HAD DISCOVERED INSIDE HIMSELF WITH ALL OTHERS, ENLIGHTENING THEM TO HIS MISSHAPEN GENIUS.

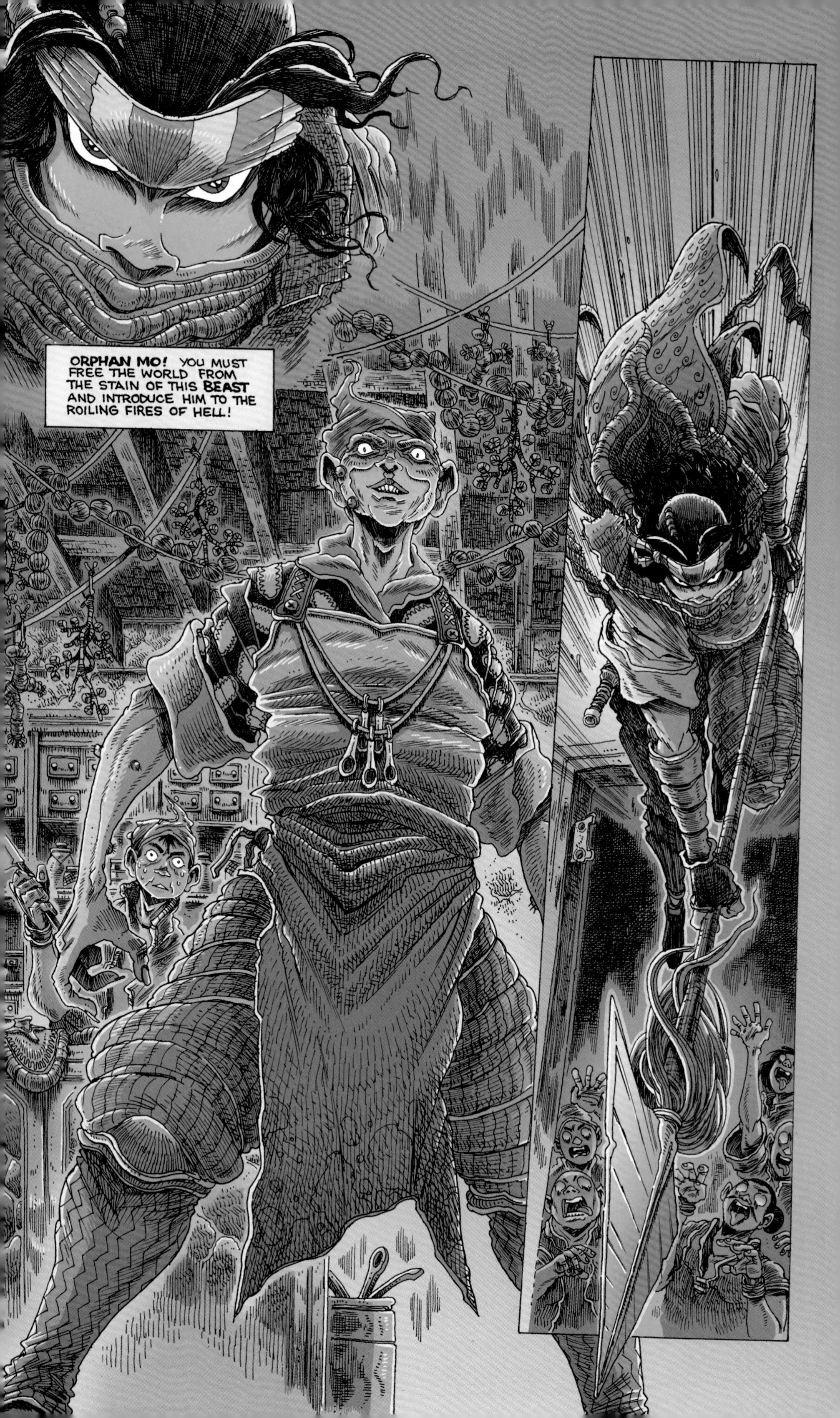
ORPHAN MO! YOU MUST FREE THE WORLD FROM THE STAIN OF THIS BEAST AND INTRODUCE HIM TO THE ROILING FIRES OF HELL!

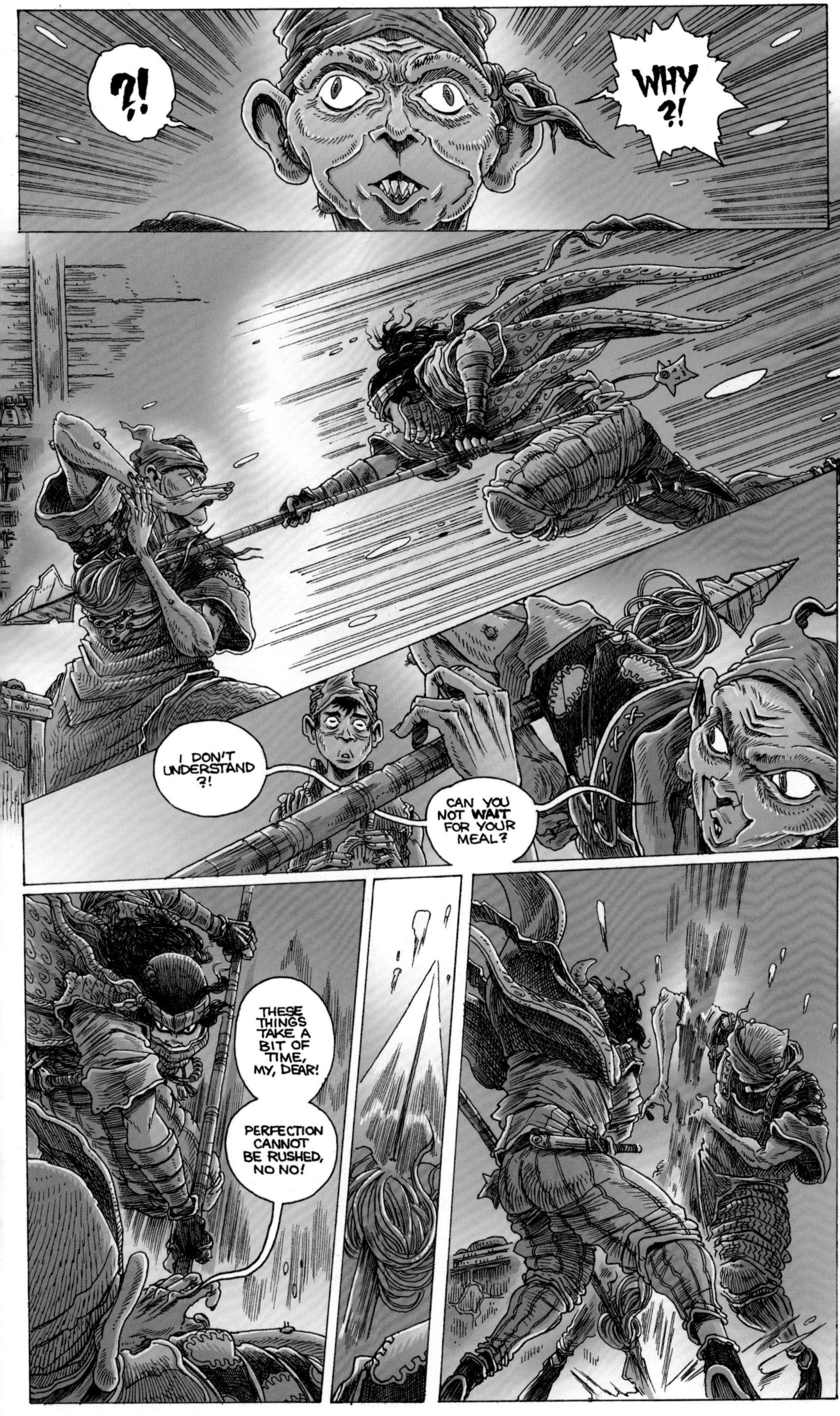

?!
WHY ?!
I DON'T UNDERSTAND ?!
CAN YOU NOT WAIT FOR YOUR MEAL?
THESE THINGS TAKE A BIT OF TIME, MY, DEAR!
PERFECTION CANNOT BE RUSHED, NO NO!

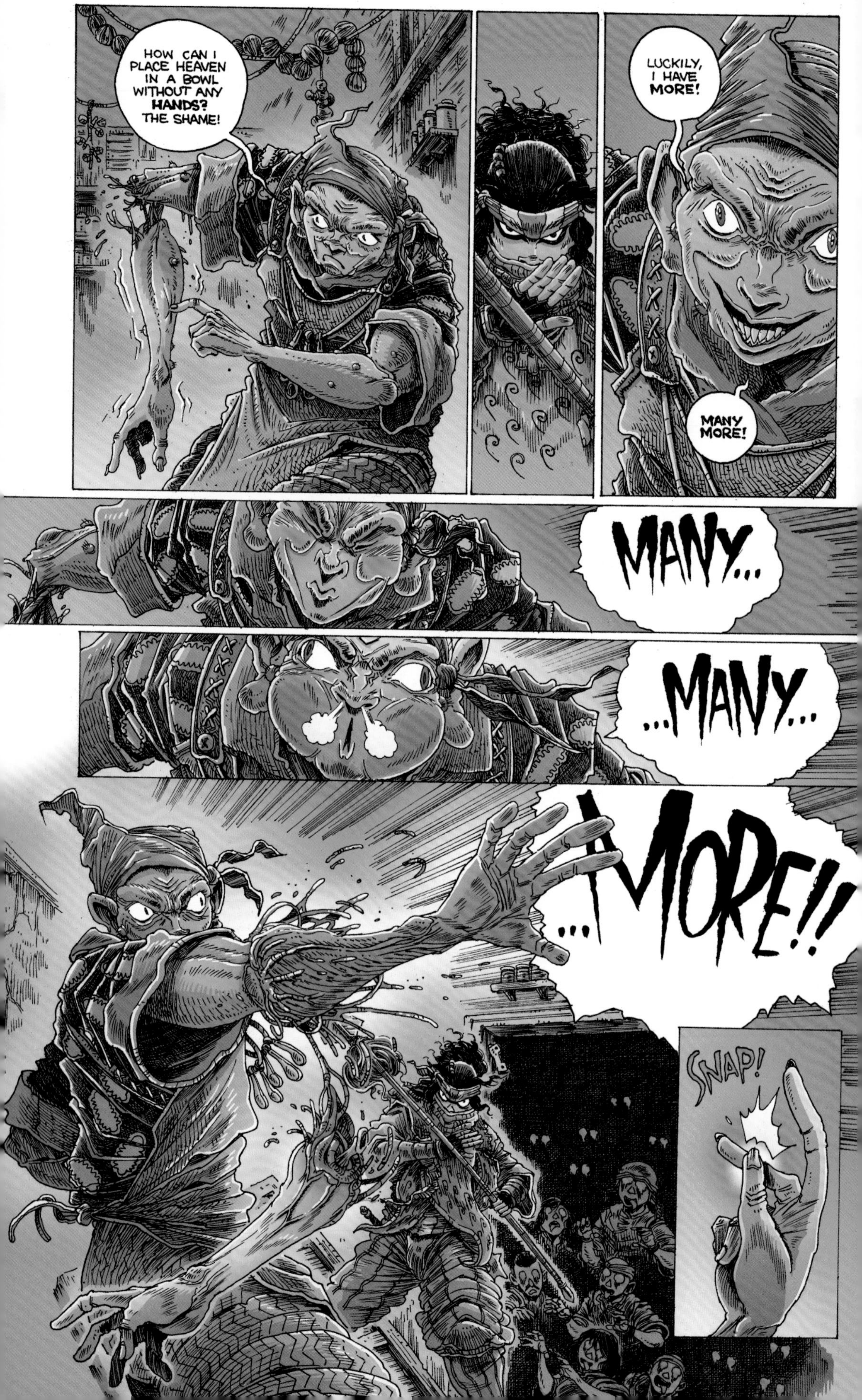
HOW CAN I PLACE HEAVEN IN A BOWL WITHOUT ANY HANDS? THE SHAME!
LUCKILY, I HAVE MORE!
MANY MORE!
MANY...
...MANY...
...MORE!!
SNAP!

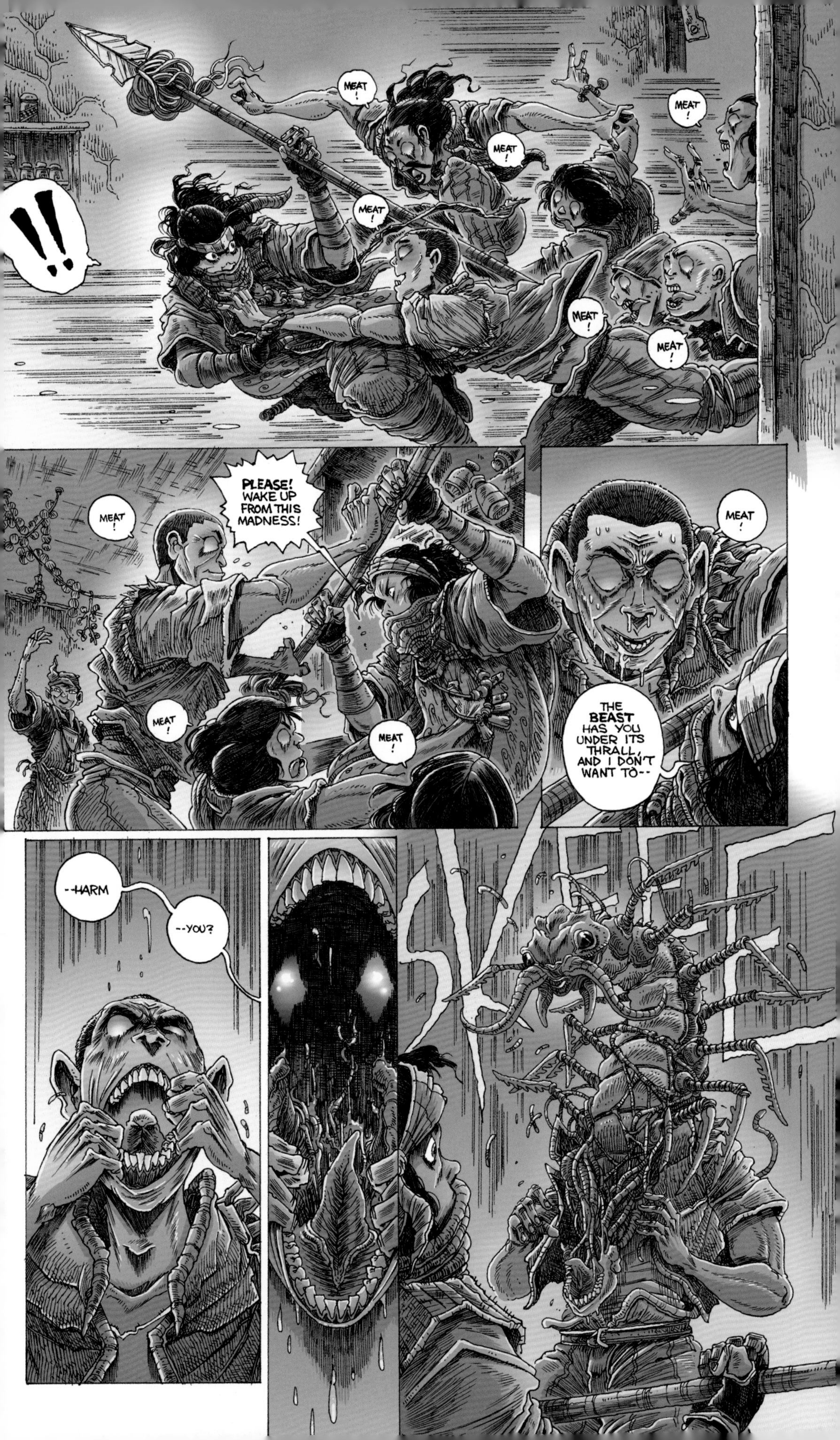
!!
MEAT!
MEAT!
MEAT!
MEAT!
MEAT!
MEAT!
MEAT!
PLEASE! WAKE UP FROM THIS MADNESS!
MEAT!
MEAT!
MEAT!
THE BEAST HAS YOU UNDER ITS THRALL, AND I DON'T WANT TO--
--HARM
--YOU?

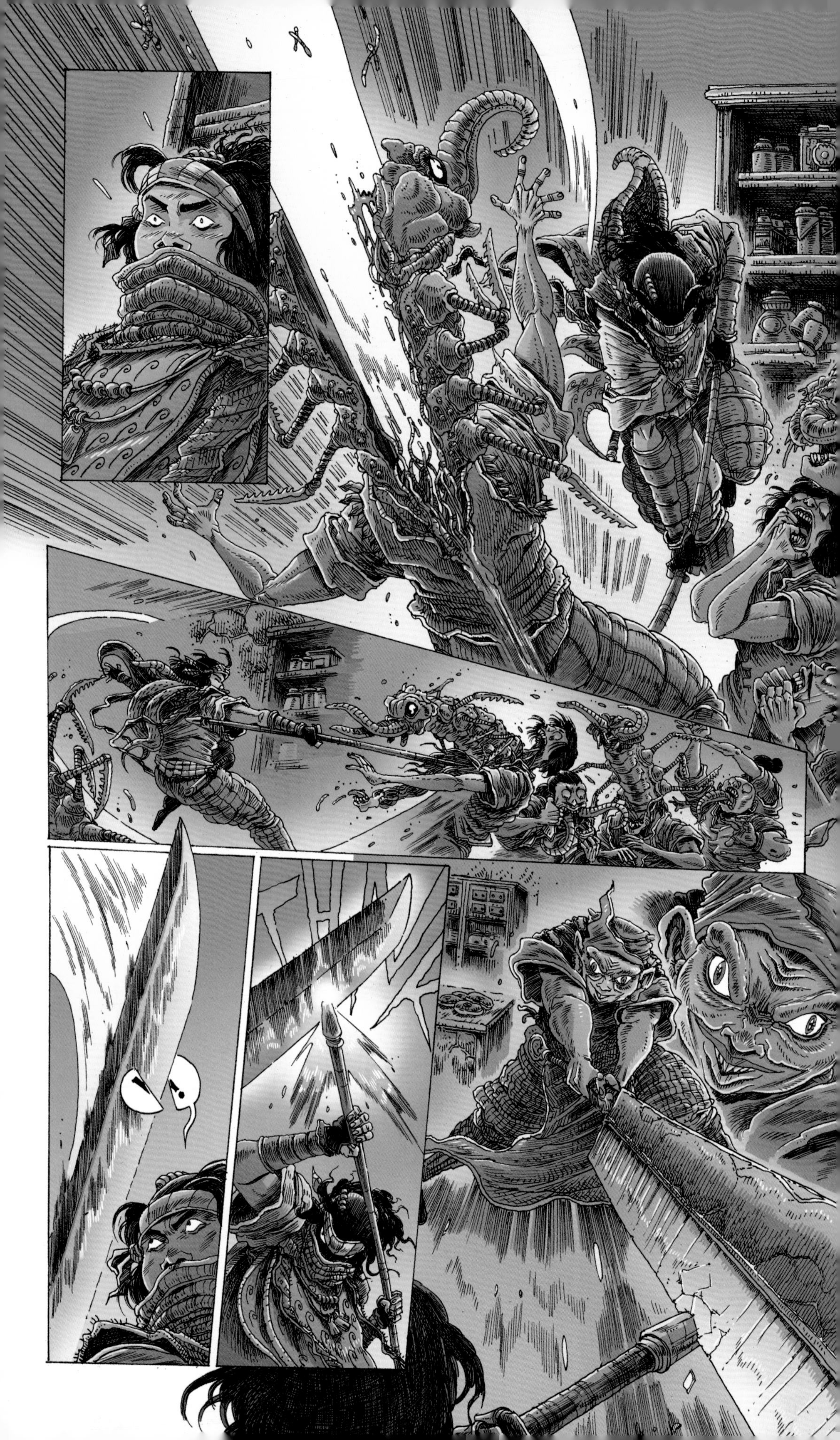
THAK

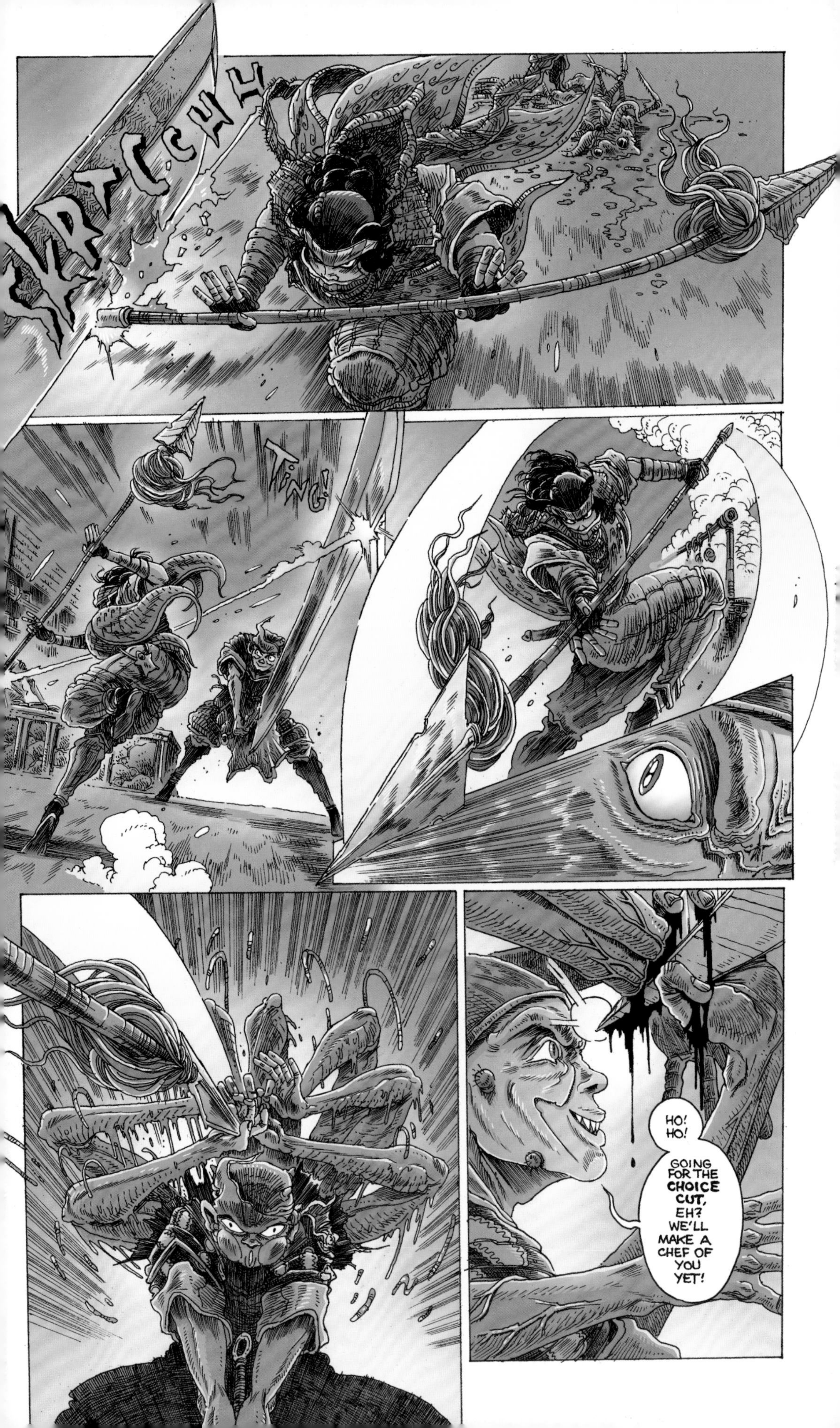
SKRTCHH
TING!
HO! HO!
GOING FOR THE **CHOICE CUT,** EH? WE'LL MAKE A CHEF OF YOU YET!

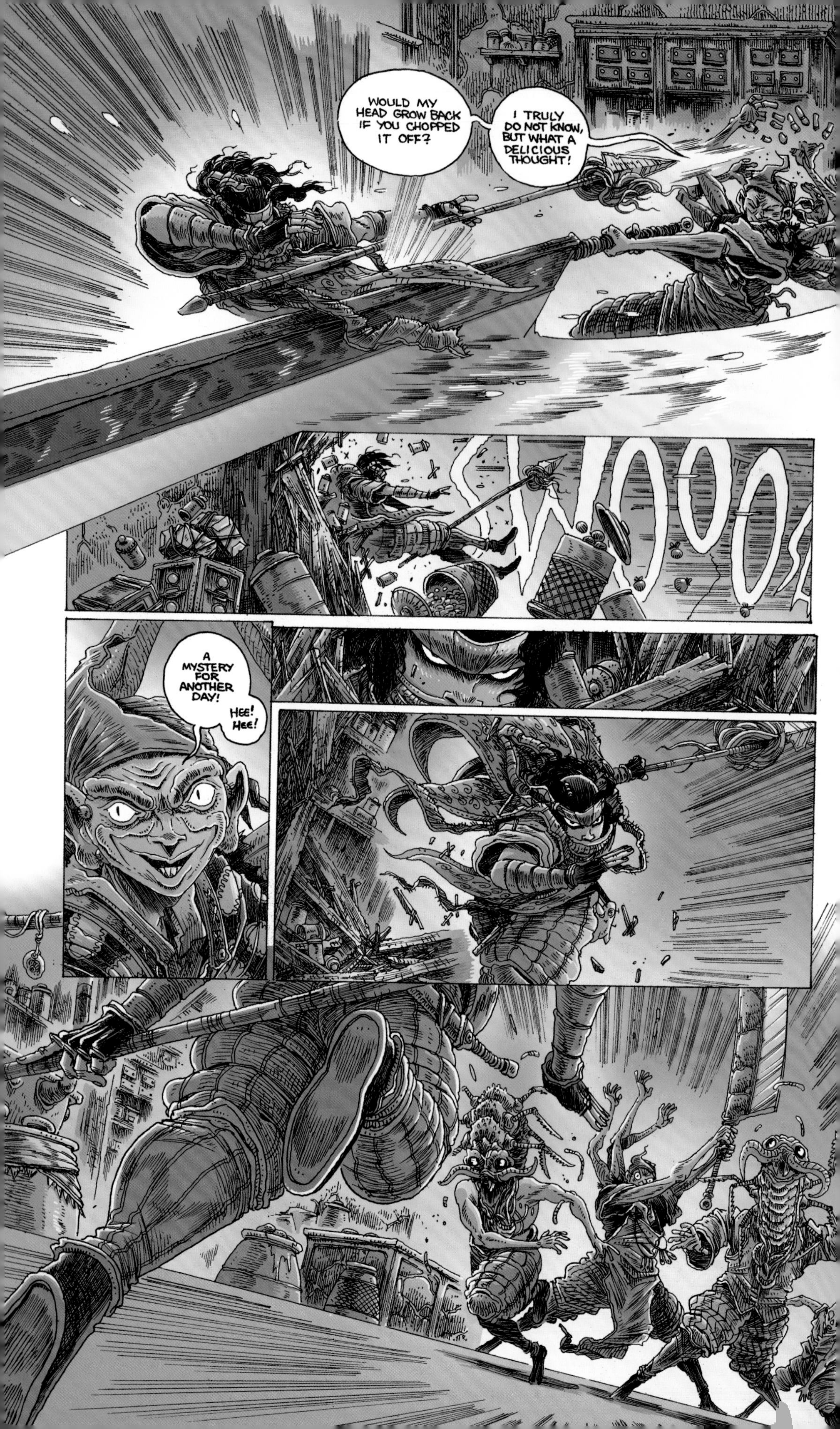
WOULD MY HEAD GROW BACK IF YOU CHOPPED IT OFF?
I TRULY DO NOT KNOW, BUT WHAT A DELICIOUS THOUGHT!
WOOOS
A MYSTERY FOR ANOTHER DAY!
HEE! HEE!

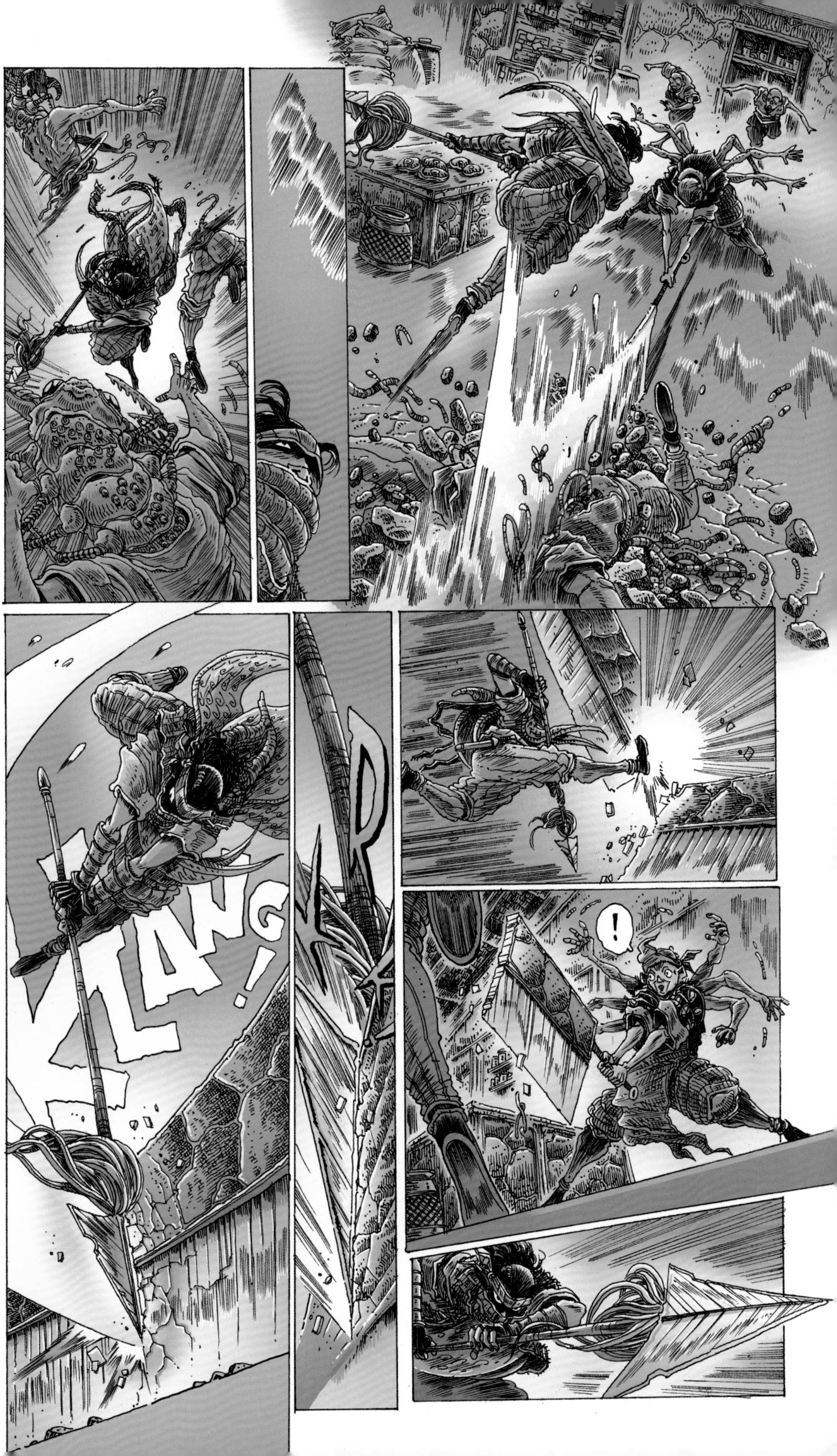
!

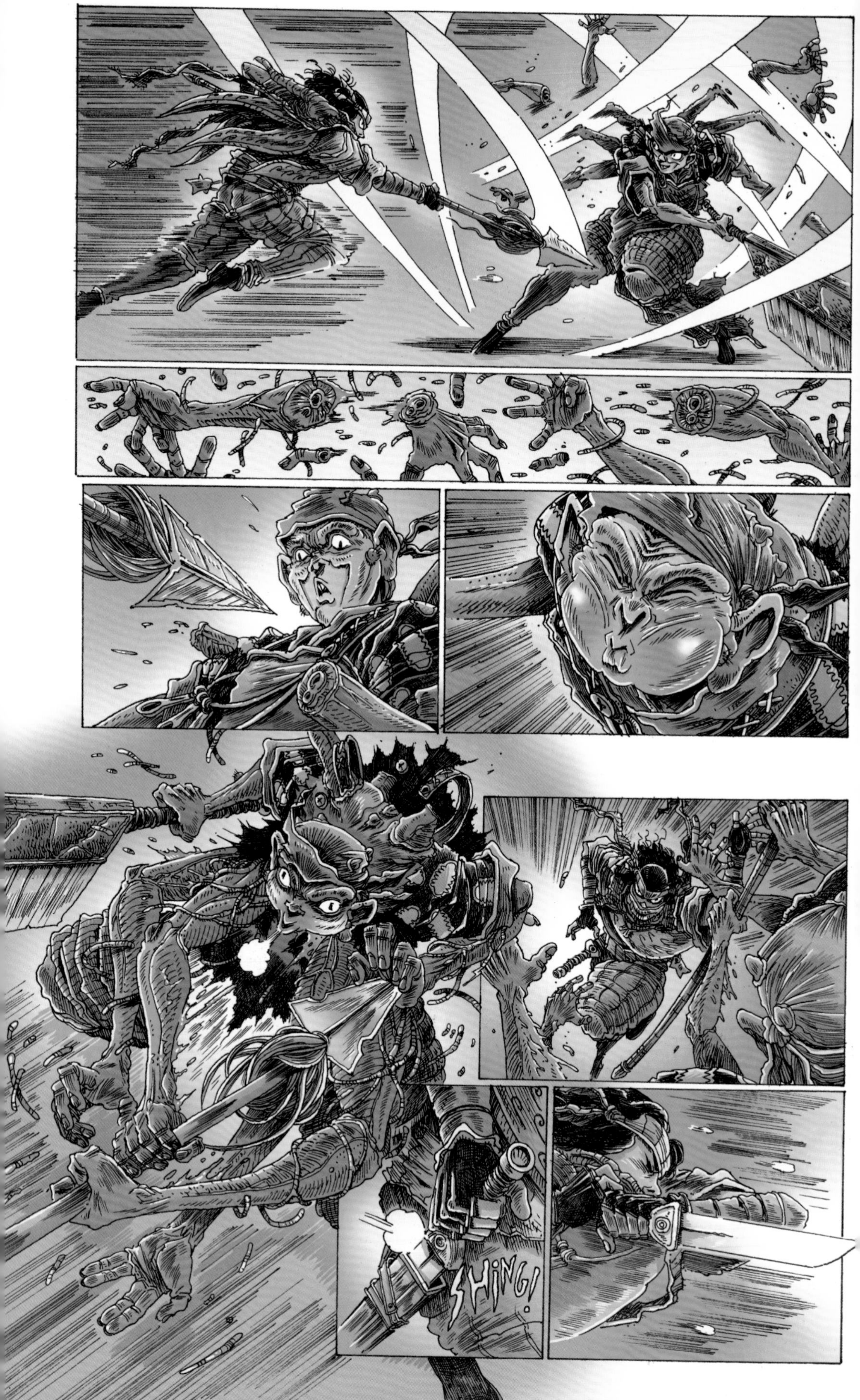
SHING!

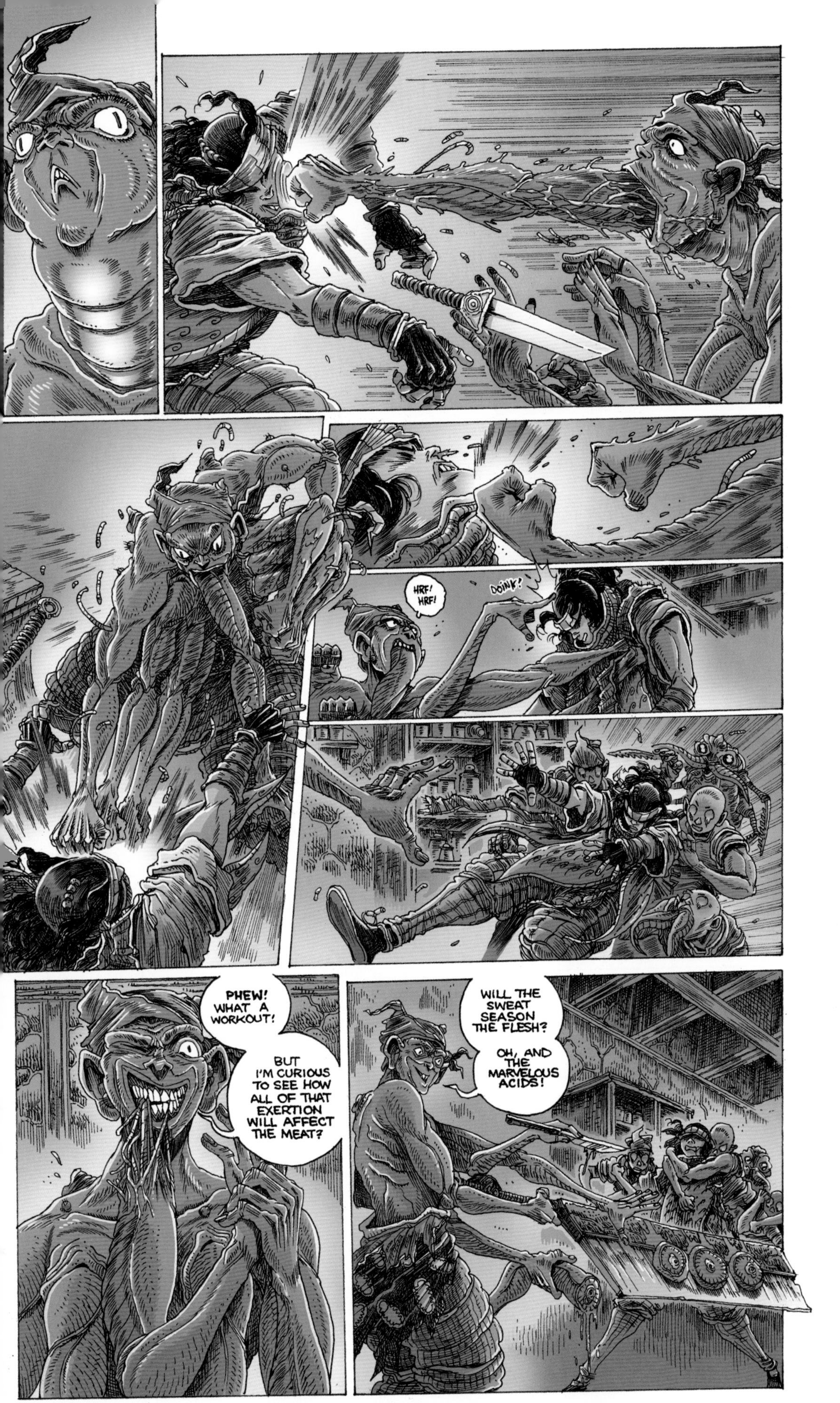
HRF! HRF!
DOINK!
PHEW! WHAT A WORKOUT!
BUT I'M CURIOUS TO SEE HOW ALL OF THAT EXERTION WILL AFFECT THE MEAT?
WILL THE SWEAT SEASON THE FLESH?
OH, AND THE MARVELOUS ACIDS!

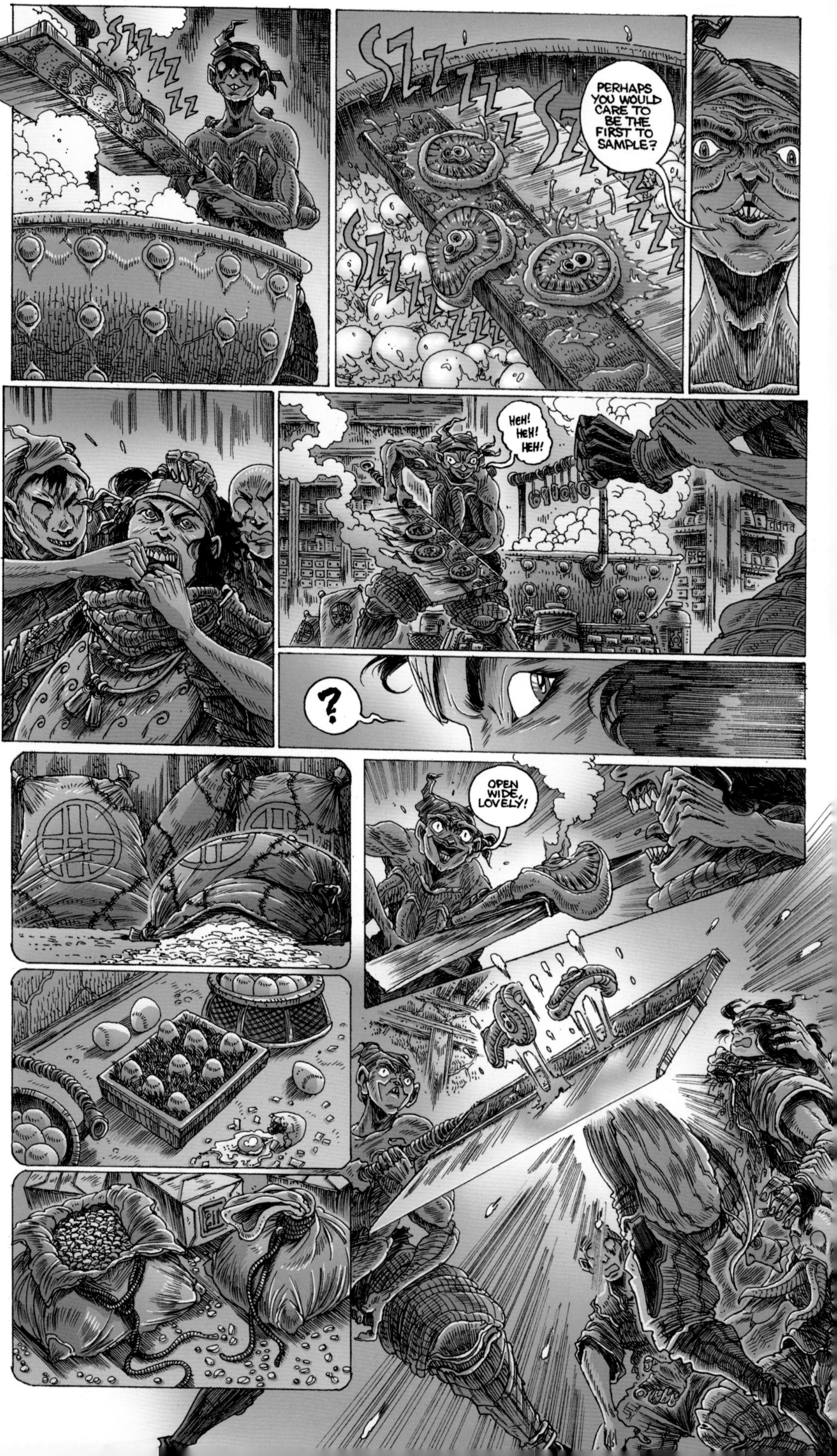
SZZZZZ
SZZZZZ
PERHAPS YOU WOULD CARE TO BE THE FIRST TO SAMPLE?
HEH! HEH! HEH!
?
OPEN WIDE, LOVELY!

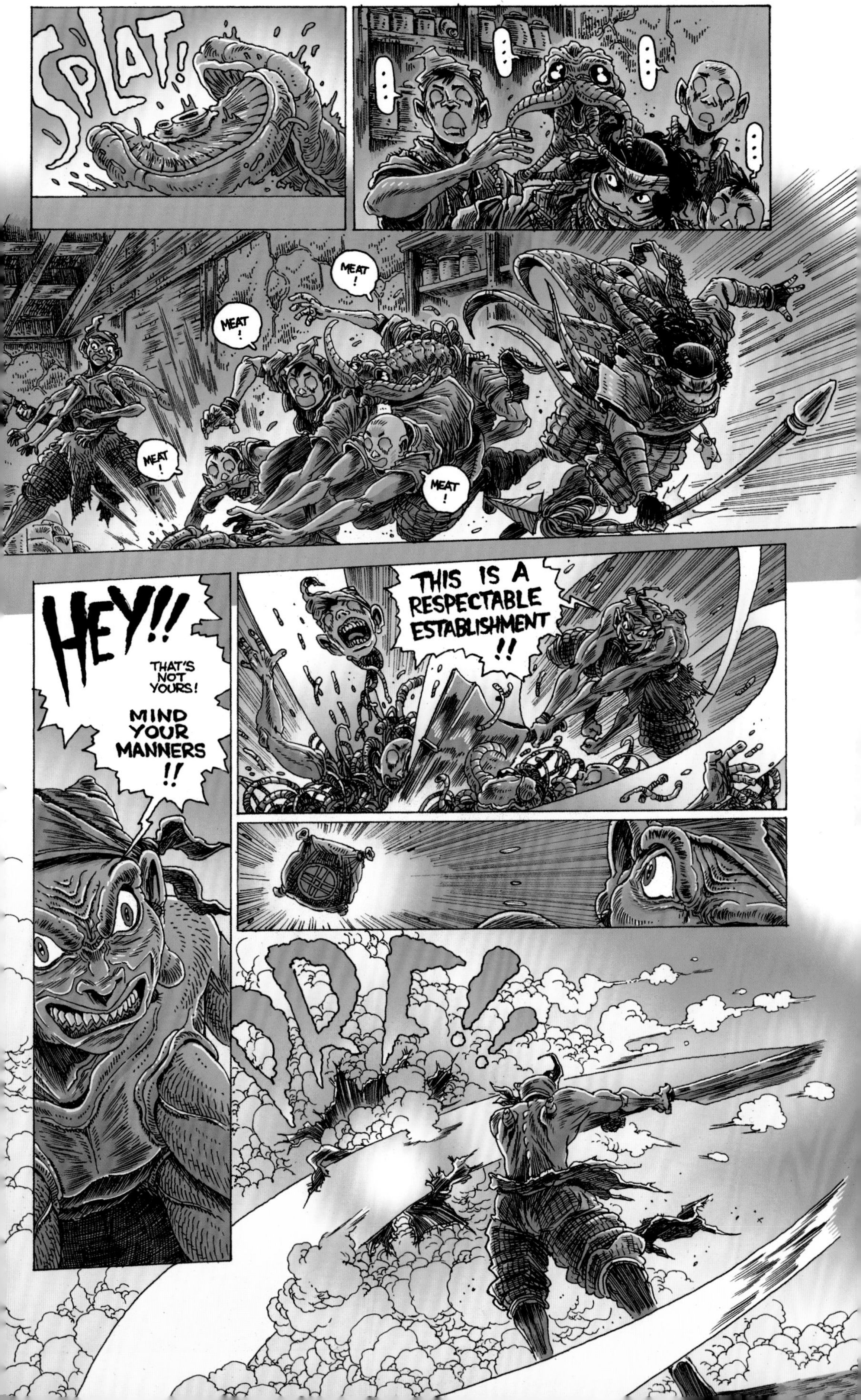
SPLAT!
...
...
...
...
MEAT!
MEAT!
MEAT!
MEAT!
HEY!!
THAT'S NOT YOURS!
MIND YOUR MANNERS !!
THIS IS A RESPECTABLE ESTABLISHMENT !!

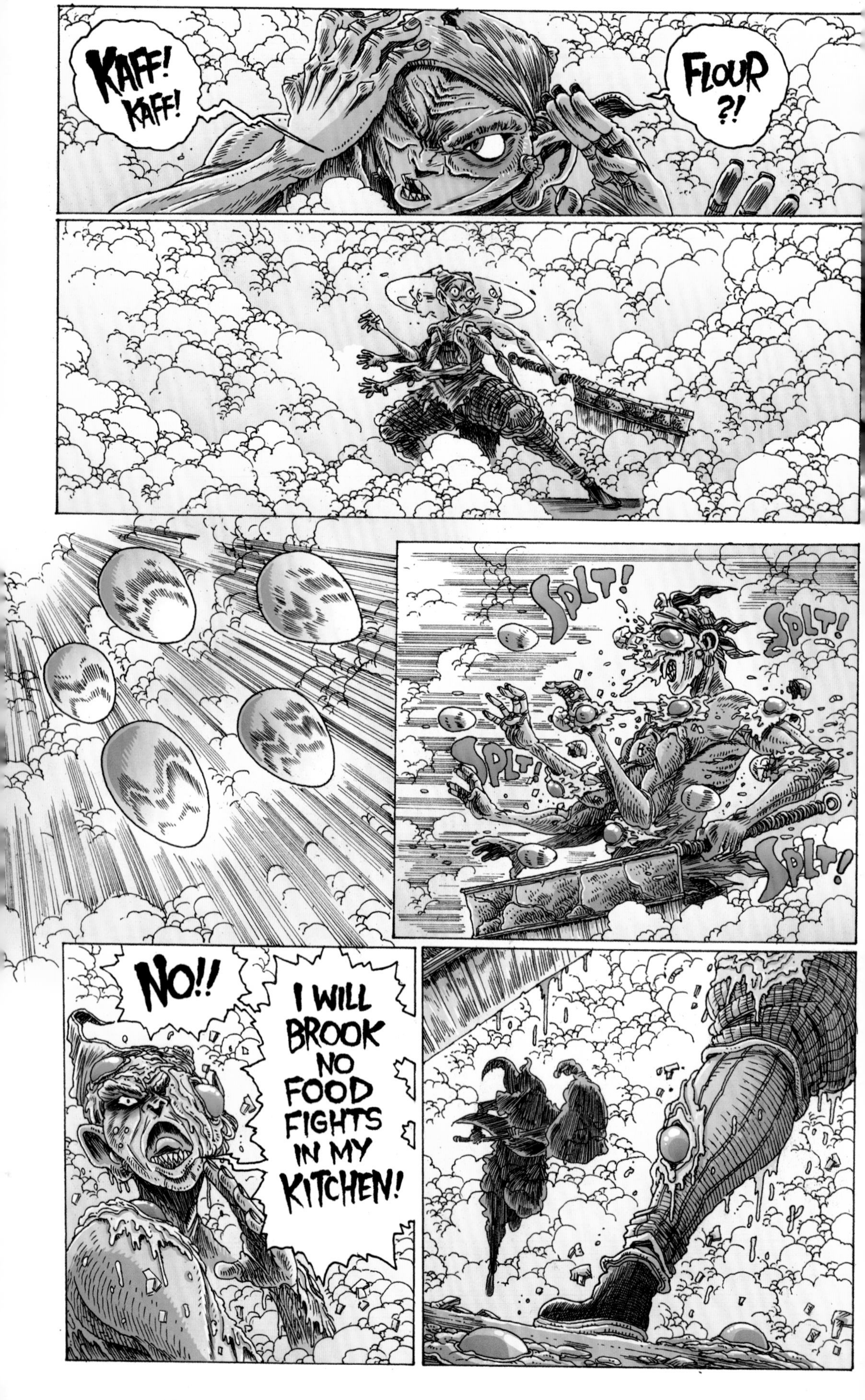
KAFF! KAFF!
FLOUR ?!
SPLT!
SPLT!
SPLT!
SPLT!
NO!!
I WILL BROOK NO FOOD FIGHTS IN MY KITCHEN!

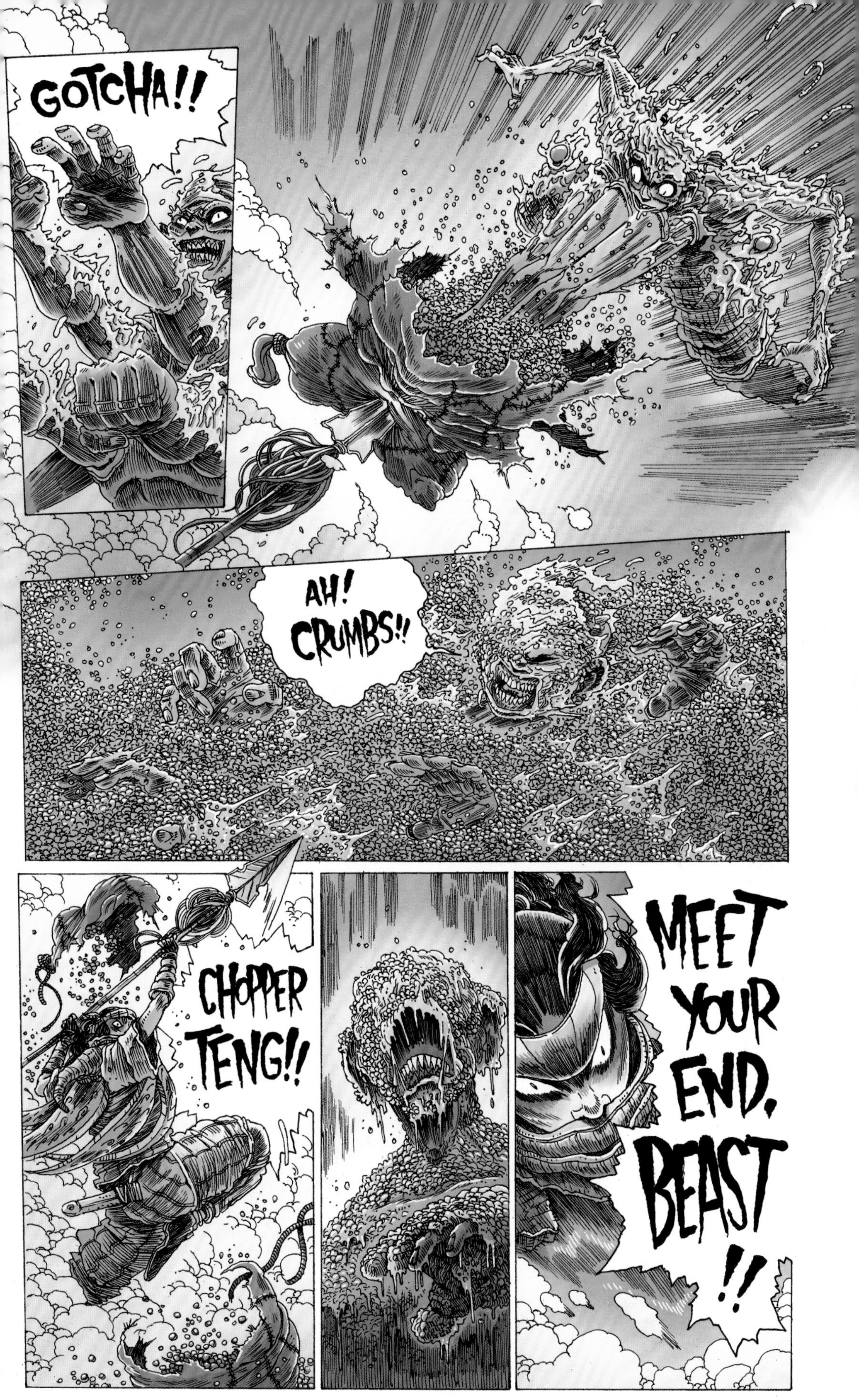
GOTCHA!!
AH! CRUMBS!!
CHOPPER TENG!!
MEET YOUR END, BEAST!!

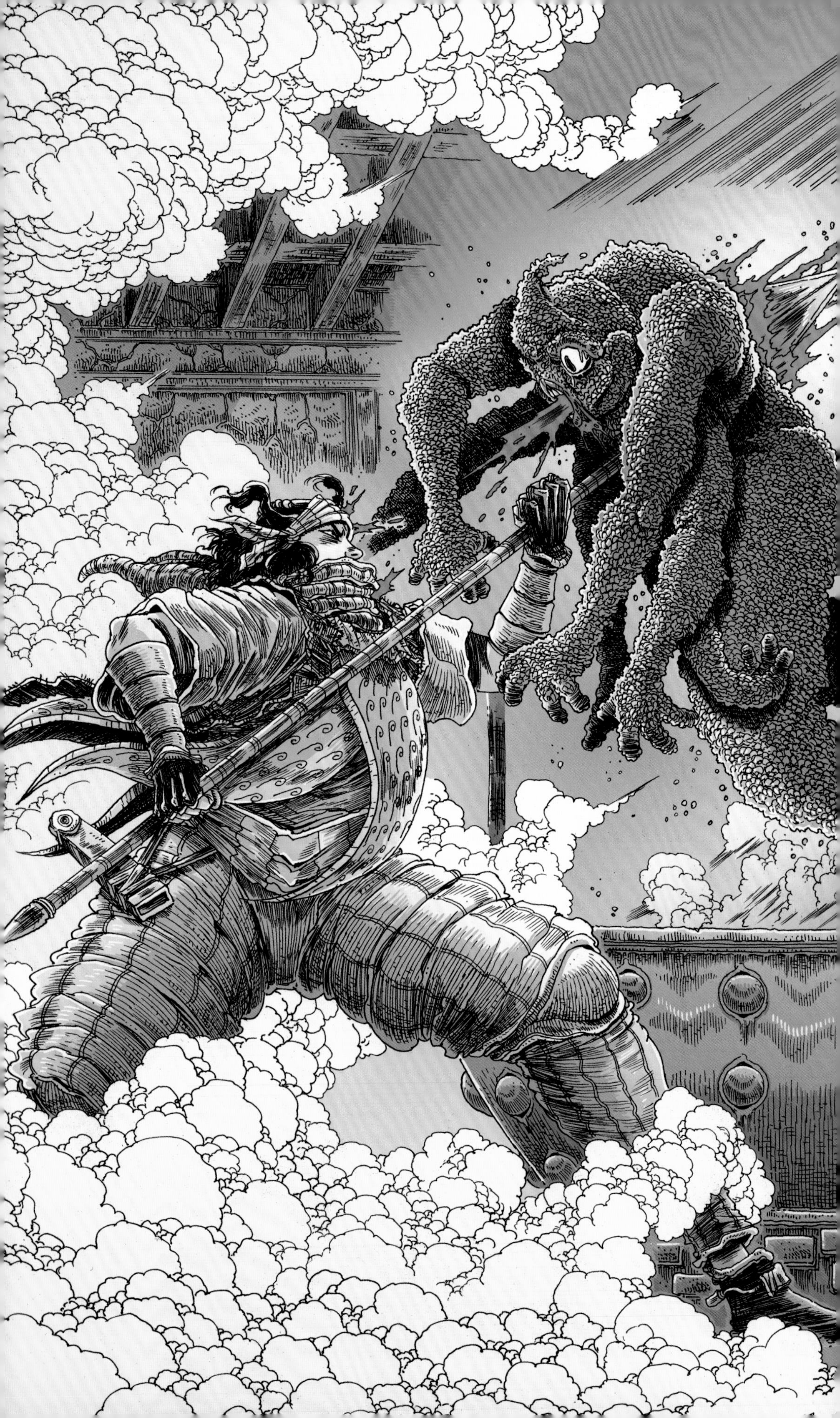

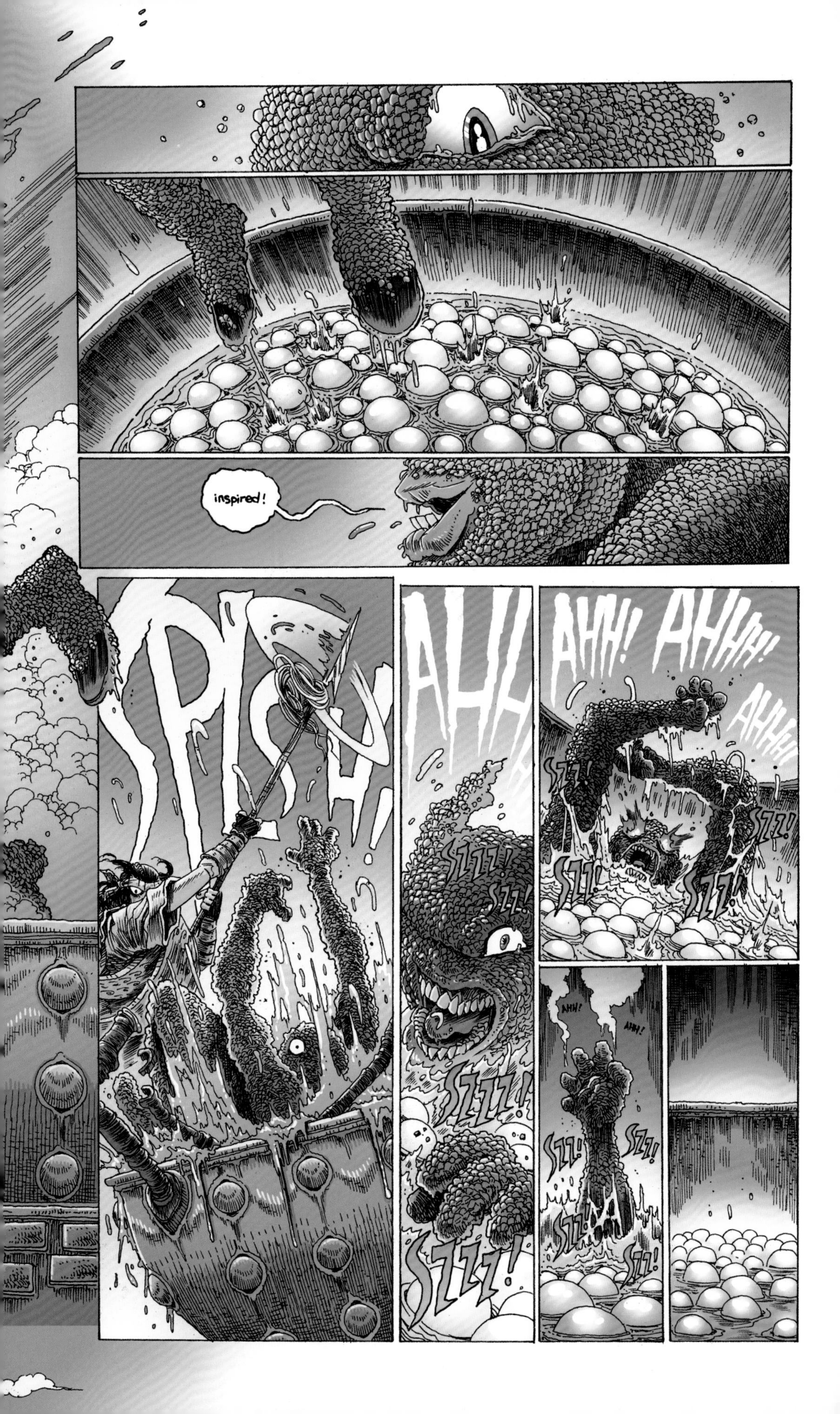
inspired!
SPLISH!
AHH!
AHH! AHHH!
AHH!
SZZZ! SZZ!
SZZZ!
SZZZ!
SZZ! SZZ! SZZ! SZZ!
AHH! AHH!
SZZ! SZZ! SZZ! SZZ!

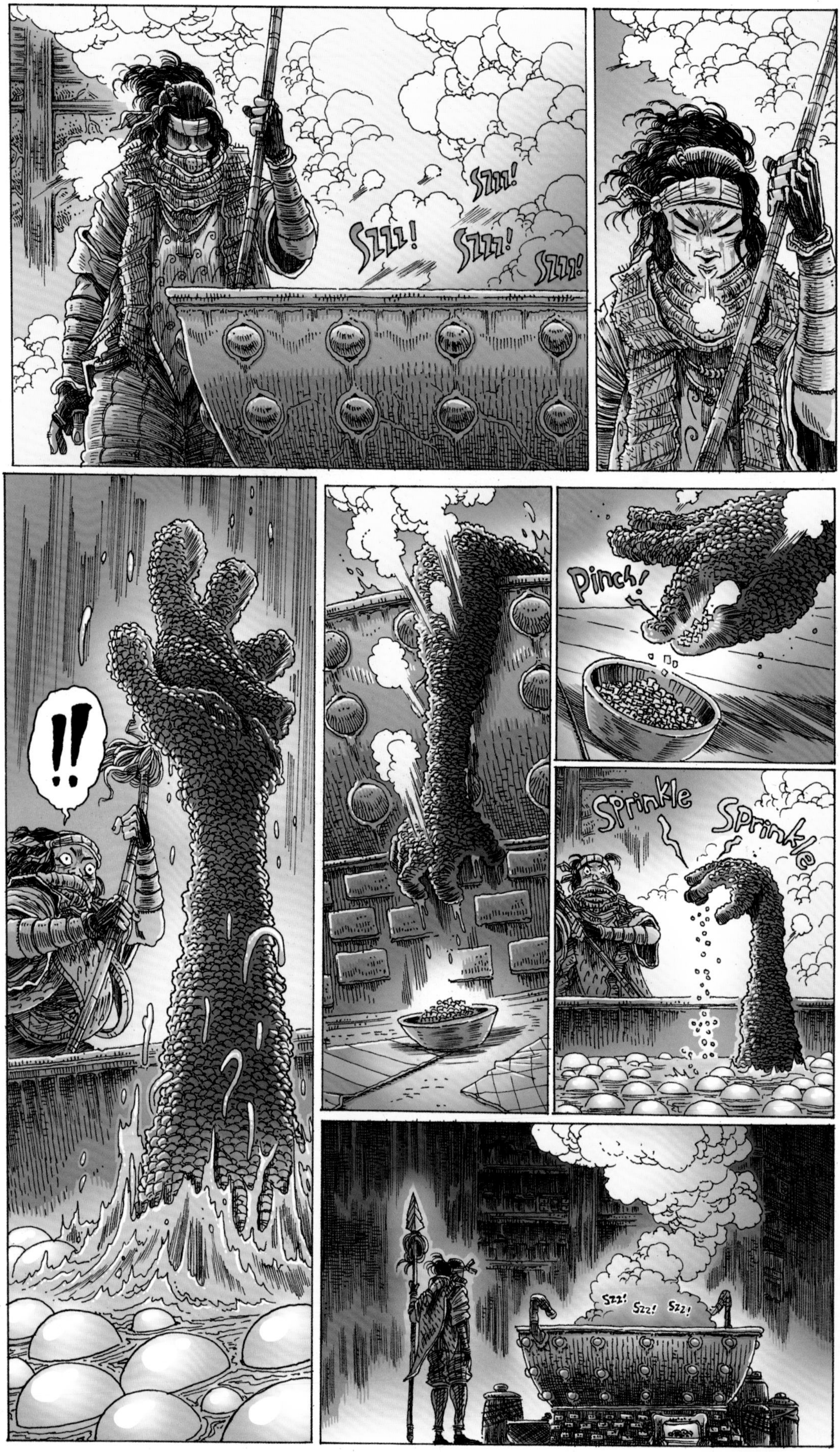

Szzz!
Szzz!
Szzz!
Szzz!
!!
Pinch!
Sprinkle
Sprinkle
Szz!
Szz!
Szz!

ORPHAN MO'S STORY DOESN'T END HERE.

Our adventure continues in the next arc of *Orphan and the Five Beasts* from James Stokoe, coming soon!

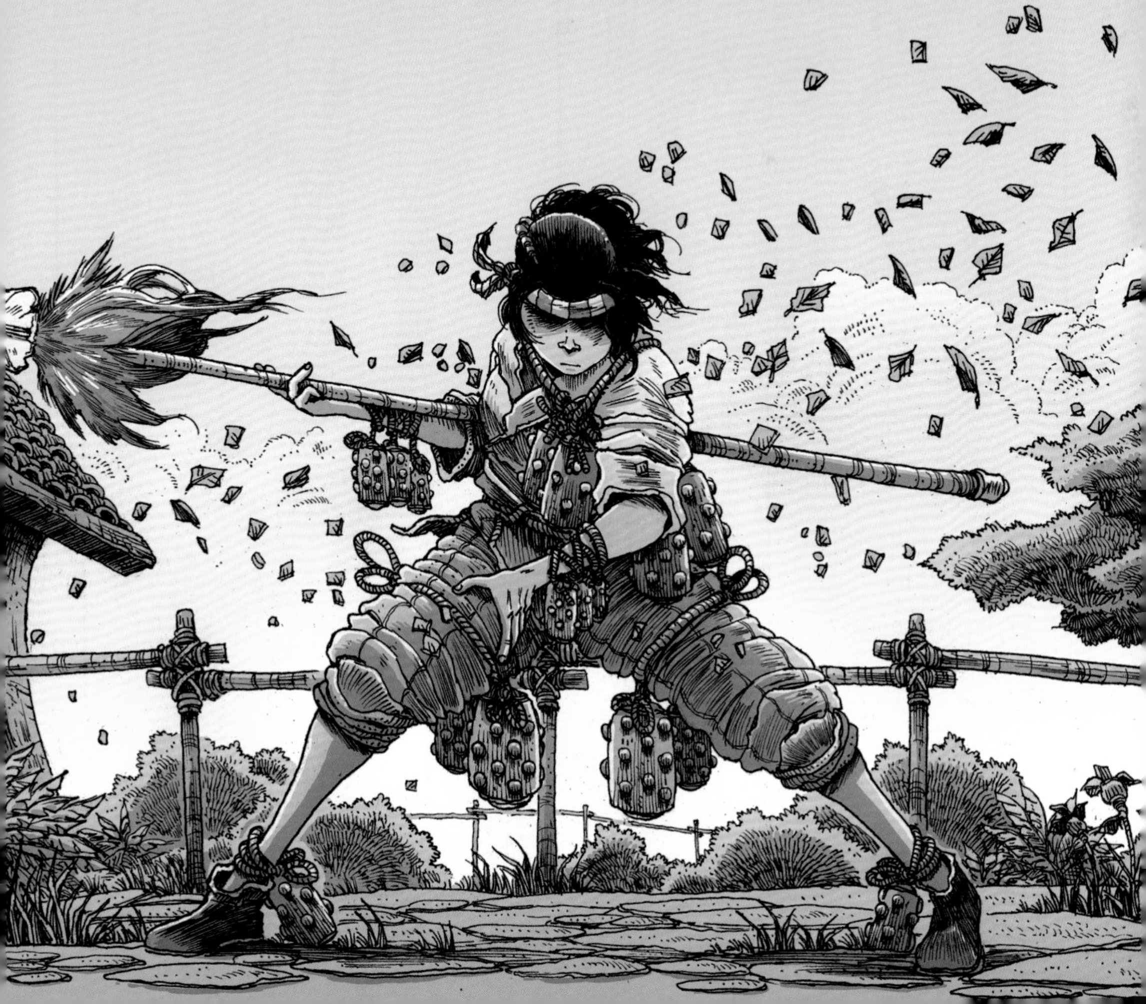

ORPHAN AND THE FIVE BEASTS™

SKETCHBOOK

NOTES BY JAMES STOKOE

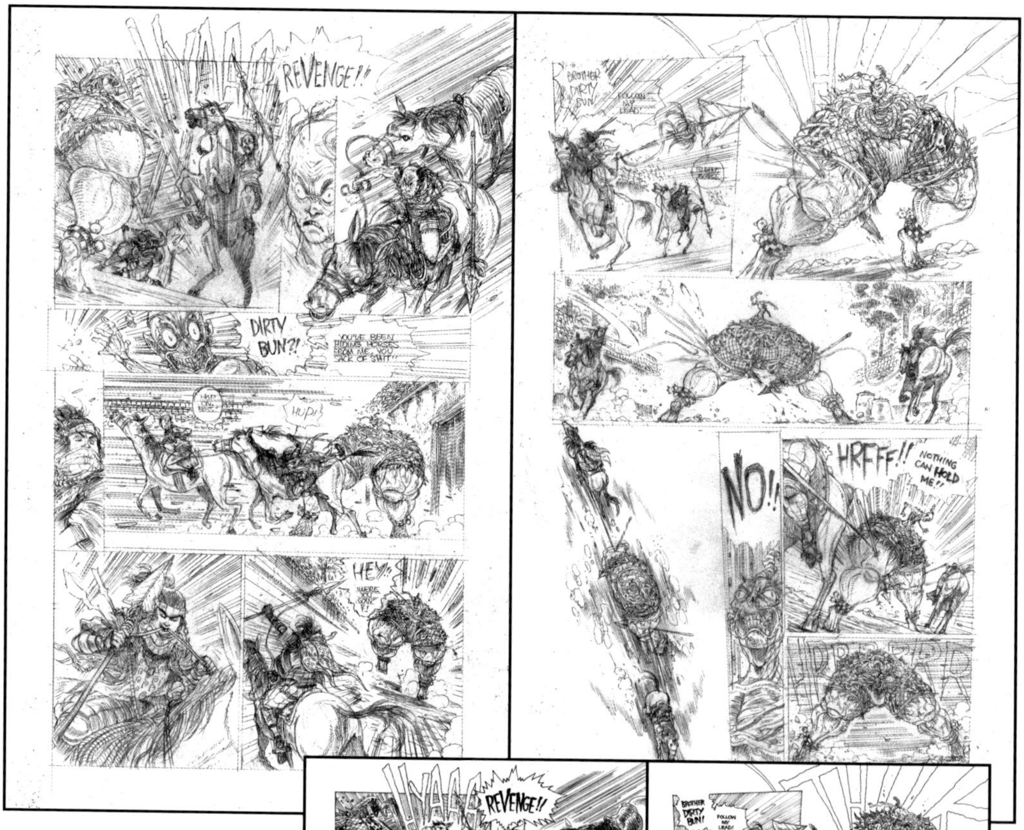

REVENGE!!
DIRTY BUN?!
HUP!
HEY!!
BROTHER DIRTY BUN!
NO!!
HRFFF!!
NOTHING CAN HOLD ME!!

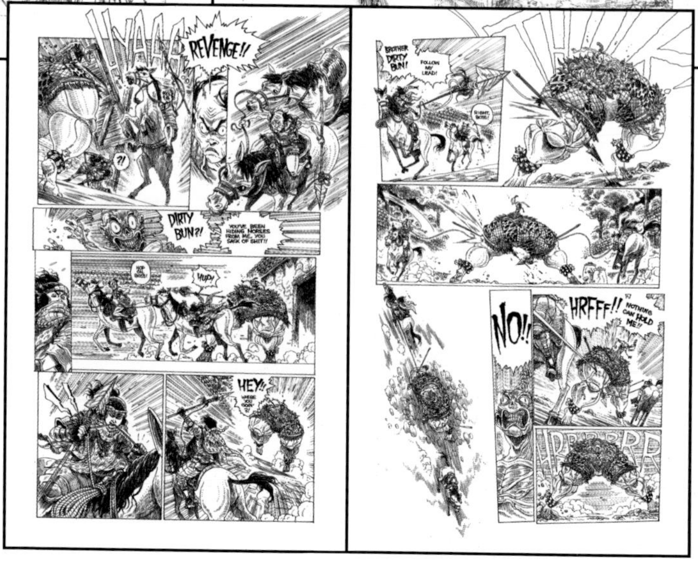

REVENGE!!
DIRTY BUN?!
YOU'VE BEEN HIDING HORSES FROM ME, YOU SACK OF SHIT!!
HUP!
HEY!!
BROTHER DIRTY BUN!
FOLLOW MY LEAD!
NO!!
HRFFF!!
NOTHING CAN HOLD ME!!

I thought that this would be one of those "easy to write/ hard to draw" scenes, but it wasn't so bad! I'll have to give Dirty Bun something to do in the next arc.

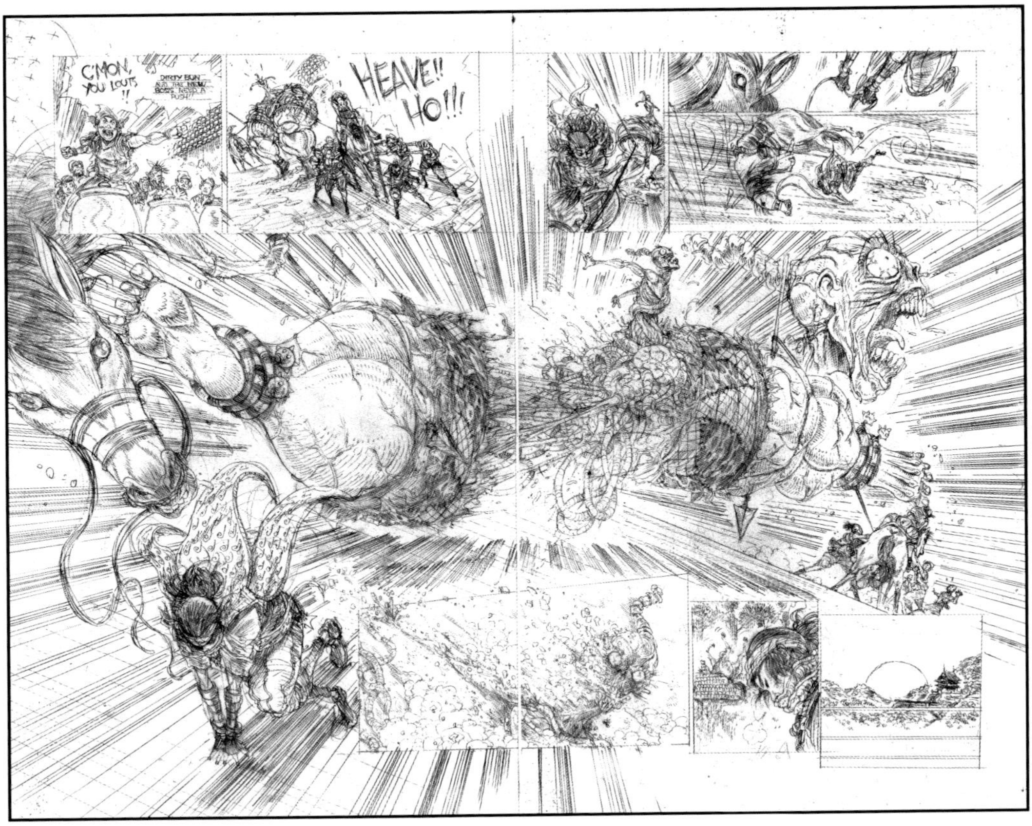
C'MON, YOU LOUTS !!
DIRTY BUN AND THE NEW BOSS NEED A PUSH!!
HEAVE!! HO!!!

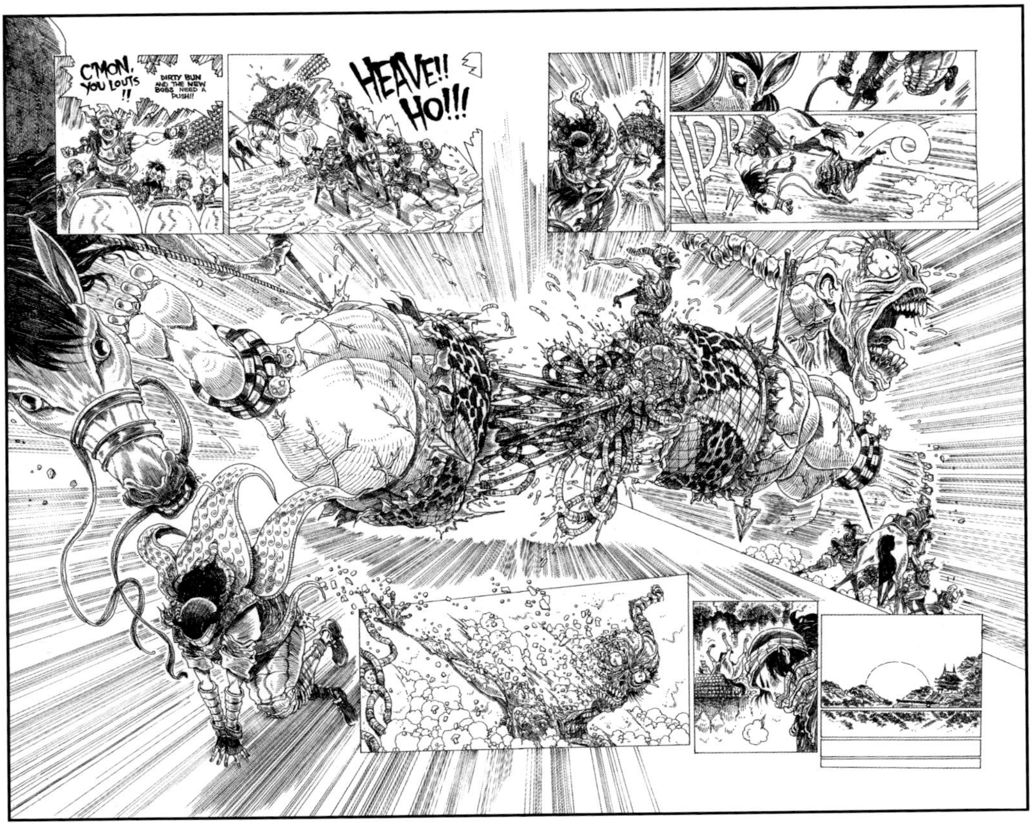
C'MON, YOU LOUTS !!
DIRTY BUN AND THE NEW BOSS NEED A PUSH!!
HEAVE!! HO!!!

Goodbye, poor Thunderthighs! This was a tricky page to figure out, as there were a lot of big actions to get through while trying to keep that big impact panel of Thunderthigh's split. That little horse butt on the second last panel still makes me laugh.

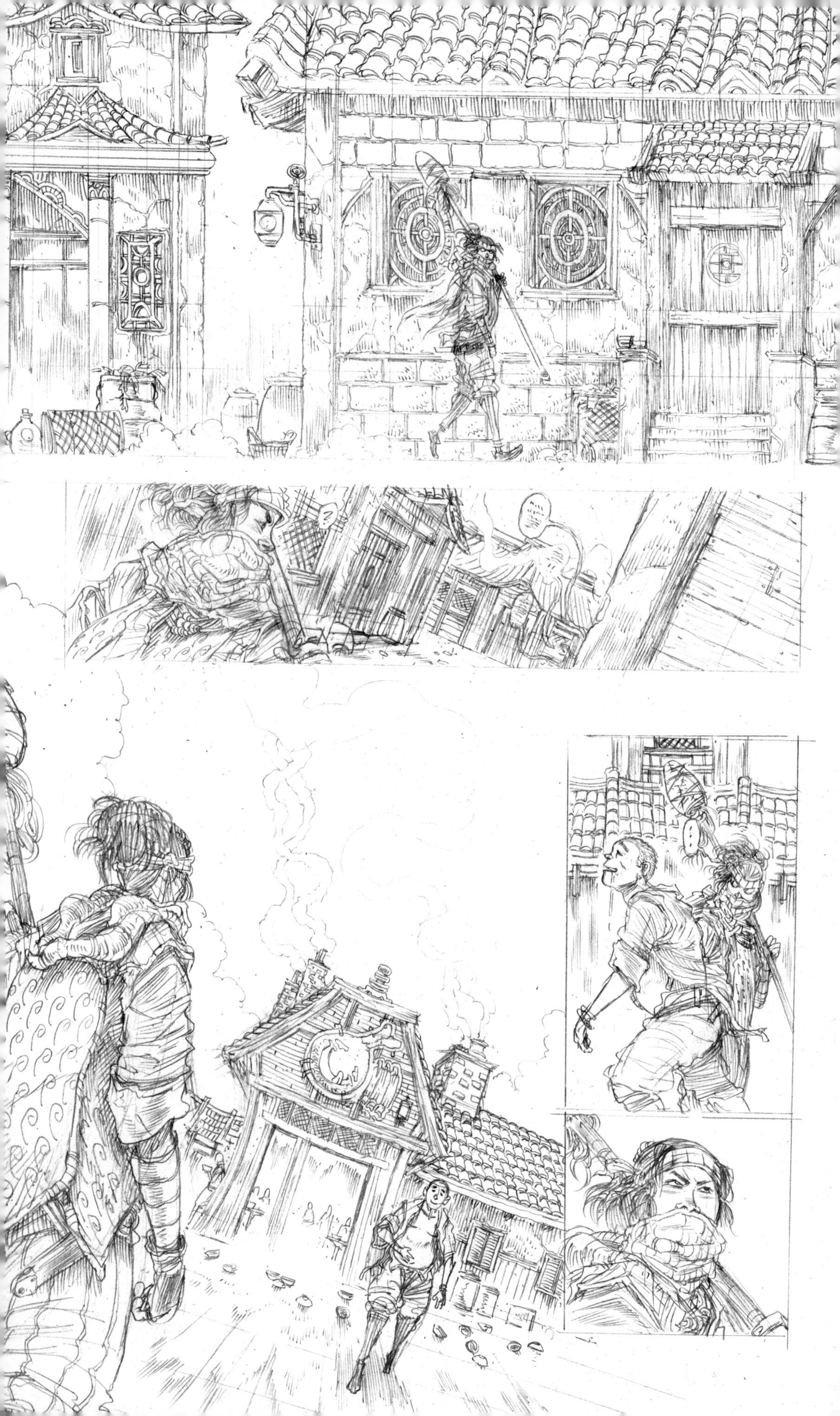
?
!

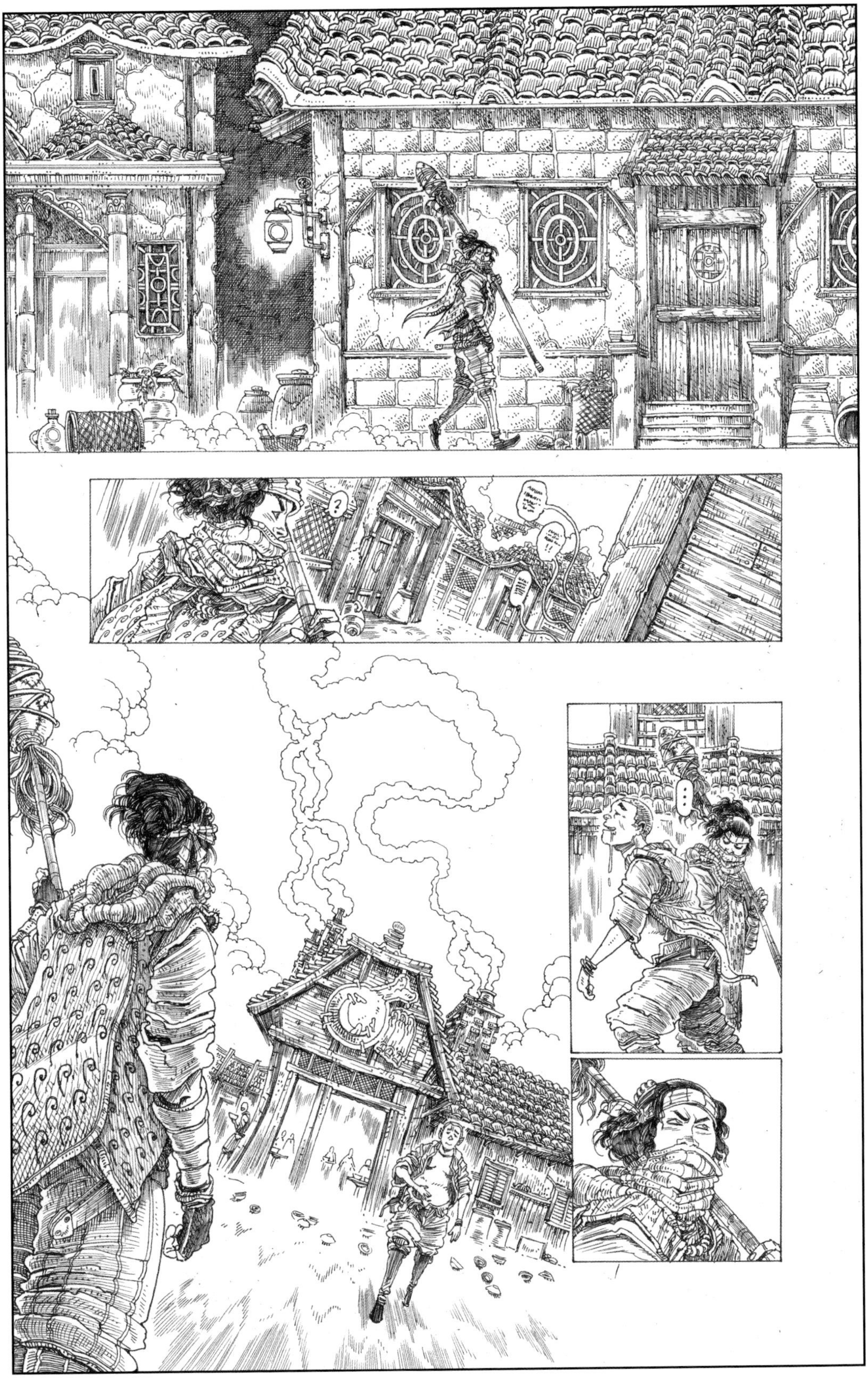
?
...

I'm not sure why, but I more often than not end up having cannibalism in my stories, though it's turned slightly on its head here. The majority of this issue was all set up for the last few pages, leading into issue four. I just hope the payoff was worth it!

Chopper Teng was so much fun to write and draw. In most panels, I tried to make him do something expressive and grandiose with his hands, which I think ended up giving him a lot of personality.

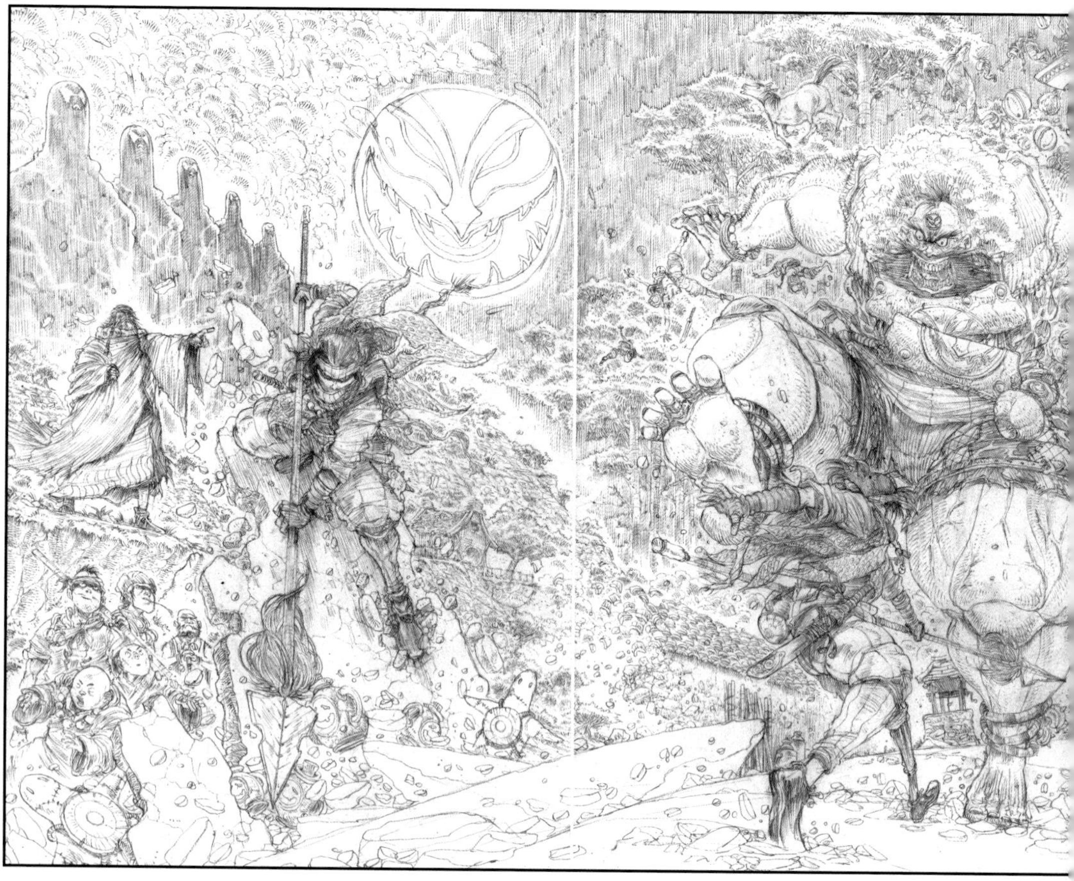

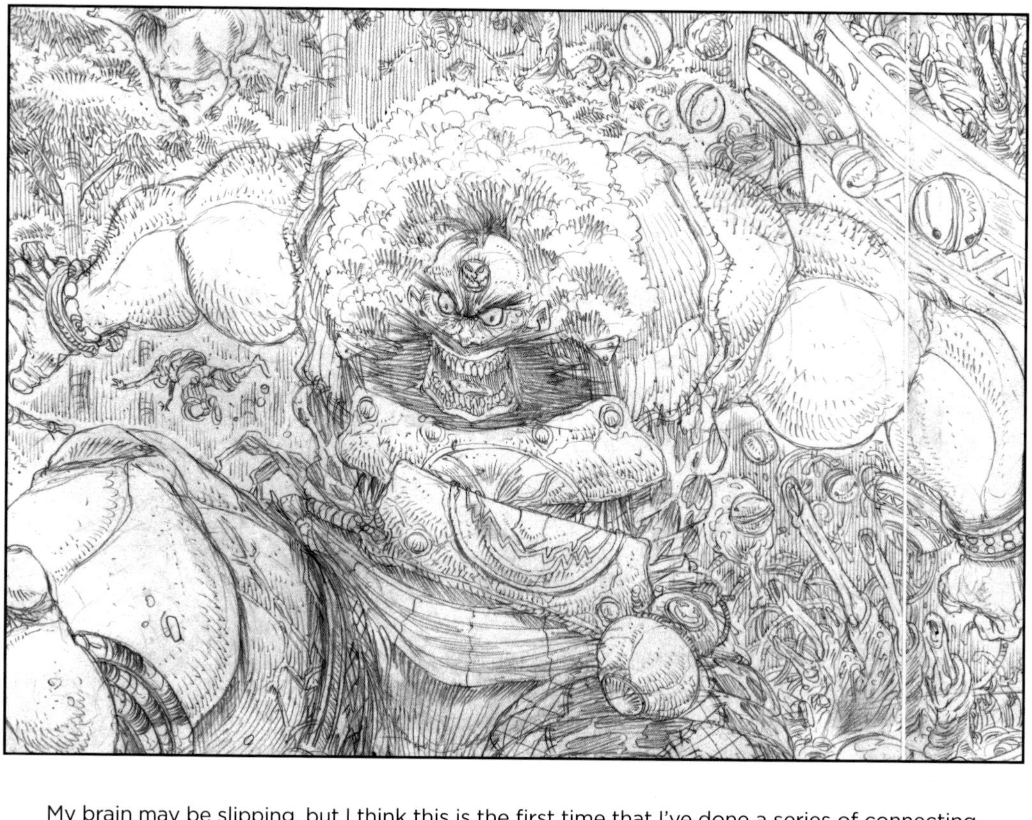

My brain may be slipping, but I think this is the first time that I've done a series of connecting covers. This would've been one of the first things I drew for *Orphan*, so some of the characters look a little rougher than they do once I had fleshed them out in the interiors.

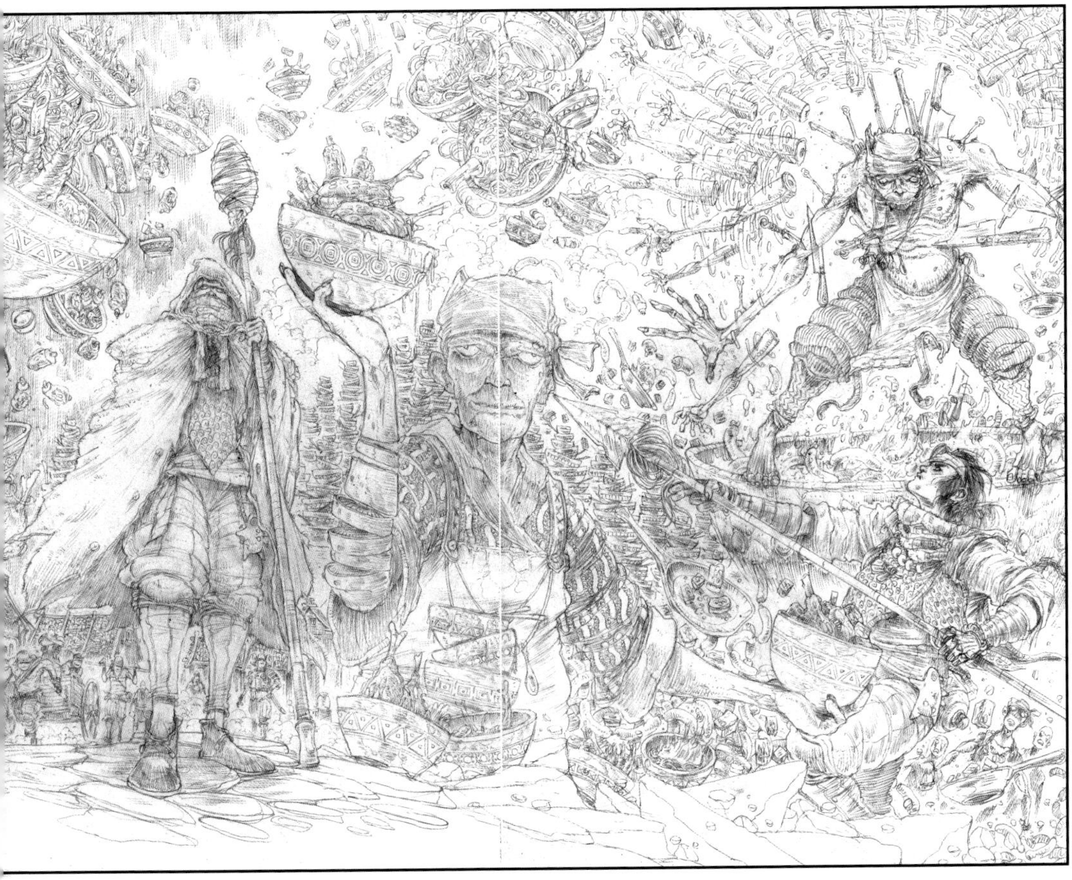

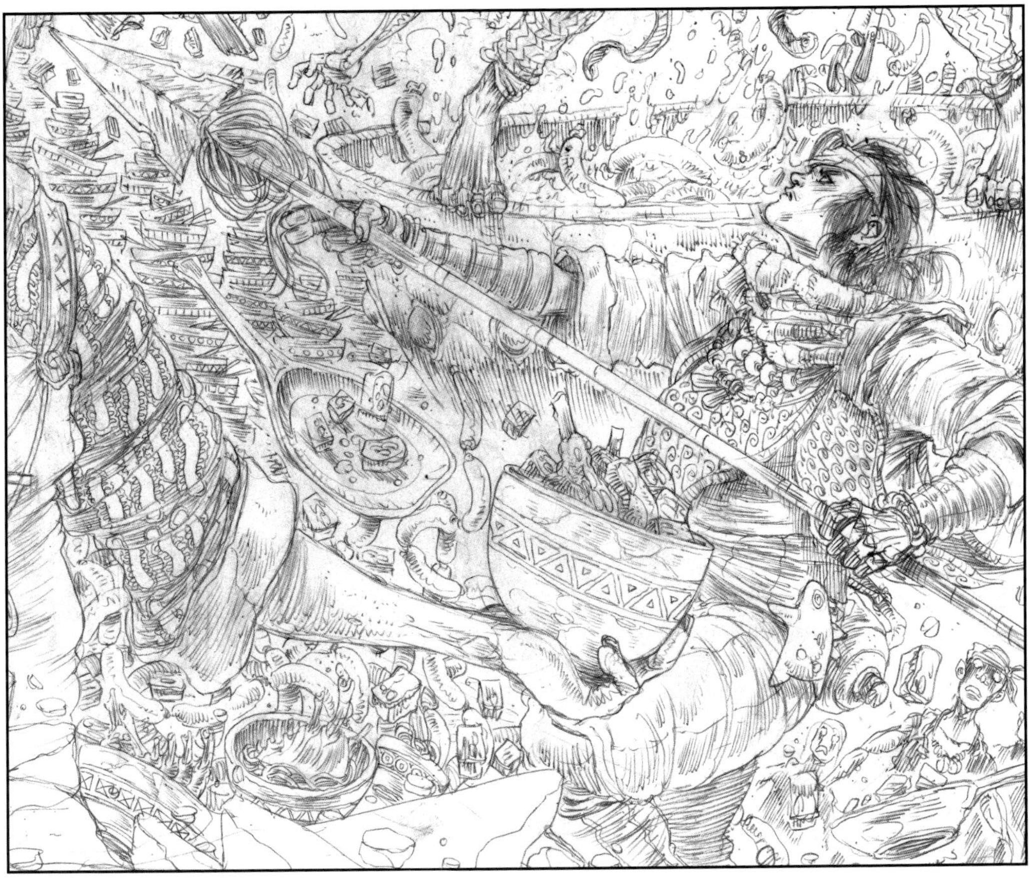

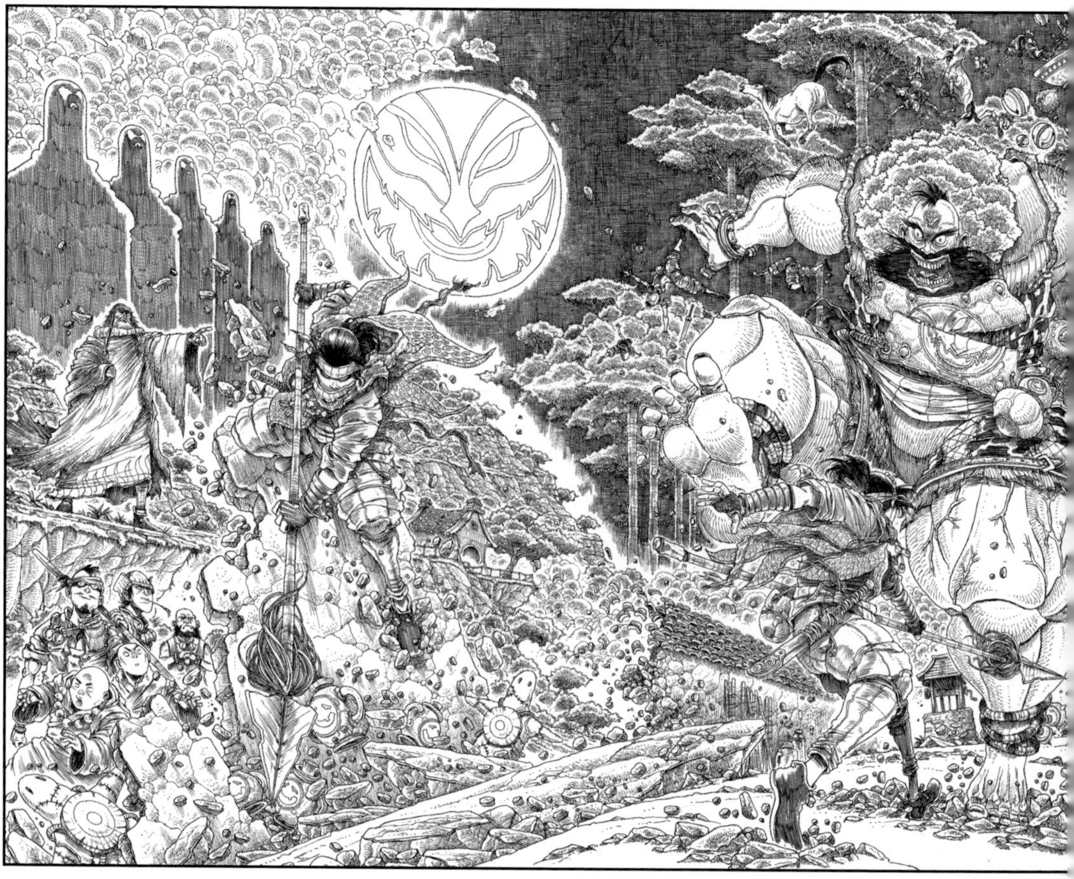

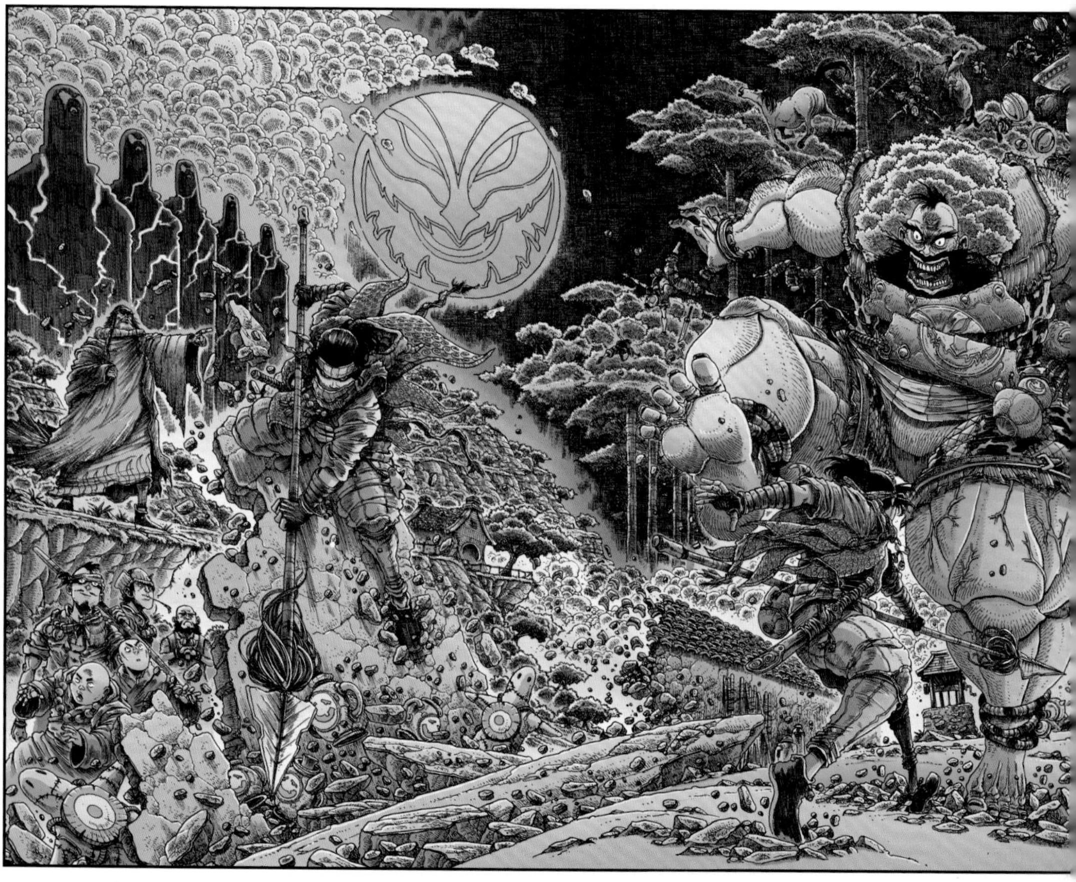

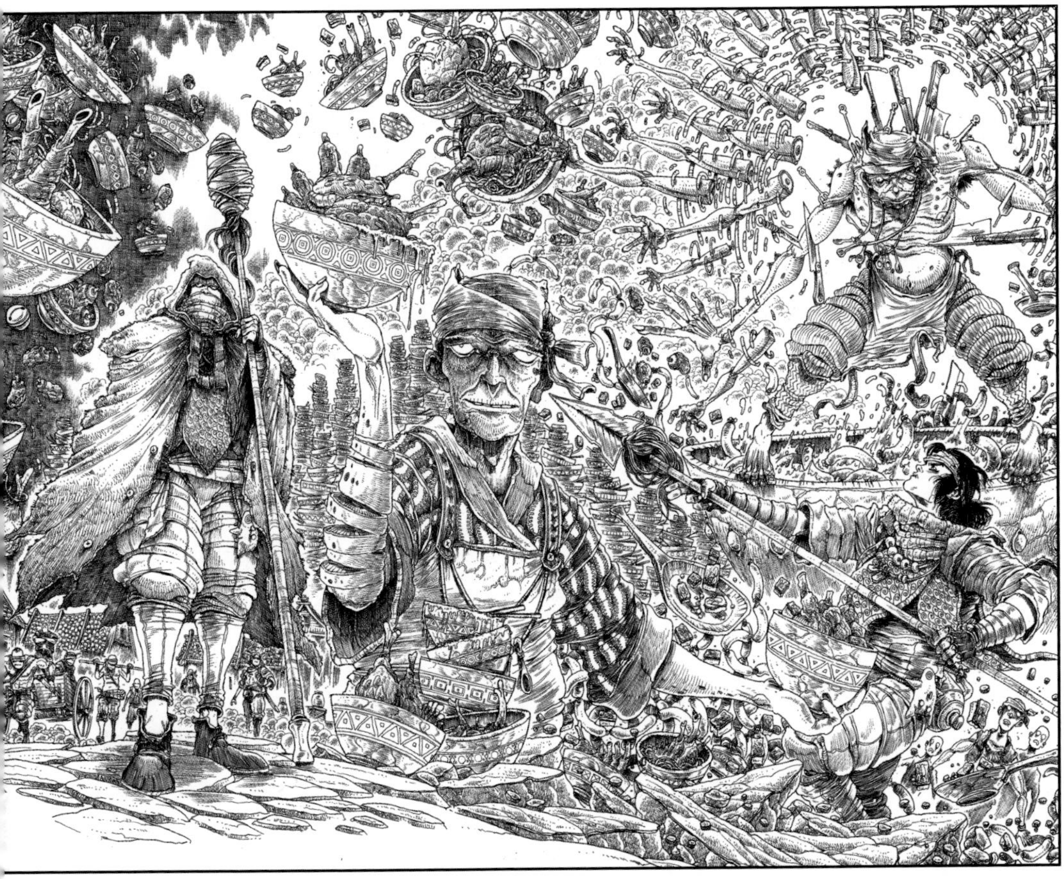

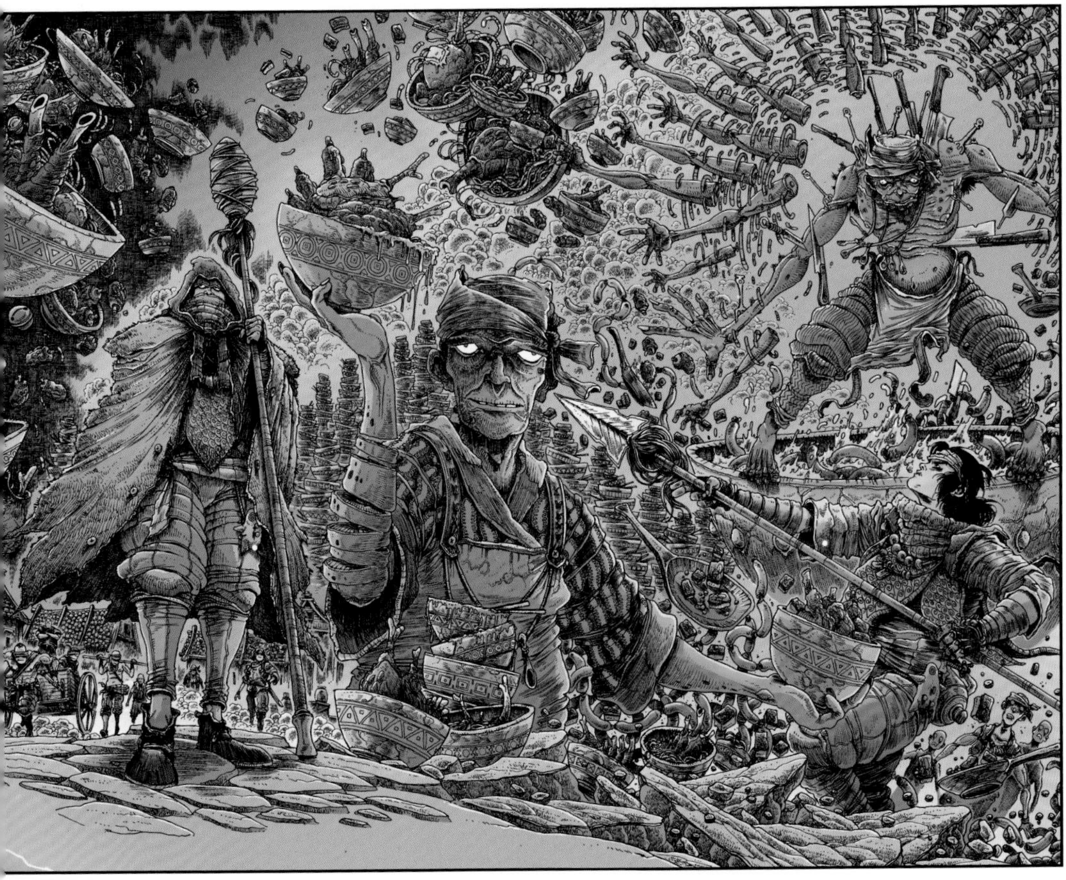

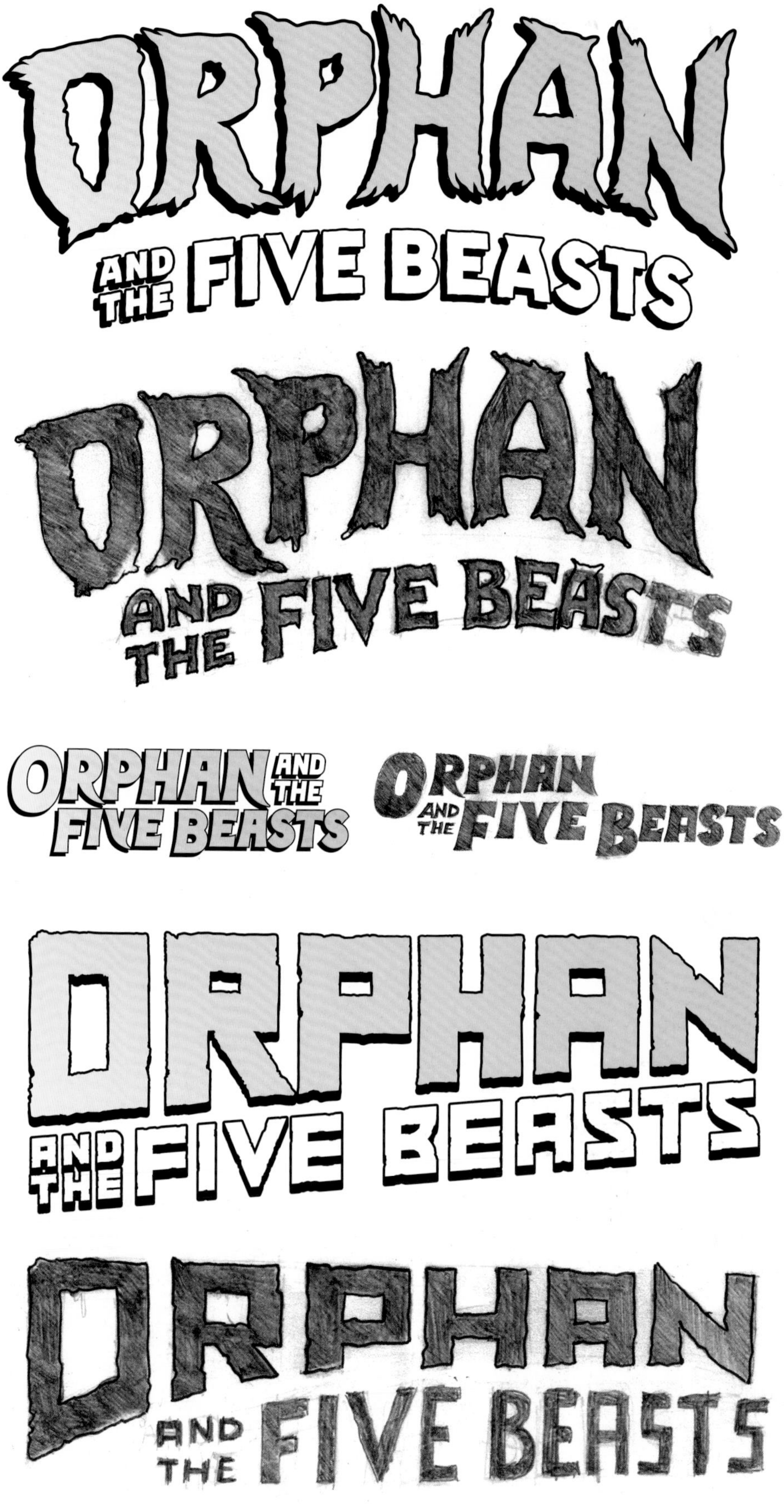
ORPHAN AND THE FIVE BEASTS
ORPHAN AND THE FIVE BEASTS
ORPHAN AND THE FIVE BEASTS
ORPHAN AND THE FIVE BEASTS
ORPHAN AND THE FIVE BEASTS
ORPHAN AND THE FIVE BEASTS

Logo Design By Ethan Kimberling